SHORTCAKE

PROPHECY FULFILLED

SHORTCAKE
BOOK 3

CHRISTOPHER GORHAM CALVIN

CONTENTS

PROLOGUE

THE HEAVY HAND OF TIME

"Amanda, it's time!" Professor Joseph Madison called across the sterile stainless steel kitchen.

It was a typical Wednesday night in the Helix Unbound Research Facility. Amanda was seated at a cafeteria table just outside the kitchen door, flipping through pages of *La Cuisine du Boulanger*, the latest cookbook by award-winning French baker Pierre Laurent. This was the first night she and Joseph had cracked open this particular cookbook, and they dove in headfirst with an attempt at making a sweet soufflé of tart apples and Saigon cinnamon. Aware of how crucial timing was for achieving the proper flavor and texture of their creation, Amanda slammed the cookbook shut and raced to Joseph's side. He had a pair of oven mitts ready, which she used to remove their ramekin from the oven.

"It's perfect," she said as she eyed their dish's pillowy golden crown. "Just like the picture in the book."

Amanda transferred the ramekin to a trivet on a nearby prep table. Then she pulled up a stool and hovered eagerly over it while waiting for Joseph to gather plates and utensils. He passed her the soufflé spatula he'd bought specifically for this night, and let her have the honor of serving them both. Amanda didn't wait for the dish to cool to what most people would consider an edible temperature. Her genetics and training had afforded her an extraordinary tolerance for heat. And while she had seen little real-world application for this tolerance, her ability to consume her and Joseph's weekly creations that much quicker was a definite upside.

"How is it?" Joseph asked, still unable to eat his portion.

Amanda's broad smile said it all. They'd had their fair share of disastrous outcomes in this kitchen, but the apple soufflé certainly wasn't one of them. Amanda finished her plate and served herself a second helping as Joseph started on his first.

"Oh, wow," he said after one bite. "We outdid ourselves."

She nodded in agreement.

"Hey, since it came out so good, maybe we should share with Doctor Vasquez and Evan."

Amanda felt a frown slip across her lips. She suppressed it before Joseph noticed, then replied, "Sure. I'll go get them."

She slid off of her stool and returned to the cafeteria. From there, she proceeded into the bland metal and white hallways of Helix Unbound and made her way to the central elevator. Along the way, she scolded herself for her initial reaction to Joseph's suggestion. It had been rude, regardless of whether he'd seen it, and completely unwarranted. Amanda loved Doctor Mary Vasquez like a surrogate mother, and she regularly received plenty of one-on-one time with Joseph. There was no reason to keep tonight exclusive to just the two of them. And Evan... well, Evan was a different story.

There had never been a time in Helix Unbound without him. Amanda and Evan were born from the same genetic experiment. They had grown up together, developed their superhuman abilities together, garnered the love of their surrogate parents together. If anything, they should have been the best of friends, two beings unique to the world and discovering its wonders hand-in-hand. But there was something wrong with Evan. Amanda sensed a darkness within him, a darkness she didn't believe—or at least didn't want to admit—existed within her as well. The boy had grown cold over the past few months, no longer spending time with her as he used to. He also seemed extra dedicated to his training, as if he foresaw *it* as his trustworthy lifelong companion, rather than the one person who could understand the turmoil within his soul. Amanda realized he had been the reason for her frown, for a fear of Evan had been swelling within her and was now nearing its tipping point.

As she rode the elevator to his floor, she told herself to push that fear aside. Fear would only drive Amanda and Evan further apart. Fear would never bring them back together as the companions they'd first been when starting life. Fear was their true enemy...

The elevator dinged, and its doors slid open. Amanda steadied her emotions and stepped out, perusing the empty labs and exam rooms that lined the hallway leading to Evan's bedroom. Since this was leisure time, his door, normally locked with three steel deadbolts, was propped wide open. Amanda peeked inside and saw Evan studying one of their combat training manuals.

"Hey," she said, trying to mask her trepidation.

Evan glanced up from his manual, but remained quiet.

"Father and I made dessert." Amanda stepped fully into the doorway, hoping her openness would spur a positive reaction from her counterpart. "We have plenty, if you want some. It's delicious."

The thought of the soufflé elicited a genuine smile from her that she couldn't otherwise force. That smile must have triggered something in Evan, for he looked back at his training manual in contemplation, then closed its cover and stood to join her. Amanda's smile grew wider, this time with surprising relief that he'd accepted her offer. She stepped aside so he could exit into the hallway, then walked back to the elevator.

"We need to find Mother along the way," Amanda told him. "She loves apples and cinnamon, so she'll..."

She drifted off, for she felt the cool breeze of Helix Unbound's air conditioning system brushing along her back where Evan's body had previously blocked its flow. When Amanda turned to learn why, she saw he'd stopped following her, and was now standing in the middle of the hallway, staring at her as if she had said something insane.

"Evan, what's wrong?"

The boy's reply was soft-spoken, with the tone a doctor might take when responding to the delusions of a mental patient. "You know we can't do that. Mother's gone."

Amanda didn't understand the claim. "What do you mean *she's gone*? She told us she was going to review our test results from this morning before going to bed."

"Amanda," Evan said, the imposter medical professional within him taking a more authoritative tone. "Mother's dead. Don't you remember? I killed her."

An icy chill crept down Amanda's spine. It hadn't been Evan's revelation that had caused the frosty feeling, but rather her realization that she had indeed known about Doctor Vasquez's death, only she also knew that death hadn't happened yet. It wouldn't happen until years after she escaped Helix Unbound. Amanda felt another chill. Escape? What escape? Helix Unbound was her home. She had no reason to leave it... at least, not yet. Fractured recollections rushed through her mind, commingling in a stew of mishmashed memories that couldn't be disentangled from one another. *What was going on here?*

The cool air blowing against her back was replaced by an intense heat. Amanda felt a powerful rumble in the ground beneath her feet, which was no longer the smooth floor of Helix Unbound, but rather a pile of broken concrete, steel beams, and ash. She turned just in time to see a gothic tower of twisted figures rising from a lake of bubbling lava only a hundred feet away. It was Evan's tower, concocted from the warped recesses of his dark mind. It was the manifestation of all the wrong, all the destruction, all the death the boy had taken part in since breaking free from his childhood prison.

"Evan, stop," Amanda pleaded. The tower continued rising into a smoky sky, blocking out the sun. "You need to stop," she repeated. She faced her counterpart, who was staring at his tower with conflicted pride. "Please, Evan. You're better than this!"

His eyes shifted to her, and Amanda felt the lava's heat dissipate. When she glanced over her shoulder, the tower and lake were gone, replaced by the majestic woods of Soul Wind Forest. When Amanda looked back at Evan, she found that he had aged considerably. He stepped up to her, caressed her cheek, and stared at her with loving eyes. Amanda now saw that she had aged as well, into the young woman that had experienced more pain in life than any person should ever have to endure. Evan leaned in for a gentle kiss, which Amanda accepted with a yearning she knew could never be fulfilled. And when the kiss was over, he pulled back, the glow of stained glass windows washing over him.

"Evan," Amanda choked through stinging tears, already too aware of what was coming next. "I'm so sorry."

Then the first blood stain appeared. It was the darkest red Amanda had ever seen, and it spread uncontrollably across her lover's chest. The other stains followed, each the result of another bullet wound, fired by an assailant who Amanda would go on to kill, but not before he had taken the life of the one person she never wanted to be without. Evan collapsed, his body disappearing into a sea of red ash. Hatred flared within Amanda. She felt it consuming every particle of her unstable body as her genetic abilities and soldier-like training took hold of her once more. She pushed back against them, unwilling to let them have her again, but unable to do anything to stop them. Then her surroundings went black, and an unnerving silence filled her ears.

"She was perfection…"

Amanda spun in the darkness, seeking the source of the booming voice.

"Did none of you ever question why she was given the Alpha moniker?"

Amanda spun again, but the blackness around her was impenetrable. She recognized those words. They had been spoken by One, a member of the Plainclothes who had been with Helix Unbound and Project Impulse from the start. Amanda had tried so hard to ignore his claims, but no matter how deep she buried them, they always found their way to the surface of her thoughts.

"You are the Alpha child."

No, she wasn't, Amanda told herself. She was Amanda, the innocent girl who had grown up as a member of the Desmond household, who never wanted to cause others pain, who never wanted to be a source of suffering.

"Like it or not, you've still got a destiny to fulfill."

Amanda rocked her head from side to side, as if trying to literally shake the thoughts loose from her mind. She heard that last phrase echoing through the blackness, repeating over and over again as if taunting her with a reality she so desperately wanted to pretend wasn't true. But destiny wouldn't let her off the hook so easily, and no matter what name she went by, she would always be the Alpha child at heart.

"It's time..."

Amanda froze. That wasn't One's voice from the night she and her family and friends had interrogated him. Nor was it Joseph's voice from the night they had made the superb soufflé. In fact, that voice was unlike any other Amanda had heard before. It wasn't even spoken in the traditional sense of sound waves transferring from the source's vocal cords to the recipient's ear drums. It was more of a mental voice, one that had snuck into Amanda's mind without her permission or desire, but which now had free rein to violate her thoughts at will.

"It's time..."

That was no memory Amanda was hearing, either. That was something new, something insidious and incomprehensible, save for its desire to force her destiny upon her. And now Amanda knew exactly from whom it had originated. She opened the eyes of her mind, not to see through the surrounding darkness, but to see it for what it truly was. A shape materialized: the outline of a human body, though its humanity was questionable at best, with features obscured by persistent shadows. It was the Dark Man, one of the central figures behind Project Impulse, though one whose true allegiances and motives were unclear. The Dark Man had never spoken to Amanda before, yet his presence had attempted to influence her on more than one unwanted occasion.

"You," she said, feeling her body tense.

The Dark Man started toward her, so Amanda instinctively retreated. She took one step back after another, keeping her eyes focused on her nemesis as she cautiously fled into a blackness that knew no end. The Dark Man followed, never in a hurry, never speeding up to match Amanda's pace, but slowly closing the gap between them nonetheless. Panic creeping upon her, Amanda turned her back to the evil entity, prepared to break into a sprint to escape him, but there he was, blocking her path at the exact same distance at which he had stood before. Amanda turned again, but the Dark Man was still where she had left him the first time, still stepping forward, a hand now outstretched toward her.

She strafed to her left to avoid him, then nearly toppled head over feet as her toes clutched the invisible ground to prevent her from running in to her stalker, who had somehow teleported into her path once more. Amanda looked to her right instead of sprinting blindly again, and saw the Dark Man awaited her there as well. There was no escaping him. The blackness was his domain, and she was his progeny, the final Impulse child, on the run from a destiny that would never let her go. The Dark Man reached out again. It wasn't an aggressive gesture, and yet it may as well have been a mortal threat, for Amanda knew if she allowed him to take her, she would never be free of him again.

She crouched back, but she could feel the Dark Man behind her as much as she could see him in front of her. His hand neared, behind it, a terrifying force Amanda didn't want to embrace. She closed her eyes, wishing him away as she might a figment of her imagination. For a moment, she even thought she'd succeeded, but then she felt the icy touch of death in his fingertips, and she knew, no matter how much she fought from that point forward, she was his...

———

Amanda screamed as she bolted upright. Her chest heaved behind sweat-soaked pajamas, and her body trembled in the moonlight. She saw the familiar walls of her temporary bedroom, heard the familiar ticking of the clock that hung nearby, and confirmed that, despite how real her nightmare had felt, it had been just that: a nightmare. She wasn't back in Helix Unbound as a child, nor in Eden during its downfall, Soul Wind Forest when she and Evan had consummated their feelings for each other, or the attic of Renewed Hope when she'd lost him to Judas. She wasn't trapped in blackness, either, and though she still felt his presence haunting her, she wasn't under the control of the Dark Man.

Amanda fell back against her pillow and waited for her breathing to regulate. Once it did, and once she felt she had full control of her senses, she rolled out of bed and crept across the hall, to another bedroom that awaited there. She confirmed her scream hadn't woken the person asleep inside, then did the same for a second and third bedroom farther down the hall. This wouldn't have been the first time Amanda's night terrors had disturbed the family that had taken her in during this past year and a half, but luckily, tonight, she had bothered no one but herself.

She returned to her own bedroom, changed her pajamas, and stripped her damp bed sheets. She would wash everything in the morning, but this had become such a common occurrence that her temporary family had provided her with two backup bedding sets she could swap whenever needed. Amanda remade the bed, leaving the comforter and top sheet turned down so she could crawl back in when ready. She then used the bathroom and took a side trip to the kitchen for a glass of water. Along the way, she passed through the living room, where a laptop was propped open on a coffee table. A digital camcorder on a tripod was attached to the laptop, as was the receiver for a wireless lapel microphone. Amanda had set these items up over a week ago, but she had yet to use them, repeatedly finding reasons to procrastinate making a recording that had been on her mind for several months now. Having no intention of making this night more painful than it already had been, she ignored the devices and continued into the kitchen.

She retrieved a glass from a cupboard and filled it with pre-chilled water from the refrigerator dispenser. Amanda downed the glass, the cool liquid calming her insides, then filled it again to bring back to her bedroom. A strong wind howled outside the kitchen window. A thunderstorm was coming, or so the weatherman had said, and though the preceding wind could be unnerving, the predicted rainfall would serve as welcome background noise while Amanda tried to recoup her lost night of rest. She stared out the window, watching the wind rustle nearby trees, whose shadows danced along the sidewalk and street of the peaceful neighborhood in which she had taken residence. Then one shadow shifted atop another, forming a rough outline of a human body, prompting Amanda to shut her eyes tight as she shook off her lingering memories of the Dark Man. Whether by his own hand or her imagination, he was in her head now, ready to seize any opportunity to remind her of his presence.

Amanda turned away from the window. Then, with a steadying breath, she opened her eyes. She confirmed she hadn't spilled her water during her blind retreat, then passed back through the living room with a conviction to keep her brain from focusing on anything of significance until she had crawled back into bed and fallen asleep. She had gotten as far as her bedroom hallway before she lost that battle, at which point a nagging voice told her she shouldn't go any further. Amanda wasn't certain what the voice had meant, for her temporary bedroom had been her safe haven for so long now, she nearly considered it her second home. There was no danger there, no reason not to return and salvage what sleeping hours remained of this night.

But then Amanda realized the voice hadn't told her she couldn't go *farther*; it had said she couldn't go *further*. And with that realization came sudden clarity. Amanda returned to the living room and set her glass on an end table coaster. She then stared at the recording setup that had been awaiting its on-camera star for over a week. If she ignored it, the setup would still be there the next day, and the day after, and so on. But Amanda's burden, the reason she had set the camera up in the first place, would keep weighing on her. And if she didn't address it soon, she might lose her opportunity to do so. For one thing was becoming increasingly clear: it was time. And Amanda couldn't sit on the sideline any longer. She sat on the couch, booted the laptop and camera, clipped the microphone to her shirt, and launched the computer's recording software. When an on-screen light confirmed the recording was underway, Amanda stared into the camera lens, the heaviness of her heart tugging at the edges of her face. Then she spoke, each word weighed down by an agony only she understood.

"Hello, Father. If you're watching this, there's something you need to know."

CHAPTER 1
LOOMING DARKNESS

Stacy Fitzgerald moaned in sleepy protest as she rolled over in bed. She didn't know what time it was, only that she wasn't ready to get up. Though the details were hazy as her mind wakened, she knew she'd been having a pleasant dream. She recalled something about a party—a birthday or wedding perhaps—at a quaint outdoor venue in the countryside. Her family and friends were all there, even those long since missing from her life. They were happy, as was she, something about the party holding extra special meaning for her. Stacy instructed her mind to fight against consciousness, to hold on to what she remembered in hopes of dozing back off and returning to the blissful dream world she had conjured. She gripped her pillow tight, burying her head in its plush filling. Then she curled her body, feeling her bare legs sliding beneath warm sheets, her feet touching the equally warm body next to her, and an even warmer ray of sunlight drifting over her face...

Wait. Stacy's brain fired into gear. *Sunlight?!*

She opened her eyes to the sight of crisp, bright light infiltrating window shades. Stacy then grabbed her phone and checked the time. "Derek!" she said with hushed urgency. "We overslept! You're going to be late for work!"

Initially groggy, Derek turned his head as if he hadn't heard her. Then he saw the sunlight peeking through his bedroom window, and a shot of adrenaline coursed through him. "Oh, shit. You've got to get out of here."

"Yeah, no kidding."

Stacy was already halfway out of the bed, her eyes darting around Derek's bedroom floor for her pants. She knew they should have picked up before falling asleep. Derek wasn't the neatest boyfriend a girl could ask for, and his room typically fell somewhere between crime scene and natural disaster zone. Finding a generic pair of blue jeans among the other laundry scattered around was near impossible.

"Here," Derek said, tossing her pants to her.

She forgot she had taken them off on his side of the bed. Or had *he* taken them off? Stacy wasn't sure. All she remembered about last night was that it had been an exhilarating reunion after not seeing each other since early March. She slipped her legs into their respective holes. "How long until your dad comes to check on you?"

"Any minute now," Derek said as he scrambled to find clean components of his police uniform. "He gets aggravated when I run us late. What about your parents?"

"They'll assume I'm sleeping in." Stacy zipped her jeans and straightened her shirt, double-checking that she was still wearing her bra. She tied a wrap around her hair, slipped her phone into her pocket, and performed a sweep of Derek's nightstand and bed to ensure she hadn't left any personal belongings in plain view. "Okay, I'm good."

Derek crossed the room and raised his window blinds. He then slid open his window and extended an emergency escape ladder his dad kept under every second-floor bed in case of a fire. Stacy joined him at the window, glanced at the ground below, then lifted one leg after another onto the first rung.

"Remember," Derek said, "make a soft landing. You don't want to draw my dad's attention if he's on this side of the house."

Stacy smirked at him. "I think I've done this enough times to know the drill."

"It's been a while. I thought maybe you were out of practice."

"Did I seem *out of practice* last night?"

Derek blushed. Stacy leaned forward and kissed him on the lips. "You look sexy in your uniform."

He was only in half his uniform by then, but he knew what she meant. "Want to meet for dinner tonight?"

"I don't know what my parents have planned. Call me when you get off of work. We'll figure something out."

They heard Vincent Desmond's voice yelling from downstairs. "Derek, let's go! I'm going to start docking your pay if you keep this up!"

Stacy giggled. "Go catch some bad guys, Officer."

"Aye aye, Captain."

She slithered down the escape ladder like a pro. It ended six feet off the ground, but she lowered herself to the last rung, dangled her feet, then dropped softly onto Derek's lawn. She made sure she hadn't been spotted through the nearest first-floor window, then blew her boyfriend a kiss and took off down the sidewalk. Derek had just managed to shut the window and return the escape ladder to its under-bed storage when Vincent rapped twice and opened his door.

"What's taking you so long?"

"I overslept," Derek said, hoping his guilt wasn't written all over his face. "I'll be down in ten minutes."

"Make it five." Ever the law enforcement officer, Vincent's eyes scanned Derek's room suspiciously. He paused ever so briefly on his son's bed, then on his nightstand, before backing out of the doorway with a leery look about him. "See you downstairs."

———

Derek split the difference at seven and a half minutes. He was fully dressed in his Eden PD attire and had even brushed his hair while swirling mouthwash. His stomach was grumbling, but he knew better than to ask for a time extension to satiate it. This was one of the drawbacks of carpooling with his father to work on most days. Understandably, the sheriff's schedule trumped his own, that of an entry-level patrolman, and it was only a problem when Derek overslept or otherwise farted around when he was supposed to be getting ready. But those days were probably a little too frequent for Vincent's tastes. Derek considered ending their carpooling arrangement to limit the tension it created, but parking at Eden PD was insufficient for its size, leaving late arrivers settling for paid street and garage options. Derek had no desire to waste his paycheck on an avoidable expense. Besides, he and Vincent's carpooling commute was the sort of father-son bonding time he still appreciated, even as he grew older and into his own manhood.

"What's on tap for today?" Derek asked as they pulled out of their driveway.

"Standard patrol duty for you," Vincent said. "I need to start prepping for the Rose Parade."

"Mayor Collins asked you to ride again this year?"

"Thankfully, no. He found some other sucker to do it. But just like last year, he wants security as tight as it can be. He still worries that one day we're going to have another incident like The Red Room."

Derek noticed the shift those final words incited in his father's tone. Just like the annual Rose Parade, The Red Room, as it was unofficially known, was supposed to be a symbol of Eden's rebirth following its collapse nearly five years earlier. It was a majestic performing arts center, a gathering spot for the culturally inclined to enjoy world-renowned concerts, stage plays, and other similar modes of entertainment. It was also the place where Judas Sparrows, in a last ditch effort to save himself from an incurable disease, had launched an attack upon the city that ultimately led to Evan's death and Amanda's departure from Vincent's and Derek's lives. His father hadn't been the same since. It wasn't that Vincent moped about in misery or harbored some inner anger at the hand fate had dealt them; it was more like the cup that contained his happiness had been permanently downsized. A joy was missing within him, and Derek suspected nothing but Amanda's return to their family would bring that joy back.

"If you need help, just let me know," he told his father. "There are rumors of a new drug making its way around the usual gangs, but other than that, the streets are pretty uneventful these days. I've got time to spare."

"Don't worry," Vincent said. "It'll be all hands on deck for parade day. That should give you at least a few hours of excitement. In the meantime, there is one critical thing you could do for me."

"What's that?"

"Tell Stacy to use the front door when she spends the night. I wasn't worried about it on her shorter breaks, but if this is going to go on all summer..." He paused a moment for Derek to process, then continued, "The girl has had enough trips to the hospital on our watch."

"How did you—"

"I've been doing this job a lot longer than you, son," Vincent said. "You don't become sheriff without having some minimal degree of observation skills. Besides, did you really think I wouldn't be the first person her parents call when she sneaks out at night?"

That caught Derek by surprise. Stacy had assured him her parents were blissfully unaware of their late-night extra-curricular activities. "They know?"

"They've got her bedroom window wired with motion sensors. Well, not just her window. Every window and both exit doors. They've also got more cameras around that house than Eden First Financial."

"They have that little trust in her?"

"On the contrary," Vincent corrected, "they trust her implicitly. You too. That's why we talk behind the scenes instead of putting a stop to it. But you've got to realize, they almost lost their daughter twice to circumstances beyond any of our control. Keeping tabs on her is just their way of having comfort that she's all right. They've got the same setup at her dorm room at school... though she doesn't know that." Vincent eyed Derek from the corner of his eye. "She doesn't need to know it, either. Got it? Let her parents have their peace of mind."

"Yeah, sure," Derek agreed. He kicked himself for being so naïve to think he and Stacy had been getting away with their tryst for well over a year without anyone catching on. He wondered whether their respective parents would take it in such stride if they knew how most of those nights together ended. It's not like Derek and Stacy hadn't slept at each other's houses before. In fact, it had been common practice while Stacy recovered from the wounds she'd sustained in The Red Room. But those sleepovers were public knowledge, and except for a few risky endeavors during the witching hours, they had been relatively G-rated. In the interest of maintaining the status quo, maybe Derek needed to plant the seed that nothing had changed. "You know, Dad, we don't do anything—"

Vincent's glare, the type of glare that said *don't bother bullshitting me*, stopped that lie in its tracks. "We all know what the two of you do up there. I'm not saying we approve, but it's only natural. You've almost lost each other twice, too, and except for summer breaks like these, it's not like you get to see each other often."

Derek squirmed uncomfortably. "I suppose this is where you lecture me about being safe?"

"It's a little late for that, don't you think?"

It was, but Derek wanted to reassure his father anyway. "We use protection."

"I know," Vincent quickly cut in. "I saw the condom wrapper folded in your bed sheets this morning. Also, have you ever asked yourself how a twenty-pack of condoms has lasted you this long?"

What had already been an embarrassing conversation for Derek had now turned downright humiliating. "I thought the foil used to be a different color..."

"Clean your room," Vincent ordered. "And start restocking your bathroom yourself. If you want to be an adult, you need to act the part. And yes, that means staying safe—no slip ups—at least until you put a ring on that girl's finger."

Derek responded the best way he could. "Yes, sir."

What Vincent didn't know was that he'd been strategizing how to get a ring on Stacy's finger for a few months now. He had no doubts about wanting to marry his long-term girlfriend. Nor did he have any doubts that she would accept his proposal, though likely not before yanking his chain with a fake denial. The problem was one of finances and logistics. Stacy was still in college, and probably would be for at least two to three more years. The distance had once been a heavy strain on their relationship, but following her second brush with death in The Red Room—and Derek's subsequent rescue of her—distance was no longer an instigator of what both of them now realized were childish and pointless fights. Nonetheless, a few more years of distance wasn't ideal for an engaged couple, especially if they intended to get married in a shorter timeframe than that. Also, there was no telling where Stacy's career would take her once she graduated. Derek had dropped out of college to join Eden PD after his brief stint as a deputy. If Stacy didn't return to Eden full-time, would he be able to foster his own career somewhere else?

Underlying all of that, engagement rings weren't cheap. Of course, they could be, and Derek was confident Stacy would marry him no matter the money invested to adorn her finger. In this case, it was his own baseline of acceptance he needed to appease. Stacy was his *one*, the girl he had always wanted, who could have had anyone else, but ultimately chose him. Derek couldn't bring himself to propose unless he did it right, and in his mind, *right* meant showing Stacy he loved her enough to put in the work necessary to buy her a ring worthy of her beauty. An entry-level patrolman salary did little to help accomplish that goal. Then again, if his father wanted him to put a ring on Stacy's finger sooner rather than later...

"You know, a little raise would go a long way to getting that ring," he said, adding a joking grin so Vincent wouldn't get suspicious.

"You'll get a raise when you earn it," Vincent replied, his face stoic. "We can't have anyone accusing us of nepotism. But I can give you some advice to get you there quicker if you'd like."

If it meant more money in his bank account, Derek would take whatever advice Vincent had to offer. "Sure."

"Start getting to work on time." He shot his son a playful wink. "When you live with the boss, it's a little hard to hide when you're slacking on the job."

It wasn't as helpful as Derek had hoped, but his father had a point. Instead of arguing or making excuses, he took the playful suggestion to heart, and once again responded in the best way he could: "Yes, sir."

———

Senator Victoria Riley's laptop screen woke from its dormant state. The text beneath her password entry box indicated a secure video call was incoming. Soon, a digital ring emitted from the laptop's speakers, filling her kitchen and drifting into her living room. The call wasn't planned, otherwise Victoria would have been waiting for it instead of putting the finishing touches on her attire for the day. She had her bedroom television turned to *Patriot Talk*, a morning show focused on politics and divisive issues around the country. It was one of several such shows Victoria would cycle through each morning. She didn't care for the talking heads that regularly hosted the show, nor the panels of so-called experts they would bring in to reinforce their personal views. But her more career-driven colleagues did care, and knowing the hot-button issues of any given day helped prepare her for whatever annoyances might come her way.

Patriot Talk was winding down a one-sided criticism of the current presidential administration as Victoria slipped into her suit jacket and flipped the end of her hair over its collar. A banner flashed across the screen that read *Next Up: America's New Drug Crisis—Who's to Blame?* Victoria rolled her eyes and searched for wherever she left the television remote. She wasn't soft on drugs, but the current crisis had been growing for over a year now. The common belief was that it stemmed from the DeMarco empire, which already had a stranglehold on most major cities, but had since expanded to even the most rural of locations. But *Patriot Talk* wouldn't blame Thomas DeMarco or anyone else in his supply and distribution chains for the declining situation. The hosts were going to blame any politician who had ever made a comment suggesting they didn't take illegal drugs seriously... as long as they were on the other side of the political chasm, that was.

Victoria found the remote and flipped channels. Then, in the quiet lull between stations, her ears picked up the ringing coming from her kitchen. She dropped everything and ran to intercept the call before it ended. Moments later, she was staring at a laptop screen containing three boxes: one with a live video stream of herself, one with her long-time friend and now clandestine partner General Francisco Javez, and the third with a still image of an official government seal that read *Office of the Senate Black Book Committee*. Once both Victoria and General Javez were on, the seal flashed to black and was replaced by a live stream of Alison Drexmore, head of said committee. The woman didn't bother with morning pleasantries nor apologies for interrupting with an unscheduled call. Instead, she dove straight into business.

"I need an update on last night's planned raid. The summary report I received this morning indicates it was a success, but its details are lacking."

Victoria suspected this was coming. She had assembled the report in question around three o'clock that morning, after General Javez and a small team of loyal soldiers had conducted an off-book operation at a chemical manufacturing plant just outside of Philadelphia. Given the time of morning and how little sleep Victoria was going to get before her day job came calling, she had skimped on the finer details. Luckily, it appeared General Javez had also anticipated Alison's call, for he lifted a note sheet into view.

"We raided the facility at 0100 hours, as planned. A skeleton crew of two security guards, one chemist, two lab technicians, and a janitor were present at the time. We subdued the security guards with non-lethal force, then systematically cleared the facility's five floors. The janitor surrendered willingly on floor two. We took the lab technicians by surprise on floor four, but were spotted by the chemist while securing them. He made a run for an emergency failsafe button that we believe would have either flushed or incinerated the contents of their production tanks, had we not caught him first."

"And those contents?" Alison asked.

"The evidence we collected suggests Trizorapine, though we'll have to wait for the full chemical analysis to come back to say for certain. I've got men holding down the building and detaining workers as they arrive for their day shifts. We're conducting interrogations, but so far it doesn't appear these people knew the full context of what they'd been working on. Even the chemist who went for the fail-safe told us he'd only done so because that was a strict protocol he'd been given. He doesn't know *why* it was the protocol."

"Digital records?" Alison asked, switching subjects.

This was Victoria's wheelhouse. "Francisco's men installed a remote tap so our cyber group could siphon through them. My last check-in with them was a little after seven o'clock. They had cracked the facility's encryption and were sorting the records by type: supply orders, shipping manifests, human resource documents, and such. They've got a long way to go, but the initial shipping manifests don't look promising."

The disappointment on Alison's face was visible. Attacking Project Impulse's supply chain had been her idea. The location of Helix Unbound's final sister facility, Complex E, remained an elusive secret. Records retrieved from Helix Unbound and its three subsequent sister facilities, B, C, and D, confirmed that plans had been drawn to develop Complex E, and even implied that some construction efforts had been put into motion. But that was the extent of record-keeping for the potentially non-existent facility. Nonetheless, Alison knew those who were trying to see Project Impulse through to its endgame must have set up shop somewhere. If not in Complex E, then in somewhere else equally capable of supporting their genetic tampering. Wherever that happened to be, they would need supplies to remain operational. And one of those key supplies, Alison had learned from scouring Helix Unbound's records, was a manufactured steroid called Trizorapine. If she could locate the sources of Trizorapine, then logically, she could trace their shipments to their secret destination. But while the idea had merit, it unfortunately hadn't played out so easily in practice.

The previous night's raid on a Trizorapine manufacturer had been the fourth of such raids in the past six months. During the first raid, General Javez hadn't anticipated the implementation of failsafes. To the best of anyone's knowledge, these manufacturers weren't a part of Project Impulse, as Helix Unbound's sister facilities had been. They were private firms contracted to produce Trizorapine under confidentiality agreements. They had no skin in protecting Project Impulse or its whereabouts. So it took General Javez and his team by surprise when the chemical tanks of that first manufacturing plant went up in flames, and its networked computer storage initiated a self-wiping routine. The operation had been a total loss.

However, it put General Javez and his team on guard when they performed the second raid. They prevented any failsafes from being triggered and secured a sizable batch of Trizorapine that had just been barreled for shipping. The problem was that this was the facility's first batch produced, and it hadn't yet received a destination for the shipment. General Javez tried to maintain the ruse that the facility was still operational, in hopes that they could still intercept the shipping information once received, but it never came. Someone from Project Impulse must have been watching the facility from afar and reported its compromised state.

The third raid had introduced its own set of challenges. General Javez and his team had prevented the failsafes from being triggered, secured the facility's staff and current Trizorapine production, and even tapped their cyber group into its robust shipping record archive. The problem this time wasn't too little information, but rather too much. The third manufacturing plant had been the largest of the four, and its capacity wasn't dedicated to Trizorapine production alone. By the cyber group's rough estimate, there were nearly eight hundred distinct chemicals being produced by the facility at the time of the raid. And all eight hundred had international shipping destinations. Given the logistics of transporting chemicals around the globe, the Trizorapine never traveled alone. With every batch, it and at least a couple of hundred other chemicals were packaged together and shipped to the same international port. From there, cargo ships would further group the chemicals with an assortment of other manufactured goods, then distribute their wares among other global ports. The goods would be further distributed by delivery trucks, planes, and even other ships, at some point reaching their final destinations. The Trizorapine had a unique strand in that spiderweb of interconnected transportation networks, but isolating it had proven to be an impossibility. By design, the manufacturing plant didn't track it beyond its initial domestic destination port. On top of that, cargo ship records Alison had procured revealed the shipping company used its own identifiers to track its cargo, with no mapping to the identifiers used by the manufacturing plant. Again, this was likely by design.

"What's the problem this time?" she asked with a hint of annoyance.

"It's not so much a problem as it is a contradiction," Victoria answered. "Well, two contradictions, really. Even though we couldn't isolate the destination of Trizorapine from our last raid, we at least gathered enough evidence to know that destination was international or, at a minimum, not within the mainland United States. Last night's facility, as far as we can tell so far, only shipped within the mainland United States. The destinations don't align."

"Maybe the destination was a domestic distribution hub," Alison proposed.

"I assume the cyber team is still collecting those details. Perhaps the Trizorapine was being gathered from multiple smaller production facilities into one centralized location before being shipped to its final destination."

"Yes," Victoria confirmed, "our cyber team is still working on that info. But therein lies our second contradiction. The Trizorapine didn't ship to a single destination; it shipped to twenty-six of them. One for each state east of the Mississippi River."

Alison tilted her head into her hand, rubbing her eyes in subdued frustration. She had thought tracking Complex E's location through its supply chain would go smoother than this. But either the former government officials behind Project Impulse were really that smart, or there was something else to their actions she couldn't quite see yet. Alison hoped it was only the former, for the latter introduced an entirely new set of headaches she might not have the time or resources to deal with. This clandestine operation had been underway for well over a year now. Even though Alison largely had carte blanche with her Black Book budget, she was still expected to produce results. Playing the long game to get those results was acceptable, but squandering a long-term allocation of resources was not.

"We should consider the upside here," General Javez offered. "This is yet another Trizorapine manufacturing plant we've taken offline. There must be a finite number of them, given the special circumstances under which the chemical needs to be produced. Eventually, we'll take out enough that it should cripple Project Impulse's next move, whatever that happens to be."

Alison returned her cold eyes to the screen. "I don't want it crippled, General. I want it dismantled. Those people are toying with scientific breakthroughs none of our other military research groups have come close to replicating. The power they've unleashed was supposed to be under our control. Instead, it's become a direct threat to our national security. If you don't believe that, ask Jacob Riley."

The reference to Victoria's deceased husband had been unnecessarily harsh. For Victoria, it stirred painful memories of the day she'd learned he'd been shot to death in his own senatorial office. She'd been distraught, sad, angry, and vengeful all at the same time, and it was that hurricane of emotions that had spurred her pursuit of Project Impulse in the first place. For General Javez, Alison's words were a reminder of the day he'd stood on Victoria's front porch and agreed to help her carry out her vengeance. Jacob had been a good friend and hadn't deserved the betrayal that had gotten him killed. Despite so much progress since then, achieving their end goal was still far from certain.

"I understand," General Javez said, forcing his professionalism ahead of any personal distaste he might have for Alison's methods. "We'll keep extracting whatever information we can from last night's raid and start honing in on our next target."

"See that you do," she replied. "At some point, we're all going to have to answer for what we've been doing these past eighteen months. Between Complex B and your more recent failure in New York, you can't afford another display of incompetency, General. As for the senator and I... well, I'm not looking to go to prison for misallocation of government resources. I assume she's not, either."

Victoria saw no reason to confirm the obvious. Alison must have sensed she had pushed enough buttons for one call, for without apology or cordiality, she told the others to follow up with her once they knew more, then ended the call. Victoria stared at her empty laptop screen for nearly a minute, debating what to do next. She considered calling General Javez privately, but other than unloading their shared feelings about Alison, the call would serve no purpose. He was doing his job, and Victoria was doing the same. At some point, they were bound to have a breakthrough. They would hit that one production facility that wasn't so clean at covering its tracks. Then they would trace it to Complex E with as much firepower as they could muster and wipe Project Impulse from existence. But Victoria knew the clock was ticking. If not her own from a pending review of her, General Javez's, and Alison's clandestine activities, then Project Impulse's. For someday soon, it would reach its endgame and unleash whatever hell it had been cooking up upon the world. Victoria could only hope they would find and stop it before then.

Inside a sterile, nondescript bunker, which itself was located inside the bowels of Helix Unbound, Complex E, Colonel Davis stared at the alarm clock next to his bed. He wasn't waiting for it to trigger; it had done that hours earlier, when his morning routine had kicked into gear to ensure he was ready by the time the science staff began their shifts for the day. It was his duty to oversee their safety, doing everything from monitoring their progress from bed to lab table, to ensuring they remained well fed, to watching for any signs of depression or other mental illness being confined to this high-tech hamster cage might induce. He was a glorified babysitter, a far cry from the elite commander he'd once been. But there wasn't much he could do about that.

The army that had once been under his command was down to only two men. Many had been killed by Evan when he'd first returned to Helix Unbound seeking revenge for his treatment as a subject of Project Impulse. Of those who'd survived, nearly all had been killed in the military's destruction of Complex B and subsequent caravan attack by Judas. The loyalty of those who remained was questionable, at best. They had witnessed their comrades fall in an unofficial war that had no end in sight, and for which it was unclear whether they were fighting on the morally correct side. Though they had never taken action against Colonel Davis, he wouldn't risk turning his back to them, for fear of a mutiny he was certain someday would come.

The alarm clock's digits flashed as a new hour began. Colonel Davis had fifteen minutes before the first morning break, at which time he would escort the facility's science staff to the cafeteria for refreshments. That meant he had fifteen minutes to place the phone call that had been on his mind for the past few weeks, a call he didn't want to make until the turn of the hour out of respect for time zone differences. He picked up the receiver next to his alarm clock and dialed. There was a brief delay as the call was routed through Complex E's cyber-infrastructure, rerouted to a dummy line in a far off country, then connected to its dialed recipient. The phone rang three times before a woman answered, her voice harboring trepidation at what undoubtedly appeared on her end as an unknown number.

"Hello?"

"Hi," Colonel Davis said, trying to sound as natural as a hard-nosed military official could. "May I speak with Demetrius Jackson, please?"

"Who's calling?"

The colonel couldn't give his real name, so he considered lying. But the last time he'd tried that, it hadn't worked in his favor. Instead, he fell back to vague truthfulness. "An old friend."

Momentary silence, then, *"Hold on."*

Colonel Davis heard the phone on the other end being shuffled around. Then he heard heated whispering, unable to make out much beyond what sounded like the woman saying *I think it's him.* Nervous that his call would be denied, Colonel Davis fiddled with a bedside pen and pad of paper, scratching incoherently to distract himself from growing frustration and anger. There was more silence, then a familiar male voice came on the line.

"You need to stop calling me, Colonel. This is the fifth time I've changed my number. I'm not coming back."

"Jackson," Colonel Davis said, relief overtaking him as he heard his former soldier's voice. "How have you been?"

Jackson didn't seem in the mood to humor small talk. *"I'm the same as the last time you called. Crippled, but surviving. Now I need you to leave me alone. I'm not a soldier anymore. I'm a family man just trying to move on with life."*

"I know," Colonel Davis said. "I know what you've told me. And... I'm sorry I keep tracking you down. It's just... things are getting tough over here. I don't know my purpose anymore. I don't know who I can trust. I'm on an island, with no one but myself to rely upon. I need my right hands back."

"Your right hands are gone," Jackson said bluntly. *"One is dead, and the other is confined to a wheelchair. What could I possibly do for you in this condition?"*

"You could be my sound mind, my voice of reason. You could be my tether to —" Colonel Davis paused, partly because he didn't know how to vocalize what he wanted to say, and partly because he wasn't sure if he should. Since the destruction of Helix Unbound, he had felt himself slipping farther and farther from mental stability. He had avoided thinking about his shift in mental state by drowning himself in work at Complex B. But that work had ultimately led to the destruction of that facility, the betrayal of Judas, the death of his men and Evan, and a hasty retreat to a half-built complex in which he had even less control than before. There was no more avoiding the shift within him, and facing that reality was now taking a heavy toll. "I just need someone I can trust."

"You chose the people you trusted," Jackson said, confident Colonel Davis would pick up on his reference to the Dark Man and Woman in White. *"If something's changed, then walk away. Do what I did and get out while you still can."*

The colonel's instinctual reaction to Jackson's words was not one he intended to voice, but it slipped out anyway. "I'm not sure I can anymore."

And there was the cold, hard truth of the matter. Colonel Davis was in too deep. He was a key component of an unholy trinity that had commandeered Project Impulse for its own goals. Only those goals had been relatively benign compared to what they were now. A little global chaos, an unseating of the United States as one of the world's greatest military powers, was nothing compared to what he suspected the Dark Man would do if left unchecked. As far as Colonel Davis could tell, the Woman in White had already succumbed to his will. The colonel had felt pressure to follow suit, but he was fighting back, unwilling to give up control of his own actions and destiny. Yet, with each passing day, and each mental slide away from stability, he felt himself losing that fight. He felt himself being swallowed by the darkness that had overtaken Project Impulse, and soon there would be nothing of his own free will left to guide him.

After a long, tense moment, Jackson replied, *"I don't know what to tell you, Colonel. Maybe you should turn yourself in to the government. Maybe you should face the penalties for your past actions, and then maybe... just maybe... you'll find redemption."*

Colonel Davis felt a twitch of hopelessness. Somewhere deep inside, he knew he was already beyond redemption. "Jackson, please..."

"I'm changing my number today. Don't look up the new one."

There was a click, and the line went silent. Colonel Davis could have been angry. In fact, the old him *would* have been angry, pissed even, that a person who had once been so loyal was now unwilling to help him. But he didn't feel anger. Instead, he felt nothing. He felt only emptiness, and some far off longing to have for himself what Jackson had found. Colonel Davis set both the phone and his scribbling pen down, then dropped his forehead into his palms. He had been such a prideful man at one time, and now look at him... pathetic, weak, paranoid, and ineffective. He had become a nobody, a figurehead of a genetic experiment in which his partners called the shots, and he obeyed like a lapdog. He needed to get away from them. He needed to get away from this place. He needed—

Colonel Davis's thoughts cut out as lights do when someone flips their switch. An alien thought slithered into his mind: don't run away. Don't disconnect. Embrace the destiny that awaits. Be part of the change that was coming to the world. Seal a legacy as one of the harbingers of greatness that awaited on the other side of catastrophe. Colonel Davis groaned as the new thoughts embedded their claws into his brain. They were positive on the surface, a tempting reprieve from the negative cloud in which he had lived these past eighteen months. But the way they had invaded his mind and now ripped at opposing streams of consciousness revealed their true nature. There was something malignant behind those thoughts, a dark force that wanted Colonel Davis on its side. He winced and pushed the thoughts away, thinking of Jackson's voice, about his encouragement to seek redemption. Maybe it wasn't too late after all. Maybe there was still something he could do. He just needed to fight a little longer...

The thoughts of embracing catastrophe fled, leaving him to his prior, though more exhausted, mental state. Colonel Davis let his head drop from his hands onto his nightstand, where it landed upon the pad he'd been scribbling on with a dull thud. The colonel took several deep breaths to reclaim control of his mind, then opened his eyes and slowly pushed himself back into an upright position. It was then that his gaze fell upon the notepad. Though he'd been scratching unconsciously, a nervous tick to counter the array of emotions he knew would accompany the call with Jackson, his pen strokes had taken on a familiar shape. It wasn't a shape Colonel Davis had seen with his own eyes before, but it was one both he, the members of Project Impulse, and every resident of Eden would easily recognize. It was a hieroglyphic eye, the symbol Raymond Holmes had left time and time again while carrying out a murderous crime spree. It was the symbol of Eden's destruction, appearing from the magma tunnels that ran beneath the city and had contributed to its downfall. And it was the symbol Judas had co-opted to isolate the other Impulse children before betraying all who'd supported him. It was a symbol of death, a symbol of darkness, and now it had found its way into

Colonel Davis's mind. He ripped the top sheet of paper from the notepad and crumpled it tightly before tossing it in his waste bin.

"Colonel Davis?" a voice said over his in-room intercom speaker.

Trying to brush off the implications of his drawing, the colonel jammed the intercom's response button. "Yes?"

"We need you in The Hive. There's been another breach."

Go fuck yourself, is what Colonel Davis wanted to say. These breaches were getting out of hand, preventing Project Impulse from reaching its final stage of evolution. Maybe if he stopped dealing with them, the project would fall apart, securing him the freedom he desired. Then again, if he ignored the breaches completely, he probably wouldn't survive to enjoy that freedom. He was screwed either way, so he would do what he'd been doing these past eighteen months: he'd keep pushing forward and let the chips fall where they may.

"I'll be right there."

CHAPTER 2

CONNECTIONS IN DEATH AND LIFE

Joseph Madison strolled down the quiet sidewalk, the warm morning sun a pleasant complement to the cool breezes that still frequented these late May days. He carried with him two roses, one red and the other white, each fitted with a small vial of water and plant food, ensuring the blooms would stay fresh for at least a few days after he placed them. The professor had taken this walk more times than he could remember since The Falling of the Tides, and it had become a regular part of his weekly routine following Evan's death a year and a half earlier. He passed row after row of concrete headstones, some bare of decoration and slowly deteriorating from exposure to the seasons, others well-kept and adorned by floral arrangements more extravagant than he had ever brought with him. There were no other visitors to this portion of the graveyard this morning, which was how Joseph liked it. It gave him the opportunity to speak and act freely, without the fear of observation or eavesdropping, both of which could lead to reporters subsequently hounding him. He was a known figure in the disasters that had plagued Eden over the past five years, and as much as he tried to put the past behind him, less-satiated and more curious minds were determined not to let that happen.

Joseph made a right turn down an intersecting sidewalk, then a left onto the freshly cut grass that ran between parallel rows of headstones interspersed with periodic gaps. He recalled a time when there had been no gaps, here or anywhere else in this graveyard on the border of Eden and Lakeview Bay. The plots had all been reserved to honor the memories of those killed during The Falling of the Tides. For many of the deceased's family members, Lakeview Bay had only been a temporary home on the way to the farthest place from Eden possible. When they'd moved to more permanent residences, a large number had their relatives' headstones—most of which weren't accompanied by a body—transferred to local cemeteries to make visitation easier. But like most residents who'd returned to Eden to rebuild their previous lives, Joseph hadn't bothered moving Mary Vasquez's headstone. Cemeteries hadn't been a top priority on the infrastructure list during Eden's reconstruction, and by the time they'd proliferated, residents who occasionally visited their departed loved ones had gotten used to the infrequent drive to Lakeview Bay.

Though Joseph couldn't have predicted it at the time, and though he would give anything to reverse how his children's lives had played out a year and a half earlier, the extra graveyard capacity near Mary's grave had given him the ability to bury Evan next to her. He'd feared Amanda would frown upon it, given Mary wasn't actually a casualty of The Falling of the Tides, but rather a victim of Evan's rage when he'd returned from vicious challenges on Sunrise Isle to exact revenge on Helix Unbound. But she'd given her approval without hesitation before departing Eden to protect her family from the ongoing activities of Project Impulse. In hindsight, Joseph shouldn't have been surprised. Despite Evan's dark origins, Amanda had found the goodness within him. She had fostered that goodness and, in turn, grown to love him. She would want her Evan, the Evan that wasn't consumed by rage nor filled with hatred and a thirst for death, to be buried somewhere meaningful, even if she wouldn't be around to visit him herself.

"Hi there," Joseph said softly when he stopped in front of Mary's headstone. "It's me again. But I guess you expected that." He laid the red rose on the grass in front of the headstone, noting the one he'd brought the previous week, which had surely wilted days ago, was no longer there. "I see the caretaker is still cleaning up after me. One of these days, I'll run into him and thank him."

Joseph twirled the white rose nervously between his fingers, then set it on the grass in front of the neighboring headstone, which read *In Loving Memory of Evan Madison-Vasquez*. In truth, Evan had no last name, but the cemetery had requested one, and given he was the product of Joseph and Mary's work on Project Impulse, Joseph thought the addition was fitting. "Hi Evan. How have you been?" The professor scoffed at his own ridiculousness. "Look at me: chatting as though you're going to climb out of that grave and respond. What a foolish old man I've become."

He sat on the grass between their graves. He knew the moisture in the underlying dirt would leave him looking like he'd had an accident during his visitation, but he didn't care. His mind was preoccupied by the inherent conflict it often faced during these trips. Joseph was a man of science, an intellect trained to assume disbelief until proven otherwise. As he had once expressed to Evan, that left him at odds with religious concepts such as God, faith, and, relatedly, a belief in life beyond death. Yet he visited these graves week after week, and week after week he spoke to Mary and Evan as if they were there with him. In Evan's case, his corporeal remains were actually there, though by now heavily decomposed. Joseph had a dream one night that Evan's Omega Genome had somehow survived his mortality, that he wasn't truly dead, but rather in a state of deep hibernation from which he would one day wake to reunite with his surrogate father. Joseph knew the idea was scientifically infeasible, and yet, even after learning it had been a dream, he had held on to a sliver of hope that he was wrong.

But as expected, Evan had never risen from his grave. Nor would he, Joseph repeatedly reminded himself, because all that made Evan was gone from existence. He was a corpse, a collection of organic compounds fertilizing the earth in Mother Nature's never-ending cycle of life. And yet, despite this knowledge...

"I'm thinking of returning to my job," Joseph said, continuing his one-sided conversation. "I've been on sabbatical for nearly three semesters now. At some point, my supervisors are going to pull my line and hire someone else. But I think I'm ready. I miss the students. I miss prepping the next generation of scientists for the greatness they'll one day achieve." He paused in self-reflection, then added, his tone growing more melancholy, "I've been squandering myself this past year and a half. I've been living a life of pity and remorse, holding on to the things I've lost instead of looking to what remains. I'm having trouble giving you up... both of you." Joseph's gaze drifted to Mary's headstone. "I still think about the good days at Helix Unbound. I think about all those nights we stayed up late trying to overcome some unexpected obstacle in our preliminary genetic code. I think about how we used to raid the vending machines and set up makeshift snack buffets in our lab. I think about the misery we put ourselves through running through iteration after failed iteration of code, and then how the eventual thrill of success overcame that misery plus some."

Joseph shifted his eyes to Evan's grave, focusing on the ground where his body lay rather than the headstone that bore his fraudulent name. "I still think about the paternal conversations you and I had whenever you and Amanda visited Eden. I think about how proud I was to see you battling your demons with the intellect and awareness of a mature mind. How proud I was to learn you had given your life trying to protect Amanda..." Joseph paused, the memory as painful as the day he had learned of Evan's fate. He closed his eyes, and the bloody scribble *Joseph in E* flashed across his mind. "How bittersweet it was to know you had thought of me before you died..."

Joseph opened his eyes and chewed on his bottom lip, the message an unsolved mystery to this day. "I did what you asked, Evan, assuming it's what you even intended. I stayed in Eden, as hard as it was to do so. But if I'm going to keep staying, I need something more to fill my life. I need to find peace, insomuch as I'm capable anymore. Returning to Pine Ridge may do that for me. Surrounding myself with bright young minds instead of living in isolation... let's just say it's something I need right now. Without you—" He looked at Mary's grave again. "Without both of you, and without Amanda, I have nothing." Joseph took a steadying breath. "I've been stopping at this local bakery every Friday night to pick up a piece of strawberry shortcake. They've gotten so used to me coming that they wait to make it fresh just before I get there. I bring it back to my house and wait until ten o'clock on the dot to open its container. Then I imagine myself back at Helix Unbound as I eat it, all the while praying that my front door will open and Amanda will be there with those innocent eyes so wide and so excited for her weekly treat." His voice cracked, and Joseph felt the warmth of a tear streaming down each cheek. "She never shows."

He swiped forcefully at the tears, flinging them from his cheeks, which were red with embarrassment. Why did he keep putting himself through this? Why did he insist on acting like a lunatic and talking to the dead, as if they could still hear him or cared to be his spiritual psychiatrists? Even as Joseph asked himself these questions, he knew the answer: because it was cathartic. Despite his lack of faith in what lay beyond mortality, he never felt alone when he visited Mary's and Evan's graves. He felt like they were there, listening to him, empathizing with him, comforting him. Joseph told himself it was just his own brain releasing endorphins in response to memories of his loved ones. But something inside of him didn't want to believe that. Something wanted to believe there was more to it, maybe scientific in nature, maybe not, but beyond his understanding either way. Joseph had yet to crack why he felt that way, and he wasn't going to figure it out today. He stood and brushed loose grass blades from his pants.

"I'm sorry to end on such a downer," he said to the headstones before him. "I know I need help. Returning to Pine Ridge will be the first step. If that doesn't work, I promise I'll seek professional care. I've got to remain strong, if only to be there for Amanda when Project Impulse eventually comes for her." He frowned in the direction of Evan's plot. "You gave your life to protect her. I'll do the same if needed. Whatever those bastards are planning, they'll need Amanda to ensure success. She's the last Impulse child. I promise I won't let them have her."

Joseph paused, giving Evan one last chance to signal he'd received the message. But he didn't, as the professor knew he wouldn't. Joseph said his goodbyes to his loved ones, then returned to the sidewalk that would take him to the cemetery's exit. As he walked, he put his questions of faith, mortality, and all related subjects aside. He focused on the thought of Amanda, living in seclusion to avoid endangering him, the Desmonds, and all others who'd been entangled in Project Impulse's web. His thoughts then drifted to Project Impulse itself, still out there, lurking in the shadows, waiting for the opportune moment to launch its endgame. Joseph hadn't been lying when he'd told Mary and Evan he'd been squandering his life. He'd done tantamount to nothing since Evan's death and Amanda's departure. But what he should have been doing was preparing a defense against Project Impulse. How he would do that, given he knew nothing about the current state of the project, was something he needed to figure out. But it was something he should get started on sooner rather than later, so with renewed conviction, he started his drive back to Eden.

———

"You're late," Diana Claiborne said as Vincent and Derek approached her reception desk in the lobby of Eden PD. She stood, her body rigid and eyes fixed nervously upon them, as if their tardiness had caused her unnecessary angst. "Cases have been piling up for the last hour." She handed Vincent the first computer printed sheet of a stack waiting on her desk. "We've got multiple gunshot victims in a downtown skirmish." She handed him the next sheet. "There was a speeding incident that ended in a fatal collision involving five cars on the east side of the city." She then motioned to the remaining stack. "And I've got numerous call-ins about burglaries, domestic disputes, and even a house fire the owner swears was arson."

Vincent scanned the details of the two sheets Diana had handed him. "What the hell's going on this morning? Did the city decide to make up for months of being quiet all in one day?"

Derek glanced over Vincent's shoulder at the reports. While not unheard of, this type of activity was certainly out of the norm for Eden these days. But the details were just as Diana described: three gunshot victims—one in critical condition at Eden Medical—and a host of witnesses queued for interviews, as well as the five-car crash, which apparently had also occurred in a school parking lot while kids were present. It was odd that Diana hadn't called Vincent in early to handle that severe of an event. Derek's eyes drifted to the stack of remaining reports on her desk. The top one covered one of the burglaries she had referred to, and by the exposed corner of the next one down, it looked like the case after that was nothing more than a flyer for the upcoming Rose Parade. Derek looked at Diana, whose lips curled into a mischievous smile.

"No," she said playfully as she snatched the reports back from Vincent. "But just think if it had, and you weren't here to deal with it. That's why it's important to get to work on time."

Vincent blinked in confusion. "Those aren't genuine cases, are they?"

Derek laughed and patted his dad on the back as Diana crumpled the false reports and tossed them in her wastebasket. "You're getting gullible, old man. I'll be in the briefing room if you need me."

As Derek slinked away, Vincent called after him, "You'll be my age one day!"

"Yeah, yeah..."

The sheriff turned his attention back to Diana. "Do we have any *real* cases waiting for us?"

"Oh yes," she said with professional obedience. She opened one of her desk drawers and removed a paperback novel with a tasseled bookmark sticking up from its center. "The Case of the Vanishing Clockmaker. It's a real nail-biter."

Vincent blinked again, this time with tested patience. "I'll be in my office."

He wanted to smile, but then again, he didn't want to give Diana the pleasure of tricking him twice, so he quickly turned from her and marched toward his open office door. His desk was clean, its wooden surface devoid of paperwork backlogs, and his computer, keyboard, and drink coaster all positioned at perfect angles to his seat. This wasn't Vincent's doing; as long as his stuff was there, he didn't really care how perfectly it was arranged. But Diana had a habit of straightening up after him, which he silently appreciated, even though he would never exert such effort himself.

Vincent woke his computer from sleep, checked his calendar for the day, which was clear except for his meeting with Mayor Collins that afternoon, then scanned through his email, none of which required his immediate attention. It was going to be a boring day at Eden PD. But, Vincent supposed, boring was better than the alternative, as Eden's catastrophic history had shown time and time again. The phone at reception rang. Vincent could see Diana's desk through his office window, and he watched as she answered with a smile and cordial tone that came naturally to her easy-going personality. He felt his heart flutter, then a nervous unease overtake his stomach, the two emotions battling for dominance as they had done so many times during this past year and a half. Vincent bit his bottom lip and looked away from Diana. Then he took out his wallet and retrieved from it the worn photo he had stared at more often than he cared to admit during that same timeframe.

The bright eyes of Abigail Desmond stared back at him from a memory long since lost to the sands of time. She was radiant, a young wife and mother more beautiful and kind-hearted than Vincent could have ever asked for. Where had she gone so wrong? The white flowing top and matching sunhat she'd worn the day that photo had been taken wasn't a part of her wardrobe any longer. Neither was the smile, nor the eyes so full of life. In their place was a cold, manipulative ghost, a woman who'd traumatized Vincent with her tragic *death* to secretly join a government project that would ultimately lay waste to Eden and eventually—well, that was something Vincent didn't know yet. He often wondered what Project Impulse's endgame was, and more importantly, what role Abigail served toward it. He sometimes wondered whether she could be saved, redeemed from the turn to darkness she had taken so many years ago. If so, could he ever forgive her for what she'd done? Could they be a family again?

Vincent recalled the night he'd learned Abigail was still alive. Colonel Davis had a gun to Derek's head, and it was clear he was intent on pulling the trigger. But then Abigail had intervened. She had saved Derek's life, her motherly instincts rising to the surface of her otherwise emotionless being. Was it possible that the true Abigail Desmond, the spirited young woman who had once loved Vincent and given him a son he cherished each day, was still alive? Could she be freed permanently from the white shell of a woman that smothered and suppressed her? Or would any attempt at freedom result in additional heartbreak that Vincent wasn't sure he could survive twice? Over and over he asked himself these questions, and over and over his answer remained: *I don't know.*

"Knock, knock," Diana said from his open doorway.

Vincent shuffled Abigail's picture back into his wallet, but not before she caught a glimpse of it. "What's going on?"

Diana frowned. She had a fresh report in her hand, but she slid it atop one of Vincent's filing cabinets and quietly shut his office door. Then she closed his window blinds, leaving the two of them with only the faint light that peaked in between their slats. Without saying a word, Diana crossed the office and sat on Vincent's desk. Then she leaned toward him and planted a soft kiss on his lips. He was hesitant to receive it, but as soon as he let his guard down, Diana kissed more forcefully, one after another, stealing his attention from the glum memories that had consumed it. When the two came up for air, she addressed the elephant in the room. "What do I have to do to make you let her go?"

"I've told you," Vincent replied, "she doesn't mean anything. Not anymore."

"But you still can't stop thinking about her." Diana leaned her forehead against his, her eyes closed to hold back tears welling in them. "You said you wanted to move slowly, and we have, but at some point we've got to change lanes."

"I know," Vincent whispered with understanding. "And we will. The ghosts of the past are just—"

"Ghosts," Diana finished for him. "They don't exist anymore. They aren't flesh and blood like you and me. They aren't real, no matter how much we might sometimes want them to be."

She was right. Vincent had already come to that conclusion on his own, even going so far as to tell Derek that the woman they had seen at Complex B the night his life was in jeopardy wasn't his mother, that she had given up that right upon choosing Helix Unbound over them. Nonetheless, the question of *why* she had abandoned those who loved her, and who she apparently still had buried feelings for, kept nagging at him. Vincent tried to ignore the question, and had even held his last remaining photo of Abigail over an open campfire flame at one point, willing himself to turn it to ash so his painful memories and the questions they harbored could blow away in the nighttime breeze. But he hadn't been able to follow through then, and he was still struggling with letting go now.

"I'm sorry," Vincent said. "Please bear with me a little longer."

Diana opened her eyes and smiled affectionately. "I suppose it's the least I can do. After all, you've borne with my horrendous cooking for the past year and a half."

Vincent chuckled. "It is pretty horrendous."

Diana shared in his laughter, no qualms with the validity of his statement. Then she planted another kiss on him, this one slow and sweet, and finally enough to tear Vincent away from his conflicted thoughts. The office door opened, flooding the space with light.

"Hey, Dad—" Derek started before pausing at the sight of Diana seated on his father's desk.

Her face reddening, she scooted off the side edge and straightened her outfit as Vincent did the same to his.

"Derek," the sheriff said as professionally as a politician caught with his hand in the cookie jar, "we were just—"

Derek cut him off with a raised hand. "I know exactly what the two of you were doing in here." He smiled, a shiver of a rush passing through him. "Whew, that felt good to say!"

Vincent glared at him with a silent *touché, smart ass* look. Then he vocalized, "What can I help you with, son?"

"Honestly? It wasn't important."

Before Derek could retreat, Diana grabbed her report from the top of Vincent's filing cabinet. "Well, in that case, I've got a disturbing the peace call for you to deal with... Officer Desmond."

Oh boy, his potentially future stepmom-to-be was pulling out the formal language. Derek told himself that's what he gets for being in the wrong place at the wrong time. Dutifully, he took the report and scanned it. This time, he didn't need to question its authenticity, for he was all too familiar with the parties involved and exactly what was going down. "Maybe you should give this to someone else."

Diana looked at Vincent, who asked, "Again?"

She nodded.

Vincent sighed with disappointment, then issued his official, yet paternal, orders. "Take care of it, Derek. Don't bother locking him up; it hasn't done any good so far. Try talking to him. Maybe encourage him to seek help. I hate to see him wasting his life like this."

Those were the last things Derek felt like doing, but he would give it a shot. "Fine. But if we come to blows, I'm putting him in handcuffs."

"Fair enough."

Derek shot Diana a *thanks, but not really* smile, to which she responded with a friendly wink. Once he was gone, she re-opened Vincent's blinds. "Well, so much for our whole *let's keep it professional in the workplace* agreement."

Vincent scoffed. "You haven't kept it professional in the workplace since the day I hired you."

Diana's breath caught in her throat in dramatic fashion. "You finally noticed!"

He shook his head, laughing. "Get back to work."

"Dinner tonight?" she called over her shoulder as she obeyed.

"It depends. Are you cooking?"

"Guess you'll have to show up to find out!"

Gladly, Vincent thought. Though at the rate things were going, it was likely to be the most dangerous part of his day. He sat there watching Diana for another minute as she returned to her desk just in time to answer another call. Then he retrieved Abigail's picture once more. Vincent fortified his emotions as he examined the image of his former love, determined not to let it consume him again. His eyes passed over hers, then took in her summer smile and wardrobe, before finally settling on the diamond ring on her finger. Vincent remembered the day he had placed that ring there. It had been one of the happiest days of his life, and though their marriage eventually met a tragic end, he was finally realizing that nothing would ever reverse the happiness he'd once experienced, and that tragedy shouldn't hold him back from experiencing it again. He nodded to himself, an affirmation that he knew what needed to be done. Then he tore Abigail's photo in half. He halved it again, and then let the pieces flutter into the wastebasket beside his desk.

One of Abigail's eyes landed face up in the bottom of the bin, staring at Vincent as if to ask, *how could you?* For a moment, the sheriff considered reversing course, gathering the pieces of the photo and meticulously taping them back together. But then he caught himself before descending into the spiral of regret his memories of Abigail now carried. He tossed off the notion of salvaging the photo, and to ensure the temptation never arose again, carried his wastebasket to the nearest break room, where he dumped its contents into the large trash bin that stood beside the coffee machine. Soon, officers would cover the photo remains with used coffee grounds, paper cups, and leftover food they consumed during their breaks. Vincent's ability to recover it would be nullified. He returned to his office, replaced his wastebasket, then leaned back in his chair. For the first time in a long time, he finally felt at peace.

———

Detective Frank Holmes was also having a boring morning at Jericho PD, though, unlike Vincent, this was definitely out of the ordinary for the relatively more unruly Jericho City. There had been a handful of violent confrontations in the early morning hours as drunks and drug-addicts fled from the approaching sunrise to clear the streets for Jericho's more civilized residents. For a change, though, none of the confrontations had led to hospitalizations or, as sometimes was the case, homicides. A pair of prostitutes had been brought in for soliciting their bodies to an undercover officer, a vagrant was in custody for exposing himself to a young lady as she got out of her car at her office, and a handful of gang members were being held for possessing illegal firearms. New calls were coming in every ten to fifteen minutes, but even they weren't pushing Jericho PD's capacity to handle each incident with officers to spare.

Frank looked at a cardboard box sitting on his desk. It was loaded to the top with manila folders and clipped packets of mismatched paperwork. Jericho PD was on the tail end of a spring cleaning exercise, and part of that cleaning required each employee to tidy the loose odds and ends of paperwork they had filed over the years. Frank had already *tidied* five such boxes. He had also given the municipal waste management workers five boxes worth of trash and a large enough tip to cover their lunch if they ensured those five boxes never made their way back to Jericho PD. But this last box wouldn't be disposed of so easily. It contained a few loose records about his deceased brother, Ray, and Frank wanted to ensure those records were secured before tossing the rest.

But not right now. Right now, he would take advantage of the lack of criminal activity in the city to handle more pressing—at least in his mind—business. Frank opened the box of paperwork, placed a few random pieces of its contents onto his desk to give the appearance that he was going through it, then left his office, propping the door partially open so anyone passing by would think he had temporarily stepped away. It wasn't completely untrue. He would return... eventually. But he wanted his co-workers to think he was simply in the restroom or on a coffee run, rather than where he was actually going. He wouldn't lie to them about his activities, but he also couldn't help it if they jumped to faulty conclusions.

On his way out of his office, Frank caught the attention of his partner, Billy Meadows, who was chatting casually with a younger officer down a nearby hallway. Frank made a *be on the lookout* sign by pointing two fingers at his eyes, then a *call me* motion as he stretched his thumb and pinky finger across an ear. That was his silent way of asking Billy to keep his eyes peeled for Captain Tipps and to warn Frank should their supervisor come looking for him. Billy returned a subtle nod that went unnoticed by his conversing officer. Then Frank slipped into an adjacent hallway and made his way toward a rear stairwell rarely used during Jericho PD's day-to-day operations.

He took the stairwell down to a decommissioned part of the basement that used to house their forensics team before that entire department got upgraded to its own state-of-the-art facility. He wound his way through dusty hallways until he reached the door to a conference room buried so deep inside Jericho PD he suspected most employees didn't even know of its existence. Billy called the conference room Frank's *Bat Cave*, a not-so-subtle nod to the operating headquarters of the fictional world's greatest detective. Frank unlocked the door with a key he had unofficially *borrowed* from Jericho PD's janitorial team. When he flipped on the light inside, he found himself surrounded by a scene straight out of a stereotypical crime-of-the-week drama.

To one side of the room, stacked sloppily against a nondescript concrete wall, were the evidence boxes Jericho PD had collected on Raymond Holmes from the time he'd first become a suspect in a series of grisly cross-country murders to the day he'd blown his ass to hell while taking Eden with him for the ride. Next to these boxes was another that looked the same, but had been singled out by Frank due to the unique nature of its contents. In it was a letter Ray had written to Frank during a moment of lucidity and had delivered posthumously by Alma Hernandez, a woman originally thought to be his victim, but who had, in fact, been spared to be his voice after death. The box also contained several personal articles that belonged to Ray, which Frank had unearthed from his old childhood home in an attempt to understand his brother's descent into madness. Finally, there were documents obtained from Doctor Laura Guiles, who Frank had learned served as Ray's childhood therapist. He had also learned her husband was one of the key figures behind Project Impulse, and that Ray's prophecy of Eden's destruction may have had more basis in fact than he'd originally imagined.

Missing from that box was a drawing Frank had taken a particular interest in since first discovering it. It was a drawing of Soul Wind Forest, with a building he presumed was Helix Unbound hovering on its horizon. Marching out of the forest was an army of stick figures, and at their center, a leader... a female leader, guiding them on their path of destruction. That drawing was currently on display on a five-by-twelve-foot pinboard mounted along one of the conference room's other walls. Spiderwebbing from it were colored strings, scraps of newspaper, photographs, and notecards, an investigative work that could just as easily be confused for the artistic production of a madman. This was Frank's pet project, a personal endeavor hidden within the bowels of Jericho PD, his final attempt to make sense of his brother's destructive acts, to understand the true meaning behind Ray's prophesied *Falling of the Tides*, and to figure out, hopefully before it was too late, what role Amanda was destined to play in that prophecy, lest disaster strike Eden again.

Frank leaned against the conference room table, his eyes fixed on the pinboard's eerie centerpiece. He had racked his brain over how much credence to give it when first starting this investigation. Logic told him it was silly to treat the creation of a crazed child's imagination as fact, much less a credible prediction of the future. But experience had taught him not to take his brother's lunatic rantings for granted, and learning of Ray's tangential connection to Project Impulse had created smoke that, if ignored, Frank feared might turn out to be a raging wildfire. So he'd promised himself that no matter how ridiculous it seemed, he would treat the drawing as gospel, then try to fit the rest of the puzzle pieces into place around it.

The first puzzle piece was Ray himself. His name was on a notecard attached by string to the left of the central drawing. Beneath his name was the word *deceased*, and though Frank had originally considered putting a question mark beside it, he told himself re-opening that can of worms was a wasteful use of his mental faculties. Besides, he'd already been burned by doing so once before. Next to the notecard containing Ray's name was another containing Frank's. He wasn't the subject of his own investigation, but he'd be lying to himself if he pretended he hadn't become a relevant player along the way.

Multiple strings branched upward from Ray's notecard. One connected to a pair of skyline photographs, one of Eden before its collapse and one more recent and reflective of how the city looked today. Another string connected to a notecard with the name *Leonard Guiles*, which was then followed in parentheses by *The Suited Man*. The nickname had been provided by Joseph after Frank shared what he'd observed about Leonard's preferred wardrobe. The word *deceased* also accompanied this picture. Another string originating at Ray's notecard ended near Leonard's, where the name *Laura Guiles* was written. Other than being the conduit through which Leonard had first noticed Ray, Frank had determined Laura Guiles had little to do with Project Impulse, and so no other information branched from her card.

The final string branching upward from Ray's notecard ended in a large sheet of paper on which Frank had written *Project Impulse*. Above it was a connected notecard that read *Helix Unbound*. Above that was a second that read *HU Industries, Incorporated*, and at the apex of the web was a final notecard that read *Lilith International*. This series of notecards represented the layers of corporate identities beneath which the government had hidden Project Impulse. Two of Joseph's brightest students from Pine Ridge University had uncovered the trail when digging into their instructor's past. The HU industries card branched to the left to a photograph of a prison-like building below which Frank had scribbled the word *Waxhill*. Branching to the right was another notecard, this one which read *Complex B*, followed in parentheses by *destroyed*.

There wasn't much else Frank knew about the upper tiers of this interconnected hierarchy, but once he'd reached the Project Impulse layer, things became much more complicated. Branching downward from that card was not only the string connecting to Ray, but one connecting to Leonard Guiles, another to Abigail Desmond, a fourth to Colonel Davis, a fifth to a notecard marked simply with a question mark, and then a sixth to a group of five notecards, in the middle of which Frank had written the phrase *The Plainclothes*. One of those five notecards had a bold X through it, Frank assuming the member he'd left unconscious inside of Complex B just before its destruction was most likely dead. Based on everything he had learned over the years from conversations with Joseph, Amanda, and Evan, as well as his own evidence gathering, the detective had concluded this was the core team behind Project Impulse. Of course, they were just the puppeteers. In the next layer of his board came the puppets themselves.

First up was Mary Vasquez, also marked as deceased, but who Frank now knew was the original scientist tasked with bringing Project Impulse to fruition. Connected to her was Joseph, the missing ying to Mary's yang. Together, they had bred the first two Impulse children, Amanda and Evan, both stringing downward from there. But they'd also been succeeded by another scientist, Angela Sparrows, who had artificially imprinted her terminally ill son, Judas, with a genome that had transformed him into a third, highly unstable, Impulse child. Both Angela's and Judas's cards were noted with the word *deceased*, as was Evan's, all three of them victims of Project Impulse's deadly game.

There were a handful of other cards on the board that weren't as immediately pertinent to Frank's investigation. The names *Jackson* and *Finch* were attached to Colonel Davis. Joseph had witnessed Finch get killed during Eden's collapse, and though Jackson had survived, all signs pointed to him having resigned from duty. Two cards stacked to the side and disconnected from all others read *Omega Genome* and *Trizorapine*. The former was what gave the Impulse children their abilities. The latter was an aggression hormone that could stimulate those abilities. The two were tied to Helix Unbound, Project Impulse, all the puppets and puppeteers involved with them, and God knew what else. But they were also exhausted topics, with no further information to shed on Frank's deconstruction of Ray's drawing. So he saved himself some string and instead let them float ominously over everything else.

There was also a card that read *Sunrise Isle*. Frank knew little about the government-owned landmass other than its role as an extreme military training ground where Evan's abilities had first been put to the test. As such, he'd stringed it to both Evan and Project Impulse, but with no reason to suspect it still played an active role in the project, Frank hadn't allocated it much attention since. He gave the same treatment to a newspaper clipping that was headlined *Disgraced General Released From Custody* and contained a black-and-white photograph of General Francisco Javez, who Frank had deduced led the unsanctioned military assault on Complex B. The detective had no clue why General Javez had attacked the Helix Unbound sister facility, nor whom else he might have been working with, nor whether they were still pursuing action against the remnants of Project Impulse. But his sudden release from custody after being hammered with allegations that would have sent him to prison for life caught Frank's attention. So he added the general to his board, strung him to Complex B, and added a notecard with a question mark next to him to represent any unknown parties with whom he might be collaborating.

That left one final, notable card, this one at the end of a red string running downward from Ray's card, and then further webbed to the skylines of Eden and the card representing Evan. On it was the phrase *The Falling of the Tides*. Surrounding it were photos and newspaper clippings from Eden's collapse. Frank had stewed over this card and his related research material for far more hours than any psychiatrist would have deemed healthy. He had replayed his brother's prophecy in his mind, over and over, seeking hidden meaning beyond what was obvious on the surface. He had paired each phrase of the prophecy with events that had unfolded the day Eden fell, trying to convince himself that there was nothing more to it, that despite death rearing its ugly head, Eden had survived, Ray had not, and the prophecy was no longer a threat. He had tried to focus on Project Impulse, on an endgame that likely had nothing to do with Ray's mad rantings and that represented a snake hiding among the brush that could unexpectedly strike at any moment. And yet, both his eyes and mind kept getting drawn back toward the bottom of the pinboard, where those haunting words his brother had spoken on so many occasions still loomed. Frank couldn't shake the feeling that there was something greater at play, something he had spent the past year and a half inwardly knowing, but avoiding admitting to himself.

He grabbed a spool of string from the conference room table, pinned its loose end to Ray's notecard, then unwound enough to reach Amanda's notecard. This wasn't the first time he had linked the two. In fact, he had done so four times already, only to remove the connecting thread days or weeks later. Amanda had played no role in Eden's collapse, but a female Impulse child was at the center of Ray's visualization of the event, and the list of those potential candidates was exactly one name long. Frank had searched for something more to justify connecting Ray and Amanda on his investigation board, but he had always come up empty, leading to him reverting the board to its prior state.

But perhaps he was being too short-sighted. Perhaps the link between Ray and Amanda was contingent upon something else, another piece of information Frank had initially posted to his investigation board, only to later remove it, chalking it up to unreliable at best and falsely manipulative at worst. Maybe Frank needed to reconsider that assessment with a greater scope of interconnected relationships in mind. He stretched another piece of string from one of the Plainclothes' notecards—the one he had mentally assigned to the Project Impulse team member he had interrogated on the way to Complex B—down to Amanda's notecard. Once pinned, he set the spool of string aside and grabbed a black marker, which he then used to draw a solid line through Amanda's name. In the empty space beneath it, he then wrote *The Alpha child*.

Frank stepped back and stared hard at the moniker. He didn't like thinking of Amanda that way. She was a powerful creation of science, bred with destructive capabilities rivaled only by Evan and Judas, and with a will to survive surpassed by none. She was also a gentle, compassionate, and all around good-natured young woman, no doubt influenced by the upbringing of her equally good-natured fathers. Amanda was one of the good guys, and Frank had felt so ashamed for thinking of her otherwise that, after he had replaced his first Alpha child notecard with her real name, he'd silently forbidden himself from ever changing it back. He had sought other females connected to Ray and Project Impulse that could fill the role of the central figure in his brother's prophecy. His prime candidate was Abigail Desmond, but as far as Frank knew, Abigail had no special abilities herself, nor an army of super soldiers under her command. He reconsidered Laura Guiles, but quickly reaffirmed his previous position that she was a mostly innocent bystander to this affair. That left Mary Vasquez and Angela Sparrows, but they were both dead, so leading an army to destroy Eden was going to be quite the feat for either of them. Frank had identified a handful of other females with extraneous connections to Ray and Project Impulse in the months since then, but none were solid enough to give serious consideration.

Desperate to push beyond his investigative rut, he now violated his vow to give Amanda the benefit of the doubt, and instead grabbed his spool of string once more. Frank pinned one end of the string to his newly christened Alpha child notecard, then pinned the other end to the Falling of the Tides notecard. He then swapped for his marker and added a bold question mark to the end of the prophetic phrase. This had been the mystery boggling his mind since first discovering Ray's drawing. Had Eden's collapse truly been The Falling of the Tides, or was an even more destructive event on the horizon? If so, it wasn't beyond reason to assume Project Impulse—and its last remaining genetic creation—would have something to do with it. Maybe Frank needed to find Amanda, to make sure she was still the innocent young lady he believed her to be. Maybe—

"So this is the Bat Cave, huh?" a deep, humorless voice said from the conference room door.

Frank spun, startled at the sudden appearance of his captain. He had rehearsed this confrontation in his mind many times over the past year, assuming that one day he'd be caught in the act. Only now, with the disapproving eyes of his superior staring him down, his mind went blank, forgetting every excuse he had planned to use to justify his side hustle.

"I've ignored this as long as I can, Frank," Captain Tipps said as he meandered into the room and perused its contents. "But people are starting to talk upstairs. And that talking is getting unwanted attention."

"How long have you known?"

Captain Tipps cocked his head as if to say *please...*

"That long, huh?"

"You and Billy aren't as sneaky as you think you are." Captain Tipps paused before the pinboard and traced his gaze along the spiderweb of string, paper, and ink. "This is good detective work, Frank, but it isn't Jericho business. You know I normally wouldn't care as long as you were still getting your job done, but the entire department is under extra scrutiny right now. City council is clamping down on budgets, and they've got their eyes set on us as a source of significant wasteful spending."

"That's ridiculous," Frank said. "This might be the first time ever our budget has consistently been where it needs to be to properly serve this city."

"I don't disagree, but unfortunately, it's not my call to make. We've been doing a great job with the day-to-day safety of Jericho, but we haven't had a big win in a while. And the last one we had led to the incarceration of one of our own."

His words struck a nerve. Captain Tipps was referring to Frank's bust of Thomas DeMarco, the type of high-profile police action that put budgetary questions to rest without a second thought. DeMarco's imprisonment would have been a boon for the department, but his right hand, Dietrich Wessler, made sure it never came to fruition. He coerced one of Frank's go-to teammates into releasing DeMarco, who quickly fled the city to avoid recapture and hadn't shown his face in public since. The teammate in question, Carter, was arrested in DeMarco's place and subsequently sentenced to a five-year stint in minimum security with an opportunity for parole after three years. He was dismissed from Jericho PD—his pension revoked—and barred from returning to the force. It wasn't fair, but it was life, and it had turned an otherwise bright star for Jericho PD into a black mark that wouldn't soon be forgotten.

"We can't control how often a big win opportunity presents itself," Frank said.

"True," Captain Tipps agreed, "but irrelevant. Other cities of our size handle the day-to-day with two-thirds of our budget."

"Size doesn't equate to criminal presence."

"Also true, and sadly, also irrelevant. That's the benchmark city council is using."

Frank shrugged. "What do you want me to do about it, Captain?"

"They're sending inspectors in to evaluate our costs. We've got to minimize anything they could consider wasteful... in fact, and in appearance."

"So my investigation—"

"Needs to be out of here by end of day," Captain Tipps finished for him. "You can take anything that's not Jericho PD property home with you; work on it there. But you can't keep spending our resources or your clocked man hours on it."

Frank considered the order. Then he considered all the early mornings, all the late nights, and all the unanticipated calls he regularly experienced as part of his contribution to keep Jericho City safe. "I don't really have much personal time outside of this job."

Captain Tipps nodded, already well aware of that fact. Then he responded, "You'll have a lot more of it if the city council inspectors deem you a waste of money. Catch my drift?"

Frank caught it, then took one shot at diverting it. He grabbed a notecard and scribbled fiercely on it with his marker, then slapped it onto his pinboard right next to the floating Trizorapine card. He pointed at the newly added name: *DeMarco*. "Would this help?"

"Do you have any evidence linking him to... whatever the hell this is?"

Frank sighed in contemplation. "How strong of evidence are we talking?"

That was all Captain Tipps needed to hear. "Get it out of here, Frank," he said as he left the conference room. "By end of day. Batman's been fired. I need Bruce Wayne back tomorrow."

Though Frank appreciated the reference, he still wasn't thrilled with the order. Defeated, he sat on the conference room table and stared again at the Falling of the Tides notecard. Something was happening; his gut told him so, and it was rarely wrong. If only he could figure out what that something was... He clicked his tongue and stood, admitting to himself that getting fired wouldn't help Jericho PD, himself, or his ability to investigate Project Impulse. He had no choice but to shut down his basement operations, so he reached for the newly added DeMarco card and pulled... then stopped. Frank pondered on the name, hanging there next to the Omega Genome and Trizorapine cards, and surrounded by people and events that didn't involve the criminal. The detective's gut was churning, picking up on something, a clue perhaps, that wasn't obvious on the surface, but which was there nonetheless.

He opened his mind, slowly scanning the rest of his investigation board, waiting for whatever his senses had picked up to manifest before him in a tangible way, but it never did. Frank studied the spiderweb, and more importantly, the newly added notecard, for nearly ten minutes before finally calling it quits. He chalked up this particular gut feeling to a false alarm, an attempt by his brain to reconcile two outstanding mysteries by erroneously combining them into a single criminal endeavor. Frank unpinned the DeMarco notecard and tossed it aside. Then he grabbed his box of Ray's personal items, made room to one side, and proceeded to disassemble his investigation board, setting its contents into the box in as organized a fashion as he could. As he packed, he couldn't shake a nagging feeling that among his spiderweb of connections there had been an important detail he'd missed. For his own sanity, though, he eventually pushed the feeling aside, unaware as to just how close to the truth he had almost been.

CHAPTER 3
EVOLVING THREATS

After multiple attempts at remembering the most recent combination of numbers in a frequently rotated passcode, Colonel Davis passed through the digitally secured door that protected The Hive's control room. Before him were two rows of high-end computer terminals, most manned by Project Impulse's remaining scientific staff. Past them, spanning from edge-to-edge of what should have been a solid wall, was an oversized observation window that provided a view of The Hive itself. It was a cavernous chamber of sterile metal and wiring containing fifty identical pods the size of small vehicles. Each was suspended from the ceiling, powered and monitored by independent cabling, and each was also wired to a fifty-first containment unit that currently sat empty in the center of the chamber. Yellow warning lights spun in their casings along the chamber walls.

"Is it safe to be in there?" Colonel Davis asked a nearby scientist after spotting the Woman in White loitering along a distant chamber wall.

"Yes, sir. According to our systems, the outer wall has been breached, but the inner layer is currently holding strong. We'll let you know if anything changes."

The colonel took a heavy breath. He despised entering The Hive. Every moment spent in there felt like a moment trapped behind enemy lines, surrounded by fifty enemy combatants of superior ability, all waiting for their moment to pounce. He confirmed his pistol was secure at his hip, then proceeded to the air-locked door embedded in the observation window.

"Going in," he announced to the science staff.

The subordinate closest to the door tapped on his keyboard. A moment later, the airlock hissed, and the door slid upward, opening the path for Colonel

Davis to step into what could best be described as an oversized phone booth. Glass panels surrounded him on all sides, permitting him view of, but not access to, The Hive's main chamber. The door to the control room slid back into place, and its airlock hissed once more. Colonel Davis heard a motor roar to life and felt vacuumed wind blast around him as it cleansed him of any intrusive particles large enough to damage the semi-fragile network of hardware beyond. When the cleansing process was complete, an airlock opposite the entry one hissed, and a second door leading into The Hive's central chamber opened. Colonel Davis passed through it, then descended the subsequent metal staircase that led to The Hive's main floor. In the distance, he saw the Woman in White, who was accompanied by a scientist named Albert and an engineer Colonel Davis was pretty sure had once introduced himself as Diego. She spotted him and waved him over.

Just turn around, he told himself. *Just turn around and leave. Let the place fall to shit. It's bound to happen eventually...*

Seeing his hesitation, the Woman in White waved again, this time with more urgency. Colonel Davis ignored his inner voice and complied, starting his journey across The Hive's smooth, metallic floor. Overhead, the suspended pods provided periodic shade from both the chamber's persistent fluorescent glow and pulsing warning lights. Colonel Davis saw wisps of vapor seeping from the seals between each pod's lower metal body and glass upper lid. This wasn't abnormal, as the pods weren't airtight, and the cold preservation fluid within them evaporated at a predictable rate that required regular replenishment. Nonetheless, the vapor seepage reminded him that within each pod waited a living organism that, if granted consciousness, could tear him to shreds in the blink of an eye. The thought didn't help his already negative state of mind.

"Any day now, Colonel," the Woman in White said with a hint of irritation.

He paused out of pure petulance, then gritted his teeth and joined her along the chamber wall. "What's the rush? They told me the inner wall is holding."

"It is," the engineer, whose name badge confirmed he was, in fact, Diego, said. "At least for now. But that's precisely the problem. Since the intrusion can't get through to the main chamber, it's scouting the perimeter, searching for a weakness."

The *intrusion*, as Diego called it, had done this before, nearly instigating a catastrophic failure within The Hive. But its inner wall had been subsequently reinforced to prevent any such catastrophic breach again, and it sounded as though it was doing its job.

"I don't see the issue," Colonel Davis said.

"The issue isn't The Hive itself," Albert said. "It's the chemical tanks buried just outside of it. The intrusion is close to reaching those tanks, and they don't have the reinforcement we have in here."

Now Colonel Davis saw their concern. Burying The Hive's chemical tanks instead of hosting them inside the surrounding infrastructure had been a proactive measure taken to ensure the safety of its workers. Should the tanks fail, their contents would filter into the surrounding subsoil. It would cause contamination for sure, but nothing that should endanger human life... or so Project Impulse's engineers had thought. In hindsight, they'd learned it was the burying of the chemical tanks that had ultimately led to these repeated breaches. No one could have predicted how what was originally considered an acceptable level of spillage would permeate so drastically through the surrounding earth. And no one in their right mind could have foreseen the consequences that would stem from that permeation...

"Where's the closest access point?" Colonel Davis asked.

Diego pulled a folded blueprint from his back pocket and pointed to a hallway that was just beyond and above the adjacent wall. Colonel Davis looked at the Woman in White, who stood emotionless, waiting for his dutiful response.

"Tell Lance and Maddox to meet me there."

———

Derek parked his patrol car in the near-empty lot outside Lucky's Liquor and Billiards. He straightened his uniform as he stepped into the late morning sun, confirming his pistol was secure in its holster and the less lethal tools at his disposal, such as the pepper spray hanging from his belt, were in their expected positions. He then reminded himself that his dad wanted a calm and friendly end to this matter—a request that was inherently painful and in opposition to Derek's personal wishes—before opening the bar's front door and stepping inside.

The interior of Lucky's was dark, so dark, in fact, that it took Derek's eyes nearly half a minute before acclimating to the environment. Windows to the sunny world outside were clogged with liquor advertisements and event flyers, and any exposed glass had been frosted to diffuse penetrating light. Incandescent bulbs highlighted a wooden bar, fully stocked and lined with vinyl stools. Empty tables and chairs sat in the shadows nearby, and behind them was a row of booths, each with its own hanging bulb overhead and vinyl seating that matched the bar stools. Farther back was the pool room, where Derek saw a pair of regulars sinking ball after ball through a haze of cigarette smoke. Televisions were mounted periodically throughout the business. They were tuned to the day's sports news, with captions scrolling across the bottom of each screen for anyone more interested in that than the classic rock playing over the building's sound system.

Derek caught the bartender's eye after he finished pouring a drink for another regular, the only person currently taking up stool space in the establishment. The bartender nodded graciously to acknowledge his arrival, then pointed to a booth midway down the row. It was sad, Derek thought, that this had happened enough times that he and the bartender could communicate in this unspoken manner. It was also sad that the person responsible for his frequent calls to Lucky's was always the same, and never one of the less unruly regulars Derek had come to recognize over time. He strolled toward the indicated booth, eventually hitting an angle where he could see its inhabitant. It was a young man, about Derek's age, wearing the clothes of someone who came from privilege, but was also doing his best to mask that fact from the world.

"Mark," Derek said with a firm and objective voice.

The young man's sunken eyes peered at him through a curtain of disheveled hair. "Shit... you again, huh?"

"That's exactly what I thought when I saw your name on the call sheet this morning." Derek motioned to the empty seat across from him. "Mind if I sit?"

"Yes, I mind," Mark snapped. "I mind a lot. In fact, what I wouldn't mind is you getting the hell out of here and leaving me be. I haven't done anything wrong and I'm not bothering anyone."

Derek decided it was best to remain standing. "That's not what was reported to us."

Mark hollered over his shoulder. "That's because Jack or John or Jimbo or whatever the fuck his name is behind that bar doesn't know how to mind his own business!" He lowered his voice as he turned his stare to the empty beer glass on the table in front of him. "All I did was ask the waitress for another drink. No crime there."

"Where is she?" Derek asked, glancing around, but not seeing another employee.

"Jackass told her to wait in the back." Mark thumbed toward a swinging door near the bar. "He didn't want me *harassing* her... whatever that means."

"Were you harassing her, Mark?"

Mark fiddled nervously with his empty glass. "I just wanted another drink."

"That she refused to give you," Derek added, connecting the dots.

"That she *denied* me," Mark shot back with emphasis. "Everyone is always trying to deny me the things I want... the things I deserve!" He backhanded the empty glass, knocking it over with a loud *thwack* that splashed droplets of beer onto the table. "You should know that better than anyone," Mark growled. "You denied me my girl. Then that Cannes idiot denied me my internship and future job opportunity. Then my school denied me the education I'd been promised. They told me to take a break, get myself in order. I told them I didn't need a break. I just need people to stop *denying* me!"

Derek could see Mark's veins swelling along his forehead. He picked up the overturned glass and set it out of his former classmate's reach. "Mark, I won't pretend to know what you're going through."

"Thank God for that..."

Derek caught himself before he replied with choice words, once again recalling his father's instructions. "What I mean is, losing your internship and free ride into an awesome job must have sucked. And you're right, that was completely out of your control. But as for me, I didn't deny you anything. Stacy's her own person. You two had your time together, but she moved on. It happened to be to me, but it could have just as easily been to someone else. The point is, you need to respect her decision and move on yourself."

"Is this where you tell me there are plenty of fish in the sea?" Mark sneered. "Thanks for the unsolicited advice, asshole."

Derek felt his patience straining. "No, but it is where I tell you that the only one denying you anything at this point is you. Not moving on from Stacy is your choice. Not taking your university's offer for probationary leave was your choice. And getting shitfaced in this bar and harassing whatever employee cuts you off every few weeks instead of making a plan for your future is your choice." He was being harsher than intended, but he also knew Mark could use a good slap of reality. "You want to stop being denied? Get your life back on track and make something of yourself. Because at the moment, you're a pretty pathetic excuse for a human being."

Derek wasn't sure whether his former classmate would yell at him, sucker punch him, or go for his gun, so he braced for all three possibilities. But Mark was civil, and instead processed Derek's words for a moment before reaching for his back pocket.

"I think I'd better pay my tab." He dug in his pocket for just a second before surprise overtook his face. "Oh wait, what's this back here?" He brought his hand around to Derek's eye level, his middle finger raised straight into the air. "Oh, I was wondering where I'd misplaced my *fuck you.*"

Derek eyed the outstretched finger, all the while thinking how his police training would make breaking its skinny bone a breeze. But that's what Mark wanted. He wanted Derek to overreact and cross the ethical line that could cost him his job. Luckily, Derek was smart enough to recognize that, so he kept his cool.

"Come on, Mark," he said, waving his former classmate out of the booth. "Let's get out of here."

Mark retracted his finger. "Throwing me in jail again?"

"I'm taking you home. You're in no condition to drive."

Mark bobbed back and forth as if contemplating whether to capitulate. Then he threw his hands up in defeat and slid from the booth. "Don't even think about having my car towed."

"It'll be here," Derek assured him. "You can pick it up when you come back to pay your tab... and apologize."

"Whatever."

Mark stumbled past the bartender, waking his middle finger from its temporary slumber to say goodbye as he tripped over the leg of a stool and hobbled toward the exit.

"Why don't you make all our lives easier and just ban him from coming in?" Derek asked.

"We tried that," the bartender told him. "And instead of causing a ruckus in here, he did it out there, scaring our other clientele away. Nine times out of ten he comes in, drinks himself stupid, maybe meets up with a friend, and then goes on his way without issue. It's just the tenth time when things get out of hand."

Mark pushed open the exit door and groaned in anguish as the late morning sun slammed into him.

"If he doesn't come settle up—" Derek started.

"He will. We don't serve him again until he does." The bartender extended a hand. "Thanks, Officer Desmond."

Derek shook it. "Let's not do it again too soon, huh?"

They shared a chuckle, then Derek joined Mark outside. In the brightness of daylight, he got a much better look at his former classmate, who had apparently fallen significantly farther from grace than Derek had initially thought. Mark's hair was not only disheveled, but greasy, as though he hadn't properly showered in days. His fingernails were at least a few weeks overdue for a clipping. His teeth were showing signs of staining, and his arm trembled the way one's arm might when low on blood sugar... or craving satiation of some other unnatural deficiency. Derek walked Mark to his police cruiser and opened the rear door.

"I thought you weren't arresting me," his former classmate said as he looked at the steel fence separating the front seat from the back.

"I'm not," Derek reiterated. "But you're crazy if you think I trust you enough to ride up front with me. Now watch your head and get in."

Mark grumbled unintelligibly, but obeyed. Once he was seated, Derek leaned in for a closer examination.

"If you want a kiss, you'd better call my *former* girlfriend," Mark hissed. "I can attest to her sucking abil—"

"Finish that sentence and I'll be dropping you off at the hospital instead of home." Derek was trying to contain his anger, but enough of it must have slipped through that Mark got the message. He finished his exam and stood back. "What have you had?"

"I think I emptied the tap of Guinness."

"I'm not talking about alcohol," Derek clarified. "Your eyes are sunken and bloodshot. Your pupils are dilated, you don't focus on any one thing for more than a second or two, and I can see your rapid pulse twitching in your neck. You've got more than alcohol in your system. What is it? Is it that new drug rumored to be going around?"

"Why, Officer Desmond, I have no idea what you're talking about."

"This isn't a game, Mark. No one knows what's in that stuff. If you're not careful, you're going to end up on a gurney or in a body bag."

"Thanks for the public service announcement," Mark said without care. "Can you take me home now? You keep me in this cruiser any longer and I'm going to be the one phoning in a complaint for unlawful detainment."

Realizing this was going nowhere, Derek slammed the door. He would bring Mark home as promised. After that, he would return to Eden PD and note Mark's name in the growing stack of circumstantial evidence on the new drug infestation cropping up in the city. Despite their tumultuous relationship, Derek didn't wish ill on his former classmate and adversary. And if Mark was an early user of this new drug, he wanted it in the official log, so they could get him help once a path to recovery was established. Derek climbed behind the wheel, plugged Mark's home address into his GPS to check whether any unexpected traffic was blocking their usual path, then eyed his passenger in the rearview mirror, wondering how someone with such a bright future could have crashed down so hard.

———

With an assault rifle slung around one arm, extra ammo strapped across his chest, and a machete draped from his waist, Colonel Davis turned the corner to the hallway Diego had shown him on The Hive's blueprints. Flickering LED lights greeted him, their wiring no doubt compromised by the intruder within The Hive's walls. At the far end of the sterile hallway stood two soldiers, Lance and Maddox, the last survivors of Colonel Davis's original command at Helix Unbound. They were armed with the same arsenal as their superior, but carried a nervousness not shared by him, their comfort with the ever evolving threats of

Project Impulse wavering over time. But they were all Colonel Davis had, so he made the best of it.

"Have you identified the source?" he asked as he joined his men.

Lance pointed. "There."

A hairline crack marred the indicated spot on the corridor's wall. Several feet beyond that wall was the reinforcement layer that surrounded The Hive, and close by were the chemical tanks that would wreak havoc on the facility if breached. Colonel Davis neared the crack and listened cautiously. At first, there was nothing but quiet. But then he heard the scraping, a deep, expansive scraping similar to those he had heard when dealing with previous breaches. Powdered concrete fell from the crack as it widened just enough to be visibly perceptible. Colonel Davis extended an open palm toward Maddox.

"Charge."

Maddox handed him a rectangular slab of putty wired with a blasting cap. It was slightly larger than a deck of playing cards, a size that had been refined through trial and error during prior breaches—large enough to provide access to their intruder, but small enough to avoid unnecessary damage to the facility. Colonel Davis placed the explosive at the midpoint of the crack, which was now branching off into multiple splinters. If he waited long enough, he wouldn't even need to waste one of his rapidly depleting explosive munitions. Then again, if he waited that long, Colonel Davis would have to switch modes from breach prevention to chemical containment, and he had little confidence in his ability to successfully achieve the latter.

"Clear the blast radius," he ordered.

He, Lance, and Maddox retreated around the far corner. Then Colonel Davis gave the signal, and Maddox triggered the explosive. The blast was deafening in the tight corridor, but experience had taught the trio to prepare for it with earplugs. When they felt the shockwave of the detonation pass, they removed those earplugs and returned to the breached hallway, which was now obscured with concrete dust and smoke. The flickering light hindered visibility further, glare reflecting sporadically off the ever-swirling smoke trails. Colonel Davis slid his assault rifle into ready position, Lance and Maddox doing the same. He motioned for his men to follow, silently wondering whether one of them would put a bullet in his back before he had a chance to complete his assignment.

But Colonel Davis reached the blast site with his life intact and body injury free. He still couldn't see well, but he could hear the deep scraping continue with greater intensity than before. The intruder was pulling back—or so he hoped—an indicator of its ability to remember what came next if it continued its assault on The Hive. The smoke began to clear, and soon Colonel Davis could see his opponent. Rough, brown, fleshy material appeared through the jagged hole left by the explosive. It was moving, worming its way past the opening as it pulled back through the tunnel it had dug to get this far into the facility. Lance pointed his rifle at the fleshy surface.

"Wait," Colonel Davis said. "It's retreating. Only engage if it stops."

These breach encounters were as much about armed combat as they were about military strategy. The Hive's opposition wasn't a singular entity, but rather an army of disjointed units that had learned to communicate and coordinate, as well as to react in kind to whatever defenses Colonel Davis levied at it. If he and his men attacked, it would do the same. But if they allowed it a safe retreat, there was a possibility it wouldn't engage, and that was the safest scenario for all parties involved. Lance lowered the tip of his rifle, but only slightly. Like his commander, Maddox had his weapon at the ready, but without the aggressive stance his partner had taken.

The fleshy brown surface continued sliding through the exposed tunnel. Its diameter was shrinking, as if funneling down toward a much smaller tip. A cloud of concrete dust shot from the blast hole, temporarily obscuring Colonel Davis's view once more, and when it cleared, the fleshy surface was gone. The scraping sound faded into the distance and eventually became inaudible. Colonel Davis freed a hand to grab his radio.

"Diego, are you on the monitor?"

The reply came after a moment's pause. *"Yes. According to our sensors, it's still in the system. I think it's waiting to see what you'll do next."*

"Roger that." Colonel Davis hooked his radio back to his belt and raised his rifle toward the breach hole. "Lance, give it some warning fire."

Lance nodded in acknowledgement and approached the hole. He gripped his rifle tighter, almost hiding the tremble in his posture as he angled its barrel into the hole, pointing toward the blackness into which The Hive's intruder had retreated. Then he fired a quick burst. The muzzle blast briefly illuminated the darkness, revealing no threat in the immediate vicinity. Lance pushed closer to the hole, angling his aim deeper into the tunnel beyond, and fired two more bursts. This time, the intruder responded. Its scraping resumed, not in an advance toward Lance, nor in continued retreat. Instead, it pivoted overhead, into a tunnel crossing the corridor's ceiling. Colonel Davis trailed its noise with both his eyes and rifle barrel, alarm bells ringing in his head as the intruder demonstrated behavior he had never seen before.

"Should we blast again?" Maddox asked.

Colonel Davis shook his head firmly. "No."

The scraping was too intense to indicate the intruder was burrowing a new tunnel. It was worming through a tunnel it had already prepared, which meant it had anticipated Colonel Davis's response, and that blasting another access point might be exactly what it wanted. The scraping stopped once more, its source not fading into the distance, but lingering directly above them.

"What the hell is it doing, Colonel?" Lance asked, his voice quivering.

Wondering the same, Colonel Davis ignored him. He scanned the ceiling of the corridor for any signs that its integrity had been compromised, but saw none. Then a new sound arose. This one was a rapid, repetitive tapping, echoing from the deserted blast hole. Eyes wide with fear, Lance backed away from the hole, indecisive whether to focus his aim toward it or the looming threat overhead. The tapping grew louder, and the increased volume revealed that there wasn't a single source of it, but rather multiple, overlapping sources, all traveling down the abandoned tunnel, traveling toward Colonel Davis and his men.

"Retreat," the leader said with the calm of an experienced soldier, but with the body language of someone who knew he was on the losing side of an impending skirmish.

Maddox stepped backwards, his rifle aimed at the ceiling. Lance followed, still swinging wildly back and forth between the ceiling and blast hole, his nervous trigger finger ready to squeeze at the slightest movement from either. Then, without further warning, a figure scurried from the darkness. It was an ant, though unlike any ant Lance had seen before. Its body was the size of his largest finger, so large that he could make out the individual lenses composing its compound eyes. The ant raced across the floor faster than Lance could chase it with his onslaught of gunfire, tapping past Colonel Davis, who jumped back as bullets ricocheted off the floor at his feet.

"Don't take your eyes off the hole!" he screamed at Lance.

But it was too late. Lance was so fixated on the mutant ant now climbing the opposite wall that he failed to notice the small army of ants that had emerged behind it. Maddox adjusted his aim and opened fire on the dark swarm, his bullets searing through hairy legs and antennae, but doing nothing to slow the movement of the army as a whole. Lance turned to join the assault, but not before the first of the swarm reached his feet. Several ants were already climbing his legs, their mandibles slicing through his thick pants and drawing blood from gashes in the skin underneath.

"Arms up!" Colonel Davis yelled.

Lance abandoned his attempt at personal defense and raised his arms as Colonel Davis swooped in with his machete. The blade passed along the front of Lance's body, nearly taking off his nose, before severing through the legs of the ants that had attached themselves to him. Colonel Davis pulled his soldier away from the swarm as it broke apart, its insect members scurrying in every direction and along every surface. Maddox's rifle clicked as it hit the end of its clip. He reached for a spare, and only then noticed the rogue ant that had snuck onto his body during his firing spree. The ant hadn't bitten him, and instead had climbed to his next slab of plastic explosive. Maddox watched in stunned horror as the ant simultaneously lifted the slab into its jaws while knocking its trigger to the floor, where another two ants waited to grab it. The ant with the explosive then jumped off of him, scurried past the retreating Colonel Davis and Lance, and tossed the explosive to another ant hanging upside down from the corridor's ceiling. The trigger ants each took an end of the device and pushed toward each other.

"Take cover!" Maddox yelled, dropping into a fetal position.

Colonel Davis and Lance barely had time to comply before the explosion thundered behind them. Chunks of concrete, torn insulation, and shredded wiring fell from the ceiling into a new cloud of smoke and dusty debris. Colonel Davis had no time to think. He felt scurrying around his feet and slashed wildly with his machete as he hobbled away from the blast. He stumbled into Maddox, who was rising with a distant gaze in his eyes and unresponsive to his colonel's muted orders. Colonel Davis gave the soldier a slap to wake him from his daze, then grabbed Maddox's rifle and pushed it into his hands. He then stood at Maddox's side and replaced his machete with his own rifle, which he aimed toward the flickering dust cloud still lingering in the corridor. The remaining ants weren't advancing. Colonel Davis tried to think through the ringing in his ears, asking himself why they had stopped, but no answers came. Then the dust cloud settled, revealing the aftermath of their surprise attack.

A new hole, this one bigger than the last due to the assistance of gravity, was now open in the corridor's ceiling. Hanging down from the darkness within it was the thick tentacle of rough, brown flesh. It was a root, Colonel Davis knew, just one of many that had mutated along with their attached plants in the grounds surrounding The Hive. The root had wrapped itself around Lance and was squeezing him like a boa constrictor as the remaining ants sawed off chunks of his flesh. This was flora and fauna working in unison to defend its terrain and survive... the unnatural insanity that had developed through years of exposure to chemicals that would one day lead to the development of Trizorapine. It was the norm for Sunrise Isle, but it was increasingly becoming a thorn in the side of Project Impulse. These abominations of nature knew what The Hive was harboring, and they wanted it for themselves. Addicts in search of a fix, they had tried to take it by force before, and there was little doubt they would try again, over and over until they picked off every last member of The Hive and claimed the chemical stimulants within for themselves.

"Colonel?" Maddox asked, seeking advice.

Colonel Davis assessed Lance. He was still alive, but even if they could find a way to rescue him, what little life he had left would be spent in painful misery. "Charge," he said to Maddox, opening his palm once more.

Maddox reluctantly handed off his final explosive. Colonel Davis guided them down the corridor, far enough that they wouldn't sustain further injury from the next blast. Then he instructed Maddox to detonate the explosive as soon as it reached the swarm of intruders. He assumed a pitcher's stance and threw the clay brick down the length of the corridor. It landed at Lance's feet, drawing an immediate reaction of fear from the ants gathered there. Maddox followed through with his orders, igniting the explosive before the ants could retreat from the blast radius, its concussive blast shredding human, animal, and plant flesh alike as it ended Lance's suffering while simultaneously crippling the attacking army.

Colonel Davis adjusted the grip on his rifle and advanced toward the remnants of flora and fauna that hid behind a barrier of smoke. He fired a burst, then another, taking out two remaining ants that were scrambling to safety. After a brief hesitation, Maddox joined him, taking out three ants himself as the smoke cleared enough to reveal what was left of the instigating root. It was dangling from the ceiling hole, too damaged to retreat, a gash splitting all but a fourth of its diameter, and burns masking its previously brown surface. Colonel Davis watched the tip of the root twitch with life, curling and uncurling as if still jonesing for a chemical fix as it dangled on death's door. He stepped close enough to draw the root's attention, then unloaded every bullet left in his clip into the intruder's remaining mass. When he was done, the fleshy tentacle fell limp. The intruding army had been defeated, though not without cost.

"Diego?" Colonel Davis said into his radio, no hint of emotion to his words.

"I'm here. Sensors are still showing a presence in the system, but no movement."

"It's dead," Colonel Davis confirmed. "But we've got extensive damage down here. You'll need to get your team on it immediately. There's no telling when the next attack will come."

"We'll get down there right away," Diego replied.

Colonel Davis didn't bother responding, and instead slipped his radio back onto his belt before silently abandoning the interior battlefield. Maddox hung back, observing the carnage. Human flesh, foliage, and splintered exoskeletons smoldered all around, an unholy spattering of man and monstrous abominations.

"This is how it's going to end for all of us, isn't it, Colonel?" he called after his superior. "One second we're fighting the good fight; the next second we're a single misstep from eternal nothingness."

Colonel Davis paused, but didn't look back. "We were never fighting the good fight, Maddox. If that's what you've been telling yourself, then you'd better get out while you still can."

Maddox didn't intend to gulp loud enough for the colonel to hear, but he was aware he'd done so. "Can we still? Get out, I mean. Because it sure seems like that ship sailed long ago."

Colonel Davis shrugged. "There's more than one way to escape. Don't believe me? Ask Lance."

And that was the dour note he left Maddox on as he turned the corridor corner to find the Woman in White for their usual post-breach debrief. Maddox hung back for another minute, unsure what to make of Colonel Davis's response. Then he said a silent goodbye to Lance and followed after his superior, forging onward with his duty to Project Impulse, if only because he saw no other viable option to pursue.

CHAPTER 4
EXPOSURE

Amanda had finished her video message to Joseph long before the sun rose. She'd known it was going to be difficult to record, hence her repeated procrastination, and yet she was still unprepared for the way each word twisted her gut, her insides crying in pain as she fought not to do the same on digital film. When the message was complete, Amanda had played it back to confirm she'd communicated all the pertinent details she'd intended. She had played it back a second time, this time studying her own face to ensure her expressions hadn't betrayed her in a way that would make the message harder on her surrogate father. Then she'd played it a third time, this time with her eyes closed, more of a reiteration to herself that she was doing the right thing than anything else.

The video wasn't long, but the words within it were heavy, and Amanda worried what toll they might take on Joseph. Nonetheless, this was an action that couldn't be avoided. So she'd saved the reviewed file to the laptop's hard drive, saved a second copy to a flash drive seated in one of its ports, and, for good measure, saved a third copy in a secure online repository. Afterwards, she had quietly packed her belongings, focusing only on a few days' worth of necessities and leaving everything else behind for her temporary family to keep or dispose of as they saw fit. Then, as the sun peeked over the horizon, she prepared breakfast, timing it to hit the table just as those who had cared for her this past year and a half woke to begin their day. She explained it was time for her to leave and showed the family where she had stored her video message, so they could deliver it when the appropriate time came. Then she exchanged goodbyes that tore at her soul more than she ever could have imagined they would, and left.

Amanda took a bus over three hundred miles to Atlanta, for she wanted to shield her temporary family from any fallout that might arise from her subsequent actions. Then she set out on foot from a downtown transit depot, walking the streets of the city as any other resident or tourist might do, her eyes and ears attuned to activity taking place near and far. She saw and heard the joyful squeals of children at play during recess, the tense conversations of businesspeople on their cell phones or in their offices, exchanges between friends and lovers meeting for midday excursions, and the often pleasant, but sometimes rude orders customers gave at their favorite coffee shops and lunch spots. There was a time when such sensory overload would have been too much for Amanda to handle. But she was different now, forever altered by both the trauma that had plagued her life and the genetic and chemical manipulations to her body and mind. Taking in all around her was par for the course, not because she engaged in it frequently, but because doing so was no more difficult than watching a movie or reading a book.

Amanda caught the sound of what seemed to be a growing dispute between agitated parties. There was one man and one woman involved, and a child crying in the background. She changed directions and picked up her pace, honing in on the luxury apartment complex in which the dispute was underway. It was coming from the nineteenth—no, twentieth floor—and now Amanda could make out aggressive movements through the street-facing windows of the apartment in question. They weren't the type of movements that the average passerby would have noticed, especially with the midday sun glaring off the clean glass panels, but they were perceptible to Amanda, who sensed both tension and fear from the parties within. This hadn't been the type of activity she'd been seeking, but she couldn't ignore it, either. She sped up again, nearly breaking into a run before halting at the next intersection.

A third and fourth party had entered the dispute. Amanda heard the words *officer* and *calm down*. Someone was now comforting the crying child, and the man and woman had been escorted to separate rooms, where much more level-headed conversation was underway. Amanda smiled, comforted to know there were still others in this world fighting the evils perpetually trying to overtake it. These were people like Vincent and Derek Desmond, like Frank Holmes, Lamar Reed, Joseph... those who Amanda looked at as her family, those she missed ever so greatly...

A shout gripped her attention. The source was a male, likely in his late teens or early twenties, maybe a half-mile to a mile away. His words were fueled by agitation, agitation met in kind by a second male. Others were present, though how many Amanda wasn't quite sure, and they were doing little to reign in the other two. This was the type of opportunity she'd been seeking, so she angled toward the source of the shouting—somewhere on the outskirts of the city's main hustle and bustle—and launched into a sprint. Amanda processed continuous updates as she ran. The original male was leveling accusations at the other, something about *encroaching on his territory*. The second male was responding with hostility fueled defense. The others had taken sides, wielding shouts of support for their chosen teams and verbally attacking those who stood in opposition.

Her speed easily besting even the greatest of athletes, Amanda was now only thirty to forty-five seconds away from the combative group. She used the angles and relative volumes of their voices to triangulate everyone's position. The two original combatants were at the center of the group, likely facing one another. Five additional people of similar age had gathered behind one of them; four behind the other. They were a mix of male and female, standing in loosely formed lines. So many were screaming at each other in unison that Amanda had trouble distinguishing which person was saying what. Then, all at once, everyone grew deadly quiet, a new emotion rising above all others: mortal fear.

The second male had pulled a gun on the first. He hadn't fired, but Amanda could sense he was willing. The weapon's appearance was what had silenced everyone else. Still about twenty-seconds out, Amanda debated whether to dematerialize into energy particles so she could race into the fray even quicker. She hadn't already because she didn't want her entry to be so astounding that it frightened the group away. She was hoping to strike a balance between exposing her abilities and freaking out those who witnessed them. But now someone's life was on the line, and she had to put that above her own wants. As Amanda's body broke into subatomic specks of blue light, she sensed the original male revealing his own weapon. The situation was spiraling quickly. She just needed a few more seconds...

Shots rang out, several from each weapon, the bullets spraying with such imprecision that they would have hit both shooters and at least two or three of their supporters had Amanda not landed in the middle of them first. She formed shields of blue energy to intercept the deadly projectiles, then allowed her arms, body, and finally, head and legs, to follow. She had forgotten how much pain taking bullets could inflict, the sear of their heat and brutality of their impact disseminating throughout her loosely formed atoms. Nonetheless, she held her ground firmly, unwilling to give the armed males any reason to doubt the power of the girl who now stood between them. She stared each of them down in turn, the fire in her eyes dissuading further violence. One dropped his gun to the concrete; the other lowered it to his hip. But Amanda wanted to make it clear their behavior wouldn't be tolerated, so she converted one of her energy shields into a tentacle of blue light that whipped the guns away from their owners, tossing them far out of sight, where Amanda would retrieve—and dispose of—them later.

"Holy shit..." one of the males muttered. "You're like a fucking superhero or something."

Amanda reformed her hands to show the group her humanity. Surprisingly, none of them had run, probably because they were too stunned by what they'd seen. Amanda hoped none of them would keel over with a heart attack, as that would put quite a damper on an intervention that had so far played out exactly as she had wanted.

"Straighten your lives out," she said to the combative males. "Both of you. Before you and your friends wind up as statistics on the evening news."

Her words triggered one of the observing supporters, just as she had hoped it might. A cell phone emerged, propped in a vertical position, with its rear camera pointed directly at Amanda. She pretended not to notice so she wouldn't scare the phone holder off, and instead allowed her body to dematerialize once more. She could have walked away like a normal person, in which case the video being recorded wouldn't have held much interest to anyone outside of this group. But that would have defeated the purpose of this little excursion. Instead, Amanda let her energy particles linger in a rough outline of her body as she looked back and forth between the combative males, brightening the particles that represented her eyes with extra electricity so they would know exactly what she was doing. Then she took off, streaming into the sky at a slow enough pace that her ascent could be digitally captured.

As she departed, Amanda could sense the shift in emotion she had instigated in the crowd. No one was harboring feelings of violence, or even anger, for that matter. They were instead sharing feelings of astonishment, of wonder, of curiosity at having witnessed an action that could only be described as superhuman. They would share those feelings and their tale with others, and at least in the short-term, they would unite over their experience. That was the best Amanda could hope for. She couldn't monitor the group—and especially the combative males at its center—forever. But she had defused the ticking time bomb that had nearly detonated between them; now it was up to them to not build another.

Amanda made sure to pass close by surrounding windows as she left the scene, to give others an opportunity to catch what certainly appeared to be supernatural phenomena on video. She made a brief stop to pick up the guns she had flung out of reach, then dismantled them in flight, dropping their various parts into open garbage bins over a two-mile stretch. Afterwards, she landed near the transit depot she had used to first arrive in Atlanta. She reformed her body—this time away from curious eyes—and entered the depot, where she purchased a ticket, then waited patiently for the ride to her next destination. Sure, she could have flown all the way there, but she needed time for her plan to play out anyway, so she conserved her energy, knowing she would eventually need every ounce at her disposal for the confrontation that lay ahead.

———

That afternoon, Mayor Samuel Collins sat in his office, leaning back in a shiny leather chair with a phone to his ear as he brokered a favorable deal for a new construction project in the southern part of the city. He was having a sports park built on prime real estate, not because he cared about his citizens having access to outdoor recreational space, but because the contractors had agreed to put his name on the complex in exchange for its premium location. With all Eden had been through during his tenure as mayor, Samuel knew he couldn't count on holding the office forever, so these days he was focused more on solidifying his legacy than on the day-to-day operations of the city. His portrait had already been allocated a permanent spot in the mayor's office, just to the side of his desk, where it could watch over the actions of his eventual successors, a ghost of the past rivaled only by Jacob Marley. Then there was the hedge maze, Eden's most popular tourist attraction, at the base of City Hall. The entrance to the maze bore a plaque with his name listed in bold letters as the party responsible for its commission, something the original incarnation of the maze had lacked, but that Samuel had ensured wasn't overlooked during its rebuilding. There was also Eden's Rose Parade, the one city event for which Samuel actually deserved credit, and he'd secured ironclad contracts requiring an annual acknowledgment of the city's gratitude for his efforts each time the parade started rolling, even once he was out of office.

Each of those tributes to his legacy was fine and dandy, but their reach was inherently limited. Only future mayors and their guests would ever see Samuel's portrait. A minimal number of tourists and residents would bother reading his name on the plaque at the entrance to the hedge maze. And only those residents crowded around the Rose Parade's kickoff point would hear the city express its ongoing appreciation for his time in office. Samuel wanted his name somewhere it couldn't be ignored. He'd been working on a scheme to get it plastered above the entrance to City Hall, but had faced a surprising amount of pushback, with opponents arguing that City Hall should be neutral ground, not tainted by the sponsorship of any one individual, corporation, or political party. Though he would never give up the endeavor, Samuel could see the writing on the wall, that it was a battle he was unlikely to win.

That's what had first taken him down the sports route. One certainty in this country was that sports captured eyeballs, and most stadiums, fields, and arenas carried sponsored names that were repeatedly absorbed by those eyeballs. They were usually the names of large corporations with limited term contracts that required ungodly sums of investment, sums of investment Samuel didn't have in his personal bank account, no matter how much he might like to. Adding to the problem was that Eden didn't currently have any professional sports teams. There had been talks of establishing both a baseball and football franchise since before the city's collapse, but those talks had been suspended for obvious reasons. Though Samuel had reignited them during the past year, it was unlikely either would come to fruition during his time in office.

So he set his sights on smaller-scale sports exposure. Maybe Eden would one day have its own professional teams. Maybe it wouldn't. Regardless, opportunities existed for talented kids to join the ranks of professional sports, and their vote-placing and money-donating parents were more than happy to support their endeavors. The kids had their usual school practice fields and gymnasiums to play in, but if they really wanted to stand out on the crowded national stage, they needed a higher-profile venue in which to display their skills. That's where the idea for the sports park had come from. Its core design would support football, baseball, basketball, and soccer. Pre-planned expansions for a year or two down the line would then appeal to less popular activities such as swimming, gymnastics, martial arts, and ballet. Foundations would be in place to temporarily convert unused outdoor space into ice rinks and festive displays during winter months, which would have the extra benefit of enhancing tourist appeal. And Samuel's name would be on all of it. The contracts he'd signed would ensure that for the foreseeable future and long after he had left this world. He could die happy, knowing his legacy would live on.

The intercom on Samuel's desk buzzed. *"Mr. Mayor?"* It was the voice of his newest secretary, Louise. *"Sheriff Desmond and Doctor Reed are here to see you."*

Samuel checked his wall clock. They were five minutes early, not egregious, but annoying nonetheless. His old secretary, Noreen, would have made them wait until their appointed time before bugging him. Samuel wished he could find someone who understood him as well as she had. But he had already gone through seven different secretaries since her untimely passing, and none of them, including Louise, had met his admittedly high expectations.

"Tell them I need two minutes. Then you can send them back."

Samuel needed two minutes like he needed Eden to undergo another catastrophe. There was nothing pressing on his plate, nor nothing he could accomplish in such a short period. He was making Vincent and Lamar wait on principle, if for no other reason than to establish that his time was more valuable than theirs. He stretched, his leather chair creaking under his weight, then sat up straight and cleared his throat as he heard his office door click open.

"Good afternoon, Mr. Mayor," Vincent opened with an outstretched hand.

The trio exchanged greetings, and Louise confirmed they didn't need anything further. Then Samuel motioned for Vincent and Lamar to take seats across from him as he poured himself a glass of whiskey from a near-empty bottle he kept in one of his desk drawers. He didn't offer to share.

"So, give me peace of mind over this week's parade. What are you two doing to ensure it goes off without a hitch?"

That question covered far more than Vincent's responsibility, and he was pretty sure it covered more than Lamar's as well. "We're only handling safety measures. The functioning of the parade itself is someone else's department."

Samuel abruptly cut off his pour and stared at Vincent as if to say *no shit*. "Fine. What are you two doing to ensure *the safety* of everyone in attendance?"

This was yet another contentious start to one of Vincent's meetings with the mayor. After going through so much together, he thought Samuel would have warmed up to him by now. But they came from different worlds and different mentalities, and apparently it wasn't meant to be. Even so, Vincent had at least hoped for some professional politeness. Based on ongoing conversations with Lamar, however, he knew better than to hold his breath.

"I've got most of Eden PD scheduled to be on duty starting four hours before parade kickoff and lasting up to an hour after it ends," he said.

"Most?" Samuel asked as he gulped back half the contents of his glass. "Why not all?"

Did he remember nothing from the previous year they did this? Or was he still that shaken by Judas's attack on The Red Room, and therefore being extra cautious? Vincent hid his aggravation. "We'll need to keep a barebones crew at the station to deal with anything that might arise away from the parade route. We've also got a handful of officers who already had approved vacation requests." He saw Samuel's right eye snap toward him from behind the crystalline cup at his lips. He treaded lightly. "And we're letting whomever worked the midnight to morning shift off the hook so they can relieve everyone else when the parade is over."

Samuel finished his first glass—of the meeting, not the day—and set it down with measured contempt. "Cancel the vacations. The parade's been scheduled for over a year. They should have never been approved in the first place."

"We have plenty of manpower—"

"And screw the barebones crew," Samuel said, cutting off his response. "Nearly everyone in the city will be at the parade. That's where the police need to be. You can clean up any minor infractions that occur elsewhere when the celebration is over."

"I don't think you want to set that type of precedent," Vincent advised. "If criminals start associating the Rose Parade with a free-for-all in the rest of the city, we'll see surges in crime that won't look good for any of us." He hoped the optics appeal would resonate with Samuel.

"That's a future problem," the mayor retorted. "It's not precedent this year, so I want everyone there. You can leave that receptionist you've been dating to monitor the phones, but if I find out anyone else stayed behind, I'll have their badge. If I find out they did it with your permission, I'll have yours, too. It's nothing personal, Sheriff."

It sure as shit felt personal. "Mr. Mayor, you tasked me with keeping Eden safe. I need you to let me do my job, and that includes resource allocation."

"Not on parade day," Samuel said. "There's too much risk." He emptied his bottle of whiskey, which only filled a third of the once-emptied glass. He then shifted his gaze to Lamar. "Speaking of..."

Ever since Eden's collapse, Lamar had been a frequent visitor to City Hall. He was in charge of the tunnel reinforcement efforts underneath the city, a project that carried with it immense financial burden and required city official signatures far more often than he cared for. He knew Samuel had never really liked him, and only tolerated him for his knowledge of Eden's deadly substructure and initiatives to stabilize it, which had, so far, been quite a success.

"I've already got a routine coded into our system to provide live monitoring of the sensors along the parade route," the wiry geologist said. "I've also had my team double-check that each sensor is working properly and that there are no blind spots."

"You're talking about detection measures," Samuel said as he stared at his last swallow of whiskey with a tempting eye. "I want to hear about preventative measures."

Lamar shrugged. "They're no different from what we've been doing. The entire route is contained within our reinforced tunnel system. There's no reason to suspect—"

"The Red Room was over the reinforced tunnel system, Doctor." Samuel's tone signaled a mix of frustration and thinning restraint. "It's not the natural disasters I'm worried about this year. It's the manmade ones."

"Um," Lamar looked at Vincent, who shrugged with frustration. "Well, we did add a security camera system to the tunnels. It currently only covers main junctures, though, not every stretch."

"Can you reposition the cameras? At least for parade day?"

"I suppose we could, but—"

"But what, Doctor Reed?" Samuel asked, his restraint nearly gone.

Lamar knew it wouldn't go over well, but there was no point beating around the bush. "The system is monitored by Eden PD. So even if we move the cameras, if no one is at the station—"

Samuel held up a trembling hand, silencing him. He closed his eyes, took an audible breath, then returned his attention to Vincent. "You can hold back the required number of men to monitor Doctor Reed's cameras, but not one more. Understood?"

Vincent saw no point in fighting. "Yes, Mr. Mayor."

"And Doctor Reed?" Samuel said, shifting his gaze again. "I expect you and your team to personally patrol the tunnels during the parade, so there are no delays should one of your sensors detect unusual activity."

"We were planning on it."

"I can pair an officer with each of them," Vincent suggested. "That way, we combine detection with deterrence."

"Deterrence will be greater if those officers are visible to the general public," Samuel argued back. "So will confidence. I want your men at street level and above."

Vincent was getting really tired of being told how to do his job. But for the sake of keeping the peace, he bit his tongue. "Okay."

Samuel swung his eyes back and forth between his guests, as if waiting for additional pushback on his requests. When there was none, he smiled. "Well then, is there anything else you gentlemen need from me today? Any paperwork to sign or reports to peruse?"

"Not from me," Vincent said.

Lamar shook his head. "Me either."

Samuel downed his last gulp of whiskey, released an obnoxious sigh of satisfaction, and tossed the empty bottle into his waste bin. It landed with a loud thud, reflexively drawing Vincent's eyes. The weight of the bottle had shifted the other refuse in the bin, pushing what appeared to be the tip of a syringe to the surface. Vincent looked away quickly, pretending as though he hadn't seen the object, and he probably would have let it go at that, had Samuel not suspiciously dragged his waste bin behind his desk, where it was obscured from Vincent's view. Rumors had been circulating for years that Samuel occasionally engaged in extracurricular behaviors that would necessitate the use of a syringe. But with no proof or reason to investigate, Vincent had always ignored the rumors until they eventually faded away on their own.

Of course, his glimpse of the syringe in the mayor's waste bin still wasn't proof that anything illegal was transpiring here. Maybe Samuel had recently received a diabetes diagnosis and was now taking insulin shots. Maybe he was on a steroid treatment for some other condition. Or perhaps he was toying with a new weight loss craze. If it was the latter, it wasn't obvious. But the first two options weren't something Vincent could assess from a brief visual exam alone. Though he had yet to make eye contact, he could feel Samuel's fiery stare daring him to say something about what he'd seen. Vincent didn't come here seeking a fight, nor did he have the ammunition to win this particular one at this time, so he remained silent. A tense minute passed, and then finally Lamar broke the silence.

"I guess we'll get out of your hair, Mr. Mayor. Unless you need something else from us?"

Vincent looked at Samuel, and sure enough, those blazing eyes were already in position, waiting for him. "Yes," he seconded, hoping to defuse the situation, "if there's anything you need while we're here…"

Samuel blinked, and the flames in his eyes snuffed out. "No, gentlemen. I don't need anything else from you today. I will expect a full report after the parade detailing anything, and I do mean *anything*, that didn't go buttery smooth. That applies to both of you."

Vincent and Lamar both agreed to the request, then offered their hands before leaving. As Samuel shook Vincent's, the sheriff fought the temptation to yank up his suit sleeve in search of track marks. He knew that wouldn't get him anywhere. He would investigate Samuel, revisiting the last round of rumors that had circulated about the man's drug use, but he would do so in secret, tasking a small, but reliable group from Eden PD to work with him in confidence. Then, when the time was right, he would return to City Hall and escort its overbearing monarch from his throne on high to a cell down below. Samuel's obsession with his legacy was common knowledge. With any luck, Vincent would help him seal it in history forever.

———

The abnormal quiet at Jericho PD didn't last as long as Frank had hoped. He didn't even get to finish dismantling his Bat Cave before reports of criminal activity started flooding in from all across the city. First in was a string of vandalism calls stretching from northeastern Jericho and moving south along its eastern edge. Each report had the same *modus operandi*: a shattered driver's side window of a luxury car accompanied by a pried-open glove box, from which any items of value had been taken. Multiple home security cameras had picked up a group of masked teens committing the acts, so those calls were relegated to lower patrolmen. Several reports of public intoxication had come in at the same time, and one of those was then updated to include a ten-person public brawl, which required sending at least ten men to deal with, even though the skirmish would likely fizzle out before they arrived on scene.

Reports of shoplifting, disorderly conduct, and trespassing followed. Then came a multiple-car pile-up on one of Jericho's major thoroughfares, with first-hand accounts suggesting an intoxicated driver may have been the cause. Frank watched as Jericho PD quickly emptied of its on-duty patrolmen. If the frequency of calls didn't slow down, they were going to run out of bodies, and he was going to find himself working a case that was far below his pay grade. So when a report of a potential crime-in-progress involving sketchy figures, duffel bags, and at least two guns came through, Frank jumped on it. He grabbed Billy and another of his go-to teammates, Gibbs, and ensured he made enough noise for Captain Tipps to notice Bruce Wayne was back in action. With a squad of experienced patrolmen in tow, they raced for the scene of the crime.

While in transit, Frank received word that gunfire was now being reported, though witnesses claimed it sounded more like hunting rifle fire than pistol fire. He ordered half of the patrolmen to disburse from the pack and to take position on routes the gunman or gunmen might use to flee. He warned the others that they were headed into a potential hot zone, and that they should prepare accordingly. Seven minutes later, the squad pulled up to the scene: a rundown warehouse situated among other abandoned buildings, the only cars in its parking lot plateless and sporting tinted windows far darker than the legal limit. Frank checked with headquarters to confirm whether any of the potential criminals had been spotted leaving the warehouse. They hadn't.

"What are you thinking?" Billy asked as he fastened a kevlar vest around his torso.

"Rifle shots, if that's indeed what they were, in an enclosed environment... someone in there is having a really bad day."

"And someone else is still armed," Gibbs pointed out. "Why aren't they running?"

"Maybe they got hit too," Billy suggested. "Maybe one of the victims returned fire."

Frank was listening to them, and processing their back-and-forth, but his mind was silently communicating with his gut, which told him there was more to this scene than met the eye. He looked to the head patrolman, Jim Rivera, who had seen his fair share of field action over his career. "I don't want us barging in there blindly. See if you can safely get a visual."

"Sure thing, Frank." He motioned for three other patrolmen to follow, then set off on foot for the side of the warehouse, where it appeared a line of cloudy windows waited.

Frank scanned their surroundings. There were no residential buildings, and the only active business he could see from their position was a twenty-five floor office building more than half a mile away. That must have been where the reports had originated from. But that was awfully far away to hear gunfire discharging indoors, even if that gunfire had come from a high-power rifle. Frank eyed the open-air parking garage next to the building, then traced a line of sight from the top of that garage to the warehouse...

"Frank, come in," Jim said over his radio. *"We've got a visual on the interior."*

"Let me guess," Frank replied as his eyes focused on what would undoubtedly turn out to be bullet holes in the upper front wall of the warehouse. "They're all dead in there."

"As far as we can see. We've got eleven bodies in view, but there could be more."

"Roger that. Hang tight until further notice."

Billy's mouth was hanging ajar. "Son of a bitch."

"I want you to take a squad to the top of that parking garage over there," Frank told Gibbs. "I assume the shooter is long gone, but be on alert just in case. Look for shells, gunpowder residue, or anything else that can confirm our suspicions. Be careful not to contaminate the scene."

"You got it," Gibbs replied.

Frank turned to Billy. "Care to find out who our victims are?"

Despite evidence suggesting there was no longer an active threat inside the warehouse, Frank, Billy, and the remaining patrolmen took standard precautions. They breached the front doors in assault formation with weapons raised, then identified themselves as Jericho PD before proceeding onto the open floor. The warehouse clearly hadn't been operational for quite some time. Cobwebs spanned overhead rafters and catwalks, debris was piled in corners and at the base of support columns, and dried animal feces littered the ground. Frank took a quick tally, noting the eleven bodies Jim had reported and adding another two farther from the pack, victims shot while trying to make a getaway. There was an abandoned office off to the side that Billy confirmed was empty, and an adjacent break room that another officer cleared. Otherwise, the warehouse was a wide open space with nowhere to hide.

"Stand down," Frank ordered, holstering his own weapon. "Everyone get a look at the victims. Visual only; no touching the bodies. Let's see if we recognize any of them."

As the patrolmen dispersed, two things quickly became evident. First, these weren't average citizens that had been in the wrong place at the wrong time. Each of them was strapped with a weapon, and several wore gang colors. The duffel bags they had carried into the warehouse contained either money or sealed packs of a white powder Frank was fairly sure wasn't all-purpose flour. Second, whomever had carried out their assassinations—and Frank was pretty certain that's what the murders had been—was a professional. Nine of the thirteen bodies had only a single, perfectly placed kill shot. The other three had a wounding shot that preceded the kill shot. The sniper hadn't had a visual of its victims, suggesting the use of infrared scoping technology. Not to mention the raw skill to successfully hit moving targets through a wall from over half a mile away...

"I know this guy," a patrolman called from the far side of the warehouse. "I busted him a year or so ago for possession. His name's Will or Wayne or something like that. He's a low-level street pusher."

"He *was* a low-level street pusher," Frank corrected. "Anyone else?"

"Yeah," a second patrolman called. "This one here went by the name G-Dawg. He's part of the Ricci clan. Rumor was, he handled their core narcotics distribution in Jericho, though the most we ever busted him for was illegal firearms discharge."

Billy eyed Frank. "The Ricci clan?"

"DeMarco's competition," he confirmed. "This is suddenly making a lot more sense."

"I take it you're feeling the handiwork of Dietrich Wessler?"

Frank nodded. DeMarco's right hand had both the resources and skills to pull off the mass extermination. But if Dietrich had been responsible, it left Frank bothered by one question: "Why now?"

"What?" Billy asked.

"The Ricci clan was operating in Jericho before DeMarco had a foothold. And it's been losing market share to DeMarco ever since. What incentive was there to knock off its head of distribution and several gang feeders now?"

"Maybe it's not business related," Billy suggested. "Maybe there's a personal rift between DeMarco and Ricci."

"We would have heard about it," Frank countered. "Personal rifts escalate. They don't begin with mass murder. We would have known something was brewing before it reached this level."

"Frank, Billy, it's Gibbs," their fellow officer said over the radio. *"It's just as you predicted up here. We've got bullet casings and what appear to be burn marks on the ledge facing the warehouse."*

"Great job, Gibbs," Billy replied. "Tape off the area so forensics can sweep for prints." If Dietrich was behind the murders, it was unlikely they would find any, but they had to try anyway. Billy turned his attention back to Frank. "So, if it wasn't personal, and it wasn't business, then what do you have in mind?"

Therein lied the problem. Frank didn't have a clue, but there had to be a motivation beyond the obvious. "Let's stew on it."

Billy's eyes brightened. "Mel's?"

Frank twisted his face in thought. Then he said, "Let's grab it to go. We've got a Bat Cave to repurpose."

———

That evening, Colonel Davis and Maddox passed through a series of security doors that protected Complex E's primary command center. They'd been summoned to an unscheduled meeting, and by the looks of it, they'd been last on the guest list. The Woman in White and Diego were already there, with the former seated at a large conference table and the latter logging into a computer attached to an overhead projector. Diego had two subordinate engineers with him, though they were standing like statues near the wall, as if under orders to stay quiet unless called upon. Near the subordinate engineers was Albert, who was holding a clipboard and observing Diego as if evaluating his ability to operate a computer. Also standing in the room, though by himself and in the shadows, was the Dark Man, who glanced at Colonel Davis upon entry, but, as usual, made no further acknowledgement. Despite years of similar interactions, these silent exchanges were beginning to give Colonel Davis the creeps. Maybe his nerves were finally shot. Or maybe there was something more to the feeling...

"Thanks for coming, Colonel." The Woman in White motioned to a nearby chair. "Please, have a seat."

He did so, but not without noticeable hesitation. Maddox shared in that hesitation as he sat next to his commanding officer, both of their eyes scanning the room for potential threats. Colonel Davis cut to the chase. "Why are we here?"

"Diego and Albert have been discussing the recent breaches. They feel we need to hear what they've concluded."

Colonel Davis swung his eyes to the scientist, then the engineer. Though they were both long-standing employees of Complex E, he'd made little effort to socialize with them on a personal or professional level. He'd almost wished he had, because unlike his neutral-colored partners, they seemed to have sound heads on their shoulders. "Well?"

"Just a moment," Diego said. He tapped on his keyboard, and the overhead lights dimmed as the projector bulb burned with life. A blueprint of Complex E appeared on a pull-down screen hanging at one end of the room. "Ah, there we go." Diego tapped a few more keys, and the projection zoomed in on The Hive. "I assume everyone recognizes this. As you know, over the past two years, we've been dealing with an exponentially increasing number of breaches from surrounding plant and animal life." A collection of red dots appeared in scattershot across the blueprint. "We've managed to fend each one off, mostly thanks to the efforts of Colonel Davis and his men." Diego nodded gratefully to the military force in the room. "Unfortunately, those efforts have taken their toll on both our human resources and defensive stockpiles. They've also caused major setbacks to our Hive project."

"This is old news," the Woman in White said. "I thought you had something new to share."

"We do," Diego assured her. "If you'll bear with me." He tapped again, swapping the blueprint for a bar chart. The x-axis represented a sequential breach count. The y-axis was a raw number count. And for each breach, there were three bars, the first of which trended exponentially upwards, and the second and third which trended linearly downwards. "The first bar on each of these plots represents the magnitude of the breach. It's a rough calculation, of course; an estimate of the number of flora and fauna lifeforms that attempted entry into the facility, scaled by their respective strengths. But Albert and I have reviewed the calculations, and we feel it's factually representative."

Colonel Davis had long suspected the breaches were becoming more difficult to deal with, but he couldn't be sure if his suspicion was driven by reality or his own deteriorating mental state. Now it looked like data was on his side. "And the other two bars? The ones trending downward?"

"Personnel and supplies," Diego said with a frown. "We don't put it in perspective at the time of each breach—we lose an engineer here, a scientist there, now a rare soldier—but when you analyze what's happening at a macro level, we're running out of bodies. Pretty soon, we won't have enough staff left to keep Complex E running, much less defended."

The Woman in White exhaled, an audible stutter to her breathing. "And the supplies? What's going into that analysis?"

Diego shook his head as if it was obvious. "Everything." He tapped more keys, and a new bar graph appeared, this one with five bars per plot, all trending downwards. "That's food," Diego said, pointing to the first bar in a series. He then moved down the line. "That's water. Trizorapine. Arsenal. Miscellaneous. We're running out of everything. Even if we could maintain our current personnel level, the facility would become inoperable in a week, maybe two, and that's assuming we don't have another breach that consumes more of our dwindling resources during that time."

The Woman in White looked at Colonel Davis for support. He could tell she was nervous, but all this news did was confirm what he had already believed: that Project Impulse and all those involved were damned to failure. He wouldn't even try to comfort her.

"Solutions?" she asked Diego.

He turned the computer over to Albert, who changed the display to an overhead view of Sunrise Isle. Blue dots flashed over various parts of the island from one end to the other. "I tasked a portion of my team with finding viable sources of food and fresh water on the island. We've got six high-probability extraction points, and another four that could prove viable, but require further investigation. That would alleviate two of our resource constraints." He tapped on the keyboard, switching the display to a chart with pictures of large predators on the left and select plant varieties on the right. "With our imports of Trizorapine dwindling, we need to consider recovering what's been lost from the local biome. Based on their physiological makeups, these eight plants and animals should have the greatest densities of Trizorapine in their systems. If we can hunt them, we should be able to harvest at least eighty percent of that Trizorapine for reuse in The Hive."

"That alleviates a third resource constraint," Colonel Davis said. "But to hunt requires manpower and an arsenal, which, as Diego pointed out, isn't looking good."

"No," Albert agreed. "I'm afraid you're going to have to find a way to replenish that yourself. We're scientists and engineers, not soldiers and arms dealers."

As was often the case, there was the Achilles' heel in the plan. Colonel Davis had no more resources to tap. Maddox was his last soldier, and whatever guns, grenades, and bullets were currently in their storeroom was the only arsenal they currently, or ever would, have at their disposal.

"I'm sure we can work something out," the Woman in White said with false sincerity. Colonel Davis wasn't sure what game she was playing, until she proceeded into her next line of questioning. "But even if we're successful at everything you just proposed, that still only solves half of our problem. The breaches are getting worse, this latest one nearly catastrophic. How do we stop those, for good?"

Albert looked at Diego as if hoping the engineer would deliver the bad news. Then, realizing it was on him, he stated what had by now become obvious: "We can't." He then hit them with even worse news. "In fact, harvesting Trizorapine from the local biome will likely have the opposite effect, spurring even more flora and fauna to attack. That's why obtaining more manpower and arsenal is so critical."

A task that has zero probability of success, Colonel Davis thought to himself. He refrained from sharing his musings with the others in the room, but he was pretty sure Maddox read into his facial expression.

"So we have one to two weeks," the Woman in White stated, no longer humoring Diego and Albert's proposals as realistic. "If we can recover the Alpha child before then, do we have everything we need to proceed?"

Albert's face was grim. "If you can recover her in the next ninety-six hours, yes. After that, it's a crapshoot."

"It's really a crapshoot, regardless," Diego added. "Because even if you recover her, and we're successful at incorporating her into The Hive, we'll only be able to maintain stability for another few days at best. Then all bets are off."

The Woman in White considered their revelations. A few days wasn't nearly enough time, but she would take what they could get. "Let's pla—"

Before she finished her sentence, the command center door buzzed and opened. Four rushed in, a tablet playing an obnoxiously loud video in his hand. "Sorry for interrupting, but you need to see this."

He pushed Albert out of his way and swapped the A/V cable for the overhead projector from the computer to his tablet. The video, a live news broadcast from downtown Atlanta, appeared on the pull-down screen. The voice of the in-studio reporter emitted from the conference room's ceiling speakers. She was mentioning something about another eyewitness coming forward. Then the scene shifted to a different reporter, this one out in the field, holding a microphone toward a teenage girl that looked either frazzled by stardom or high as a kite; it wasn't clear which.

"I'm telling you," the girl shouted into the microphone, "she was like a young Wonder Woman or something! A Supergirl... or Superman's younger sister! She turned her body into these electrical balls and shit. Oh, and she was bulletproof too!"

The Woman in White and Colonel Davis exchanged a curious glance. The scene shifted back in-studio, where the desk reporter apologized for the live airing of profanity. She then mentioned that a clip claiming to have captured the incident in question was going viral online. The clip began moments later, a shaky vertical video taken with a phone that showed the blurry backside of a teen girl's hair. Then bright specks of light overtook the screen as the girl dematerialized into tiny energy particles that floated into the sky. The clip ended, and the in-studio reporter noted that numerous online commenters were claiming it must have been faked, while others in the Atlanta metro area were reporting having seen the energy particles floating through the city.

"Holy shit," Maddox muttered. "It's her."

"It *might* be her," Colonel Davis said, unwilling to let himself be taken by the prospect that something was actually going their way for a change. To Four, he then said, "I want you and the others monitoring news broadcasts twenty-four seven. Report immediately if there's any new information that could be related to the Alpha child."

"Sure thing."

He grabbed the A/V cable as if about to unhook his tablet, but then froze. Something wholly uncharacteristic had caught Four's eye. The Dark Man had stepped forward, leaving behind his shadowed refuge, exposing himself to the light reflecting off the projector screen. Colonel Davis held his breath in anticipation as the Dark Man strolled past him, slowly, methodically, stepping up to the screen, where the news broadcast was replaying the cell phone video of the Alpha child's dematerialization. He stared intently, his face unable to mask the insatiable longing he felt, longing for a power that had eluded him these past seven years, a power that was in the open once more, ripe for the taking.

Colonel Davis watched the Dark Man with trepidation. Would he suddenly start talking, too? Would he hike up his pants and do a jig to celebrate the Alpha child's resurfacing? Or would he simply shut down, unable to process the anomalous emotion that had slipped free of the black hole that resided within him? Colonel Davis wasn't sure he wanted to be around for any of those options, and by the looks of it, neither was Maddox. The colonel was about to make a silent break for the exit; after all, if that was the Alpha child on that news report, there were plenty of preparations for him to make. But then he saw something else, something that made him cringe with unease. The Dark Man had extended his hand, and the Woman in White had embraced it. She tilted her head upward, staring rapturously at her shady partner, an eerie smile spread across her lips. They were a singular unit, a yin and yang of chaos hellbent on achieving Project Impulse's endgame at any cost; the rest of the world be damned.

Colonel Davis stifled his inner commentary and tapped Maddox's arm. He then motioned for them to get the hell out of there, and unsurprisingly, Four,

Diego, his subordinates, and Albert all followed. The Dark Man and Woman in White seemed oblivious to their exit, and out in the hallway, each man looked at one another, as if challenging someone to speak what was on all their minds. But though they had the strength to walk away from the command center, walking away from Complex E and Project Impulse was another matter altogether. None of them was strong enough for that, so after a moment of tense silence, the group broke apart, and everyone went their separate ways to conduct business as usual.

CHAPTER 5
DEVIATION

Vincent felt out of his comfort zone as he stepped through the doors of The Cellar Prime, one of Eden's fancier steakhouses that catered to those with much higher paychecks than his own. He was still in his uniform, whereas most of the other clientele were wearing suits, dresses, or other similar evening wear. But Vincent's failure to meet the expected dress code didn't deter the lead host from greeting him as though he fit right in, nor the waitress he was passed along to from escorting him to his table among the city's elite. There, Diana waited, her body wrapped in a sparkling evening dress Vincent was pretty certain he'd never seen in her closet. She stood as he approached, putting the dress on full display, then welcomed him with a kiss. Overwhelmed, Vincent didn't respond with his typical passion.

"What's wrong?" Diana asked.

Afraid of giving the wrong impression, he stammered to explain himself. "N-nothing. It's just... you're stunning."

Diana blushed. "I can be when I try."

She reclaimed her seat, and Vincent took a chair next to her. He declined the waitress's offer of wine and perused the menu, which was stacked from top to bottom with succulent sounding dishes he rarely consumed outside of special occasions. Each dish was accompanied by an equally succulent price Vincent couldn't imagine paying for a single meal.

"When you suggested we have dinner earlier, I figured the fanciest we were going to get was one of those mail-order do-it-yourself kits."

Diana giggled. "I figured I'd tortured you enough lately."

"Yeah," Vincent agreed, "but a good burger and fries, or maybe even some fried chicken from that hole in the wall near your house, would have sufficed."

"Ignore the prices," Diana said. "I'm friends with the owner, and he's a friend of Eden PD. They're going to ring up our bill at cost." She squeezed his arm gently. "Just try to enjoy the evening."

From there, he did. It wasn't as though Vincent minded paying for a nice evening out, but he and Diana were still in the dating phase of their relationship, and whenever she arranged their night, she also insisted on covering whatever bills they racked up. God knew what she had already spent on that dress. Vincent didn't want her emptying her bank account to satiate his stomach, too. Given that everything sounded wonderful, he still opted for one of the lower-priced dishes on the menu: a sampler of three fresh cuts of meat with two sides of choice. Diana went with a custom surf-and-turf dish: a filet paired with lobster bisque and a salad. Vincent filled her in on his aggravating visit with Samuel while they waited for their food. In turn, she filled him in on the back half of The Case of the Vanishing Clockmaker, which had apparently lost steam before the climax and ended with a whimper. Diana hinted Vincent could thank her for dinner by restocking her office reading material.

The meal itself was just as delicious as described in the menu. Vincent cleared his plate. Diana requested part of her steak be packaged to take home, but otherwise emptied her bowl of soup and finished off her salad. The two then shared a dessert: a fresh slice of cheesecake drizzled with strawberry syrup and topped with nuts and berries. When the bill came shortly thereafter, Vincent caught a peek at the total. Not counting tax and tip, it wasn't much more than their bill would have been had Diana treated him to fried chicken instead. That left Vincent wondering what other discounts he'd been missing out on from friends of Eden PD all these years.

"Thank you," he said sincerely while they waited for the waitress to return Diana's credit card. "This was just the relaxing evening I needed."

"I know," she replied coyly.

Ever the policeman, Vincent picked up on her playfully devious tone. "What exactly do you know?"

Diana stared at him with eyes that held such care, yet also an undertone of sadness.

"You saw me throwing out Abigail's picture, didn't you?"

"You weren't exactly subtle about it," she said. "I mean, since when do you empty your trash can in the break room?"

Vincent should have known. Nothing that happened inside the walls of Eden

PD got by Diana. The problem was that she also had her own way of *helping* when she felt the need to intervene. "Please tell me you didn't retrieve it."

"Absolutely not! In fact, I had a sudden urge to clean the coffee station. And you know how much I hate cleaning that coffee station. All those used coffee grounds and spills and half empty cups lying around..." She shrugged innocently. "I just don't know what got into me."

Vincent wasn't sure whether to laugh or cry; either way, he was grateful, and he gave Diana a smile that showed it.

"Sometimes we have to let the past go," she said. "You see this dress I'm wearing?"

"How could I not?"

Diana blushed again, then continued. "I had no intention of buying a new dress today. But I wanted to look good for you, so I dug out an old bridesmaid's dress I'd packed away years ago. It was a gorgeous little number, and it had some great memories attached to it."

"But?"

"But it also would have required me to lose twenty pounds to squeeze into it. I honestly don't know how I was ever that skinny..." She shook her head, her thoughts temporarily trailing elsewhere. "Anyway, it was in great shape, so I took it to a local consignment shop, did a little bartering, and walked away with this number instead."

Vincent had no idea she'd gone to such lengths for him and, hearing her story, worried she'd paid too high a price. "What about those great memories?"

Diana sighed. "That's the funny thing. The memories are still up here." She pointed to her brain. "Sure, the dress was a reminder of them. But it's not like I was ever going to fit into that thing again. And getting rid of it didn't magically make its memories disappear from my mind. They're still there; and by bartering for this new dress, now I'm able to make new memories... with you."

Vincent stared, his gaze a mixture of admiration, love, gratitude, and respect. Diana was a simple person, and yet sometimes she amazed him with her innate wisdom. That wisdom had sparked its own inspiring ideas within Vincent on an occasion or two, and tonight was no different. Though he'd kept it a secret, he had his own metaphorical bridesmaid's dress to dispose of, and now he knew just the way to do it. He leaned across the table and gave Diana a kiss worthy of her personal sacrifice. The waitress then returned with her credit card, thanked them for coming, and encouraged them to take as much time as they needed before leaving.

Vincent didn't need more time, however. He was stricken by the way that dress looked on Diana, and he would be even more stricken by the way it would look slipping off of her. Diana must have had a similar thought, for she pocketed her credit card and shot him a sultry glance that said *my place or yours?* before sliding out of her seat and allowing him to escort her to the door. They were so engrossed with each other that neither took notice of the muted television mounted above the restaurant bar on their way out. Nor did they notice the blurry images of the back of Amanda's head, or her blue energy particles as she dematerialized and floated into the Atlanta sky. Having not stopped to catch up on the news that day, Vincent was still unaware that his adopted daughter had resurfaced. But, given her current course of action, that would change soon enough...

———

Amanda crouched in the shadows, watching the criminal activity unfolding before her. She had arrived in St. Louis a couple of hours earlier. The sun had already descended below the horizon, and most commuters had already gone home for the day. That left the city's bars, restaurants, and dance clubs to serve as gathering spots for energetic locals and tourists alike. Amanda had walked the more popular venues, seeking activity worthy of making a second public appearance, but surprisingly, she had found none. She then shifted to less popular venues, and it was in a dark and fairly empty bar that she'd overheard the plan currently being executed.

A group of four males in their late thirties and early forties had received a tip from one of their girlfriends that the downtown branch of Mackey and Sons bank was receiving an after-hours deposit from one of its business clients tonight. The client had publicly disclosed it was completing an acquisition of a rival local business in the morning, and that one of the key influential factors in the deal was a promise to cover twenty million dollars of the purchase price in cash. It didn't take a rocket scientist—which these men certainly weren't—to put two and two together.

From what Amanda could gather, two of the men had amassed a small collection of firearms to help take the bank by force. One had contacted an old military buddy to get his hands on plastic explosives they could use to breach the bank and any vault the money might be stored in. The fourth had purchased and staged a series of unregistered cars they could use as part of an elaborate getaway strategy. And the tipping girlfriend, who apparently worked inside the bank's security department, had sabotaged the camera system before leaving that day to ensure there would be no video evidence of the crime. The plan wasn't foolproof by any means, but Amanda had to give them credit for covering their bases.

She loitered outside the bar, listening to their whispered scheme, until the foursome ordered a final round of drinks to steel their nerves. Then Amanda retreated to the shadows so she could monitor the group as they retrieved the first of the unregistered cars from the bar parking lot. They drove it to Mackey and Sons, parked on the street a half-block away, then donned black ski masks, empty duffel bags, and their hodgepodge of weaponry. Amanda watched from afar, questioning whether this was even the type of situation in which she wanted to involve herself. Yes, this was a crime, and sure, she had the ability to stop it; but her current course of action was more deliberate than that. She was trying to draw attention to herself, and stopping four lowlifes from robbing an empty bank in the dark of night wasn't exactly an attention-grabbing feat. Only, as the men approached the bank's front doors, Amanda learned it wasn't as empty as she had assumed.

She saw a security guard patrolling the lobby. He had come from a side hallway and was now pacing from one end to the other, guiding himself by the dim nightlight that glowed inside the bank, rather than by a more noticeable flashlight. He stopped at the front doors to confirm they were locked, did the same to a handful of offices to the left of the lobby, and performed a check of the security shutters that covered each teller station. The security guard then appeared as though he was about to return to the hallway from which he came when something diverted his attention from the opposite side of the lobby. It was a second guard, accompanied by a man in a suit that Amanda assumed must be the bank manager, there to oversee the after-hours deposit. An armored car pulled up to a red light in a nearby intersection, its trajectory suggesting it had come from the alleyway behind the bank. The deposit had already been made.

The four masked men pressed themselves against the shadowed wall of a building as they waited for the armored car to leave. A few seconds later, the light turned green, and it was on its way, no sign that its driver had noticed them stalking its most recent drop-off location. The men closed the gap between themselves and the front entrance of Mackey and Sons. One peeked through the glass windows and motioned for the other three to hold their positions until the manager and two security guards had cleared the lobby. Amanda almost took them out of play there, but then she considered they hadn't actually committed a crime yet. As backwards as it might have seemed, intercepting them now would make her guilty of assault. And though she had no reason to fear the charges themselves—after all, she would be long gone before anyone could identify her—a story about four men being assaulted in the dark of night by an unseen assailant on the streets of St. Louis wouldn't exactly rock headlines. She would wait for a more fitting time to intervene.

The manager and two security guards strolled out of sight together. The peeking man signaled to another of the group, who jogged forward and placed a strip of explosive along the seam of the front doors. They stood clear and detonated the plastique, blowing the doors open and triggering an audible alarm. The men appeared to understand their time to act was short, for they stormed the lobby at double the speed they'd been moving and went straight for the hallway into which the manager and his guards had departed. Amanda leaped from her concealed position onto the roof of the bank. She located a maintenance hatch and merged her energy particles with it to disengage its interior lock. Then she dropped inside, landing in a utility closet lined with electrical wiring. Amanda heard tense, muffled shouting, then a gunshot—only warning fire, by the sound of it—followed by the scrambling of feet.

A jumble of conflicting emotions swept over her. She could feel the nervousness of the manager and security guards, who were now disarmed and praying they wouldn't get killed tonight. She could also feel the anxiety of the men as they listened for police sirens while awaiting the next detonation of plastic explosive. Waves of exhilaration rose and fell among them as they advanced closer to their prize. An explosion went off, and Amanda knew the men had breached the holding area where the night deposit had been stored. She hustled down hallways, using her abilities when needed to open her path, until she found the secondary vault where the robbery was occurring.

The manager and security guards were on their knees in the hallway, one of the men holding them at gunpoint. His partners were inside the vault, scooping tightly bound stacks of cash into their duffel bags. One of the security guards spotted Amanda from the corner of his eye. He glanced at her, confused at why a teenage girl had suddenly shown up inside the bank, and his reaction caught the attention of the criminal watching over him. That criminal turned and fired blindly. Amanda deflected his bullets with small shields of energy particles, then disarmed him and threw him against the remnants of the gate that had once secured the vault hard enough to knock him unconscious.

By then, the other three had taken notice of her. But they were so stunned by what they saw, they didn't know how to react. Amanda advanced toward them, her genetically enhanced brain having already calculated the most efficient manner of incapacitating the group. Police sirens resonated in the distance, and in a panic, the explosives-handling member of the team punched the trigger of a detonator he'd been secretly palming. Amanda had mere seconds to respond. It was too late to prevent the explosion about to take place, and there certainly wasn't enough time to find the plastique and dispose of it. But there was just long enough for her to sense the rush of fear that overtook the manager and security guards, to instantly atomize her body into a swarm of energy particles, and to cocoon them from the concussive blast that tore into her at close range, scattering her essence across the interior of the bank.

Amanda's particles were slow to regroup. Every ounce of her seared with pain as she recomposed her physical form. Her brain throbbed, and her vision was blurry, but both passed quickly. When Amanda reoriented herself, she saw through dust and smoke that she had saved the trio of bank employees from what had been certain to be an explosive death. The two security guards stared with immobilizing shock. The manager passed out, and Amanda couldn't be sure if it was from his brush with death or his witnessing of her miraculous rescue. Either way, she could hear his pulse thumping steadily, confirming he'd be okay. Amanda returned her attention to the infiltrated bank vault, where only the crumpled form of an unconscious criminal lay. The other three were gone, having escaped into the night through the fresh hole that crumbled behind her in the building's wall.

Like a predator on the hunt, Amanda sprinted after them. She spotted their first car peeling down an adjacent street, the silhouettes of all three men inside. The car made a sharp right turn four intersections away. Amanda darted down a parallel street, opening herself to the sounds of the night. The police sirens were louder now, on track to arrive at Mackey and Sons within the minute. Amanda ignored them and instead honed in on the roaring engine of the getaway car, which was still ahead of her, but losing ground. She projected its course, which would take it straight to the garage where the second getaway car waited. Her energy recovering from the concussive blast, Amanda readied her leg muscles, and at the next intersection, she leaped onto the roof of a cater-corner building. From there, she traversed a diagonal of rooftops that, at her current pace, would intercept the men during their car swap.

She reached the building across the street from the nondescript garage the men had mentioned earlier that night and listened. They were inside, arguing about leaving their fourth member behind as they transferred duffel bags of cash into the second getaway car. One was concerned the fourth member would rat them out to the police. The explosives-wielder argued he had probably been killed in the blast, so they had nothing to worry about. The third member of the group insisted they both be quiet and focus on the task at hand if they didn't want to get themselves caught. Amanda heard a trunk slam shut, then three car doors clicking closed, and an engine firing to life. She braced herself as the garage door lifted on an electric motor.

The second unmarked car pulled out as casually as if driven by someone who hadn't just robbed a bank. Amanda jumped from her rooftop perch and landed on its hood, drawing yelps of surprise from the men in the front seats. She atomized her hand as she punched through the hood, then cinched her energy particles around the battery cables until they snapped, stalling the vehicle. A bullet cracked the windshield. In an autonomous reflex, Amanda's body absorbed the projectile into its own atoms, then released it and the majority of its kinetic energy out her backside. Though the bullet left no lasting physical damage, Amanda had felt the full force of its impact, and it wasn't a feeling she wanted to experience again. The driver had been the one who'd shot at her. He was now shaking with fear-induced panic, his finger squeezing once more around his weapon's trigger. Amanda punched through the windshield with a hand of pure energy and ripped the gun from his grip. She then pressed him against his headrest as she used her energy particles to bound his hands to the wheel with his own seatbelt.

"What the hell are you?" the man shouted as he yanked on his restraint. "Let me out of here!"

Amanda ignored him and turned her attention to the final two criminals, who had fled the vehicle and were running on foot down a nearby side street. She launched into a run, then leaped, sailing over their heads and landing in front of them. One man toppled backwards upon seeing her touch down. The other froze on the spot. Amanda unfurled leashes of energy particles that wrapped around their waists. Then she dematerialized her entire body and floated into the sky, carrying them screaming behind her.

A minute later, Amanda recalled her energy leashes, leaving the men to free fall ten feet onto the street outside Mackey and Sons. They landed with hard thuds, their screams turning to pained groans and then whimpers, all of which drew the attention of patrolmen who had arrived on scene to respond to the bank's alarm. The patrolmen seemed confused by the sudden appearance of the men, until the bank manager pointed at them with an accusatory finger.

"That's them!" he shouted. "That's two of the group that robbed us!"

"You'll find the fourth one tied up in a car several blocks from here," Amanda announced. "If you have trouble finding him, these guys can show you where to look."

No one acknowledged her words. They were too busy staring dumbfoundedly at her partially dematerialized body still floating high in the sky. Amanda made no attempt to hide her extraordinary abilities; that would have defeated the purpose of playing superhero tonight. Instead, she let them stare for a few more seconds, then flew away to avoid serving as a continued distraction. She didn't stick around to confirm the patrolmen arrested the two criminals she'd deposited near their cars; she was confident they would. Nor did she linger to make sure the driver who had taken a shot at her was also rounded up. He wasn't breaking free of his seatbelt handcuffs anytime soon, so the patrolmen would either find him now or when someone called in a suspicious vehicle stalled in the road the next morning. But by not hanging around, there was something even more important Amanda had missed...

An errant energy particle, one blown free of her chaotic mass of atoms during the bank explosion, hadn't returned upon reconstituting her body. It had settled under building debris, hidden from sight, but still glowing with life. Its bond to its owner was no longer strong enough to voluntarily command it, but as long as Amanda remained in the area, the particle also couldn't break loose of her unconscious grip. Once she departed, however, the energy was free to follow its own course. It rose from the debris, dropping dust particles off of it as though it were a celestial body, and continued onward, snaking through air ducts until it emerged from a rooftop vent. From there, it floated into the night, seeking its own, yet inherently familiar, path.

———

Victoria rocked quietly in the dark, the sounds of heavy wind and rain filling her ears as she bided her time. She was hungry, having not had a chance to eat dinner yet, and her stomach growled to remind her of that fact. Victoria held her breath, worried that the guttural noise would derail her current mission. But nothing stirred, and after a few moments, she eased. She checked the nearby clock. It had been thirty minutes. Sometimes that was long enough; sometimes it was but a third or fourth of the time she needed. She checked the body sprawled across her lap. It was breathing heavily, rapidly, but its eyes were shut tight. This was the moment of truth. Victoria stopped rocking and lifted the body ever so slowly. She carried it through the dark, careful to watch her footing, then gently lowered it into the crib that awaited. Victoria tiptoed to the sound machine on the nearby nightstand and adjusted its volume. Then she blew a kiss to her sleeping grandson and slipped out of his room. Mission accomplished.

At the bottom of the stairs, her daughter, Elizabeth, extended a questionable thumb. Victoria responded with a silent thumbs-up and saw Elizabeth's muscles relax. She then whispered that she'd be down in a second. Victoria stopped in a guest bathroom to freshen up, checked that no urgent messages had come through during Operation Night Night, then proceeded down to the kitchen to answer the call of her stomach.

"I can't believe you got him down so fast," Elizabeth said as she took the foil off casserole dishes lining the countertop. "He's been so fussy lately with Adrian out of town. I swear the child thinks his father carried him for nine months instead of me."

"It's a boy thing," Victoria said. "Your brother did the same to me."

Elizabeth shot her a tired smile. "Well, I really appreciate you stopping by to help tonight. Lord knows I could use some sleep." She pointed to the casserole dishes. "Now, as repayment, you can have your pick of dried out mac and cheese or really dried out mac and cheese."

"Set the wrong oven temperature again?"

"It's like my brain isn't fully functional these days. The doctors warn you about the physical toll having kids takes on the body. They conveniently leave out the mental toll it takes during those first few years after they're born."

Victoria put a comforting hand on her shoulder. "I've got bad news for you. It lasts more than a few years."

"Great..."

She then evaluated the two dishes of nearly identical looking mac and cheese before her. "I'll take the one on the left. And a spoon of whatever side dish you ruined to go with it."

"You mean my famous burnt-tip broccoli? Coming right up."

Victoria chuckled, Elizabeth's ruined meal a reminder of her younger days, when her kids were babies and life seemed as though it couldn't get more hectic. That was an exhausting time, perhaps the most exhausting time of Victoria's life, and yet she would do it all over again, for no exhaustion, stress, or lapses in brain function were enough to overshadow the joy of watching her children grow. Elizabeth was in the midst of the storm right now, but one day, she would look back and feel the same. Victoria poured a glass of soda and sat at the kitchen table as her daughter reheated her plate of leftovers.

"Make sure you dry it out a bit more," she joked.

"Have no fear," Elizabeth replied in equal jest.

Victoria took a sip of her drink as she waited for the microwave to do its job. Then she felt her phone buzz. She ignored it, assuming it was one of many pointless mass government emails set to automatically fire off after-hours so it wouldn't interrupt the work day. But then her phone buzzed two more times in rapid succession, and Victoria knew those weren't emails.

"I'll be back in a minute," she told Elizabeth.

She stepped into her daughter's living room and checked her messages. Three texts awaited, all from General Javez. The first said he'd uncovered new information, and that he and Victoria needed to talk. The second was an apology, General Javez remembering that Victoria was visiting her daughter that night. And the third amended the first message, letting her know they could connect first thing in the morning instead. Victoria heard the kitchen microwave beep, so though she was itching to learn what news General Javez had to share, she forced herself to put her phone away. But on her way back to the kitchen, she heard her daughter returning her plate to the microwave for a second round of warming, which bought her a couple of minutes to touch base with her military friend.

"You didn't need to call tonight," General Javez answered after a single ring.

"It's okay," Victoria assured him. "Elizabeth's fixing dinner. What have you got?"

He didn't waste time. "Two things. First, a follow-up on the chemical analysis from the Philadelphia raid. Our lab technicians confirmed it was Trizorapine being manufactured there, though not in its natural liquid form. The plant had implemented an additional step to convert the liquid into a dry powder, essentially creating a solid Trizorapine variant."

"Why would they do that?"

"Your guess is as good as mine. But it's the solid variant that was being distributed around the country. I've got men looking into it, but like everything else, it'll take time."

This was what Victoria referred to as *a wrinkle*, something in their hunt for Project Impulse that appeared to align with their prior beliefs, only to then defy them in some small, but potentially significant, way. She didn't like wrinkles, and their hunt certainly didn't need more of them. "What's the second item?"

General Javez hesitated, as if even he didn't know what to make of what he was about to tell her. "Do you remember when we first gathered intel on Project Impulse's sister facilities? When we learned the Waxhill Compound had hosted Complex C in one of its decommissioned wings?"

Victoria tried to recall the details of that long-ago conversation. "It was another chemical factory, right? One of the main feeders for the original Helix Unbound. But it was deserted when Complex B was brought online."

"Yes," General Javez confirmed. Then, "Do you remember there were also rumors about cutting-edge science experiments happening there before its abandonment?"

Victoria thought hard. "Cellular cloning or something like that, right? But we could never substantiate the rumors."

General Javez was silent.

"Don't tell me..."

"It turns out the chemist we apprehended at the Philadelphia factory used to run the Trizorapine production line at Complex C. When we pressed him about his time there, he admitted that some of the Trizorapine was produced for internal use."

Victoria felt a tension headache coming on. "More Impulse children?"

"It doesn't sound like it," General Javez said, much to her relief. "Complex C's infrastructure didn't mirror that of Helix Unbound and Complex B. It was built for manufacturing, not super-soldier development."

"So what then?"

"This chemist claims there was a section of Complex C that he and the rest of the Trizorapine group didn't have access to. But he befriended one of five geneticists who worked there. Apparently, after a few too many drinks one night, the geneticist slipped up and mentioned something about having a breakthrough that would enable his team to mass produce dormant organic lifeforms."

"The cellular cloning," Victoria deduced.

"It would seem so. Our chemist didn't learn anything further from his friend, but over the following weeks, his team was asked to increase their internal Trizorapine production tenfold. He also said Complex C began receiving unusual shipments of large crates that were delivered straight to the genetics group. He doesn't have an exact count, but he's confident there were at least thirty or forty of them. Maybe more."

"Contents?"

"He doesn't know," General Javez said. "But he said the crates were big enough to hold commercial refrigerators. More concerning is that those same crates were shipped back out over the two weeks prior to Complex C's shutdown."

Victoria worked through the implication. "So whatever they grew in there—thirty or more dormant organic lifeforms—got transferred to another facility. Nothing in our Complex B files suggests the lifeforms went there, but we've got blueprints for Complex E detailing a gymnasium-sized hub-and-spoke device that requires massive amounts of electricity to run." She tried to picture the blueprints in her mind, then realized she probably didn't need to. "You've checked them already, haven't you?"

"There are fifty spokes," General Javez replied, confirming her suspicion. "And each one is approximately the size of a refrigerator."

Victoria felt a weight pressing down on her. "So Complex E was always Project Impulse's final destination. Every other facility was just a stepping stone toward the endgame." A thought struck her. "Is there any way we can backtrace the shipping manifests?"

"If we can find them, maybe. I've already got a team working on it."

"Perfect. I—" Before she could complete her next sentence, a beeping indicated another caller was trying to reach her. Victoria checked the caller ID and saw it came from a restricted number in Washington, D.C. "Francisco, it looks like

Alison Drexmore might be calling. I'll patch her in so you can share what you've learned." She clicked over to the other line to confirm it was indeed Alison and not another colleague or cleverly disguised spam. Then she merged the calls. "Okay, Ms. Drexmore, you're on with both of us."

Alison skipped a cordial greeting. "Have either of you been watching the news?"

Victoria hadn't. She'd had a busy day of senate meetings, and when those were over, she'd rushed to her daughter's house to lend a hand with her grandson's bath time and Operation Night Night. She hadn't looked at a television screen all day, and by his silence, she suspected General Javez hadn't either.

"Turn on channel seven," Alison commanded. "Both of you."

Victoria took a moment to locate her daughter's television remote amongst the scattering of baby toys and gear in the living room. She turned to channel seven as instructed, where she joined a replay of an interview with a frazzled-looking security guard that was already in progress.

"*She saved us,*" he said with a despondent stare. "*We would have burned alive in that explosion, but she just—her body—I can't explain it.*"

A voiceover from a reporter kicked in. "*Some of the police officers who responded to the bank's alarm shared similar tales.*"

The video switched to a patrolman being interviewed outside of a branch of Mackey and Sons. His name and the phrase *St. Louis, MO* briefly appeared on the lower third of the screen. "*She was floating, up there above us. Her body... well, part of her body... it was surrounded by these bright blue... fireflies or something. She told us where the last member of the crew was, then flew away.*"

"*Flew, as in a vehicle?*" the reporter on the ground asked.

The patrolman shook his head. "*She was like an angel or something. I don't know. Maybe I need to have my brain examined.*"

The voiceover resumed. "*This strange sighting comes only a day after a similar sighting out of Atlanta that's gone viral on social media.*"

The report flipped to the cell phone footage of Amanda fleeing the altercation she'd defused the previous day. Victoria's eyes were glued to the screen as she watched the teenage girl's body dematerialize into a swarm of energy particles. She had never met nor seen an Impulse child in person, but between the knowledge Jacob had shared with her before his death, and that which she had learned on her own during her pursuit of vengeance, she knew exactly what she was looking at. The news report ended, and Victoria turned off the television.

"One of the originals survived," she said. "We'd just assumed..."

"That's why we don't make assumptions," Alison replied. "The question now is how this changes our course of action. This super-soldier doesn't appear to be doing Project Impulse's bidding. But if she has gone rogue, why the sudden public spectacles? Why expose herself like that?"

His strategic military mindset always churning, General Javez had the answer. "Bait. She's putting herself out there as bait. Instead of trying to find Complex E like we are, she's trying to draw Complex E to her."

Alison considered the suggestion. "You think we have an ally in this fight?"

"Maybe not an ally, but at least someone who shares a common goal."

Elizabeth signaled to Victoria from the kitchen that her dinner was ready. Victoria held up a finger to let her know she would only be another minute. Then she shared her thoughts on the matter. "If that's true, maybe there's a way to leverage the rogue Impulse child to our advantage. She's a weapon, after all. Only she can pull her trigger, but perhaps we can help aim her toward the target."

"How?" Alison asked. "We still don't know where that target is."

Victoria thought back to those late nights her husband spent fielding hushed phone calls with Helix Unbound. The calls were supposed to be confidential, but Jacob rarely kept their contents from his wife. This girl—the Alpha child, she presumed—had formed personal connections that had become thorns in Project Impulse's side. And if she was still alive, maybe those connections were as well. "You mentioned allies, Ms. Drexmore. Given the clandestine nature of this operation, we haven't formed many of those."

"Your point?"

Victoria took a deep breath, knowing what she was about to suggest wouldn't go over well. "Maybe it's time we start. Francisco hasn't filled you in yet, but Project Impulse is growing an army. Maybe it's time we build our own."

Silence. Victoria's muscles were tight with tension as she awaited what was certain to be a blunt rejection of the idea. But then Alison spoke, replying with much more openness and calm than Victoria was used to.

"Hypothetically, if I were to approve, where would you find these allies?"

In Victoria's mind, there was only one logical answer. "Eden."

———

Empty takeout containers and a plastic bag with the logo for Mel's Early Bird Diner were strewn across Frank's basement conference room table. He and Billy hadn't cleaned up after themselves, both detectives too deep in their Bat Cave makeover to bother. Where Frank's yarn spiderweb of Project Impulse players had once been on display was now a similar web of interconnected photographs and notecards detailing Thomas DeMarco's drug empire. Frank had placed DeMarco's and Dietrich's pictures at its center, and from there, he and Billy had constructed five connecting clusters of documentation. The first, largest, and most obvious cluster represented an outline of DeMarco's drug distribution network, which covered the entire United States and, if rumor were to be believed, had penetrated European and Asian countries as well. The second cluster represented the crime boss's supply line, fully captured by a single notecard on which Frank had drawn a bold question mark. The fact was, no one really knew where DeMarco sourced his drugs. Law enforcement agencies occasionally caught wind of one-off shipments, like the one from a year and a half earlier, when Frank had first busted DeMarco. But no one had been able to trace those shipments back to a centralized supply chain. DeMarco was smart enough to know that without supply, he had no business, and thus he protected it as if it were the Holy Grail.

The third cluster detailed DeMarco's known rivals in the drug world. This included the Ricci clan, the Botha tribe, and the Torres family. They were the only three groups with enough clout, manpower, and weaponry to hold their own against DeMarco's monopolistic expansion. Though, as of today, the Ricci clan was looking like less of a going concern. With his business organization already covered, the fourth cluster of information displayed a summary of DeMarco's arrest by, and subsequent escape from, Jericho PD. Two contrasting newspaper clippings told the whole story. In the first, a bold headline applauded Jericho PD for busting a nationally renowned drug kingpin. In the second, another headline scolded one of their own for setting him free, burying the fact that Carter had only done so to protect his family. Frank almost didn't hang that one, but he reminded himself that good detective work required objectivity.

That left the fifth cluster, one Frank had first pinned to the investigation board as a quasi-joke, but then left in place once he realized there may not be anything funny about it. At the center of the cluster was the same sheet of paper that read *Project Impulse* from his prior investigatory artwork. It was tied directly to DeMarco's picture, and from it branched all the usual suspects: *Helix Unbound*, *Trizorapine*, and the *Omega Genome*. When Billy had first seen Frank constructing the odd connection, he'd thought his partner had gone mad. But then Frank had explained he was only doing it to cover his ass should city council inspectors find their secret room and question why so many documents about Ray and The Falling of the Tides were shoved off to the side. That remained the running explanation for several hours, until Frank and Billy had gotten on the topic of DeMarco's escape, and Frank had lamented how he wished he'd been around instead of in Eden so things could have gone differently. Then he'd remembered his final conversation with DeMarco, one in which the drug lord had given him a vague warning not to chase his brother's ghost back to Eden. It was as if DeMarco had known something Frank hadn't, and given how events had played out from there...

"As unlikely as it might be," Billy suggested, "let's assume for a moment DeMarco knew about Project Impulse. By the time you arrested him, Helix Unbound was in ashes. Eden had already fallen and been rebuilt. And Project Impulse had moved to Springwater Hills. The only reason you were headed back there was to investigate your brother's letter, which DeMarco claimed to know nothing about."

Frank chimed in. "Based on Alma Hernandez's testimony, I think we can take that claim at face value."

"Agreed. But that leaves me scratching my head. One, how did DeMarco know you were headed to Eden in the first place, and two, why would his knowledge of Project Impulse make him warn you not to go?"

Frank offered a tentative explanation. "Maybe he knew about Judas. The Plainclothes we captured before raiding Complex B told us Eden was intended to be Project Impulse's testing ground. Even though the project had relocated, maybe the testing plan hadn't changed."

"But that would've only mattered if Judas had been close to completing his development. From what you've told me, he was actually regressing toward death at the time."

"Maybe DeMarco didn't know that," Frank said. "Or maybe he knew none of it. Maybe he was fishing when he mentioned Eden, just to see if I would latch on to the idea."

"But when you did, he didn't encourage it," Billy reminded his partner. "He tried to talk you out of it. That's not the response of someone fishing for a bite."

Frank had to give him that. He stared at the photo of DeMarco, his gaze trying to pierce the image's forehead as if it would magically give him insight into the drug lord's inner thoughts. Sadly, it didn't work. "Let's focus on your other question for a minute. How did he know I was headed to Eden?"

"Wessler," Billy proposed. "The man's resourceful. He probably had eyes on you even before we arrested his boss. His spies could have told him about Alma Hernandez, the letter, your emotional state, your fight with Captain Tipps... it wouldn't have been too hard for someone to piece together what was happening."

"Fair point," Frank said. "And that explanation makes sense regardless of whether DeMarco is connected to Project Impulse, so let's roll with it. Now, assuming he isn't connected, explain the warning."

Silence. Though Frank had proposed a weak explanation of the warning when assuming a connection between DeMarco and Project Impulse, neither he nor Billy couldn't explain it when assuming the opposite. Without knowledge of

Project Impulse's ongoing activities, Eden simply didn't pose the threat DeMarco had implied it did.

"And round and round we go," Frank said with a heavy sigh. "DeMarco knew something, Billy. My gut tells me that. What he knew, and whether it truly was related to Project Impulse, remains to be seen. But we can't rule a connection out, and that scares the hell out of me."

"Why?"

"Because it means there's something larger at play that has us completely in the dark. And it's been at play for a least a year and a half, if not longer. If everything was status quo, I wouldn't fret over it too much. But the Ricci clan assassination was uncharacteristically aggressive, a move that'll have repercussions throughout the entire illicit drug industry. It's no secret that DeMarco and the other three empire leaders have never liked each other, but they've always maintained an uneasy truce for the betterment of their trade as a whole. If DeMarco's willing to throw that balance away, and if his motivation stems from his knowledge of Project Impulse..." Frank shook his head. "I just don't know."

Billy saw his partner's mind sinking into that same dark abyss it often did, and was about to toss him a life raft, when Captain Tipps marched through their open door. The surly, but caring chief took turns shooting suspicious glares at Billy and Frank before turning his eyes upon the revamped investigation board. He scanned from the center photographs to each of the five information clusters, the slightest hint of a pleased grin on his lips... at least until he reached the fifth cluster. Then the bottom half of his face fell with displeasure.

"You just couldn't help yourself, huh, Frank?" Captain Tipps asked.

Billy jumped to his partner's defense. "Actually, it's a legitimate piece of the DeMarco investigation." He saw the suspicious glare hone in on him again. "Honest to God, Captain. We were just discussing it before you walked in."

Captain Tipps looked hard at Frank. "Is this true?"

He nodded.

Then the captain did something wholly unexpected. He sighed with relief. "Good. That means I can justify it to the city council inspectors when they discover you've gone back to Eden tomorrow."

Frank's eyes widened with intrigue. "What are you talking about?"

Captain Tipps pulled his cell phone from his pocket. "I figured you hadn't seen it yet. Otherwise, you'd already be on the road instead of down here doing your job." He opened a social media app, his main feed displaying a number of scantily clad women.

"Captain," Billy said, "if you need dating advice, we're probably not the best—"

"Shut up, Meadows." He scrolled down the feed until he found a video clip of Amanda's Atlanta hijinks. Captain Tipps turned the volume up and played the clip for Frank, then scrolled farther until he found a link to a St. Louis news article detailing Amanda's bank rescue. He passed the phone to Frank and waited while his detective read the column from start to finish.

When he was done, all Frank could say was: "She's back."

"Atlanta, then St. Louis," Captain Tipps said. "I assume you don't need a map to figure out—"

"She's going home." Frank spun on his heels and marched to the stack of boxes containing his Project Impulse investigation material. He dug, quickly finding the two items he sought. Then he pinned both to the investigation board, strings linking them to *Project Impulse.* The first item was Eden's current skyline. The second was the card Frank had previously rechristened *The Alpha Child.* He stood back and traced the jagged lines from her card, up to DeMarco's photograph, and back. This was the danger the drug lord had warned him about; not Judas, and not Complex B. Amanda was Eden's threat. Frank could feel it in his gut. The connection was there, even if he couldn't see it in its entirety yet.

"Listen, Frank," Captain Tipps said. "I know I've been hard on you about your extracurriculars in Eden. And, to be honest, I was starting to wonder if maybe you'd finally cracked; that maybe the job had broken you. But, seeing this video going around the internet, reading the descriptions of this mysterious girl, knowing the things you claim to have been involved in... I don't think you're crazy after all." He walked around the conference table and peered into Frank's stack of boxes. Then he removed a single sheet of paper and turned it for his detectives to see. It was Ray's drawing of The Falling of the Tides, the one in which a female figure was leading an army out of Soul Wind Forest. "Put all personal feelings aside. Based on everything you've seen, and everything you know, do you truly believe this is the girl from that video?"

Frank didn't want to admit it, but try as he might, he'd had yet to come up with an alternative. "Yes."

"And the destruction your brother predicted... do you really think Eden's collapse wasn't the end of it? Is something worse still coming?"

Again, Frank acknowledged the hard truth. "Yes."

Captain Tipps turned the paper where he could analyze its contents. Then he glanced at the investigation board, specifically on the newly added documents. He nodded, almost as if affirming to himself that he was making the right call. Afterwards, he turned his intimidating stare upon Frank. "Then get your ass back to Eden and stop it. Billy and I will cover for you here as long as we can."

Frank couldn't believe his ears. "You've never approved—"

"I've got a kid in Eden," Captain Tipps blurted, much to Frank and Billy's surprise. "He moved there after it was rebuilt. You don't hear me talk about him because, well, he and I don't exactly get along." The normally stoic captain struggled to hide his sadness. "The boy doesn't want me in his life, and I try not to think too much about it. But he's still my son. And if something happens to him, and I could've done more to stop it…"

Frank put a consoling hand on his shoulder. "Don't worry, Captain." He then hammed up his next words with over-the-top conceitedness. "Your best detective's on the case."

A smile broke through Captain Tipps's emotional veil. "You're so full of shit, Holmes."

Victorious, Frank laughed.

"Well," Billy said with a knowing sigh. "It looks like I'm back on *guy in the chair* duty. Whatever you need, Frank, just let me know."

"Thanks, partner."

Wasting no time, he took Ray's drawing from Captain Tipps, replaced it in the box of his brother's personal belongings, and carried the box to the door. As he passed into the hallway, his boss called after him.

"Hey, Frank. All joking aside, come back alive when this is over."

Frank hesitated. He'd been so caught up in the moment that the thought of his own well-being hadn't even crossed his mind. He didn't know what storm awaited him, nor the exact nature of the dangers he might face. But he had survived his brother. He had survived Eden's fall. And he had survived everything Project Impulse had thrown at him and his friends since. He wasn't about to break that streak now. "Yes, sir."

CHAPTER 6

CORRUPTED

Derek squinted at the early morning sun through Vincent's car window. He hadn't been ready to get up this morning, especially when he'd opened his eyes to Stacy snuggled warmly at his side, no longer any urgency for her to slip away before her parents discovered her missing. Derek had delayed his alarm an extra thirty minutes, then nestled against his sleeping girlfriend, debating whether to cancel the alarm altogether and take his chances that Vincent would let him sleep in. But apparently that wasn't in the cards today. Instead, his father had shaken his shoulder even before his alarm would have normally woken him. He'd told Derek they had something important to do, and even had a spare key ready to leave for Stacy so they wouldn't need to disturb her. Forty minutes later, they'd hit the road for what Derek assumed would be Eden PD. Only that didn't seem to be in the cards today, either.

"Where the heck are we going?" he asked his father.

They had bypassed their usual turnoff for the station and were now passing through one of Eden's seedier neighborhoods. Though the city's crime was minimal relative to others of its size, what crime there was often occurred here. Vincent didn't seem to care. He stared straight ahead, driving as if he had a specific destination in mind, a stupid grin plastered across his face that Derek was pretty certain hadn't budged since that morning.

"You know," he said, "just because you got some last night doesn't mean you're suddenly Superman."

"Excuse me?" Vincent asked, his face turning red.

"That's what this is, right? Diana got your testosterone flowing so much that you woke up at the crack of dawn ready to take on the criminal world."

Vincent put on a front of denial. "You don't know what you're talking about."

"Oh yeah? Then why was there a second spare key on the kitchen counter?"

Vincent gritted his teeth. "I knew I should have left it somewhere else…"

Derek chuckled. "It's okay, Dad. You deserve to get some. I know it must be difficult with your old age and everything—"

"Unless you want to spend tonight in lockup, I suggest you stop right there."

"Yeah right. What are you going to charge me with? Verbal assault?"

"Elder abuse."

The father and son shared a hearty laugh. Vincent then slowed the car and turned onto a street lined with a mix of small businesses and unoccupied buildings. It wasn't the most attractive stretch of Eden, and Derek didn't want to imagine what it would look like after a few more years of wear and tear. They pulled into a parking lot with a single-story standalone building covered in attention-grabbing signs and flashing window lights. Lettering above the entrance read *Jack's Stash*. Derek didn't know what to make of their destination.

"Ummm…"

Vincent parked the car. "Just come on."

He unfastened his seatbelt and stepped out. Derek hesitated for a moment, then followed, the stench of this more unkempt section of Eden an unpleasant reminder that not everything in the city smelled like roses.

"For future reference," he said, "I would have been okay if you had gone on your little superhero adventure without me."

Vincent rolled his eyes and opened the door to Jack's Stash, its movement ringing an obnoxious bell to alert the staff of his arrival. Derek went inside, and once his eyes adjusted to the stark change in lighting, he saw that the business had been aptly named. A stash of junk lined the floor and walls as far as the eye could see. There was little rhyme or reason to the collection—a band instrument here, a rug there, a display case full of coins, metal hooks with a variety of iron-on t-shirts that had no consistent theme—it went on and on. Somehow, Vincent was able to navigate the mess, finding a walkway that took them to the back of the store, where a clerk wearing a lanyard that read *Meathead* waited behind a desk.

Maybe Jack's Stash wasn't such an apt name after all, Derek thought to himself.

"Hey, Meat," Vincent said. "How's it going?"

Meathead replied as if they were acquaintances. "Not bad, Sheriff. How about you?"

"Can't complain." He dug into his pocket and removed a cloth pouch the size of a small cell phone. "I'd like to get a cash offer on something."

Vincent emptied the pouch's contents onto the desk. Derek saw that there had been three objects inside: a shiny gold ring that was both wide and smooth along its entire circumference, a second gold ring that mirrored the first, but was thinner and daintier, and a third ring with a solitaire diamond on top flanked by two smaller diamonds. He recognized the wide ring as his father's wedding band, which he had stopped wearing long ago. Derek had no memory of the other two rings, but it didn't take a genius to deduce they had belonged to his mother, one to signify her engagement to Vincent, and the other to signify their marriage.

"Dad, what are you doing?"

Vincent acted like there was nothing unusual about his request. "I'm getting an offer."

"Yeah, I heard that part. Why?"

Meathead scooped the rings onto a padded tray. "I'll be right back."

Vincent watched him disappear through a rear door. "Because it's time for me to let go of the past and to focus on the future. Because even though those rings were once a symbol of love, now they're nothing more than a reminder of betrayal and hurt."

Derek understood where his father was coming from, but also heard apprehension in his voice, almost as if he didn't fully believe what he was saying. "You don't have to pawn them. You could lock them in a safety deposit box or something. Out of sight, out of mind, right? And that way, if you ever decide you want them back—"

"I've already thought this through," Vincent said, cutting him off. "This is the right move."

Seeing his father's pain, Derek tried a more lighthearted tactic. "Does Diana know she's got you this wrapped around her finger?"

Vincent glared at his son with false anger, then gave him a playful push. Meathead returned from the back with the padded tray in one hand and a computer printout in the other. He set the tray on the desk, but didn't give the rings back to Vincent.

"Based on the diamond ratings and wholesale value of smelted gold, I can give you twelve hundred for the entire set."

Vincent felt a lump form in his throat. "Twelve hundred? I thought I'd be looking at two grand, minimum."

"A few years ago, maybe," Meathead said. "But there's just not a lot of demand right now."

Vincent eyed the rings. "I don't think I can let them go for that little." He then shook his head adamantly and reached for the jewelry. "I'm sorry to have wasted your time."

Meathead threw out an arm to block his hand. "Well, hold on a minute." He examined the printout once more. "Okay, it's not something I would normally do, but I'll raise my offer. How's fifteen hundred sound?"

It sounded like Vincent was still getting lowballed. He looked at the rear door. "Is Jack back there?"

Ah, Derek thought, *so there is a proverbial Jack.*

Meathead glanced back, as if putting his x-ray vision to the test. "He was on the phone a few minutes ago, but I can get him for you."

Vincent expressed his gratitude. After a brief trip to the backroom, Meathead returned with a rough-skinned, tattooed, biker-type in tow. Jack, Derek assumed, saw him first, and made a puzzled face, suggesting he didn't know why Meathead was wasting his time. But his attitude changed as soon as he saw Vincent, whom he greeted with genuine cordiality.

"Hey, Sheriff, what brings you to my neck of the woods?"

Vincent motioned to the rings. "I've got some personal jewelry to offload. I was hoping you could give me a fair price."

Jack leaned over to get a better look at the rings, then angled his face toward Meathead. "What'd you offer him?"

"We're at fifteen hundred right now."

Jack frowned as if his employee should know better. "Give me that," he said as he snatched the appraisal sheet from Meathead's hands. Jack scanned the information it contained, then scowled, "You idiot. What have I told you about transacting with Eden PD?"

Meathead stammered. "W—well you've been all over us about profit margin lately. I figured that rule got suspended."

Jack swatted him with the appraisal sheet. "That rule never gets suspended. It doesn't matter what's going on in the economy. Eden PD takes care of us, so we take care of them." Jack shifted his gaze to Vincent. "My apologies, Sheriff. Meat can be a dumbass sometimes."

"Don't be too hard on him," Vincent said dismissively.

Jack scanned the appraisal form again. "According to this, we'll be able to dismantle this stuff and sell the components for about thirty-eight hundred dollars. I've still got to cover labor, overhead, marketing... you know the deal. So how's thirty-four hundred sound? Normally, I would've tried to barter you down to an even three thousand to work in a little profit, but consider this an olive branch for my employee's stupidity."

Vincent smiled appreciatively. "I'll tell you what. Let's split the difference at thirty-two. You've got to make a living, too."

Jack extended his hand. "Deal."

They shook, after which he turned Vincent back over to Meathead to complete the transaction. It took another five minutes to fill out paperwork, then a couple more for Meathead to retrieve the thirty-two hundred dollars from a backroom safe. Vincent and Derek waited in silence, until a high-strung teenager tripped the front door bell, then stormed down the aisle like a bloodhound seeking its target.

"Where is he?" the teenager demanded as Meathead returned with cash in hand.

"He's in the back, but—"

The teenager didn't wait for an excuse. He marched past Meathead, pushed through the rear door, and slammed it behind him. Vincent and Derek could hear exchanges of muffled anger from beyond the door. Meathead heard them too, but simply shrugged.

"That's Jack's boy," he said. "He's a good kid, but sometimes he and Jack butt heads." He counted out the money, one hundred-dollar bill at a time. When he was finished, he raised his hands like a blackjack dealer to show he'd held nothing back, then motioned for Vincent to collect his winnings. "Pleasure doing business with you, Sheriff."

"Thanks, Meat." Vincent straightened the stack of money and held it out for Derek. "Here you go."

Derek eyed the cash, but made no attempt to take it. "What's this?"

"Consider it your raise," Vincent said. "Courtesy of a little encouragement from Diana."

Derek still didn't understand. "My raise for what?"

"For you to finally put a ring on Stacy's finger. That's what you told me you needed, right?"

"Dad, that was just a joke."

Vincent knew better. "No it wasn't. You've been wanting to marry that girl since the day you two met. And I'm guessing the only thing holding you back is not being able to afford a ring you feel is worthy enough."

"It's not the only hurdle," Derek admitted, "but yes, it's the biggest one."

Vincent pushed the cash into his hands. "Now it's not." He smiled affectionately at his son. "I told you it was time for me to let go of the past and to focus on the future. I wasn't talking about my future. My path in life is set, but you and Stacy... you have the whole world waiting for you. And I want to support your journey in any way I can. So, consider this a first step."

Derek felt tears swelling in his eyes, so he hurried and wrapped his father in a hug to hide them. "Thanks, Dad."

They embraced for several seconds, and when they parted, Derek could see

Vincent fighting to hold back his own waterworks. The emotional moment was broken, however, when Jack's son stormed out of the back room, apparently even more furious than before. He nearly took the door off its hinges and went out of his way to leave a trail of chaos on his way out of the building. Vincent peered through the open rear door.

"Jack, is everything okay back there?"

He responded from somewhere beyond the door. "Yeah, Sheriff. Just family issues."

Vincent looked at Derek, who nudged his head with encouragement. He then glanced at Meathead for approval to bypass the employee desk before entering the back office. Jack was seated with his back to the door, staring blankly at the office wall.

"Anything I can do to help?" Vincent asked.

Jack spun to face him, his face tight with stress. "I don't want to impose."

Vincent could see there was something he wanted to share, even if he was hesitant. He'd seen that same look on the faces of parents who'd come to the station because their kids were in trouble, and they didn't know where else to turn. He shut the office door to give them privacy. "Talk to me, Jack. What's up?"

Jack's jaw shifted from side to side nervously. "Can we talk man to man? Leave the police out of this?"

"You've got my word."

Jack released a heavy, burdened breath. "My son's on drugs, Sheriff. I caught him a few weeks ago. It's that new shit spreading through Eden. It's like a plague, silently infecting our communities. I didn't think for a million years..." He shook his head. "Anyway, we had a blowout fight over it, and I told him he needed to kick the habit, or I was going to kick him out of the house. I didn't mean it, of course, but he didn't know that. He got pissed and took off, spent a few days at a friend's house, and when he came back, he seemed like he'd cleaned up his act. It turns out he was just doing a better job of hiding it."

"You found his stash?" Vincent asked.

Jack nodded. "This morning. He was keeping it in a baggie taped behind his toilet. I only spotted it because I was collecting trash bags for garbage pickup. To teach him a lesson, I left the baggie and his tools, but took the drugs and replaced them with a note that told him if he kept buying it, I'd keep stealing it."

"I take it he just found the note."

Jack nodded again. "I don't know what to do, Sheriff. Let's face it, I'm no choir boy. I've made my mistakes, done my fair share of stupid shit in life. But I don't want that for him. He's better than me. I don't know who introduced him to this stuff, but he's not alone. I've heard stories from my friends, my neighbors… it's everywhere."

"We've heard the rumors down at Eden PD," Vincent said. "But they're just that. We haven't gotten our hands on any concrete evidence."

Jack stared at him, a secret behind his eyes.

Vincent caught on. "You still have the drugs, don't you?"

Jack turned his chair to a filing cabinet, which he then unlocked before sliding the bottom drawer open. He knelt and reached inside, past the inner edge of the drawer, and pulled something free from hiding. When he returned to his chair, he was holding a small makeshift pouch of plastic wrap secured by a twist tie. Inside was a chalk-white powder. "I didn't know how to get rid of it. If I'd thrown it in the trash, my kid would've dug it out. If I'd dumped it down the toilet or let it loose in a breeze, who knows what it might have contaminated or whom it might have affected. So I brought it here and hid it."

"Would you be willing to let me take it in as evidence?" Vincent asked. "I can log it as coming from an anonymous tipster. You and your son can stay out of it."

Jack's face grew solemn. "If it helps get this shit off the street, it's yours."

He tossed the makeshift pouch to Vincent, who said, "Believe me, that's the goal."

Their conversation over, he reached for the office door handle, but Jack's next words stopped him.

"You need to move quickly, Sheriff. That stuff's not only spreading like a plague; it's deadly, too. I haven't heard of anyone overdosing yet, but it's got people on edge. And edgy addicts only keep their cool for so long before that edginess turns to violence. I've seen it too many times in my life. I don't want to see it happen here."

Neither did Vincent. He gave Jack a nod of confidence and said, "We'll do our best."

————

"She's made another appearance," Four announced to those seated around Complex E's command center. He projected a recording of the patrolman interview from the night before on the display screen. "St. Louis this time."

He was speaking to the Woman in White, the Dark Man, Colonel Davis, and Maddox, as well as his remaining peers, One and Three, who were connected via video call. The science team at Complex E had been excluded from this discussion, their services in the matter unnecessary until the Alpha child was back under Project Impulse's control.

"Where's she going?" the Woman in White asked.

Four shrugged. "Where else?"

He swapped the projection with an overhead map of the United States. Two red dots appeared, one over Atlanta, the other over St. Louis. A straight red line extended from the first to the second, then beyond, eventually stopping at a third dot, next to which the name *Eden* appeared. Sight of the word caused Colonel Davis to shift with unease, his previous interactions with Impulse children within the city's borders having gone poorly, to put it mildly. But the Woman in White and Dark Man didn't appear to share his feeling, as they seemed to tense not with unease, but with anticipation.

"It's happening," the Woman in White said. "She's ready."

"Ready for what, exactly?" Colonel Davis asked. "I hope you don't think she's going home to embrace her role in Project Impulse."

"Well, of course she is." The Woman in White stared at him as if it were the only logical explanation. "She's been hiding from us for over a year now. Her family and friends have moved on with their lives. Why else would she suddenly expose herself like this? Knowing we're watching; knowing we'll project where she's going?"

"Because she's setting a trap for us," Colonel Davis countered bluntly. "That girl slaughtered Judas, who was arguably the most powerful Impulse child we'd created... if not for the disease that was eating him alive. And *someone—*" He glared at One's pixelated video image. "—tipped our hand that she's central to Project Impulse's success. She must suspect we're getting desperate by now. Which means she knows we can't pass up an opportunity to go after her." Colonel Davis returned the Woman in White's stare. "She's not heading home for a welcome reunion. She's heading there to have home-field advantage, to make it that much easier to slaughter us, too, should we take the bait."

That took the wind out of the room. The Woman in White sat in silent contemplation, taking Colonel Davis's warning to heart as she used to do when their relationship was more of a close partnership than an undesirable pairing of convenience. After a few moments, she turned her attention to the video feeds of the remote Plainclothes.

"Has there been any unusual activity in Eden to suggest her family is making advance preparations for her arrival?"

"No," One responded. "I don't even think they've seen the news reports yet. Of course, there's only so much surveillance I can do without being spotted. So it's possible I've missed something."

"And our friends in D.C.?"

That was Three's territory. "Senator Riley and her bulldog are slowly dismantling our infrastructure, apparently with full support from the Senate Black Book Committee. But that's nothing new. I'd be surprised if they didn't know about the Alpha child by now, but it hasn't changed their course of action in any meaningful way, at least not so far."

The Woman in White contemplated again. When she was finished, she looked to the Dark Man for approval before announcing, "Then we proceed. We've got no alternative. As soon as the Alpha child makes her presence in Eden known, we'll take her."

Colonel Davis felt his blood pressure rising. "And how do you expect us to do that? Without the Alpha child, we have no army. We have no genetic enhancements. Hell, we barely have any weapons left. And Maddox and I won't make it one round in a fistfight with that abomination of science. So, what's your grand plan?"

The Woman in White smiled coyly, then pressed a button on a nearby intercom. "Bring it in."

A few seconds passed, then the command center door opened, and a pair of engineers entered. They were carrying an oversized steel case used for transporting temperature sensitive materials. Albert followed them, the case his responsibility, and the engineers simply his muscle to lug it around. They placed the case on the conference room table and turned it toward him. Colonel Davis heard the heavy clicks of its locks, followed by a hiss as the case depressurized and released frozen gas that spilled across the conference room floor.

"Show him," the Woman in White said.

Albert removed a glass vial from the case and set it on the table. The vial contained a swab stained with purple liquid. He then removed a second vial containing a liquid of the same deep purple color, which he set next to the first. Colonel Davis was unimpressed.

"Madison's counteragent. So what? Even if I can get a shot into her, she'll murder me long before it neutralizes her abilities. Then she'll go into hiding, and Project Impulse will run out of resources well before she comes out again. We'll all be screwed."

The Woman in White nodded to Albert, who removed a third vial and put it on display for Colonel Davis. At first, the vial appeared to contain the same purple liquid as the others, but upon closer inspection, Colonel Davis saw it was thicker and cloudier, with a black substance swirling within.

"What the hell is that?"

"This," Albert said, pointing to the second vial he'd removed, "is your weaponized variant of Joseph Madison's counteragent. An effective concoction, though suffering from the same drawback as the original. It takes too long to act. Also, it doesn't have the same impact on the subject's memory as the original mixture. I was tasked with refining your weapon, but instead of working from an already inferior product, I went back to the source." He pointed a finger to the vial containing the stained swab. "And then I perfected it." Now he held up the third vial, showing it off like a proud father would his only child. "It'll neutralize any Trizorapine in the target's system in less than five seconds and put a chemical dampener on the Omega Genome. It also contains an active memory blocker, similar to the original, that should provide us with a clean slate on which to imprint our own program. For good measure, I've included a powerful sedative. That way, even if the neutralization takes longer than expected, the target will be helpless to act." Albert passed the vial to Colonel Davis with a gentle touch. "Careful. It's the only one we've got until we replenish our resources."

The colonel eyed the mixture floating in the vial with a renewed sense of power. If this truly could disable the Alpha child, then maybe they stood a fighting chance. Of course, there was one significant hiccup no one in the room had acknowledged yet. "You're presuming Maddox and I will be able to get it into her system. Even if we use the customized rifles, it's one shot, and she's a hell of an evasive target."

The Woman in White caught his eye, that coy smile still plastered across her lips. And what she said next left Colonel Davis filled with disconcerting intrigue. "That's why we're not giving that responsibility to the two of you."

———

Amanda could feel herself getting hungry. She'd gotten so accustomed to living her life with as little use of her abilities as possible that she'd forgotten what a drain they were on her energy. She would need to eat soon if she wanted to maintain optimal conditioning for the battle ahead. But she knew she was close now, too close to deviate from her course for a quick bite. After leaving St. Louis, she had taken a bus as far as Des Moines, Iowa, before she began noticing the occasional double-take or diverted stare from those riding with her. She'd been lucky to make it that far before news of her appearances garnered enough attention that she became a recognizable figure outside of Eden. Though Amanda wanted the Project Impulse team to follow her journey, she didn't want them to follow it closely enough that they could ambush her, at least not before she was ready for them. She needed controlled exposure, something she would lose the moment people around her starting posting unplanned pictures and recordings to the web. So she'd ditched her bus at the next stop and resorted to walking.

She'd maintained an abnormally fast pace for a girl of her physical age, trusting that any passerby would only notice that speed momentarily, brushing it off as coming from someone in a hurry. When she was out of visual range of civilization, she'd put her abilities to use, dematerializing so she could cover significantly more ground in a quarter of the time. And just a few minutes earlier, she had touched down from her most recent flight, triggered by the fact that her energy was waning, but also by the knowledge of where she was.

Amanda walked along the side of an empty highway road, up a steep incline surrounded by young trees, and to its crest, where a signpost waited, marking Eden's border. She paused there, staring at the distant city skyline, downtown Eden still quite a way from her current location. Amanda was overcome with familiarity. Though it had changed in appearance over the years, this was her home. It called to her, ready to welcome her with a warm hug, as if it had lost a part of itself when it had lost her, and was yearning to have her back. Amanda felt her lips curling into a serene smile, and for a moment, she was at peace.

But then she remembered cradling Evan's lifeless body on the floor of Renewed Hope. She recalled the pain and hatred that had consumed every fiber of her being. Images of her fight with Judas flashed through her mind like unwanted pop-up boxes. And when she banished them, the stark reality of why she had returned flooded in to fill the empty space. Amanda's smile faded, and her eyes drooped with gravity, as she felt the familiar ache of heartbreak once more. She took a heavy breath, then forced one foot in front of the other, and continued her journey.

An hour later, Amanda came across a roadside diner in the midst of its lunch rush. The televisions inside were tuned to either daytime soap operas or business news networks, neither of which was displaying or discussing her recent public appearances. The diner was so crowded that Amanda had little trouble fading into the background as she climbed atop a bar stool and buried her head in a menu. She ordered the fried chicken, which came with sides of green beans and mashed potatoes. It wasn't the healthiest meal, but it would keep her energized for the rest of the day. She ate and downed three glasses of iced tea without incident. Then she paid for her meal, kept her head low, and resumed her outdoor trek.

Amanda glanced over her shoulder periodically to confirm no one had followed her out of the diner. She also stayed on a straight path to keep the diner in sight. That way, she could observe if anything out of the ordinary occurred following her departure. At first, there was nothing. But then, just before the diner was far enough to fade from view, Amanda glimpsed what appeared to be a news van pull into its parking lot. She paused and turned to watch, her genetically enhanced vision enabling her to see details no ordinary person would have been able to perceive from that distance.

Sure enough, she had seen a news van. Now, both its driver door and side sliding door were open, its three passengers having already climbed out. One was a woman dressed in a pressed suit, who was currently checking her makeup in a mirror. The others were casually dressed men, and they were fiddling with camera equipment in the back. This was why Amanda had to be cautious about public appearances. She didn't want Project Impulse to know she was in Eden yet. She wanted to meet with her family first, to tell them what she was doing, to assure them that everything would be okay. But now she saw that she might have blown that opportunity. Her breath caught in her throat as she watched one of the men prop a news camera on his shoulder, as if preparing to shoot the scene. The woman, who Amanda assumed was the on-screen talent, finished touching up her lipstick and joined the other two. They chatted for a moment, looked at the diner, then chatted a little more. The second man made some adjustments to the camera on the first man's shoulder. Then they set the camera back into the van and slammed its doors shut. The woman said something that made the two of them laugh, and all three headed inside, with no equipment or anything else on them that indicated they were there for a story.

Amanda's muscles relaxed. She breathed easily and turned around to continue her hike, when she nearly bumped into someone who'd been hovering just inches behind her. So caught in determining whether her arrival in Eden had been observed, even her genetic enhancements had failed to notice the man, who was draped in layers of unwashed clothing and reeked of alcohol.

"Hey, do I know you?" the man slurred from behind a thick, unkempt beard.

Amanda tried to be polite, but brief. "I'm afraid not. Excuse me."

She walked around the man, leaving her back to him, but also keeping her senses tuned on his actions. Not that she had anything to fear. The man was dirty, but he hadn't been threatening. And even if he turned out to be dangerous, Amanda knew from experience she could take care of herself. But he was a wild-card, an interaction she hadn't planned on having, and therefore someone she needed to monitor, just like the diner news crew.

"Well, wait a minute," the man called after her. He jogged to catch up, then kept pace by Amanda's side. "You don't happen to have any of that new stuff on you, huh?"

She shook her head. "No."

But the man persisted. "Please, if you've got some, I could really use a fix. I don't need much. Just something to hold me over."

"I really don't know what you're talking about."

It was the truth, and the man must have sensed it, for he stopped and let Amanda walk ahead. "Are you sure I don't know you?" he then yelled. "You look really familiar."

Amanda kept her eyes focused on the road ahead, but she could sense the man catching up with her again. She was prepared to defend herself, but kept her cool, projecting that he was on an angle to rejoin her side, not to attack. A few moments later, there he was.

"Okay, maybe I don't know you," he said. "But can you please share some of that new stuff anyway? I know you've got some. I can smell it."

Amanda paused, taken aback by his claim. "What?"

He nodded with the excitement of a dog who'd found a treat. "I can smell it. It's all over you. It's like you've got it stashed all over your body. Please, just give me a little. I'm really struggling here."

Amanda tried to reason with her unwanted friend, if only to appease him, so he'd leave her be. "I was just in the diner up the road. You're probably smelling that. I'm happy to give you some money if you want food."

"I don't need your money," the man growled, a sudden anger overtaking his facial features. "I've got money. And I can get food. I need that new stuff. I need it right now."

"As I said, I don't know what you're talking about."

"But I can smell it!" he insisted. Then he leaned into Amanda, sniffing audibly. "Here," he said, his nose moving over her shoulder. "And here." His nose had traveled down her arm and to her hand. "And definitely here," he said with a moan of longing ecstasy. "Please... how can you be so selfish?"

It was clear to Amanda there would be no appeasing him. "I'm sorry. I don't know how to help you."

She turned away again, hoping this time the man would give up and leave her alone. But only ten seconds later, she sensed him approaching again. She couldn't let him keep distracting, and potentially exposing, her like this. So she spun to face him, intimidation tactics at the ready. But before she got a word out, the man was in her face, having gone straight for her instead of angling to the side. And instead of coming at Amanda with an attack she could have foreseen, he bent toward her and sunk his teeth into her upper arm. The pain was nothing compared to others she'd experienced, but it caught her by surprise, and Amanda responded on instinct by shoving the man away with more force than which a girl of her build should be capable.

"What the hell was that for?" the man asked from fifteen feet away as he picked himself off the ground.

Was his brain so fried that he really didn't know? Or did he think his own actions had been appropriate? Not caring to find out, Amanda resumed her walk. Her bite wound had already healed, her genetic enhancements instantly repairing the damage, which had run surprisingly deep. Amanda glanced at her sleeve, now stained with small drops of blood mirroring the arc of her assailant's mouth. She would need to buy a new shirt before passing through any heavily populated section of Eden for the sake of avoiding even more attention. She would also—

Amanda's thought process derailed as her senses alerted her of the man racing toward her. She spun, this time prepared for an attack, and caught him mid-run, lifting him over her head and dropping him on the pavement behind her in a single, fluid motion. The man groaned in pain and rocked back and forth on the hard surface.

"Leave me alone," Amanda ordered.

She resumed walking again, but again, the man rose to chase her down. Amanda braced her arm and extended a flat palm, pivoting so he would slam into it chest-first. All air escaped his lungs as he collapsed on the spot, and Amanda was pretty sure she sensed the cracking of a rib or two during the collision.

"I don't want to hurt you," she said. "Stay down and let me walk away."

But the man didn't listen. Despite whatever ribs might have been broken, he wheezed what little air he could and lunged at Amanda. She side-stepped him, this time catching one of his arms and pulling it free of its socket. The man howled in pain and stumbled away from her.

"That's enough," Amanda said.

But it wasn't. The man turned his head to her, and it was then that she saw his crazed eyes. They hadn't looked that way before, but something about their inter-action had spurred him into an uncontrollable frenzy, one that even massive levels of pain couldn't subdue. He charged at Amanda again. She dodged the incoming attack with ease and tripped the man, sending him tumbling across the street. Certain he wouldn't stay down or leave her alone, Amanda gathered a handful of dirt and gravel from the side of the road. When the man charged again, she threw it into his eyes. Then, taking advantage of his temporary blindness, she allowed her body to fully atomize and floated into the breeze. She drifted far enough away that the man wouldn't see her touch down again, all the while keeping her genetic hearing focused on his unintelligible rant.

"Where'd you go?! I need my fix! Please, come back! You smelled so good. Just give me that fix..."

The man's yells broke down into pained sobs before Amanda stopped listen-ing. She still couldn't make sense of what had happened back there. Was he simply out of his mind? Or had he really smelled something on her? If so, what was it, and how had it gotten there? Amanda already needed a new shirt; now she considered maybe she needed a new outfit altogether, along with a fresh shower. She promised herself she would take care of both. Then, as she continued her trek into Eden, she tried to put the encounter out of her mind. Yet Amanda's thoughts kept returning to it, as if there had been something more to the assault that her instincts had noticed, even if her conscious mind hadn't. What that was, however, remained a mystery.

CHAPTER 7

UNCONSCIOUS CONSCIOUSNESS

After they'd left Jack's Stash, Vincent brought Derek home. He'd recognized the nervous excitement in his son's voice and mannerisms, and knew Derek would be about as useful as a sack of wet rags at work, given his personal distractions. So he gave his son the day off to shop for a ring and get the nerves out of his system. The last thing he needed was for Samuel to get a whiff of those nerves while on duty for the Rose Parade the next day. Luckily, Stacy was already gone when they'd arrived back at the house, having left a note that she was meeting a friend for lunch and then spending the afternoon with her mother, but that she would see Derek again that night. That negated the need for excuses to ditch her, so Derek set out on his shopping journey, while Vincent headed to Eden PD.

Diana, who was also gone by the time they'd returned from Jack's Stash, read dramatically from her phone as Vincent walked through the front doors. "Have something important to do. Will see you at work. Spare key is on the kitchen counter. Feel free to have a Pop-Tart before you leave." She lowered the phone and batted sarcastic eyes at him. "What did I do to deserve such chivalry?"

Vincent felt the heat of embarrassment rush into his cheeks. "I guess I should've worked on that last bit a little more."

"Well, the joke's on you, buddy. I had two Pop-Tarts." Diana removed a thin stack of paper from a desk drawer and held it out for him. "Here's what you've missed so far today." When Vincent reached for the stack, Diana yanked it back. "Not until you tell me what was more important than having breakfast with yours truly."

Clearly, whatever was in the stack wasn't important, but Vincent played

Diana's game anyway. "You'd be proud of me, actually. I took your advice and—hey, who the hell is in my office?"

Diana turned just in time to catch the shadow he'd seen cross behind his closed office blinds. "Oh, is that your office? Maybe if you'd spend more time in it—"

Vincent held up a hand to stop her mid-sentence. She was in playful mode, which meant she would run him round and round, chasing an answer she would never give. If he wanted to know who was in his office, he was going to have to see for himself. He left a grinning Diana behind and stormed through the office door, finding Frank lounging back in his chair with feet propped up on his desk. Vincent chuckled. "I should have known."

"I knew you had a cush job around here, Sheriff," Frank said, "but I didn't know it was this laid back. Not showing up for work until lunchtime... Captain Tipps would have my ass."

"Get out of my chair," Vincent told him, not actually caring whether he did.

Frank stood, and the two shook hands before exchanging a friendly hug.

"Do I even want to know what you're doing back here?" Vincent asked. "You're like a bad omen. Life's going well, then you show up on my doorstep, and the next thing I know, we're all in mortal danger. Please tell me you came to sell your family's land or something normal like that."

Frank bit his lip, his happiness at seeing his friend giving way to concern.

"Shit," Vincent muttered. "What is it?"

"You mean you really don't know?"

"Know what?"

Frank couldn't believe it. "When was the last time you watched the news?"

Vincent shrugged. "I don't. I find life is much less stressful that way."

"Well, you should." Frank pulled out his phone and searched for social media postings of Amanda's recent appearances. He handed the device to Vincent. "Your daughter's on her way home, and she isn't being subtle about it."

Vincent watched the clip out of Atlanta first. Then, after watching the one from St. Louis, he replayed them both. "This makes no sense. She left to protect us. And she went into hiding to protect herself. Why would she endanger all of us like this? She's got to know they'll come for her. They'll figure out she's headed home and—" Vincent felt realization setting in. He fell into his chair, a hand to his already pounding head. "That's what she wants them to do. She's coming home to fight, isn't she?"

"That's a reasonable conclusion," Frank said, though his tone indicated he didn't buy it.

"You've got something else in mind? How long have you known about this?"

"Since last night."

"And what? You woke up this morning and decided it was better to tell me in person instead of making a simple phone call?"

Frank shot him a weak smile. "Waking up implies I went to sleep."

"Ah," Vincent said, cutting the word abruptly. "I see you haven't changed much this past year. So you being here isn't about informing me of Shortcake's return. You're here to do something about it."

Frank bobbed his head. "I'm here for a variety of reasons." He took a nervous breath, already knowing the effect his next words would have on his friend. "Amanda's return isn't some random event. Death is coming back to Eden, Sheriff. I know it, and now you know it."

"Don't say that," Vincent snapped, his voice shaky with a mix of worry and anger. "It won't be like before. It may not be anything at all. Joseph told us Project Impulse would be foolish to go after Amanda in her heightened state. So she's drawing them out of hiding. So what? They're no match for her. She'll put a stop to them once and for all, and then maybe she'll stay home, for good this time."

Frank stayed quiet for a moment so Vincent could process his own words. Then he softly replied, "Are you trying to convince me... or yourself?"

The sheriff didn't immediately respond. He knew the truth, but he would never admit it. "Why are you really here, Frank? We've been through too much together to keep secrets now. Are you here to help stop Project Impulse, or because you think the threat goes beyond it?"

Frank couldn't look him in the eyes. "I'm here because there's a connection between Project Impulse, your daughter, my dead brother's prophecy, and our drug-dealing pal, Thomas DeMarco."

"DeMarco? I thought he's been on the lam since his escape from Jericho PD."

"He has," Frank confirmed. "He's also started eliminating rival drug organizations. Yesterday, he hit the Ricci clan in Jericho. Billy spent the morning making calls, and he's already confirmed similar hits in seven other major cities."

"Damn..."

"That's not all. He's hit the Botha tribe in another nine cities and the Torres family in five more. We're talking coordinated assassinations that are sending the illicit drug world into chaos."

Vincent shook his head. "I don't get it. No single organization can maintain a monopoly over the world's illegal drug trade. He may as well be sealing his own death warrant. There'll be an uprising and rebalancing of power in no time."

"I completely agree with you, Sheriff. And yet, monopolistic control is exactly what DeMarco is trying to achieve. He wants his drugs, and his drugs alone, fueling addict communities around the globe." Frank swallowed hard, then brought the conversation full circle. "Now pair DeMarco's sudden self-destructive behavior with that of your daughter, and consider that both of them have ties to Project Impulse, a project my brother was exposed to as a child, and which he prophesied would destroy Eden... the very place your daughter is currently headed in a very public fashion. I can't connect all the dots just yet, but I can't ignore the facts, either."

Vincent stared at him with hard eyes. Frank hadn't declared Shortcake the enemy, but it was pretty clear which way he was leaning on the matter. Vincent needed to convince him he was wrong, and in turn, reassure himself that he was right, that Shortcake was still the innocent young girl he'd raised as his adopted daughter, that she could exercise free will and oppose her destructive roots. But pieces of this puzzle were still missing, and if Vincent wanted to win Frank over, he would need to help fill those pieces in. He threw the pouch of drugs Jack had given him onto his desk.

Frank's mouth fell open. "Is that—"

"Yes," Vincent confirmed. "Don't worry; it's not mine. A friend caught his kid with it. But that's not why I'm showing it to you. You and I are on the same side, Frank, but we're not on the same page. And if we're going to survive whatever's coming our way, we're going to need to rectify that. So, let's connect those remaining dots." He motioned to the drugs. "This is what DeMarco's self-destructive behavior is all about. This is what he wants spread around the world. If it was just about money and addiction, he'd be peddling the same stuff he always has. But he manufactured something new. Maybe we should find out what's in it."

Frank nodded respectfully. "That's something we can definitely get on the same page about. The problem is, we've seized plenty of this stuff back in Jericho. Eighty percent of it is comprised of known substances. It's the other twenty that's a mystery, and something tells me your quaint little facility here isn't more skilled at chemical analysis than my own."

"Fair point," Vincent said with an expecting smile. "So let's take it to someone who is."

———

Stacy pushed through a set of commercial glass doors and into a world of dark déjà vu. Before her eyes could adjust, her ears were lambasted by a hurricane of digital beeps and boops from arcade and pinball machines whose volume was cranked to the max. Her nose was assaulted by the smell of pepperoni pizza combined with an underlying odor of wood, oil, and air freshener. Ahead, a long perpendicular counter came into view, and above it hung an equally long sign displaying packages, prices, and the name *Big Al's New and Improved Bowl-o-Rama*. The *New and Improved* portion of the title had been given a spray-paint treatment that made it look like grammatical graffiti inserted above the bowling alley's original name. This was the first time Stacy had been back to Big Al's since The Falling of the Tides, during which the original building had been decimated. Rumor had it the newly built version was no less popular than the original, and given the crowd inside in the middle of a weekday, Stacy believed it.

She declined help from the employee stationed at the front counter and made her way down the western wall of the building. Its original layout had been restored, providing her with a sense of familiarity. Yet, it appeared all the amenities within, from the bowling lanes themselves to the waiting areas and computer terminals at the front of each lane, to the dining and alternate entertainment, had received significant upgrades. Even the building's interior paint job had received a boost, swapping what had been bright panels of bold colors for textures and patterns of those same bold colors, as well as a few additional accents. It was surreal, and it took Stacy back to the simpler times of days gone by.

She located the pizza counter and scanned the adjacent tables and booths. Most were populated by high-schoolers fresh off of their final exams and ready to jumpstart their summer plans. Some contained families with younger children whose parents had taken off of work to have a fun outing before Eden's summer camp programs kicked off. And, of course, there was the occasional loner or Big Al's regular who wished the others would return to their normal lives so they could have the bowling alley back to themselves. Stacy spotted one such loner sitting by himself along the far edge of the dining area.

"There you are," Mark said when she approached. "I was starting to think you were going to stand me up. I took the liberty of ordering."

Stacy glanced at a clock on the wall. She was only one minute late, but the missing two slices of their cheese pizza suggested Mark had taken his liberties well before their established meeting time. In the heyday of their relationship, he would've waited for her no matter how late she ran. But he wasn't that person anymore. Stacy shrugged it off and sat. "Kind of an odd place to meet for lunch, huh? I mean, there are better—and quieter—pizza places nearby."

Mark smiled as he grabbed a third piece. "I guess I was feeling nostalgic. The last time I was here was..." He trailed off, not as if he'd forgotten, but as if he didn't want to complete the thought.

Stacy, on the other hand, had no problem finishing his words. "The night I told you I wanted to break up." She observed his disheveled appearance, and how he couldn't keep the slice of pizza steady when moving it between plate and mouth. "Are you sure you wanted to relive that night? Or is this the only place in the city that serves alcohol that you haven't been kicked out of yet?"

Mark threw his slice down angrily. "That boyfriend of yours has a big mouth."

"He's worried about you, Mark. We both are."

"Yeah, right."

He angled away from her as he resumed eating. Stacy debated leaving. She had more enjoyable and productive ways to spend her time than arguing with her former-boyfriend-turned-loser. But she'd been telling the truth about being worried. Despite their romantic falling out, and then their subsequent attempt at friendship that had cratered the moment Mark accepted he would never win her back from Derek, Stacy wanted the best for him. And she knew he was capable of getting it too, if only he'd crawl out of his funk and start applying himself again. She touched his arm.

"Hey, I mean it. You know Derek could have you behind bars for much worse things than disturbing the peace and disorderly conduct if he wanted to. He lets you slide because he keeps hoping you'll turn your life around."

"Tell me more about Mr. Perfect, why don't you?" Mark grumbled as he resumed eating.

Stacy sighed in frustration. "What's it going to take? Do I need to drag you to rehab myself? Clearly, you aren't motivated to get clean on your own."

Mark swallowed the last of his slice with an audible and off-putting lip smack. "I'm perfectly fine with the way I am. If others don't like it, maybe they're the ones with a problem."

"If you really believe that, then you need more help than I thought."

Mark slammed a fist, rattling his plate. "Hey! I didn't ask you to lunch so you could criticize me. Or so you could give me motherly advice."

"Then why did you ask me?"

His attitude flipped like a switch. He tried to be suave, though it came across as pathetic given his current state. "I thought maybe we could have a little fun." Stacy assumed he meant by bowling or playing in the arcade, but Mark dispelled her of that quickly. "My friend tells me the family restrooms are extra large and always clean. He said the baby changing station will even support the weight of an adult."

Stacy wanted to vomit. "You asked me to lunch hoping I would have sex with you in a bathroom?!"

Mark shrugged. "Or the laser tag arena. I hear they don't check whether everyone exits when their time is up. I'm sure there are at least one or two dark corners—"

"I'm out of here."

Stacy stood, but Mark grabbed her arm. "What's so wrong with me that you won't even consider the idea? It's not like it's something we haven't done before."

"To be clear," Stacy said, "we've never done what you just described before. Now get your disgusting hand off of me."

Mark obeyed. "Sorry," he said like a wounded child. "I just thought maybe—"

"Maybe what? That after over a year of barely speaking to each other, I would have a sudden urge to jump your bones? What are you, twelve?" Stacy noticed other patrons watching her, so she lowered her voice, but maintained the firmness of her tone. "Listen to me, and listen good. I am with Derek. I will always be with Derek. And even if I wasn't, I wouldn't be with you. Not the way you used to be, and certainly not the way you are now. I'm willing to be your friend, to help you turn things around, but even that, you're making very difficult right now."

Mark stood, lines of anger returning to his face. "Fuck your friendship. And fuck you and Derek, too. I don't need either of you." He stormed toward the exit.

"Mark..."

He didn't look back, but he did sign-off with two middle fingers pointed toward Heaven. Seconds later, his body was awash in sunlight, and then he was gone. Stacy was done. She'd tried to make things work with Mark as both girlfriend and good friend, but it was clear now that neither was a long-term possibility. She grabbed her cell phone, intent on blocking his number, when something caught her eye. It was a small, plastic baggie, no bigger than a gum ball, filled with a white substance and secured with a twist tie. It was on the floor beneath Mark's seat. Stacy hadn't noticed it when joining him, suspecting instead that it had fallen from his pocket when he'd jumped up to leave.

She bent over casually, pretending to adjust her shoe as she grabbed the baggie and tucked it into her palm. Then she shoved it into her pocket, glancing around to confirm no one was still watching her. As she did, however, she saw something else that stole her attention. It was a replay of a news report, silent on one of the dining area televisions, with closed captions describing the scene as Amanda's body dematerialized on screen before floating over the streets of Atlanta. Stacy felt a chill run through her as her mind flooded with questions: Why was Amanda in Atlanta? Why had she allowed her abilities to be caught on video? Where was she going? And most importantly, who else was watching and planning their next move in response? Immediately forgetting about her drama with Mark, she woke her cell phone and dialed Derek. His phone rang seven times before kicking her over to voicemail. Knowing that was out of the norm for him, she dialed again, but this time got sent to voicemail after only three rings. Stacy waited for the message to play and beep to sound.

"Derek, it's me. Call me back as soon as you get this. Your sister's been exposed."

———

The errant energy particle bobbed as an ocean breeze swept past it. It was over one thousand miles from its origin, and even farther from its owner. It didn't have a mind of its own; it was still a part of Amanda, and still influenced by her will. But it was on a rogue course now, diverging from that of the rest of her body, pursuing a deep longing of which she wasn't even fully aware. It sunk closer to the ocean surface, below an increasingly strong wind current, and pushed through saltwater mist emanating from chop just ahead. Soon, the energy particle crossed over land, at first sandy, then covered in dirt and foliage that thickened the farther inland it went. It could feel the pull of its destination nearing, a magnetic attraction that had nothing to do with magnetism, but was as strong nonetheless. The particle lowered again, now skimming through low brush, past puddles and animal tracks, then through a metallic boundary overgrown with vines. The angle of its destination changed, so it veered downward, into the dirt below, merging and unmerging with nature's elements as it pushed deep underground.

The particle emerged from a concrete barrier into an unnatural space filled with clean air. It let instinct take hold, guiding it down one corridor, then another. It passed people in lab coats and uniforms, but they didn't take notice. The particle was too small and blended too well with the fluorescent lighting that lined each hall. It merged through a steel door, then floated past rows of computers that emitted so much electrical interference it had to pause and reorient itself. Then it merged into a thick wall of glass and came out on the other side, where an enormous room sat waiting. The particle's destination was upon it, but there was so much invisible noise clouding its remaining path. It couldn't isolate its target among the pulses of electricity, the streams of sterile airflow, the radio interference of an intercom system...

The particle tried to draw upon Amanda's energy, the way it always did when she allowed her body to enter its chaotic state of atomization. But she was too far away. It tried to focus her inner will, that which had guided it this far, but that yielded even more confusion. Instead of one destination, the particle sensed fifty of them in close proximity. They were all the same, likely the instinctual equivalent of double-vision, given the suboptimal conditions in which those instincts were operating. The particle floated toward the multiple destinations, and their proximities to it shifted in a pattern that confirmed they were no hallucinations. They were fifty distinct, tangible destinations. But which should the particle choose? Was one superior to the others? Was one more aligned with Amanda's desires? Having no true conscious thought of its own, the particle couldn't make that determination. And with Amanda not actively controlling it, she wasn't receiving its input to make the determination for it. So the particle chose at random. It floated toward one of its destinations, merged with the high-tech barrier blocking its path, and pushed through to the other side...

———

"These look okay for now," Albert told one of his fellow scientists. He had just finished reviewing an environmental assessment of The Hive. "Let me know if the particulate reading gets any higher. We may need Diego and his team to test the inner shell and filtration system for ancillary breach damage."

"Yes, sir."

The scientist took his assessment and departed. Albert proceeded to the nearest wall-mounted computer display and reviewed the latest stats being fed from The Hive's pod array. All appeared normal. He then strolled to the metal staircase that would take him through decontamination and back into The Hive's control room. Albert performed a cursory visual inspection of each pod he passed. It wasn't that he expected to find anything wrong; it was just his normal routine when passing through The Hive's main chamber. He would spot check for any deterioration in the pod walls, any gaps in their circumference seals, and any unexpected condensation or thermal imbalance. He noticed nothing unusual in the set of pods he'd passed on this walk, so Albert proceeded up the metal staircase and into the decontamination chamber. It was then that he spotted the vapor... or lack thereof.

Though Albert hadn't seen signs of seam damage or thermal deviation, one of the pods was shedding significantly less vapor than usual. He exited the decontamination chamber and returned to its underside, where he confirmed the observation hadn't been a trick of his eyes. Albert called the control room from a nearby intercom.

"*Yes, sir?*" one of the technicians asked.

"Check the coolant flow on pod forty-two. Something doesn't look right."

There was a momentary pause accompanied by keyboard clicking, then the technician replied, "*Good catch, sir. It looks like one of the coolant tanks is empty, but its alarm never tripped. It must be faulty. We'll change it out right away.*"

Albert was more concerned about the pod than replacing the tank. "Did we breach any critical levels?"

More typing. Then, "*No, sir. We came close, but the coolant stayed about three clicks above the minimum threshold at all times. We'll get it back to optimal range within the hour."*

"Thank you." Albert was about to let the technician go when The Hive's yellow warning lights sparked to life in their perimeter casings. He reopened the line. "Is that because of the coolant failure?"

There wasn't an immediate response, and Albert could see that all of the control room technicians were scrambling with urgency. The one he'd been speaking with received a printout from another. That was The Hive system's fail-safe in emergency situations. A diagnostic report detailing the anomaly responsible for the emergency would automatically print in hard copy. That way, even if they subsequently lost their computer systems, they would know what problem needed fixing to restore normal operations.

"It's not the coolant," the technician eventually replied. *"Pod forty-seven is showing... movement."*

The technician said the word as if it was an impossibility. Albert knew that's because it was.

"Earthquake?" he suggested.

"We've got nothing showing on seismographs. The movement is coming from inside."

Albert didn't understand how, but how became irrelevant the moment the glass lid of pod forty-seven broke open. Cooling vapor spilled from its edges, obscuring his view of the organic lifeform within as it rose on two legs, stretching muscles that had been genetically engineered and, until now, maintained through artificial stimulation. Albert could only watch, wondering what a creature with no mind of its own and no knowledge of its surroundings would do when freed of constraints. It was like a baby entering the world for the first time. Only this baby was partially matured, and far deadlier than its lesser developed peers could ever be. The lifeform's silhouette rotated from side to side behind the curtain of vapor. Then it bent its knees and launched itself upward. That was all the motivation Albert needed to get the hell out of there.

He spun on his heels, ready to make a mad dash for the exit stairwell, when his mindless creature landed in front of him with an echoing thud. The creature stared at him, not with ill intent, but with an insatiable, childlike curiosity. Albert could barely breathe. A lump in his throat prevented him from swallowing, and fear prevented him from moving. The creature observed its creator's incapacitated state, but didn't seem to know what to make of it. It then held out its hand, a hand that began dematerializing into bright blue energy particles. The creature appeared confused, even as the dematerialization proceeded up its arm, then across its chest and torso. Soon, it was nothing but a swarm of energy, energy fused with Amanda's errant particle and under its control. The swarm shot toward The Hive's ceiling, then circled its perimeter, as if seeking an easy way out. When it didn't find one, it charged straight through The Hive's wall. Each individual speck of energy then merged and unmerged with its surroundings as it pushed through layer after layer of Complex E's infrastructure, until they emerged into the open air of nature. Then they took to the sky, darted over treetops, and jetted out over the ocean with a singular, shared purpose as their guide: *they were going home.*

CHAPTER 8

THE ETERNAL HURT

Vincent counted the repetitions of Frank's right-hand fingers as they tapped in rhythmic succession on the classroom lab table. *Eighty-three, eighty-four, eighty-five...* On and on Frank went, a consistent, if not somewhat annoying, way to pass the time. A couple of hours earlier, they had knocked on Joseph's front door, thinking they'd catch the professor by surprise with their unannounced visit. But Joseph was expecting them, having already seen the news reports out of Atlanta and St. Louis, and suspecting Amanda's return to Eden would draw the old gang back together. What he hadn't expected was for Vincent and Frank to bring illegal drugs into his home, then to ask him to analyze those drugs as if he harbored some scaled-down version of Helix Unbound in his attic. Luckily, his ongoing sabbatical didn't deprive him of access to Pine Ridge. And with it being the afternoon before the Rose Parade, he was confident at least one or two student labs would be available for use.

One hundred one, one hundred two... This hadn't been the only wait Vincent and Frank had endured since arriving at Pine Ridge. First, there had been the search for guest parking, for even though Joseph was still employed by the university, he had failed to renew his parking pass since taking leave over a year earlier. Next, there had been the trek across campus and hunt for an open lab room, which had been interrupted by the Life Sciences dean, who was interested in both making chitchat and grilling Joseph about when he'd return to the classroom. Then there had been the precautions—oh so many precautions. Joseph had locked the lab door and instructed Vincent and Frank to slide a heavy desk in front of it to keep anyone from busting it open. While they'd done that, he'd lowered the shades on all windows equipped with them and blocked those that weren't with papers and equipment. He was on the verge of returning to active teaching and researching duties. The last thing he wanted was a drug scandal derailing that.

Joseph had made each of them suit up to avoid contaminating the drug sample, as well as wear masks to mitigate the risk of an unexpected cough or sneeze. Then he'd partitioned the sample into eleven separate specimens: ten for testing and one to keep as backup should some tragedy befall the others. Joseph had secured nine of the specimens in test tubes, then carefully transferred the tenth to a microscope slide. Vincent and Frank had tried to converse with him as he prepped each tube and its necessary equipment for his chosen analyses, but he'd insisted on silence so he wouldn't make a mistake. That left the law enforcement officers sitting idly by for nearly an hour. They'd been on the verge of going stir-crazy when Joseph completed his prep, and though they'd thought that would give them a welcome reprieve, the professor had then insisted on silence once again as he performed his microscopic analysis. *One hundred thirty-six, one hundred thirty-seven...*

"This is interesting," Joseph said, breaking Frank's rhythm.

"What is?" Vincent asked.

"This structure. It's too complex to have been concocted in some rogue chemist's lab. This required precision engineering, high-end manufacturing equipment, a climate controlled environment. It's the type of structure I'd see when I worked in the private sector: delicate to produce, but highly stable as a final product."

"I assume it's the type of structure you worked with at Helix Unbound as well?" Frank asked.

Joseph nodded. "Everything we did there was bleeding edge." He pointed to the slide glowing under the lens of his microscope. "This was our standard."

Given his conflict with Frank, that information provided no comfort to Vincent. "Can you tell what's in it?"

"Not based on looks. But once those test tubes are done processing, I should have a good idea." Joseph looked back and forth between his guests. He could feel the tension hanging over them. "We've got a few minutes to spare. How about you two fill me in on why this is so important? With Amanda on her way home, and Project Impulse still lurking out there, I'd assume there are more important things to do than investigate the nation's drug crisis."

"Frank thinks they're related," Vincent said.

Joseph eyed the detective. "How?"

"I don't know," he admitted.

Out of respect for his friends, and in the interest of full transparency, Frank relayed everything that had been going through his head about Thomas DeMarco, Project Impulse, and Amanda, who he caught himself referring to as *the Alpha child*, rather than her more common name, multiple times. He could tell he was on an island with his beliefs, but he couldn't fault the others for that. They were Amanda's fathers. They didn't see her as a threat, regardless of her upbringing. And any connection between her and Thomas DeMarco was still circumstantial, the strongest evidence being the unsupported warnings of a man in captivity and the crazed musings of a psychopath. Saying it aloud, even Frank began to question the validity of his assumptions.

"I take it you don't agree with his view," Joseph said to Vincent once Frank was done.

"No, but we shouldn't ignore it, either." Vincent treaded carefully with his next words, aware of the emotional impact they could have on Joseph. "Frank's instincts aren't perfect, but they do always seem to point toward a looming danger. If he thinks there's danger headed for Eden, I'm willing to trust him, even if he might be wrong about its source."

Joseph turned his glistening eyes to Frank. He didn't vocalize what he was thinking, and he certainly didn't need to. In the months following Evan's death, Frank had struggled to overcome his guilt for misidentifying the threat that ultimately took the boy's life. He'd dodged Joseph's calls, refused to visit Eden, and buried himself so deep in the DeMarco case that he didn't have time to dwell on mistakes of the past. Yet they never went away, and eventually Frank accepted he would need to face them. He attended therapy sessions with Jericho PD's in-house psychiatrist, returned to Eden at her suggestion to see how life was thriving there, and eventually called Joseph back. When the professor had answered, Frank could only manage a single phrase: *I'm sorry*.

They were cordial after that, both in agreement that if they could turn back time, they would have handled the emergence of a new threat to Eden differently. But they couldn't turn back time, and for Joseph, the pain of losing a child would never leave him. For Frank, the pain of failing to protect that child would forever haunt him, no matter how much he had come to terms with it. This was their status quo, and though uncomfortable, Frank and Joseph had accepted it, and each other.

"Okay," the professor said. Then, after a tense breath: "Well, if figuring out what's in these drugs helps us identify that danger, let's do it."

He guided the others to a different table, where a variety of machines were winding down their processing of the test tube specimens. A computer terminal sat in the middle of the table, and with a few clicks and password entry, Joseph had access to its running programs. Vincent and Frank saw streams of scientific notation scrolling by in one program window while a molecular diagram took shape in another. Joseph perused the information, able to decipher that which the law enforcement officers couldn't.

"So the bulk of this stuff is your usual narcotics blend," he said. "Illegal manufacturers don't tend to keep their different products segregated during production and packaging, so it all mixes together a little."

"I thought this stuff was complex," Frank noted. "Like it came from a professional manufacturing plant that wouldn't have those issues."

"Yes," Joseph replied. "Something in here has that level of complexity. But not all of it. Not most of it, actually. I only mentioned the complexity back there at the microscope because it was so odd. But it's only a portion of the mix, likely added as a supplement to an existing low-quality batch."

"Could it be filler?" Vincent asked. "Some sort of cutting agent to decrease potency and maximize quantity?"

Though Joseph wished that were the case, he knew better. "You wouldn't waste those types of resources on a cutting agent."

"Can you isolate it?" Frank asked.

"That's what I'm working on."

Joseph tapped a few keys, then copied lines of scientific notation from one of the text-based programs to the modeling program. Line by line, the program processed each identified ingredient, removing layers of complexity from the molecular diagram it had originally produced. The chemical structure of the mystery ingredient took shape. A progress bar to its side filled, the number beside it soon reaching *one hundred percent,* then a concluding message box popped up:

MATERIAL UNKNOWN

Frank and Vincent's anticipation deflated like a punctured tire. The detective rubbed his forehead in frustration, while the sheriff drifted away from the table, his mind already working on another solution, but unable to think of anyone more skilled than Joseph to contact. Neither of them noticed Joseph's reaction, which on the surface appeared similar, but inside was significantly different. He stared at the molecular diagram on display, unable to believe what he knew to be true.

"We were so close," Frank said before acknowledging defeat. "I appreciate you trying, Professor, even if we still don't know what this crap is."

Joseph swallowed hard, his pulse pounding. "*The computer* doesn't know what this is." He turned to Vincent and Frank, who could now see his visible unease. "But I do."

Vincent shook his head. "No." He knew what Joseph was going to say even before it left his lips, and the sheriff didn't want to hear it.

But Joseph put it out there anyway, finally connecting the dots Frank had struggled for so long to join. "It's Trizorapine. Your drug kingpin is lacing the globe *with Trizorapine.*"

"You mean the shit Project Impulse tested on my brother as a kid?" Frank asked rhetorically. "The same shit they pumped into your daughter when trying to turn her into a willing super-soldier? The same shit they corrupted Evan with? That they empowered Judas with?!" Though he couldn't fully see the implications, he knew it had to mean something. "Why? Why spread it all over the world like that? What'll it accomplish?"

Before either Joseph or Vincent could propose a hypothesis, a fourth, rather surprising, voice answered him. "It doesn't matter why."

They all turned toward the source of the voice: Amanda, who didn't need to peer through windows or bust down doors to gain entry to the lab. Her body was still reconstituting itself from a swarm of blue energy particles, a supernatural glow highlighting the firm expression on her face. She repeated, "It doesn't matter why... because I'm going to put an end to it."

———

Despite the gravity of the situation, Amanda was met with open arms by both of her fathers. They hadn't seen her since she left Eden following Evan's death, and nothing could overshadow the joy of being reunited. Amanda even received a handshake from Frank, though she could sense trepidation in his touch, as if he no longer viewed her as the trusted ally he once had. She would inquire what was behind that later, but there were more pressing concerns right now, and she knew time was limited.

"I'm sorry I didn't coordinate with you before exposing myself," she told the trio. "I couldn't risk Project Impulse intercepting any long-distance communication, and I couldn't risk them spotting me here before I was ready."

"Ready for what?" Vincent asked. "After all we've been through over the past five years, why put yourself out there like this? Why put your life on the line?"

"Even more importantly," Frank added, "why now?"

Amanda frowned, aware of how things must look, given the secrets she'd withheld from her family. "I know I owe you explanations. Please, bear with me." She pulled a nearby lab stool closer and sat. She didn't need to, but she wanted to conserve every ounce of energy possible, and she suspected she would already lose some of it to the emotional toll of the coming conversation. "This past year and a half has been... I don't know. It's hard to describe. When I left Eden, I was completely lost. I didn't know what to do without Evan by my side, but I knew I had to go, to protect all of you, and I knew I had to keep going, to keep surviving, so Evan's death wouldn't be in vain. I wandered across the country, seeking somewhere I could settle down while going unnoticed by the outside world. Eventually, I came across this quirky little hotel off the beaten path. The staff there let me stay for free. I don't know why; maybe I just looked that pitiful. But, while I was there, I felt something change within me. I felt a clarity I hadn't known since losing Evan, and when I checked out, that clarity guided me to my next destination."

Frank's inner detective told him Amanda was holding something back from this story. Maybe it was pertinent; maybe it wasn't. Either way, he didn't want to risk derailing her tale before hearing how it led to her public exposure and return. So he continued listening intently and kept his eyes—and poker face—focused on his suspect.

"I found a family willing to rent me their spare bedroom," she said. "They were good people, people I could trust to keep my presence quiet. They took care of me, providing me with food and shelter—until I decided it was time to leave and come back home."

"And what drove that decision?" Frank asked.

The way he was staring at her made Amanda nervous. He was friendly in tone, but his eyes were that of a judge gathering evidence for a verdict. "Something else changed. Not within me this time, but out there." She motioned around her.

"Out... where?" Vincent asked for clarification.

Amanda took a stuttered breath. "Everywhere." An eery silence settled over the room as the other three exchanged uneasy glances and waited for her to continue. When she did, she let it all out, despite knowing how crazy she sounded. "I don't know how to explain it exactly, but I can feel the world changing. I can feel it growing darker, as if suddenly shrouded by a growing storm. The darkness pulls at me. It calls me to it, tempting me to embrace it like I did the night—the night—" She turned away to hide watery eyes.

"The night Evan was killed," Frank said.

Amanda didn't acknowledge him, but the way she bit nervously at her bottom lip was confirmation enough. "We've all lost so much. I don't think I can take losing anyone else." She didn't say it as if it would break her spirit, but as if she was afraid of how she might respond. She continued, "The only way to ensure that doesn't happen is to take the offensive and stop Project Impulse before it achieves its end goal."

"What is its end goal?" Frank asked.

Amanda shrugged. "Death. Destruction. Darkness. Sadness. Loss. Misery. It doesn't really matter what name we assign it. The outcome is the same." She looked at Joseph. "This isn't about creating an army of genetically enhanced super-soldiers anymore. If that's all they wanted, they wouldn't have gone rogue. They wouldn't have spent years methodically planning a way to reclaim the power I took with me the night I escaped Helix Unbound. They wouldn't be saturating the world with experimental drugs. They wouldn't be haunting my dreams, invading my mind, trying to extinguish the last bit of light still within me!"

Amanda broke into a sob. Vincent and Joseph both rushed to her side, each cradling her with one arm as she touched her head with a shaky hand.

"He won't leave me alone," she cried. "He's in here now. He has been ever since I let him in, ever since I embraced his darkness. I need to stop him before he takes everything from me."

The two fathers caught Amanda's use of the words *he* and *him*. They shot each other a concerned look. What had a year and a half of isolation done to their little girl? Her departure from Eden had been in the best interest of everyone else, but what of her interest? To allow someone so grief-stricken to leave on her own, to attempt the healing process with no ongoing emotional support... it left Joseph and Vincent feeling like failures. Amanda's body went slack beneath their grips, the teenage girl's elbows propped on her knees and tearful face falling into her palms. Wave after wave of chokes and sobs broke through her mask. Months of pain, months of fear, months of stress over what to do next, were all coming out at once.

And then, it stopped. Not because Amanda had no more tears to shed, nor because her fathers had found a way to comfort her, but because Frank had placed a single finger beneath her chin and lifted so that their eyes met in an empathetic lock.

"I know that darkness well," he said, recognizing every emotion she was feeling as though Ray had brought them out of him only yesterday. "I also know that if I'm strong enough to overcome it, then you are too." He pulled a folded sheet of paper from his pocket. It was Ray's drawing of The Falling of the Tides, which he'd kept on him upon returning to Eden for inspiration should he ever waver from his purpose there. He showed the drawing to Amanda. "My brother prophesied the destruction of Eden at what appears to be your hand." He licked his lips in contemplation, updating his beliefs in real time in response to Amanda's emotional state. Then he said, "But this isn't you, is it? This is the Alpha child. This is the vessel of that darkness. And you don't have to be her. You can stop Project Impulse before that happens."

Amanda nodded. "That's what I came back to do." No longer an emotional wreck, she shared a gracious smile with each of her fathers, who let go and stood back to give her space. "As you've probably guessed by now, I exposed myself in Atlanta and St. Louis to provide those behind Project Impulse with a trajectory they could trace to Eden. I thought about making a stand in some other city, to keep the fight away from you, but I couldn't take the chance they would ignore me there, always assuming those cities were a temporary stopover rather than my final destination. By guiding them here, they know I'm coming home. And as soon as I make my return known, they'll send whatever forces they have left to retrieve me."

"What makes you so sure they don't already know you're here?" Frank asked.

"I've done my own counter-surveillance. They only have one Plainclothes monitoring Eden, and he's currently tailing Derek from one jewelry store to the next." Amanda turned her attention to Vincent. "Is there something I should know?"

He smiled. "I think you're smart enough to put that puzzle together."

Amanda felt the edges of her lips curl upward involuntarily. "Good for him." It saddened her to wonder whether she would be around to see the wedding with her own eyes, but it thrilled her to learn Derek and Stacy were going to make it after all the pitfalls their relationship had overcome. Not wanting to spoil the moment for Vincent, she redirected the conversation. "Tomorrow is the annual Rose Parade. I'll wait for the appropriate time, and then I'll make one last public appearance to show Project Impulse I'm here. Then I'll wait for them to come."

"I assume you've already got a location picked out," Frank said. "Give me the details, and I'll start working up engagement scenarios." He looked at Vincent. "How many men can you spare? Weapons, too. We need to be ready for whatever Colonel Davis—"

Amanda held up a palm to silence him. "I'm doing this alone."

"Like hell you are."

She sighed. "I didn't come back here to endanger any of you. I can handle Project Impulse. There's nothing they can throw at me that I haven't seen before. The only way they can defeat me... is through the rest of you." She frowned, but there was a strange sweetness underneath it. "You're my weakness. All of you. The most efficient way to get me to do their bidding is to threaten you. That's why I need you to stay out of it tomorrow. Let me fight. You protect each other. Derek and Stacy, too. And anyone else you can think of that they might use against me. By doing that, you'll give me the ability to fight without being handcuffed, and that's the best shot we've got at being victorious."

Frank didn't want to ask the question, but he felt someone had to. "What if you lose?"

Vincent and Joseph glared at him, aware of where his mind was headed. But Amanda took no offense and instead reached for the drawing in his hand. She stared at it for several seconds, then turned it to face the others.

"If I lose, assume the girl you know is dead. Then do whatever it takes to stop this person—" She pointed to the female figure at the drawing's center. "—from bringing your brother's prophecy to fruition."

Joseph placed a gentle hand on top of Amanda's and pushed the drawing down and out of sight. He spoke, his words soft and reassuring. "It won't come to that."

Amanda placed her free hand over his and squeezed affectionately. She put on a brave facade, a mask to give her fathers some sense of comfort that everything would be okay. But Frank saw it for what it was. And there was a moment, a brief instance lasting no longer than the blink of an eye, when she stole a glance at him to affirm what she had said before. If she lost her battle with Project Impulse, it was going to be up to him to stop her. Her fathers wouldn't have it in them, and if left unchecked, she would rain destruction upon Eden. Then the rest of the world would follow. She knew it to be true... and Frank did too.

———

Amanda visited with her family for another half hour. She kept her senses attuned for any suspicious activity outside the Pine Ridge lab, but thankfully, there was none. The young child of science didn't waste any more breath on talks of Project Impulse or the coming war. Instead, she relayed interesting stories from her time on the road, the most unusual of which involved her attempted return to the hotel that had sparked clarity within her. She'd tried to stop by on her journey back to Eden, but the building wasn't there. And it wasn't as though it had gone out of business or been repurposed or anything like that. The building literally wasn't there, and in its place were a pond and walking trail that looked as though they'd been there for quite some time. Amanda didn't know what to make of the sudden disappearance, and even admitted her hotel-induced moment of clarity might have been nothing more than a delusion of her genetically modified brain. But her fathers believed her, neither willing to revisit the topic of Amanda's sanity, given their love for her and the mental stress she had clearly been under. The time flew by faster than anyone would have liked, the short visit reminding them of the way life used to be, first for Joseph during Amanda's younger years at Helix Unbound, then for Vincent during her adolescent years in his household.

When Amanda insisted it was time for her to leave, the sadness on her fathers' faces was impossible to hide. She reminded them that the Plainclothes following Derek would only put up with ring shopping for so long, and when he shifted his surveillance back to Vincent or Joseph, and saw that they were now together with Frank, it would raise suspicions. Amanda needed to be gone before then, for the Plainclothes would likely stick with them twenty-four seven for the foreseeable future. She also reminded her fathers that by this time tomorrow, Project Impulse would be no more, and then they would have their lifetimes to share stories and spend time as a family. For now, though, they needed the discipline to see things through to the end.

Amanda shared prolonged hugs with both Vincent and Joseph. She told Vincent to share her love with Derek and Stacy, at which point he told her she should do it herself tomorrow night. That's when Vincent caught the first and only glimpse of concern on his daughter's face, and it was devastating. She wasn't fully confident she'd make it to tomorrow night. Joseph hadn't caught the concern, and Frank's eyes gave away that he was already aware, so Vincent kept the observation to himself. He hugged his adopted daughter one more time, this time even longer, unwilling to let her go. When they finally released each other, Amanda didn't say goodbye. Vincent wasn't sure if the choice was deliberate, or if she just couldn't bring herself to say it. Instead, she said she'd see the rest of them soon, then atomized her body and floated away.

She traveled well outside the footprint of Pine Ridge University before reforming. Now it was time to wait out the Rose Parade. Amanda still had a standing offer from Jebediah Steene for a home when needed at Renewed Hope. She'd had no intention of ever taking him up on it, but on the eve of her final battle with Project Impulse, it occurred to her that perhaps she needed emotional closure. That was where she'd let the darkness in; maybe if she came to terms with her loss, that was where she could expel it from her. She got her bearings and walked, avoiding the use of her abilities, as not to accidentally reveal her return to Eden. And by the time she arrived at the parking lot that had once served as its own Impulse child battleground, it was evening.

Amanda looked at the silhouette of Renewed Hope against the sinking sun. Despite the pain she'd gone through there, the building still welcomed her with warm lighting shining through colorful panes of stained glass. Amanda reached instinctively for the necklace tucked beneath her shirt. It was Evan's necklace, the fang of the first kill he'd made on Sunrise Isle, a symbol of his ability to survive, and now a symbol of him, the sole physical object that still bound Amanda to his memory. She gripped the necklace tightly and pressed ahead. As she approached the doors to the narthex, she heard the soft melody of organ music accompanied by harmonious choir vocals. She recalled how this music had once soothed her soul, whisking all worry away and filling her with a serene sense of peace. Amanda didn't think it would be able to do that this evening, but she was willing to give it a try.

She passed through the narthex and stood outside the open sanctuary doors. She could see the organ player and choir now. Their tunes waltzed through the air like dancers floating on a cloud. Amanda opened her ears and heart, beckoning them in, beckoning them to heal the darkness within her. But the darkness was strong. The music pushed at it, even pierced its wispy veil, but it could do nothing to eradicate the core. That had a grip on Amanda that would take much more than sweet melodies to loosen. She stared down at the break between the narthex and sanctuary floors. She wondered if this was how Evan had felt when he'd tried to let the music in. He couldn't bring himself to enter the sanctuary because something inside of him didn't belong there. Was that something now inside Amanda? Would it prevent her from entering that very room she had once sat in with Jebediah? There was only one way to find out.

She lifted a foot and moved it forward, past the narthex threshold, where it hovered over the sanctuary floor. She shifted her weight to put that foot down, and she was almost there, when suddenly an unexpected feeling overtook her. It wasn't a feeling of darkness, or of regret, or of unbelonging, but it caused her to withdraw her foot nonetheless. Amanda closed her eyes and focused on the feeling. She couldn't identify its nature or source, but she didn't feel threatened by it. It was familiar, almost as if it were an extension of herself...

She retreated from the sanctuary door and played an internal game of *hot and cold*, testing one direction to see if the feeling grew stronger before testing another. Her game led her back outside, then to the neighboring rectory, to its second floor, and then to the narrow staircase that led to the all-too-familiar attic door beyond which had been her and Evan's previous temporary home. The door was open, but no light shined from within. Amanda sensed the unusual feeling emanating from inside. Its source was there, perhaps her own subconscious guiding her to the closure she so desperately needed. Amanda didn't want to go inside. She didn't want to relive what had happened there. But closure required courage, so she forced herself forward, one foot in front of the other, until she reached the attic door and stepped inside.

Painful memories hemorrhaged from the recesses of her mind. She saw the pool of deep red blood. She saw herself crawling through it, over to Evan's lifeless body, which she cradled as though it would make the horror of that night fade away like a dream. Then Amanda saw herself make her way back to the ladder that led to the attic's upper floor, where she would reawaken her Omega Genome with an overdose of Trizorapine. Why had she done it? Why had she opened herself to the darkness like that? Revenge wouldn't bring Evan back. It would only serve Project Impulse's purpose. It would only serve *his* purpose. If Amanda could take it back...

She turned her eyes from the ladder, barely visible in dusk's glow. She didn't need to climb it, for her closure wasn't with her own actions following Evan's death. It was with her inability to save the life of the person she loved, the one person in this world with whom she had shared an unbreakable bond. Amanda glanced at the spot where she'd left his body behind. She had apologized for her failure in the moment, and yet she felt a compulsion to do it again, as if her previous words hadn't been enough. Only when she looked for Evan's body, she didn't see it anymore, her memory of it having already receded into the depths of her mind. What she did see, however, ripped the breath right out of her.

There was someone standing in the dark, over the place where Evan had fallen. The figure was a shadow against the light of the far window, and it was looking down at its feet, feet positioned on a carpet that didn't fully hide the red stain of the wood beneath. Amanda's game of hot and cold was over. This figure was the source of her odd feeling. It was what had drawn her out of the sanctuary and into the harsh history that lived on in the rectory attic. Amanda didn't know what to make of it. Was it an Impulse child? Was it a figment of her imagination? She shut her eyes and counted to three before opening them again, but the figure was still there, still staring at the tarnished ground.

"Who are you?" Amanda asked, perhaps with more aggression than needed.

The figure didn't respond, but she could see its eyes moving in the dark. It was aware of her presence, even though it had barely reacted to her arrival.

"My name is Amanda," she said, taking a more peaceful approach. "Can you tell me who you are?"

The figure cocked its head at her, then looked at its surroundings, almost as if unsure of where it was. Amanda took a step forward, and the figure took a step backwards.

"I'm not going to hurt you," she said. "I—"

What should she tell it? That she used to live here? That she watched her soulmate die here? That she was the central figure in a plot to overrun the world with darkness? Maybe the less said, the better. Amanda took another step, and the figure retreated in unison.

"Please, just talk to me."

She reached forward. The figure reached back. She stepped three more times. It retreated the same distance. Amanda didn't understand. Why wasn't it speaking? Why was it mirroring her movement, only in the opposite direction? Was it afraid, or did it not comprehend what she was saying? She needed a new tactic, so to show her actions were benign, she backed up two steps. This time, the figure took two steps toward her. Feeling like a puppet-master who hadn't asked for the job, Amanda strafed three steps to the right. The figure did the same to its left, maintaining a parallel position to her. Amanda backed up again; the figure moved toward her.

Fine, she thought. *If that's the game...*

She strafed into alignment with the far window. The figure, as expected, did the same. Then Amanda walked toward it, slowly, not aggressively, and the figure kept pace in its retreat. Amanda guided it straight toward the window, through which parking lot lamps provided additional illumination. She expected the figure to break from its mimicry routine once it realized she would out its identity, but it remained obedient, eventually stepping into a stream of artificial light that moved up its legs, over its naked body, and finally to its face. Amanda instantly went weak, every muscle in her body turning to gelatin.

She choked, her next word requiring every ounce of energy she could muster: "Evan?"

Then she collapsed, her heart seizing. The figure was suddenly free of its puppet strings. It looked up and down Amanda, then out the window. As if afraid of what would happen if it stayed around her, it reared back and jumped through the window, plummeting in a cloud of shattered glass toward the ground below. Amanda was frozen in a catatonic state. Inside, her mind was hard at work on rebooting her neurological system. It told her she must have been mistaken, that she couldn't have seen Evan, that he was dead and she knew that. But she also knew what her eyes had seen. That thing may not have been Evan, but it looked exactly like him... or, at least, it looked like Evan had looked before his escape from Helix Unbound and subsequent maturity. So if it wasn't Evan, then what the hell was it? That question was enough to zap life into Amanda's frozen heart. She resumed breathing, her head pounding from a combination of emotional shock and oxygen deprivation. She fought through it and pushed herself to her feet, then looked out the attic window just in time to see the false Evan flee toward the tree line of Soul Wind Forest. No longer concerned with being spotted by Project Impulse, Amanda dematerialized and raced after it.

It didn't take her long to catch the figure. She touched down on a bed of damp foliage and pursued on foot, a gap of only ten feet between them. She thought she'd have no trouble closing that gap, but no matter how fast she moved, the figure seemed to match her pace. They traveled deeper into the youthful woods that had grown following Eden's destruction, until the lights of the city faded behind them. Amanda debated dematerializing once more, but she suspected the figure would do the same. After all, it must be capable of her abilities to some degree, or else it would have crippled itself jumping from the attic of Renewed Hope. She still needed to catch up with it, however, and with no sign of it slowing down, she tried the most basic thing she could think to do.

"Stop!" she yelled.

And surprisingly, the figure listened. Amanda then realized she had stopped while delivering the order, so perhaps it hadn't listened at all, and was instead back to its games of mimicry.

"Don't move," she commanded. "Just stay right there."

And it did, even as she walked toward it, then circled around it, then faced it head on. Amanda's eyes confirmed what they had seen earlier. This thing, whatever it was, had been modeled after Evan. It had his facial features, his build, his deep, black eyes... but it wasn't him, was it? As much as Amanda longed to have her life partner back, resurrecting someone from the dead was beyond even her capability. That left this mystery figure's identity an ongoing secret.

"Who are you?" she asked again. Then, thinking of her previous experience, she rephrased it as a command. "Tell me who you are."

The figure looked at her as if she should know, but it didn't speak. Amanda wondered whether it even could speak. It was human, sort of. That much was obvious. But it wasn't natural. It reminded her of, well, herself. This thing had been grown in a lab, a lab under the control of Project Impulse and with access to Evan's genetic material from Helix Unbound. But if it shared Evan's genetic material, did that mean—

"Do you recognize me?" Amanda asked.

The figure eyed her from head to toe with curiosity. Then it made a slight motion of its head, possibly a nod, or possibly a reflex with no meaning behind it at all.

"Amanda. My name is Amanda. We—" She caught herself, realizing just how far off the deep end she had gone. Oh well, it was too late to turn back now. "We knew each other. We grew up together."

Again, the figured eyed her. It didn't appear afraid, but it also didn't appear fully conscious either, as if it were operating on autopilot with a limited set of instructions.

"Your name is Evan," Amanda said. She knew it wasn't true. This thing's name was probably Delta or Sigma or any other choice letter of the Greek alphabet. But it looked so much like him... "They called you Epsilon, back where we're from. You—" Amanda struggled for words. Then a thought came to her, and she pulled Evan's necklace from beneath her shirt. She left it hanging from her neck, but clasped the figure's hands around its dangling fang. "This was yours. You won it defending yourself from a deadly predator. Do you remember it? Do you remember me?" Then, desperately, she asked, "Do you remember *us?*"

A tear escaped Amanda's left eye, and as she felt it glide down her cheek, she saw a matching droplet escape the figure's right eye. That's when reality punched her in the gut. The false Evan didn't recognize her or the fang. It didn't know who she was, nor who it was, and it didn't have any of Evan's memories. And why should it? This wasn't Evan. This was an abomination of science, an insult to everything Evan ever was. The only recognition Amanda saw in it was her own, for now that they were in close proximity, it had resumed mimicking her in every respect. Weakness returning to her legs, she fell back onto the damp grass, the figure doing the same. Amanda stared at it, wondering what use Project Impulse had for such a basic, mindless lifeform. She'd thought they had nothing new to attack her with, but she'd been focused on attacks of a physical nature. Assault rifles, knives, counteragent rifles, grenades, pure military muscle... she'd been prepared to handle any of it. But an assault on her emotional stability... Amanda had no defense, now or in anticipation of future attacks to come.

She continued watching the figure, who watched her in return, and a portion of its blanket of mysteries unraveled. Amanda recalled how the figure had felt so familiar when she'd first sensed it. It felt like an *extension of herself*. Was it possible—

No, Amanda thought. *There was no way.*

But the figure was real, and it was sitting across from her, behaving as she, a puppet of the puppet-master. Had her longing to have Evan back in her life been so strong that she'd subconsciously sought him out? Unable to find him, had she then latched onto the closest replication? Amanda had her answer nearly instanta-neously, for in her clarity, she felt her errant energy particle residing inside this figure. She didn't know when it had escaped her, and supposed it was irrelevant, but it explained so much. She'd given this abomination life, and, on instinct, had led it home to Eden. It was a joint effort of her body and mind to reunite her with her lost love, the one person who could protect her from the darkness within.

But it was a misguided effort.

Amanda would give almost anything for this creature to be the real Evan. But that was an impossibility she now had to deal with, for this thing was a weapon of Project Impulse, and like the project itself, it needed to be destroyed. Amanda stood, averting her eyes so she wouldn't have to look into her lover's youthful face. She heard the figure do the same. Then she extended a hand and willed her errant energy particle to return. The figure mimicked her, and their fingertips touched, creating a surge of warmth that spread through Amanda's hand, then arm, and straight into her heart. Unable to fight the inner embrace, she turned her swollen eyes to the figure. It was crying, and that's when Amanda realized it wasn't only mimicking her in action, but in thought. It knew what she was doing to it. It may not have had the consciousness of a normal human being, but it understood the concept of life and, more importantly, death. Amanda pushed what she could of the realization aside, but remnants of it still tore at her. Her eyes remained locked with the creature's until her errant energy particle transferred from its fingertip to hers. Amanda felt the particle merge back into her body, then lowered her arm. The figure didn't follow suit.

She debated leaving it like that. After all, what harm could it do? It was an organic statue, and at some point, nature would take its course and consume it through decomposition. That, or it would become another creature's meal. Then again, Amanda hadn't consciously awoken the figure the first time it had come to life. If she left it intact, who was to say her body and mind wouldn't do it again? And if that happened, would she have the fortitude to revoke its consciousness once more? It was a risk she couldn't take, not with the end of Project Impulse so close at hand. So Amanda walked to the figure's backside and placed a hand on each side of its head.

No, she then told herself. *Not like that. She owed it more respect than that.*

Amanda returned to the figure's front side and assumed the same position. Those black eyes, Evan's eyes, stared at her as she braced her arm muscles.

"I'm sorry," she said, the words failing to bring the closure she'd hoped they would.

Amanda squeezed her eyes shut, releasing a final wave of tears, and contracted her arms, snapping the false Evan's neck. She couldn't look at what she'd done, so she withdrew her arms and turned away before opening her eyes again. Then, fighting nausea, Amanda took several broken breaths, each one cut short by uncontrolled hyperventilation. No bullet, no explosion, no sharp stab, nor blunt force trauma could match the pain coursing through her, and all she could do was run away from it, leaving the body of the false Evan behind for Soul Wind Forest to do with as it pleased. Through that pain, however, one thing had made itself crystal clear: Project Impulse needed to end, and as Amanda had already concluded, she needed to be the one to end it... *no matter the cost.*

CHAPTER 9
NEVER AGAIN

"Have you determined our best contingency plan yet?" The Woman in White asked over the repetitive beat of helicopter blades.

She was seated in the vehicle's dark cabin, glowing lights and the hum of electricity all around. Colonel Davis was playing pilot in these pre-sunrise hours, with Maddox in the co-pilot seat and Four accompanying the Woman in White in the back. He was holding a tablet, scrolling through an assortment of maps that ranged from individual countries, to entire continents, to the world at large. Each map contained at least one red dot, and some, including the United States and European continent, contained multiple.

"Albert says everything's stable," he responded. "We activated the tracking chip on the escaped drone so we could recover it, but there was no signal. Whatever woke it must have shorted the chip out. Albert's working on modifying the learning program to prohibit such action going forward. In the meantime—" He switched to one of his global maps and passed the tablet to the Woman in White. "—we've still got forty-nine viable subjects. We need all the European and Asian ones in play to ensure they take out any significant resistance, especially potentially catastrophic responses that might arise from the Middle East, Russia, or North Korea. The same could be said for North America, but we overloaded it to start with, so we have some flexibility there. We don't have many drones assigned to South America, Africa, or Australia, so I'd hate to reduce our numbers there. But then again, resistance should be minimal, so putting them on the back-burner shouldn't be detrimental."

The Woman in White examined the map, which periodically adjusted its display for the scenarios Four had laid out. "Let's pull back on North America.

We had a drone assigned to Eden. There's no need for it now. The city's a fraction of what it once was. We can handle it in the second or third wave."

Four reclaimed his tablet. "Yes, ma'am."

The Woman in White angled her voice toward Maddox. "What's the status of the others?" She was referring to One and Three, who Colonel Davis had ordered to abandon their posts a few hours earlier.

"They'll meet us when we're done so they can take refuge on Sunrise Isle."

"Did they have anything to report?"

"Your so—" Maddox caught his slip-up before completing the word. "The Desmond kid was acting unusual yesterday, so we thought maybe he was in contact with the Alpha child, but it turns out he was just shopping for an engagement ring."

The Woman in White remained stoic at the news, but inside, its sting was piercing.

"Frank Holmes is back in Eden. He, Sheriff Desmond, and your old colleague Professor Madison are up to something. There's been no indication they've been in touch with the Alpha child, but they must have done the same math as us. They know she's coming home."

"What about D.C.?" she asked Four.

"Senator Riley and General Javez are on the move. They've probably done the math too. We don't know what they have up their sleeves, but don't be surprised if they make an appearance in Eden soon." Four tried to read his superior's face, which was tight with concern. "Are you sure you want to pull the Eden drone? The rest of the world won't know what's hit it until it's too late, but these people..."

"Leave it alone," the Woman in White ordered. "The drones won't help with them anyway. I doubt they have the full picture yet. As long as we stay a step ahead, we should be all right."

A ring emitted from Four's tablet. He checked the accompanying pop-up, then passed it back to her. "It's Wessler."

The Woman in White answered the incoming video call. Dietrich's face filled the screen from some dark, nondescript location. "Mr. Wessler, I appreciate you getting back to me. Where's your boss?"

Dietrich shifted his camera to show DeMarco pacing nervously in the background. The Woman in White also got a better view of their room, which was barren and windowless, and illuminated by a string of incandescent lights drooping from a cement ceiling. It reminded her of an underground bunker.

"What's his problem?" she asked.

"He's paranoid that someone's contracted a hit on him by now." Dietrich resumed his place as the camera's center focus. "He's probably right. The Ricci and Torres gangs won't take our coup lying down."

"There wouldn't have been a need for a coup if you'd stayed on schedule. Where are we in terms of timeline?"

"Still behind. It takes time to usurp global competitors. We've made headways in a few of the major markets, but it'll be weeks before we take control of all primary supply lines. Secondary lines will take months after that. And the low level feeders—"

"Forget taking control," the Woman in White said. "The situation's changed. You can continue your coup to cut off alternate sources, but in the meantime, flood the market with everything you've got."

"Did she say to flood the market?" DeMarco called from off-camera. A moment later, the video feed jiggled, and then the drug lord's face replaced Dietrich's. "Flooding the market is a surefire way to go out of business. This is my legacy. I was willing to make a play for the top, but I'm not about to push the self-destruct button. I need consistent manufacturing, consistent supply, and an endless stream of customers willing to pay. If I flood the market, prices will tank. Manufacturing won't be able to keep up with the type of demand influx that'll cause. The entire business will cannibalize itself."

The Woman in White couldn't care less, and she made that abundantly clear. "You need to stop thinking long term, Mr. DeMarco. Long term has passed. It'll be a new day for all of us soon. So do what I say and flood the market. Empty all warehouses, storage units, production facilities, the works. Give the product away if you need to, but make sure you do it *now*."

Her orders took a moment to process, but when they did, DeMarco's face went white. "It's happening already, isn't it?"

The Woman in White nodded.

"But—" he stuttered, "—it's early. I was supposed to have more time. I—" DeMarco paused, his dreams of a monopolistic drug empire scattering like dust in the wind. He'd known for years where his deal with this White Devil was headed, and now it was time to prepare. "What should we do to stay safe?" he asked, motioning to himself and Dietrich.

"The same thing any smart drug dealer does. Stay out of your own stash. Beyond that..." The Woman in White shrugged. "...enjoy the ride." She didn't give him a chance to respond, pressing the *end call* button and passing the tablet back to Four.

Colonel Davis peered at his colleague through a rear-facing mirror. "Do you want Maddox or I to pay him a visit to make sure he listens?"

"Wessler will take care of it. Besides, you two are needed here."

She glanced out of the window beside her head. Previously filled with nothing but the blackness of the pre-dawn sky, it was now a display of distant pinpoints of light. The lights were artificial, beaming up from the sleepy homes and empty businesses below. Off to the side of their collection was a long stretch of young greenery, and at the collection's center was a decorative tower silhouetted by the first rays of sunlight to pierce the horizon. Just like Frank, just like the Alpha child, just like her husband, son, and the numerous other residents that had returned to rebuild following The Falling of the Tides, the Woman in White had come home.

———

Derek stirred as the soft glow of dawn fell upon his face. He'd had a restless night, emotions from the day before refusing to give his brain a rest when he and Stacy had finally settled down for the evening. After what seemed like a never-ending day, he'd found the ring he'd been seeking. It was simple yet beautiful, just like his girlfriend, with a central diamond that sparkled from every direction resting atop a band with carefully spaced smaller diamonds between decorative etchings. Recognizing Derek as a young officer with Eden PD, the jeweler had given him a significant discount off sticker price, leaving Derek without debt and three hundred dollars to return to his father. He'd wondered whether he'd be able to restrain himself from presenting the ring to Stacy the moment he saw her. But then he'd received her message about Amanda, and proposing took a backseat to concern over what her sudden appearances meant, and what danger might be headed for Eden.

By the time Derek had gotten home, Vincent, Frank, and Joseph were already there, as were Stacy and her parents. A decision had been made that they'd stick together until the threat of Project Impulse had passed, and though Derek was the last to receive the details of what was happening, he'd agreed with the call. The group had eaten dinner together, then figured out sleeping arrangements for the night. Frank, having spent many a night in locations and positions that set a new low for the word *comfortable*, had volunteered to take hind choice, letting everyone else have the more desirable furnishings of the Desmond house. Stacy's parents had taken the spare bedroom, rebuilt where Amanda's room used to be before The Falling of the Tides, and Joseph had taken the living room couch. Despite being aware of Stacy's recent nighttime habits, her parents seemed a little uncomfortable when she'd excused herself to Derek's bedroom. Perhaps knowing their daughter was safe in his arms was more comforting than physically watching her climb into his bed. But they hadn't said anything, and Derek wondered whether his dad had clued them in on how he'd spent his day.

With standard sleeping quarters already claimed, Frank had his choice of the living room floor, a chair that didn't recline back as much as he would have hoped, or Vincent's car. He'd opted for the floor, if only so his eyes would be on the same level as the crack that would form beneath the Desmonds' front door should someone open it. He'd kept his police-issued pistol nearby, and assured Joseph he would look before he shot, just in case the professor got up to use the bathroom in the middle of the night. Upstairs, Derek held Stacy tight, and waited until he'd heard her snoring lightly before slipping away to retrieve the jewelry box he'd left stashed under his driver's seat. Frank had stood watch to ensure he made it back into the house safely, and Joseph, spotting the box from his vantage point on the couch, had given the teenager an approving thumbs-up.

After quietly hiding the ring in his closet, Derek had returned to bed. But by then, his heart was once again racing with the anticipation of asking Stacy to marry him. Meanwhile, his mind was spinning over Amanda's plan to confront Project Impulse the next day. The two conflicting forces had left him tossing and turning for hours, until finally he had no energy left to sap. He'd passed out, but with only a little over two hours left before dawn, the same dawn that now woke him mid-sleep cycle. Derek checked his phone for the time and saw he only had twelve minutes left until his alarm was scheduled to go off anyway. He'd set it early, allowing extra time for him and Vincent to run a few buddy-system errands before taking their positions for the Rose Parade. Frank would remain in charge of the others' safety in their absence, and once everyone was up and dressed, they would hunker down together in Eden PD while Amanda fought her battle with Project Impulse.

Derek turned off his alarm and crept out of bed. Stacy moaned and shifted a hand to the depression where his body had been, but she remained asleep. Derek then opened his closet door and took out her ring. Even in the dim glow of dawn, it was beautiful, alleviating any concern that his successful outing had been a dream. Derek placed the ring back into its box and took a moment to conceal it better than he'd hastily done the night before. Then he stripped off his pajamas and threw them in his hamper.

They landed atop Stacy's outfit from the previous day, which, under any other circumstances, Derek would have paid little attention. But the outfit's left sleeve was exposed, and on it, he glimpsed what appeared to be an oily handprint. Derek pulled the sleeve closer and used his phone flashlight to get a better look. Sure enough, it had been stained by a handprint of oil with occasional streaks of red sauce, perhaps from pizza or pasta, maybe even ketchup. Derek recalled Stacy had met a friend for lunch the day before. Given everything else going on, he hadn't thought to ask how that lunch had gone, and Stacy hadn't volunteered anything. It was unlikely she would've been so careless to grab her own arm with a food-covered hand, and besides, the print was too big to be hers. In fact, it was so big that Derek questioned whether it could reasonably belong to any of Stacy's female friends.

He set the outfit back into the hamper and tiptoed around to Stacy's side of the bed. Her phone was on the nearby nightstand, and while Derek hated the idea of snooping, he needed to know if something was wrong, and whether Stacy had simply forgotten to tell him about it or whether she'd intentionally hid it out of fear... or worse. He entered her password, something both of them openly shared with the other, and retrieved her call history. The most recent call had been to her parents, likely to make arrangements for them to spend the night at Derek's house. The call before that had been the one Derek had missed. And then, before that, was an exchange of brief inbound and outbound calls with a number that no longer showed a name, and instead displayed in all caps *BLOCKED*. Derek clicked the information symbol on one of the call listings, but he didn't recognize the number.

So something had happened at lunch. At least Stacy was already taking steps to deal with it. Derek would ask if she needed anything from him later, but for now, she was in good hands, and whomever had bothered her the day before wouldn't get near her today. He shut her phone off and returned it to the night-stand. Then he got dressed before Vincent came looking for him.

———

The Rose Parade kicked off at noon in Eden's northwestern-most neighborhood. Twenty-five floats of floral decor were lined along the neighborhood's border, each waiting for its turn to join the procession. Samuel was on the first, which was more of a decorative platform on wheels than a true float. It was smaller than the others and designed to resemble the throne room of a flower king. The mayor sat on his colorful throne as a decree in his honor was read aloud for the citizens of the starting neighborhood. Then, when the decree was over, he stood and waved to his flock as if they should be honored he'd come down from his grand tower to grace them with his presence. The parade started rolling, and Eden's citizens danced and cheered as the first real float reached them, its riders tossing flower petals to decorate the air and treats for their children to collect.

The procession was scheduled to take three hours. It would wind its way south, initially sticking to Eden's residential zones, then turn east, proceeding into commercial districts and the downtown region. Tourists seeking a more relaxed experience would commingle with residents there, while those desiring to be in the thick of things would station themselves around City Hall, the parade's final destination. Once all twenty-five floats arrived, they would encircle the tower and perform three revolutions for everyone celebrating there. Afterwards, Samuel would deliver a rousing speech from the foot of City Hall, unable to pass up such a perfect moment for grandstanding. Then the parade would disband until next year.

Vincent shook his head as he watched the pompous official sucking in his glory. "So far, so good," he said to Derek as Samuel's float shrunk into the distance. "We'll stay here until the other floats launch, then we'll move to City Hall to keep an eye on things there."

Derek was supposed to be on duty at Primrose Path Shopping Center for the entirety of the parade, but heeding Amanda's warning, Vincent had him swapped with another officer. "You think Shortcake plans to out herself there?"

Vincent shrugged. "It was either here or there. Your sister wants publicity. The decree reading provided her first shot. Mayor Collins's speech will provide her second."

"There are cameras all along the route, though."

"They cycle during the national broadcast. She can't be certain one of them will give her the screen time she needs."

"But when Mayor Collins makes his speech…" Derek said.

"The eyes and ears of the country—and Project Impulse—will be on him."

Derek bit nervously on his lower lip as he watched the fifth float start forward. "Are we sure this is the best plan? Letting her fight Project Impulse alone?"

Vincent's response came with notable hesitation. "No. But it's what Shortcake requested. We're liabilities in that fight, so we need to stay as far from it as possible."

Derek still wasn't sure he agreed, but he let the topic rest for now, and instead focused on monitoring the crowd for suspicious activity as the parade rolled on.

———

Downtown, Frank stood in Eden PD's lobby and watched the Rose Parade on television. Having witnessed Eden's collapse firsthand, he'd never thought he'd see it prospering this way again, and it made him realize just how amazing the healing powers of time truly were. Nearby, seated on a pair of wooden benches that Diana had tried to make as comfortable as possible, were Stacy and her parents. They were watching the parade too, but their expressions made it clear they would've preferred watching from the comfort of their own house. That, or they would have preferred watching without the looming threat of a band of unsavory ex-government agents trying to use them as leverage in a coming war. Frank pegged the odds at fifty-fifty. He then checked his watch and grabbed a police-issued radio.

"Hey, you guys are ten seconds late. I need a perimeter check now."

The voices of officers pulled from parade duty responded immediately. There were eight of them, enough to blow Samuel's top if he ever found out. But they'd all sworn to secrecy, and to keep Eden PD safe until the day was over. Frank counted off the eight confirmations that all was well, then reminded the officers that even just a few seconds of being breached could make the difference between life and death. Diana walked up beside him with coffee to go around.

"Take it easy on them," she said with a friendly smile and offering of caffeine. "Some of these guys haven't been home to see their families since yesterday. All this Rose Parade prep had them working overtime."

"I just don't want any security lapses," Frank said. "I gave Sheriff Desmond my word that I'd keep the rest of you safe."

"Speaking of..." Diana tongued the backside of her teeth. She knew she probably shouldn't say anything, but she had a valid concern, so after a short pause, she spilled. "The last time you men tried this *all eggs in one basket* thing, it didn't work out so well."

Not working out so well was an understatement, considering it had left one of their own dead. "That was different. We were up against an enemy we didn't know, and had vulnerabilities we couldn't foresee." Frank could tell she wasn't buying it, so he altered his approach. "From what I recall, you were safe and sound right here in Eden PD."

Diana had to give him that. "True, but I wasn't the target. And this time, all you targets are here under my roof."

"Well, you're half right."

Diana cocked her head.

"Your relationship with the sheriff isn't exactly a secret," Frank explained. "That makes you a target, too."

She glared at him. "Very reassuring. Thanks."

Frank laughed to show he'd meant no harm. "Diana, do we have men stationed at every entrance and exit?"

"Yes."

"And in the tunnel beneath us?"

She nodded.

"And on the roof, just for extra precaution?"

She nodded again, this time a realization that she was worried for nothing coming over her.

"Everything's going to be fine," Frank said. "Let's just get through the day and hope it plays out according to plan."

————

By two o'clock, Samuel's lead float had crossed through Eden's commercial districts and set a direct path for City Hall. The mayor was still glowing from the continued positive response he received from residents and tourists alike. But something was troubling him. The police presence, the presence he'd insisted on to ensure the Rose Parade didn't run into any speed bumps, felt light. Samuel probably wouldn't have noticed if not for a few key positions along the parade route that were strangely unmonitored. Perhaps some of Eden PD was camouflaged to mix with the crowd, or perhaps his sheriff had failed to follow his instructions. If it was the former, Samuel would give Vincent a deserved scolding. The whole point of a police presence during the parade was *not* to blend in, so that it would serve as a deterrent to criminal activity. If it was the latter... Samuel felt his blood boil. If it was the latter, he would have Vincent's head on a stick. The mayor tried to put the thought out of his mind, not wanting it to tarnish this otherwise perfect day.

————

"So, as you can see," Lamar said, pointing to a line chart on printed computer paper, "every time the magnetic anomaly surges, the metals inside the magma respond. Some surges are stronger than others, resulting in an exaggerated response, and even when there isn't a surge, the anomaly continues to interfere with radio waves, electrical signals, and the such."

James, one of Joseph's students who had gotten unwittingly drawn into the Project Impulse war by Complex B, took the chart and studied it. "That is so cool."

"Seriously," his equally entangled classmate, Rebecca, added. "You should come teach at Pine Ridge. This stuff is so much more exciting than the generic textbook examples our other instructors give us."

Joseph appeared behind them, cups of coffee in hand. "Did I just hear you bad mouth your Pine Ridge instructors?" he asked jokingly.

"Not you, Professor," Rebecca said. "You're the best."

He smiled. "Flattery won't get you an A when I return next semester."

"Be careful," James warned as he took a cup of coffee. "That's a sore subject."

Joseph saw Rebecca glare at him. "Don't tell me your grades have slipped."

"She earned her first B ever," James announced. "You should have seen the way she marched into Professor Phillips's office. I thought for sure he was going to have campus security escort her out."

"Shut up," Rebecca said.

Joseph tried to make her feel better. "Professor Phillips's classes are some of the toughest at Pine Ridge. You should be proud of a B."

"I'd like to give him a B," she mumbled. "B for boredom, because that's how I felt every time I was in his class. Doesn't Pine Ridge have a mandatory retirement age?"

"Good help was scarce after Eden's collapse," Joseph told her. "Just know it's not the end of the world." He turned his attention to Lamar. "And what about you, Doctor Reed? The kids have a point. The stuff you're studying underneath this city would make fascinating subject matter. Is there any teaching in your future?"

Lamar squinted. "I'm more of a *keep my head in the rocks* kind of guy."

"Suit yourself. But if you ever change your mind, I can put you in touch with the right people." Joseph heard a commotion from a nearby television. "What's going on?"

"The mayor's float just reached City Hall," Frank said, his eyes still glued to the broadcast. "If your daughter's going to make her move, it'll be soon."

After changing venues, Vincent and Derek had planted themselves at the entrance to the hedge maze. From there, they could watch Samuel's float make the first arc around City Hall while also monitoring the rest of the parade as it completed its journey into downtown Eden. Surprisingly, this was turning out to be the least eventful Rose Parade yet. Vincent had received three reports of disorderly behavior and one of attempted pick-pocketing, but all situations had been dealt with quietly, and the parade crowd seemed none the wiser.

"Is it just me," Derek asked, "or are things going a little *too* well?"

Vincent wasn't going to complain. "The fewer distractions, the better."

He scanned the faces on the perimeter of the crowd. There was so much joy there, so much elation and upbeat spirit. They were oblivious to the danger hanging over the city, focused solely on the fluttering rose petals that showered over them and the sugary treats they collected in Rose Parade themed bags. It had been a long time since Vincent had felt that type of peace. But maybe, just maybe, if Amanda was successful today, he would find it again. Maybe next year, he and his own children would be part of that crowd, enjoying the parade without a care in the world, finally safe from Project Impulse and all those involved in it. Maybe…

"Hey, back off!" someone yelled from off to Vincent's right.

Derek sighed. "I might have spoken too soon."

They traced the source of the yelling to a small group of college students that had come prepared for the parade with folding chairs and drink coolers. Encroaching on the students' space was a bumbling kid about their age, who had apparently tried to help himself to one of their beers. Shoves were exchanged, resulting in the bumbling kid toppling over a chair and crashing onto the concrete sidewalk. Derek saw the kid's face—Mark's face—and lowered his head in disappointment.

"He's all yours," Vincent told him. "Try not to make a scene."

Begrudgingly, Derek approached the college students and introduced himself. They reacted defensively, shuffling to hide their beers and immediately lobbing blame at Mark. Derek told them he didn't need an explanation, then extended a hand to help Mark up. Vincent watched as Mark slapped it away defiantly. He'd been such a bright student in high school, and he'd had a world of opportunity going into college. It was downright sad to see all that talent and potential go to waste. Vincent scanned the rest of the crowd for anything that might need his attention. With nothing standing out, he then decided to give Derek a hand.

But something caught his eye. It was brief, a half-second at most, a glimpse of white fabric darting through his peripheral vision. Anyone else would have ignored such an insignificant flash, but for Vincent, it was as if alarm bells were going off. His eyes darted after the white fabric, which was now gone, leaving nothing but the entrance to the hedge maze in his sight.

It must have been your imagination, Vincent told himself.

But his gut said otherwise. He glanced back at Derek, who was now being assisted by another officer, with Mark still on the ground and refusing to budge. He'd be okay for a few minutes, just long enough for Vincent to confirm his eyes were playing tricks on him. The sheriff proceeded into the hedge maze, which he knew like the back of his hand from his many meetings with Amanda there. He chose the left path, aware that it would intersect with the right after a few twists and turns. The maze was empty, something that only happened during the Rose Parade or when Eden was experiencing severe weather. There was no sign that anyone had entered ahead of him, nor trail left behind for him to follow. But there was a sound: faint breathing, coming from the other side of the hedge just ahead.

Vincent placed his ear to the hedge, and that's when the source of the breathing broke into a run.

Vincent darted through a gap in the foliage to his right, then made a left turn, dashed down a thorny corridor, and then made another left. This time, he saw that same white fabric as it disappeared around a sharp right turn in the distance. Vincent raced after it, making the same turn, then following the sound of rustling foliage until he pivoted onto a path he knew led to a dead end. And that's where he found her. She wasn't running anymore, but instead awaiting his arrival, standing there in her bright white outfit, winded from the pursuit, but maintaining that same icy demeanor that refused to show weakness of any type.

"Hello, Vincent."

"Abigail," he replied, hardly believing his eyes. "What are you doing here?"

The Woman in White met his gaze, and for a moment, her facade betrayed her. "I came to warn you. It's not safe to stay in Eden. You need to take Derek and head somewhere secluded, away from major cities. There's a war coming, and while the two of you aren't targets, I don't want you caught in the crossfire."

"You put us in the crossfire," Vincent reminded her. "You and that project you abandoned us for. We wouldn't be in danger if it weren't for you."

The Woman in White didn't deny his accusation. "Nonetheless, you need to get Derek out of Eden. You still have some time, but how much..." She shrugged.

Vincent stood his ground. "We're not going anywhere. We're going to stop you."

The Woman in White shook her head as if she knew better. "You can't stop this."

Vincent saw she believed her own words. But he also saw something else, a crack perhaps, a sliver of hope that somewhere, deep inside this cold, soulless woman, was still his wife. If that was true, maybe he could reach out to her. Maybe there was a chance at redemption. After all, that's how Amanda had initially gotten through to Evan. "You say we can't stop it, and maybe you're right. But you can. You want to protect Derek? Then help us put an end to Project Impulse. Help destroy it from the inside."

The Woman in White's eyes glistened. "I can't."

"Why not?" Vincent pressed. "What is it about Project Impulse that has you trapped? Are you telling me you don't have your own free will anymore? Because I'm willing to bet your colleagues don't know you're here right now. You're defying them just by talking to me. All I'm asking is that you take it a step further."

"You don't understand."

"Then help me understand!" He approached his wife, who instinctively took a step back before planting her feet and letting him come. "What happened to you, Abigail? Why'd you leave us? Why'd you become this shell of a person hell-bent on destruction?"

She was trembling now. "You need to let me go. I'm not the wife you remember anymore."

"Fine," Vincent said. "You may not be my wife, but you're still Derek's mother. You saved his life at Complex B. And now you're trying to save him again by warning me. You've let your love for him interfere with Project Impulse multiple times. Embrace that love and put an end to it for good!"

The Woman in White frowned. "*He* won't let me."

Vincent paused, confused by her claim. "What do you mean? Who won't let you?"

The Woman in White took his hands in hers, the warmth of her touch surprising to them both. "You were a good husband, Vincent. But your wife is dead. What you see here, standing before you, this emptiness, this vessel of darkness hiding behind a veil of white, that's all that's left. I made my choice, and for better or worse, there's no going back."

"I don't believe that. The Abigail Desmond I married was one of the strongest women I've ever known. If she wanted to make a different choice, she'd find a way."

The Woman in White let his hands fall back to his sides. "There is no way. Once you let him in, there's no getting him out. There's no escape. There's only... his will... his way. I've held on to my love for Derek, my one anchor to who I used to be. But I can feel my grip slipping, and once it does, there'll be nothing of Abigail Desmond left."

Vincent had heard a variation of this story before, from Amanda, when she'd visited him at Pine Ridge the previous day. He remembered thinking she'd been hysterical, the toll of everything she'd been through finally crashing down upon her. But the Woman in White wasn't hysterical. In fact, she seemed as lucid as a person could be, and yet here she was, vocalizing the same fears as Amanda, as if the threat wasn't purely psychological.

"Abigail," Vincent said softly, "Project Impulse is—"

"This isn't about Project Impulse!" she snapped. "Don't you see that? It hasn't been for a long time now. Project Impulse was just a means to an end... and that end is coming."

Vincent didn't know what to say. First, Frank had told him that death was coming. Then Amanda had implied a darkness was coming. Now, the Woman in White was telling him the end was coming. Three different messengers, three different motivations, and yet all triangulating on the same outcome. He'd be a fool to ignore it. "How will I know when it starts?"

Having finally gotten through to him, the Woman in White released a tense breath. "You'll know. Promise me you'll keep Derek safe when it does. No running into the firefight like he did at Complex B."

"I'll do what I can," Vincent said. "He's an adult now. I can guide him, but his decisions are his own."

The Woman in White turned away, but not before Vincent caught a tear escape her right eye. "I hear he's getting married. Is that true?"

The sheriff could feel her pain, the pain of her last glimmer of humanity still holding on to what it once was. "He hasn't asked her yet. But yes. He's going to propose soon."

The Woman in White nodded with a mixture of sadness and loving approval. "Thank you for telling me." A chime played from somewhere outside the hedge maze, and the parade crowd broke into cheers. "It must be time for the mayor's speech. I imagine you and I are here for the same reason. Shall we go watch?"

It was such an odd request. Vincent knew he should probably slap handcuffs on the Woman in White, or at least interrogate her further to extract whatever information he could about the coming end of which she'd spoken. But he was only human, and as a human, bound by logic-defying emotion, he longed for just one more moment of normalcy with his wife. "Sure."

They strolled, hand in hand, reversing course through the hedge maze until they emerged from its entrance. Vincent worried about Derek spotting his mother again, knowing full well she was one of the primary architects behind the threat that loomed over them. But Derek and the officer assisting him were gone, likely busy locking Mark up in one of the temporary holding facilities that had been established along the parade route. Vincent and the Woman in White fell in line behind the last row of the parade crowd and watched as Samuel drummed up those standing in front of City Hall. If Amanda was still going to make her move, it was going to happen now. For Vincent, it would be the first step toward dismantling Project Impulse. For the Woman in White, it would be the next step toward the endgame.

The only problem, Vincent thought as he stole a side glance at his wife, *was that only one of them could be right.*

————

Samuel rallied the crowd as if he was the world's most popular pop star. He loved every minute of it, too, relishing in the cheers, chants of his name, and blown kisses from the younger, less mature females in the crowd that he would no doubt take advantage of later that day. After several minutes of letting his praises linger, he hushed the crowd and took hold of a microphone that had been added to his float following its arrival at City Hall.

"Citizens, tourists, friends," Samuel began with a wolf's smile, "thank you for coming out to celebrate our dear city's rebirth. I don't know if you agree with me, but I think this was the best Rose Parade yet!"

The crowd responded with overwhelming cheers.

"What's that?" Samuel asked, pushing them to cheer louder. "You think it was the best one yet, too? Then let's give it up for all of this year's riders, who, as you know, also design the floats on which they ride!"

The crowd broke into deafening applause. Samuel let it linger long enough to make his point, but not so long as to overshadow his own cheers. He then hushed the crowd again.

"It's been a long day already, so I promise to keep my speech short this year. All I want to say is—" His eyes darted to something coming at him from the sky: a swarm of blue energy particles unlike anything he'd seen since Evan had interrupted his speech at the Lakeview Bay Convention Center following Eden's collapse. "What the hell?!"

————

Vincent felt a nervous energy as Samuel cowered from the approaching swarm. He saw the Woman in White was just as nervous, her eyes glued to the scene as Amanda's perfect body materialized atop the lead float.

"You," Samuel's voice echoed across the awestruck crowd. Never one to miss an opportunity to spin a situation in his favor, the politician rose and approached Amanda with a presenting arm. "Ladies and gentlemen, I knew today was special, but I never thought it would be this special. You may have seen this young lady on the news recently. Rest assured, she means us no harm. I'd like to introduce you to one of Eden's saviors, Shortcake Desmond!"

Many in the crowd cheered. Others looked on in confusion, or still couldn't shake the supernatural way in which she had appeared before them.

"If that name sounds familiar," Samuel said, "it's because she's the daughter of Eden's very own sheriff, Vincent Desmond." He looked around, a hand shading his eyes from the sun. "Where are you, Sheriff? Why don't you come up here and join your daughter?"

Vincent had no intention of getting on that float to support Samuel. Luckily, Amanda stole his opportunity to do so.

"That's enough, Mr. Mayor," she said, amplifying her voice to match the power of his microphone. "My father and I won't be pawns in your corrupt political game anymore."

Samuel glanced at the crowd nervously, then put on his best shit-eating grin and responded, "I'm afraid I don't know what you're talking about."

"Yes, you do. And the people will know soon, too. You see, while you were gloating over the crowds this morning, I paid a visit to your office. I found drugs, bribe money, illegal contracts, you name it. I hand-delivered them to Eden's attorney general."

A worried chuckle escaped Samuel's lips. "That must have been planted there. I've never—" He shook his head in defiance. "Besides, you obtained it illegally. It wouldn't be admissible in court even if it was mine."

"If it had been from your home, no," Amanda admitted. "But City Hall is public property. And as you just pointed out, I'm Sheriff Desmond's daughter. That makes me a resident of Eden, with all the rights to access public land that come with residential status."

"Yeah, but you're—" Samuel caught himself. Even if he outed Amanda as having been bred at Helix Unbound, that facility had still been within Eden's borders. She was a resident, one way or another. "You little bitch."

Amanda tossed the comment aside. "You'd be amazed how many judges were willing to drop everything this morning to sign a search warrant." She glanced up the front-facing side of City Hall. "The attorney general and his team are up there right now if you want to say hi. I'm sure they'd love to ask you some questions."

Vincent smiled proudly. He hadn't known what Amanda had planned, but he couldn't imagine it being any more satisfying than this. Samuel wasn't willing to acknowledge defeat so easily, though.

"You—you're delusional. I've never broken the law. I've never done anything that wasn't in the city's best interest."

A voice left the crowd: "Yeah, right!"

It was followed by a series of boos that soon grew into a roar. Samuel would have his day before a judicial court, but he'd already lost in the court of public opinion, which, for someone like him, might actually be the worse outcome. Amanda caught her father's eye and smiled. He returned the gesture, then watched as her body dematerialized once more before it floated into the breeze. He didn't care what happened to Samuel after that; the crowd would handle him. What Vincent did care about is what Amanda's appearance meant for his conversation with the Woman in White. But when he turned to get her attention, he found she was gone.

"Dad!" Derek yelled as he ran alongside the increasingly rowdy crowd. "Did you see that? Way to go, Shortcake! It's about time someone put that asshole in his place."

Vincent tried to show his joy, but the distraction of his wife's disappearance overshadowed it.

"Dad, what's wrong?"

He wanted to be honest with Derek, but he also wanted to spare his son the pain he now felt, pain in knowing that, though there was still a part of Abigail Desmond buried within the cold shell of a woman she'd become, there was nothing he could do to bring her back. "Nothing's wrong. This crowd is getting out of hand. Let's help get it under control and then get back to the others."

Derek nodded. "And then we wait."

"Yeah," Vincent said, his mind torn between how he had hoped this day would end, and how the Woman in White had implied it would. "Then we wait."

———

It was another two hours before the Rose Parade crowd dissipated. Recognizing a losing battle, Samuel didn't keep trying to win them over. Instead, he retreated inside City Hall, where the attorney general, flanked by members of his own staff and Eden PD, informed him he shouldn't leave the city, for an arrest warrant was coming soon. Samuel ordered them out and locked himself in his office. It had been stripped of all but the most cleverly hidden illegal substances, though it still contained a significant amount of alcohol, so Samuel went to work on the stash. He refused to quit until his walls blurred and the world tumbled sideways, leaving this land of persecution for one in which he was still king, if only for a short while.

Vincent and Derek stuck around until all but the last stragglers had gone home or made their ways back to hotel rooms. Then they returned to Eden PD, which was wrapped in a cloud of celebration after having made it through the parade without incident, and after having witnessed Samuel's spectacular downfall. Frank had repeatedly reminded the officers on duty that they weren't out of the woods yet, not until they made it through the night, after which Amanda's confrontation with Project Impulse should be over. Nonetheless, he'd allowed them some celebration, a stark contrast to the bundle of nervousness still hanging over his friends as they awaited word of Amanda's success.

As for Amanda, once she'd left the Rose Parade behind, she'd returned to the one place where she knew Project Impulse would find her. There were fewer visible remnants of Helix Unbound in the overgrown field than when she had last visited with Evan. She recalled that night, perhaps the greatest night of her life, when she had beckoned him to follow her through the lush darkness of Soul

Wind Forest, when they had stumbled into a preserve of ancient pines and oaks, when, under the moonlight, they had created their own special kind of magic together, a memory she would cherish for as long as she lived. Amanda placed a hand over the imprint of Evan's necklace beneath her shirt. She asked his spirit to give her strength to face the battle ahead, a battle they were meant to fight together, but which she would now have to handle alone.

It was still bright out when she took a seat in the middle of the field. Amanda conserved her physical strength while opening her mind to her surroundings. She could feel the individual strands of wind that comprised the late day breeze. She could hear the forest animals scurrying about, oblivious to the battle they would soon witness. She could see the rustling of trees and swaying of tall grass strands, no matter how minute their movement. Amanda could smell the scents of nature, of campgrounds and barbecues, of nearby neighborhoods preparing late lunches and early dinners on this city-wide holiday. And she could sense the rumbling beneath the earth, those deep magma pits that still swirled beyond Lamar's tunnel system, no longer a threat to Eden, but unwilling to yield to the will of man.

There was no way Project Impulse would sneak up on her now. Amanda might have appeared vulnerable, seated in the middle of an open field with no weapons, no obvious defensive mechanisms, and no friends or family to have her back. But she was ready. She would sense them coming, and she would respond accordingly. Amanda hoped it wouldn't come down to bloodshed. There had already been far too much of that in the name of Project Impulse. But she was willing, should the need arise. Of that, she was certain.

More time passed, and eventually the afternoon sun gave way to a gorgeous sunset of pinks and blues that filtered through the young trees surrounding this part of Soul Wind Forest. An hour later, the sunset had fully faded, and nighttime took its place.

Of course they wouldn't attack during the day, Amanda told herself. *That would put them at an even greater disadvantage.*

Sunlight or not, however, she still felt confident she could thwart whatever attack they levied at her. She waited as the evening grew darker and darker, never letting herself tire, never letting her guard down. And then, a little after ten o'clock, she heard it. It was coming from the east, the blades of a helicopter spinning in rapid succession. The vehicle they were attached to was on an intercept trajectory. But before it made an appearance over the field in which Amanda sat, she heard its approach slow. Then the spinning slowed, and the helicopter must have landed and shut down, for all went quiet again.

Amanda couldn't be certain how far out her assailants had landed, but she couldn't assume it would take them long to reach her. She focused all five senses to the east, searching for any disturbance in the blanket of sensory inputs she'd established during her hours of waiting. There was an unexpected twig snap, something Amanda could have chalked up to the forest life, but the source of the snap had been heavy, like a person, and the snap itself had bounce to it, as if reflecting off the bottom of a shoe. Amanda smelled body odor. It wasn't repugnant, but it was strong enough that her heightened sense of smell could track it as it neared the field, then veered off along its circumference.

There were two of them now. One moving to Amanda's front, the other to her back. Try as they might to conceal themselves, she could hear their footsteps. She could sense their heartbeats. She couldn't see them through the black of night, but she knew exactly where they were. And that's why, when the first counteragent dart zipped out of the tree line ahead, Amanda was able to dodge it effortlessly. A second followed behind the first, then three more, but Amanda took each in stride, contorting her body around their paths and letting them plant into the ground at her feet or pass through the clearing altogether.

"Colonel Davis!" the child of science screamed, more anger behind her voice than she'd meant to use. She calmed herself. "Is that really all you've got? Because I can do this all night."

Amanda heard a high-pitched squeal, then saw a metallic orb fly out of the branches ahead. It landed with a thud and rolled within a few feet of her. The orb had blinking lights and small glass pills containing counteragent embedded in its surface.

Huh, Amanda thought. *That's new.*

She dematerialized and shot straight into the sky as the high-tech grenade detonated, firing shrapnel and droplets of counteragent in every direction. By heading upward, Amanda had gravity on her side, and was fairly confident she'd outrun any counteragent that had followed her way. She dropped back to the ground and reformed her body.

"Okay," she said. "I'll give it to you. That one surprised me. But how much of that could you possibly have left?"

A second counteragent grenade bounced toward her feet. Knowing what she was dealing with this time, and knowing just how much time she had to deal with it, she picked up the grenade and lobbed it back toward Colonel Davis. Amanda heard the former military official scramble. Then the grenade detonated, briefly illuminating the tree line beyond which he'd stood. Shrapnel and counteragent pierced the edge of the field, but traveled only a few feet before spiking into the ground.

"I know you're still out there," Amanda said into the night. "I can hear you breathing. Why don't you just show yourself so we can end this?"

Apparently, Colonel Davis had other plans. Amanda had been so distracted by his attacks that she'd all but forgotten about the second assailant behind her. But she remembered as soon as a barrage of bullets slammed into her spine. The teenage girl dropped to the forest floor, her body searing with pain as it expelled the bullets and started regenerating her flesh. Colonel Davis wasn't going to wait for it to finish. He fired a counteragent dart, which Amanda rolled to avoid at the last moment. Then he fired again, and again, now emerging from the woods, each projectile getting closer and closer to delivering its contents into Amanda's bloodstream. Her backside was healed enough that she could stand, but when she did, she found herself staring into the barrel of Colonel Davis's counteragent rifle. He pulled the trigger.

Click.

He was out of ammo. With barely a second's delay, the colonel reached for his live round pistol and opened fire into Amanda at point blank range. But she was ready this time, adapting her body particles around each bullet as they passed through her and continued out the other side. Amanda reached for Colonel Davis's throat. Then a subtle whistle caught her ear, and she stepped aside just in time to avoid an incoming counteragent dart from the rear. Colonel Davis hot-swapped his pistol clip and opened fire again as more counteragent darts shot forth. Amanda bobbed and weaved, dematerializing and materializing various parts of her body as needed to avoid each impact. Colonel Davis and whomever he had helping him were putting on a stronger front than she'd expected. But Amanda knew the only reason they'd lasted this long was because she'd been holding back. She'd wanted a non-lethal ending to this battle, though it was looking like that may not be a viable option.

She dodged counteragent darts until their firing ceased. She could tell the second assailant was swapping out rifle magazines, but Colonel Davis already had another fresh clip ready for use. He fired again, each shot aimed at Amanda's head, knowing if he could just land one, it might give him the leverage he needed to stop her. With no need to dodge regular ammunition, Amanda erected a shield of blue energy from one hand and pressed forward toward the colonel. He fired until she was inches away, then dropped his gun and replaced it with a Bowie knife. He swiped, not at Amanda's shield, but beyond it, leaving her upper arm with a bloody gash.

The gash began to heal, but Colonel Davis saw an opportunity in its momentary delay. He swiped again, but Amanda dematerialized around his blade. Then her backside was met with another round of automatic fire. As she stumbled forward, Colonel Davis got a clean slice across the side of her neck. Now Maddox emerged from the trees behind Amanda. He fired in periodic bursts to keep her in a constant state of injury and repair. Colonel Davis delivered additional wounds via knife, and Amanda took each one, her mind spinning for a way to win this fight without doing what she knew needed to be done. With no options coming, and her skin now vulnerable and within range should either soldier have a counteragent injection pen on them, she unleashed the anger that had peeked from within her when this battle had first begun.

Maddox fired, but Amanda sent particles of energy to intercept each bullet, which she redirected into Colonel Davis's chest. He was wearing a kevlar vest, so the bullets wouldn't kill him, but they knocked him on his rear and caused him to lose his grip on his knife. Amanda caught the blade with an extended hand of energy and beamed it into Maddox's thigh. He dropped his rifle and grabbed his wound with a scream. That bought Amanda just enough time to heal from their latest onslaught and rise. Either fearless or no longer worried about dying, Colonel Davis pushed to his hands and knees, and charged. Amanda caught him mid-advance. She scooped him up by his throat, extending her forearm with a stream of energy to lift him off his feet.

"Do you want to die, Colonel?" she asked. "Do you want to die, the way Evan died, the way my mother died, the way so many innocent people have died because of the chaos you and the others have created?!"

Unable to breathe, Colonel Davis clawed at her hand, but it was no use. Amanda told herself to put him down. She'd been pushed into using physical force against these men, but they were subdued now, and still alive, just as she'd wanted. She still needed the rest of Project Impulse's core team, but with enough persuasion, she would get their location out of Colonel Davis or his subordinate, whichever cracked first. Maddox didn't have the willpower to remove the knife from his leg, but with Colonel Davis turning blue under Amanda's grip, he was the only one left who could salvage the situation. He reached for his pistol and fired.

The bullet discharge was deafening. Amanda had turned just in time to see the muzzle flash, had instinctively raised a deflective energy shield, and now stared into Maddox's eyes as the realization of what happened settled in. He felt the warmth of his own blood as it seeped from the hole in his neck. Then, before his brain had time to process a response, life left him, and his body collapsed to the forest floor. Amanda stared at the red pool that spread from beneath him. She saw Evan, the boy lying in his own pool of blood on the floor of Renewed Hope, one of so many pools shed in the name of Project Impulse. She turned reddening eyes upon Colonel Davis.

"You're the reason he's dead. You're the one who promised Judas a new life.

You're the one who sent him after us like an attack dog released from its leash. It may as well have been you who pulled the trigger."

Colonel Davis still couldn't respond. Amanda wasn't sure he could even comprehend her, for that matter. His eyes were rolling into his skull, and his cheek was twitching uncontrollably. If she didn't release him now, he would certainly die.

But that's exactly what she wanted. She might not have begun this fight with a lethal outcome in mind, but this man... he was the reason Evan had been taken from her. He didn't deserve to live. He didn't deserve her forgiveness. And he didn't deserve her mercy. Amanda felt that familiar darkness swelling within her, feeding her with the strength necessary to stay the course. She tightened her grip to ensure not a single molecule of air would reach Colonel Davis's lungs. Then she watched him hang there, his entire body twitching violently. It was repulsive, and yet it satiated Amanda's primal needs. It fed the darkness, darkness which filled her soul, encompassed her very being, extended outward from her, amassed... behind her?

Amanda's fatal mistake became instantly clear. Project Impulse hadn't sent Colonel Davis and his subordinate to capture her. They'd been sent to distract her. And the moment she felt that needle prick her neck and unload its contents into her carotid artery, she knew she had lost. The effect hit her like a truck. She lost immediate control of her Omega Genome, her body withdrawing its particles as an inherent defensive mechanism, letting a gasping Colonel Davis fall to the damp ground below. Amanda spun, knowing all too well who she would find standing behind her with the needle in hand, but needing to see him with her own eyes, needing to give him one last message that she would never do his bidding. But even that was impossible, for Amanda's muscles had turned to jelly, and she fell forward, into the Dark Man's arms.

He scooped her up like a groom would his bride before crossing the threshold. He then stared into her emerald green eyes as though he'd been longing for the day he'd see them again. Amanda's vision was going blurry already. Her thoughts were escaping her. Her memories... *oh God, her memories...* they were leaving her once again, just as they had the night she'd escaped Helix Unbound. She saw Colonel Davis rise, then felt her body bounce as the Dark Man carried her across the field and to the eastern tree line. Amanda tried to hold on to something, anything, that would prevent everything she knew from being trapped behind a chemical barrier from which there might be no escape. But it was a futile effort. She no longer remembered what had happened during the past few minutes. She no longer remembered outing Samuel as crooked or playing public superhero as she made her way across the country.

Please... I don't want to forget...

But she couldn't stop it. Soon, she no longer remembered Evan's death, nor Joseph's embrace to comfort her in her time of need. She forgot the events of Complex B, and then of Eden's original fall. She forgot about Frank and Raymond Holmes, about her adopted family and the loving friends she'd made during her short life. Then, as she heard helicopter blades spinning up for flight, she forgot about Joseph, Mary, Evan, and Helix Unbound. The only thing she still knew, and only because she was watching the blurry silhouette of its majestic young forest pass by, was Eden. But even that memory would flee her soon. Amanda's inner conscious screamed at her to hold on, to not let the city go, but it was screaming into the void. And as the Dark Man loaded her onto the helicopter, and as she got one last look at the life she was leaving behind, Amanda knew that she would never see Eden again.

CHAPTER 10

THE PROPHETIC ENTITY

Frank watched the sunrise from Vincent's office chair. It had been over twelve hours now, and there'd been no word from Amanda about her confrontation with Project Impulse. At some point, they would have to assume the worst. But Frank wasn't there yet. He'd returned to Eden thinking Amanda had become the enemy. But knowing she was still on their side, especially after that little stunt with the mayor... he had to give her as much time as she needed to see things through to the end. He pulled Ray's folded drawing from his pocket and stared at it, asking himself just how much he trusted the illustration of a madman as a predictor of the future.

"Hey, what's that?" James asked, plowing into the office without knocking and kicking back in one of its guest chairs.

Frank tucked it under a stack of paperwork on Vincent's desk. "Nothing. Just something my brother made when we were kids." He then noticed the chocolate donut James was cramming into his mouth. "Where'd you get that?"

"Break room," the boy responded through a muffled mouthful. "There's a whole case of them left over from the Rose Parade. They're a little stale, but ten seconds in the microwave makes all the difference."

Frank hopped up, the needs of his stomach calling.

"Hey!" James called after him. "Do you mind if I look at your psychopath brother's drawing while you're gone?"

"Knock yourself out, kid."

Eden PD was quiet. Vincent had reduced his officers to a skeleton crew—just enough to guard the building and respond to emergencies, should they arise. Frank would've never gotten away with that during an overnight stint at Jericho

PD, and he was kind of envious. He passed a series of conference rooms with turned-down blinds. That's where the others were currently sleeping on the cleanest cots they could requisition from Eden PD's holding cells. They had been taking four-hour rotating shifts, each shift led by someone involved with law enforcement—Vincent, Derek, Frank, or Diana—and accompanied by someone who wasn't—Joseph, Lamar, Stacy and her family, and the Pine Ridge students. How Frank had gotten stuck on babysitting duty was beyond him, but he was trying to make the best of it.

"Looking for the donuts?" Rebecca asked from a lunch table as he entered the break room.

"How'd you guess?" he asked dryly.

She rolled her eyes. "Check the pantry, second shelf down, behind the canned goods."

Frank followed her instructions, finding the box of donuts stashed like a pirate's buried treasure. "What kind of idiot would put them there?"

"James. He figures if they stay out in the open, they'll be gone by first shift. This way, he can keep sneaking snacks all day."

Frank had to give him credit; his reasoning was sound. "Smart kid. Do you want one?"

"No thanks. I've got class in a few hours. I don't want to sugar crash in the middle of it."

"You have class on a Saturday?"

Rebecca released an aggravated sigh. "Why does everyone always ask me like that? Is it such a crime to want to excel at my education?"

"No," Frank said without judgment, "but it will burn you out. Trust me when I tell you to enjoy your college years. There's enough burnout in the real world you'll have to deal with."

She shot him a knowing smile. "I've already had a pretty brutal glimpse of the real world. It sucks."

"Amen to that."

"*Detective Holmes, are you there?*" It was the roof squad, making radio contact well before the next designated check-in.

"Holmes, here," Frank replied. "What's going on?"

"*It may be nothing, but we see two government sedans heading our way. They're federal, not local.*"

There was no way that was *nothing*. Frank raced out of the break room and along the row of conference rooms, banging on each window and door to arouse those within. Vincent was the first to pop his head out.

"What's going on?"

"Government vehicles, heading our way."

That got Vincent and Derek scrambling, too. They ordered the others to stay in the conference rooms and keep the doors closed. Frank instructed James to grab Rebecca and join them.

"They're stopping out front," the roof squad reported. *"What do you want us to do?"*

"Provide backup," Frank said. Then, "Front door patrol, don't let anyone inside this building until we vet them first. We're heading your way now." Frank tossed Vincent the radio. "I guess you're the senior officer again. Do you want to do the talking, or should I?"

"That depends," Vincent said with a sly smile. "Are you going to talk or shoot?"

Frank raised his brow. "That depends on who's in those sedans."

That's what Vincent figured. "I'll do the talking."

They marched across the lobby, each with a hand on his gun holster, then stepped through the front doors of Eden PD, where they found the front patrol holding their new arrivals at gunpoint on the entrance steps. There were three of them, two women dressed in expensive business suits, and the third a man in casual military garb. Vincent thought he recognized at least one of the women, though he couldn't place from where.

"Identify yourselves," he said.

"My, aren't we jumpy this morning?" the woman Vincent didn't recognize asked. "I'm Alison Drexmore. This," she said, pointing to the other woman, "is Senator Victoria Riley. And our muscled companion over there is General Francisco Javez. We're unarmed." She glanced at General Javez. "Check that. Two of us are unarmed. The third is allowed to carry in an official capacity. May we come in?"

Vincent shared a glance with Frank. What was a United States senator, general, and whatever the hell the woman named Drexmore was doing on their front steps? They weren't with Project Impulse; he was nearly certain of that much. That made them neutral parties, or maybe even friends. There was only one way to find out.

"All units," he said into his radio, "stand down."

Alison smiled with false perkiness. "Thank you."

She then marched past Vincent, Frank, and Derek with an air of authority none of them were used to, her heels clacking against every step into Eden PD. Victoria and General Javez followed, bearing far graver demeanors than that of their colleague. And in that moment, Vincent wondered just how in over their heads his little crew had gotten.

The morning sun was already beaming over the horizon when Colonel Davis and his replacement co-pilot, the Woman in White, landed their helicopter on a discrete helipad in one corner of Sunrise Isle's abandoned military compound. The Plainclothes had transferred Amanda's unconscious body to a portable stretcher during transit, and as soon as they had her unloaded, Colonel Davis requisitioned one of them to help cover the helicopter with a camouflage tarp. Then the entire group proceeded past the compound's auxiliary bunkers and vehicle depots, which were even more overgrown with aggressive plant life than they had been when Evan had made this same trek nearly five years earlier. They entered the compound's central building. It was a useless structure, its walls and ceiling cracked open by the forces of nature, its computer arrays overturned and busted by animals that had long ago raided the building for food and water, and its floor covered in dirt, stains, and debris from long-term exposure to the elements. Project Impulse couldn't have designed a more perfect cover for its operations.

The Woman in White broke from the group and stood before a security camera. It was the same camera that had monitored Evan's movements through this very building during his Sunrise Isle test. She waved at its lens, and moments later, a series of underground gears turned. A wide section of flooring that had been artificially tarnished to match the rest lifted on angled hinges, filling the building with Complex E's fluorescent lighting. When the gears locked into their open positions, the Woman in White lead the retrieval team below ground, into the fully operational compound that resided there. The Dark Man fell into line directly behind her, Amanda's stretcher carried by the Plainclothes behind him, and Colonel Davis taking up the rear, keeping his feet at a safe distance and his hand on the grip of his pistol.

"Ah," Albert said with delight as he met the group in the entrance hallway, "the queen bee has arrived." He was joined by two other scientists, at whom he directed his next sentences. "Let's get her to sanitation. We'll need to strip her clothes and any accessories, scrub her down, and change her into a hospital gown."

The scientists nodded before taking Amanda's stretcher from the Plain-clothes.

"Is that really necessary?" Colonel Davis asked from his rear position. "Will it interfere with the device to leave her as she is?"

"Well, no, but we do try to keep The Hive as sanitary as poss—"

"Skip it," the colonel ordered. "I'm not giving that thing any chances to wake up prematurely. We've got no defenses left. If she wakes, with no other thoughts to guide her, she'll react on defensive instinct. And then we're all dead. Hook her into the machine... *now.*"

Albert looked at the Woman in White, hoping she might override the rash order.

"Just do it," she said, supporting Colonel Davis.

Albert took an uncomfortable breath, then adjusted his own orders. "Skip sanitation. Bring her straight to The Hive's cargo entrance."

The scientists acknowledged their new orders and carried Amanda's body down the hallway and around a right-hand turn. Albert stuck with Project Impulse's officials, who proceeded past that turn and wound their way to The Hive's control room. By the time they arrived, the reinforced steel cargo door embedded at ground level along one of The Hive's side walls was lifting. Beyond it, the scientists carrying Amanda's stretcher waited in a glass box the size of a small moving truck. It was an oversized version of the air-locked chamber that separated the control room from The Hive itself. It wouldn't provide the degree of sanitation Albert desired of his new pet project, but it would protect The Hive's equipment from any particulate matter large enough to do significant damage. Once the cargo door was fully open, a seam seal released in the front wall of the glass box, allowing the two panels that comprised it to slide in opposing directions, like an elevator door.

"Lower the central pod," Albert ordered one of the control room technicians.

The technician entered a series of commands in her terminal, and through the observation window, everyone present saw mechanical movement along The Hive's ceiling, followed by a release of pressurized gas, and then the descent of the middle pod. It was larger than the others, serving as their connective hub, and it didn't contain preservation fluid or the vital hookups necessary to sustain a dormant organic lifeform. This pod was designed to hold a living, breathing, conscious person. It contained what could best be described as a padded chair in its current configuration, though the headrest, back, seat, armrests, and leg supports could be repositioned as needed. Most of the chair was augmented with metal restraints: cuffs for the wrists and ankles, a lap belt, and a chest strap, all of which would lock into place around their subject, then retract into the chair to remove excess wiggle room. The headrest was augmented with a high-tech helmet and goggle setup, the next generation of similar technology that had been used to manipulate Judas Sparrows's mental responses in Complex B's Learning Room.

Beyond the chair were tubes and needles necessary to keep Amanda's body alive. There were IVs that would provide hydration and caloric sustenance, a catheter to remove waste from the girl's body, and a number of feeds dedicated to the delivery of Trizorapine. The scientists were joined by floor technicians, who helped position Amanda inside the pod. She wasn't a person to them. She was an object, the missing cog in their machine, and they treated her as such as they secured her into place and violated her body both inside and out in pursuit of their end goal. When she was ready, the scientists and technicians stood back, one of them signaling a thumbs-up toward the observation window.

"Let's start the program," Albert said.

The technician who had entered the commands to lower Amanda's pod now retracted it. Those next to her activated Amanda's IVs, while others launched the virtual simulation environment that would mold her mind to serve Project Impulse's desires. By design, the child of science was still asleep. She was being influenced on a subconscious level, prepared to accept the harsh environment into which she would awaken. And that's when the real training would begin. That's when the Alpha child would be drawn forth to reclaim her bodily vessel from the weaker being that had stolen it from her seven years ago. That's when she would assume her place as The Hive's queen, and when she would awaken her drone bees to do her, and Project Impulse's, bidding.

Colonel Davis saw Amanda's pod lock into place among its peers. His job was done. What happened next was in the hands of this freak show he'd somehow aligned himself with, and he had little desire to watch.

"Where are you going?" the Woman in White asked when he stepped toward the exit door.

"To get some rest. You don't need me here for this."

No one put up an argument, so Colonel Davis continued his departure. It was only when he was clear of the control room, its security door sliding shut to cut him off from his colleagues, that he felt an immense tension in his muscles ease, and noticed what must have been labored breathing returning to normal. To date, the colonel had survived the wrath of three different Impulse children, but if something didn't give soon, he wouldn't survive the stress this venture was taking on his own body. He had to find a way out, and preferably not the same one most of those under his command had found. He marched the nondescript hallways of Complex E until he located one of its lesser-used storage rooms. The others he knew contained the day-to-day supplies required to keep The Hive functioning: Trizorapine, preservation fluid, water reserves, machinery lubricant, and the such. But all Colonel Davis wanted was some aspirin to relieve his growing tension headache. And he was pretty sure he recalled it and any other supplies of lower importance being congregated here.

He flipped on the storage room light, which illuminated rows of metal shelving down both of its sides. Sure enough, the shelves were stocked with items

Complex E rarely needed: spare tarps, miscellaneous tools, a couple of gas cans, some canned goods and MREs, and, as he had hoped, an assortment of over-the-counter medicines and first aid supplies. It took Colonel Davis only a few seconds to locate a bottle of aspirin, but it had an expiration date from over a year ago. He would take it if it was the only option, but suspected there must be something more current in the medical collection. He scanned the names adorning each bottle, which covered a multitude of common needs, from decongestant to laxative. But apparently his luck had run out, for there was no more aspirin or alternative such as acetaminophen or ibuprofen. He read the expiration date on the bottle in his hand again.

Fuck it.

Colonel Davis returned to the storage room entrance and flipped off the light. He was about to close its door when his brain gave him a nudge. It was telling him he'd ignored a viable alternative his eyes had seen, even if Colonel Davis himself hadn't processed it as such. He turned the light back on and scanned the rows of metal shelving. What had he overlooked? It wasn't like some canned fruit or vegetables would alleviate his headache. The gas cans could, but only if he filled them and then burned himself alive, thus defeating getting rid of his headache in the first place. But there had been something—

He finally saw it. It was out in the open, clearly visible, yet deceptively benign, its malignant contents known to a select few. Colonel Davis retrieved the small steel briefcase from a top shelf. He not only knew what was in it, but he had the code to its latch locks, for he'd been the one to put it there. He scrolled the combination tumblers into position, then popped the briefcase open. Inside, nestled into a well surrounded by foam padding, was a glass vial containing a white powder. It was just as Colonel Davis had left it the day it had first been delivered to Project Impulse. It was a proof of concept, showing them that Trizorapine could indeed be produced as a solid variant and successfully mixed with DeMarco's narcotics for worldwide distribution. They'd only needed a few micrograms of the mixture to chemically confirm its potency. The rest had been locked away, out of sight and out of mind... until now.

Colonel Davis needed to find a way out, but perhaps if he couldn't muster the courage to do it physically, a mental escape would serve his purpose equally well. His only prior experience with drug use had been some occasional steroid experimentation in his younger days. He'd never done hard narcotics, and especially not those laced with unapproved hormonal stimulants, and the dangers weren't lost on him. This stuff could kill him in more ways than one, but at this moment, he just didn't care. So he returned the expired aspirin to its shelf, closed the drug sample case, and took it to the privacy of his room. Twenty minutes later, his head was swirling in a conscious dreamland, and shortly thereafter, his body followed, as Colonel Davis fell into the deepest, most relaxed sleep he'd had in years.

———

Trust wasn't something Alison Drexmore would easily extend to a group of unvetted civilians. And it wasn't something Vincent, Frank, nor anyone else who had lived through Eden's trials and tribulations had imagined offering a group of government outsiders. Yet they had to start somewhere, and since this allying of forces had been Victoria's idea, she proposed she go first. Seated in one of Eden PD's rarely used oversized briefing rooms, she reintroduced herself for all those present, then offered apologies on her deceased husband's behalf, and revealed everything she knew about his role in Project Impulse, which ultimately led to his untimely death. Joseph extended an olive branch by then filling in missing details in her story with knowledge he was privy to from his time working at Helix Unbound. Vincent and Derek picked it up from there. They recounted their discovery of Amanda the night of her escape and shared tales of her childhood as a part of their household.

Vincent passed the baton to Frank when the story approached Eden's destruction. He saved the group some of the more gory details from his brother's backstory, but hit the highlights of how Ray had once been a subject of Project Impulse, had formulated a crazed prophecy about Eden's destruction, and had been determined to bring that prophecy to life. Lamar assisted with the scientific explanation behind Eden's collapse, then Vincent and Joseph closed out this chapter of their tale with a play-by-play of what happened at Lakeview Bay and how they, Amanda, Evan, and Derek had almost died in the carpet-bombing of Eden that followed.

The first time General Javez took the floor was to offer his side of the events leading up to that bombing. He then advanced the timeline to when he and Victoria had formed a pact to destroy Project Impulse, the investigatory work they'd performed as a result of that pact, and the small, but ultimately incomplete victory they'd achieved in the destruction of Complex B. That opened a whole new can of worms when Frank bitterly revealed it had been the very people in that room on the ground at Complex B when General Javez's troops opened fire without a single consideration that there might be innocents on the scene. Tempers flared, but with everyone already clear that all parties present, those from Eden and Washington alike, were on the same team, the flare was short-lived. Soon, the sharing of knowledge resumed.

It was a group effort relaying what had happened in the aftermath of

Complex B's destruction. Though every word that left his lips cut like a razor blade, Joseph took it upon himself to recount how Evan had been murdered, how Amanda had killed Judas in an emotional, chemically-fueled rage, and how the world was now down to one extremely powerful Impulse child. From there, the conversation pivoted to Project Impulse's retreat to Complex E and the pieces it had been putting in motion to achieve its endgame. The Eden crew shared what it had learned about DeMarco's drugs being laced with Trizorapine, providing closure to Victoria and General Javez's investigation into the manufacturing plant distribution contradictions. The Washington group shared its discovery of the cellular cloning project at Waxhill, and of its subject relocation, supposedly to the hub-and-spoke system that existed within the bowels of Complex E.

And that was it. All cards, from both sides, were on the table. No one had previously had a clearer picture of how the actions of Project Impulse had unfolded to date, nor of the pieces still on the board, taking up strategic position for a final strike. And yet, for Frank, and he suspected for most others by the concerned looks on their faces, the dots still weren't connected. What did the cellular cloning have to do with Amanda? It wasn't as though Project Impulse would have time to clone her before its resources ran dry. It also sounded like they already had an army of clones at their disposal, but then why did they need Amanda? And what did any of that have to do with dousing the world in Trizorapine? There was still something none of them were seeing, at least, not until James clicked on an overhead projector at one end of the briefing room and displayed Ray's prophetic drawing across the wall.

"You all look like you're asking yourselves the same set of questions," he said. "Here are your answers." He crossed through the oversized projection and pointed at its female leader. "You have a hub." He then motioned toward the army behind her. "You have spokes." He looked at General Javez. "You said the cloning project created—what was the term—*dormant organic lifeforms*? They're going to need something, or in this case, someone, to wake them from their dormant state." He shifted his gaze to Joseph. "You said Evan had the ability to control others. You saw him scatter his energy particles into the minds of snipers and force their hands into shooting at their own forces."

"That's right."

"And you, General Javez, you told us your men saw Judas hypnotize Complex B's soldiers into almost committing suicide during a recon mission. Correct?"

General Javez nodded.

"I think it's only prudent to assume Amanda possesses that same ability." James stepped back to emphasize his point. "Hub. Spokes. They're planning on using her to make their military wheel turn."

Holy shit, Frank thought. *He was right.*

"How does this explain the Trizorapine distribution?" Alison asked in a surprisingly respectful tone, considering James was one of the least qualified people to even be in this room.

He bit his lip, having not quite made that mental connection.

"Energy," Rebecca said, coming to his aid. She joined her classmate at the projection. "You said the hub-and-spoke device draws the power of a small city. That's to power the machine. You still need to power the lifeforms inside of it, both when they're inside... and once they're out." She pointed to the female figure. "Think of Amanda like their wall outlet. She'll give them the juice needed to bring them to life. She may even serve as a motherboard of sorts, guiding their actions the way Evan and Judas did others. But once they leave the physical confines of the machine, those clones will be running on internal energy... battery power, if you will. And if they're going to be exercising Impulse abilities, those batteries are going to drain quickly. They'll need constant replenishment."

"My God," Joseph said. "They've turned the world's addict population into a near-endless supply of refueling stations. This... Impulse army they've created... it won't need to eat; it won't need to sleep. It can march across the world in perpetuity, feeding off human-sourced Trizorapine until there's no world left to destroy."

Alison had heard enough. "Okay, then." She stood, her mannerisms indicating she was done with the conversation. "I feel like this should go without saying, but can we establish for the record that we're all friends now? Any dissenters?"

Silence.

"Good." She started for the door. "Officially, I was never here. You need something from me, you talk to them." She pointed to Victoria and General Javez. "I'll be in Washington, getting preliminary defensive and counter-offensive resources lined up."

"You might be wasting your time," Derek said. "We still haven't heard from Shortcake. She might have already stopped all of this." He tried to sound hopeful, but he knew the others could hear his doubt.

"That encounter was expected to occur, what... fourteen, fifteen hours ago?" Alison gave him a consolatory frown. "If you want to find out what happened, be my guest. I genuinely hope you learn something favorable. But I need to prepare for the worst." She turned and clacked out of the room, calling over her shoulder, "You have my number!"

Once Alison was gone, the others stared at each other as if not knowing where to start. The Eden crew had its own special dynamic to it, a dynamic that didn't involve outsiders. Victoria and General Javez had also grown into their own hybrid dynamic of personal and professional interactions, one that only Alison Drexmore had previously violated. But if these two groups were going to work as a team, they would each need to find the flexibility to intertwine their dynamics with the other.

"So..." Lamar said, sensing the tension in the room. "What should we do?"

Frank looked at Vincent, their shared law enforcement background already putting them on the same page. Then he looked at General Javez, a man of a different background, but one with similar goals, and he could see they were at least reading from the same chapter of the book. These teams needed a connecting bridge; this might be the best they were going to get. "We do exactly what Ms. Drexmore suggested. Let's find out whether Amanda succeeded."

CHAPTER 11
INITIATION

Colonel Davis was lying on the beach, a cold beer in one hand and a tablet live streaming that evening's basketball game in the other. The sun was on its way out for the day, leaving the sky streaked with gradient hues of deep orange. The ocean waves were gentle, lapping quietly at the sand while sea birds sailed overhead. Kids played in the distance, building sand castles and throwing frisbees, while parents watched, and couples took strolls along the tide line. This was just the vacation Colonel Davis had been needing. He couldn't remember why he was so desperate for one—something to do with his job, perhaps—but he knew he'd found paradise, and he wasn't going anywhere for a while.

A resort waitress dropped off a tray containing a fresh beer, as well as a deli sandwich and bag of potato chips to go with it. She was cute, if a little young for his age, and Colonel Davis made a mental note to leave her a decent tip for trekking this far down the sand to serve him. He popped open the new beer, took a mouth-filling swig, then sighed and rested his head, letting the warmth of the falling sun bathe his shirtless body. What he wouldn't give to truly be here. What he wouldn't do to escape those cold, metallic walls of Complex E and leave his past behind.

What are you talking about? Colonel Davis asked himself.

He was here, right? The beach sure seemed real. The sand was grainy and stuck to his forearms every time he lifted them. The sound of the waves was serene in the way it rushed in toward his ears, then swept away to near-silence before rushing in again. The beer—oh, that beer—it was the best Colonel Davis had tasted in a long time. And that sun; its warmth was such a stark contrast to the underground dampness no amount of air filtration could fully eliminate. How could this not be real?

And yet, something about it was artificial. Like the way the sun had yet to set, despite sinking into the horizon for well over half an hour. Like the way the resort waitress had replenished the colonel's beer, even though he didn't remember phoning in an order. And like the way those kids squealed and giggled with eerily repetitive sounds and motions, almost as though they were trying to play through a scratch on their record of life. This wasn't real, and Colonel Davis could see that now. He sat up and tried to spot the resort hotel behind him, but anything beyond fifty feet was a murky blur. He tried calling to a passing couple along the water, but they either didn't hear him or purposefully ignored him. Colonel Davis stood and brushed the sand off of him. He yelled for the attention of the nearest sand-castle building children, but they, like the couple, paid no attention. He chucked his open beer in their direction, nailing the castle, and yet the kids kept on laughing and playing as if nothing had happened. Then he looked back at the tray the waitress had brought him. His beer was still there.

What the hell is this?

Colonel Davis took off walking down one direction of beach. He focused straight ahead, ignoring the pedestrians around him, not worrying about the blurs that existed in the distance, and marched until he left everything—the couples, the waitress, the kids—behind. He checked the status of the sun and waves, finding they still hadn't changed. Then he shook his head, and caught sight of his beer, meal, and tablet, all awaiting his return to the sand just inches from his feet. With nowhere else to go, Colonel Davis plopped back into place. Only this time, the sand felt springy. It had a cushioned bounce to it, and when the colonel dug his hand in to investigate, he pulled out the edge of a bedsheet. It was a bland, no-frills type of bedsheet like those used throughout Complex E, he recognized.

But he also saw an unfamiliar red tint to the bedsheet, so he pulled further, exposing more and more of its sandy hiding spot. The tint grew darker, so dark it reminded Colonel Davis of blood. Then he realized it was blood, and his sheet was drenched with it. But what was the source? He exposed more of the sheet, now fully soaked from end to end, dripping thick globules of blood onto the sand. He pulled and pulled, but the fabric seemed endless. There was a pile large enough for two beds already gathered on the sand, and yet more was coming, all of it dripping with dark red. Colonel Davis didn't understand. He pulled the section of sheet in his hands tight to examine its surface, to figure out what witch-craft was preventing him from reaching its other end. Then something moved on that surface. Something pressed against the blood, first forming random wrinkles, then taking shape... the shape of a face... Colonel Davis's face. And it spoke.

"Great job killing yourself, asshole."

Colonel Davis screamed as his eyes popped open. He let them do the moving, scanning his surroundings before risking even the slightest motion of his body. As far as he could tell, he was back in his bunker at Complex E. He was in bed, his head still resting upon his pillow, and the open briefcase and partially empty drug vial he'd helped himself to were right where he'd left them a few feet away. Part of him was relieved his bit role in Bloody Beaches 18 had been a dream. Part of him wished he was still there, still listening to that serene water, still feeling that warm sun. Colonel Davis closed his eyes and tried to picture it once more. For a moment, he returned to his original sandy getaway, where he could see that cold beer within his grasp. But he couldn't taste it. The dream was over, and though he could picture it in his mind, he couldn't feel the physical sensations it had offered.

That was, except for the warmth. Colonel Davis could still feel that. But only on half of his body. He rubbed his eyes and looked toward his legs, wondering if they were in the current of a heating vent, and that's when he saw the bloody sheet of his dreams. Only this wasn't a dream at all. This was real, and there was only one person that blood could belong to. Colonel Davis ripped the sheet away, and what he found defied even his worst expectations. Wrapped around each of his legs was a jungle green vine the thickness of a garden hose. Running along the inner surface of each vine was a line of flappy suction cups that reminded Colonel Davis of those found on an octopus's tentacles. But these weren't normal suction cups; they were lined with microscopic teeth, teeth that had already gnawed through his pants and consumed enough flesh to reach his dermis layer. In fact, based on the amount of blood soaking his bed, they'd probably reached his dermis layer quite a while ago.

Colonel Davis grabbed his Bowie knife from his nightstand and hacked at the base of the vine wrapped around his right leg. It tried to uncoil itself after only the first slice, but the colonel didn't let up, and before it could fully release him and retreat, he'd cut straight through it. A shriek of pain came from somewhere beyond his bedroom wall. The severed vine flopped wildly, and it was in that moment Colonel Davis saw the slimy tube running down its center, spilling his blood onto the floor. That thing hadn't been eating his flesh for sustenance. It had been doing it to reach his blood.

The second vine retreated before Colonel Davis could turn his knife on it. He watched as both vines pulled back through a hole they'd made in the wall at the base of his bed. Then he slid himself free of the partial vine still wound around his leg, grabbed his pistol, and moved in to investigate. It was funny, Colonel Davis thought, that despite his legs being ripped into fleshy tatters, and his blood flowing freely enough to drip down his shoes, he felt no pain. All he could imagine was that those vegetation vampires must inject their prey with a numbing agent of some sort, so they can feed without being noticed. He wondered whether they would have drained him dry if he hadn't woken when he did. Then he realized he already knew the answer to that question.

Colonel Davis fired a warning shot through the hole in his wall. Hearing no movement, he then leaned in to assess. There was light within the hole, negating the need for a flashlight, and though the opening itself was barely big enough for his head, the cavernous space that existed beyond was shocking. It was only two or three feet deep, but it extended in every direction, creating a hidden air gap that ran the height and length of this edge of Complex E. Occasional breaks at surface level allowed light in, and that light showed Colonel Davis more than empty space. It showed him that within this gap, no matter which direction he looked, was another writhing threat biding its time to infiltrate Complex E. One of them, some sort of oversized groundhog with two sharp fangs protruding from the center of its lips, spotted Colonel Davis and scurried forward.

He retracted his head, glanced around the room for something he could use as a distraction, then tossed the vial with the remaining drugs into the hole. Now, more than the groundhog was scurrying. It sounded like armies of nature's mutated creations were racing to claim the prize he'd given them. As for Colonel Davis, he wasn't sticking around to find out which was victorious. He was getting the hell out of this house of cards before it came crashing down. He stripped his bloody pants, hastily rolled each leg with gauze from a first aid bag he kept in his closet, then put on fresh pants and shoes, and bolted from the room before something else came looking for him.

He beelined it for the compound surface exit, well aware that he was probably going to have to battle his way off this island. But that was better than staying put and waiting for a death that would inevitably come. He passed the hallway leading to The Hive's control room just as one of the Plainclothes was heading inside. In that brief moment, he could see that Amanda was awake. Her body was no longer limp inside her pod, and it was trembling uncontrollably as her blood was pumped full of Trizorapine and her brain rewritten to accept her destiny as Project Impulse's weapon of mass destruction. Colonel Davis questioned how he'd ever gotten so deeply ingrained in this insanity, and if anything were confirmation that it was time to get out, it was the sight of that science-bred freak being primed to do what she was born to do. The thought crossed his mind that perhaps he should try to free her. Perhaps he should be the one to burn this place to the ground instead of leaving it in Mother Nature's hands. But that would go against his sense of self-preservation. And right now, that was the only sense he had left. So Colonel Davis continued on until he reached the surface exit. Then he gripped his pistol in one hand and knife in the other, and set out to face whatever obstacles awaited him there.

———

Amanda hadn't told anyone where she was planning to confront Project Impulse, but it didn't take much for Joseph to figure it out. She wouldn't have chosen the Desmond house, his own, or anywhere else in Eden's outer neighborhoods, for fear of putting innocent bystanders in harm's way. Likewise, she wouldn't have chosen Pine Ridge, Renewed Hope, Eden PD, or popular sites in downtown Eden to avoid similar risk. She could have chosen to battle it out in the underground tunnels, which would've given her a strategic advantage, since Colonel Davis and whatever army he had at his disposal would have limited space in which to make tactical maneuvers. The problem was that it was unlikely Colonel Davis would yield such an advantage, and thus he would wait Amanda out instead of chasing her underground. She needed somewhere open to draw in Project Impulse's forces, somewhere they would deem a fair battleground. After eliminating most other public venues, Joseph determined that only left Soul Wind Forest as a viable engagement zone. And given its expansiveness, there was only one logical location in the forest where Amanda could guarantee Project Impulse would find her.

Vincent, Frank, and General Javez led the trek into the wilderness. They followed a GPS locator into which General Javez had loaded Helix Unbound's coordinates. Joseph went with them to provide on-site analyses should they be needed, while Derek stayed at Eden PD with the rest of their group's civilian members to ensure they remained safe. It was an easy walk through the woods, both because of the youthful size of its regrowing trees and because daylight made obstacle avoidance a breeze. And after only forty-five minutes on a straight shot to their target, General Javez announced they were close to arrival.

"Keep your eyes peeled for a clearing, or debris, or anything else that would indicate a space where a manmade structure once stood," he said.

The group fanned out, forming a wide line to ensure they didn't bypass the location. Frank, a few steps ahead of the others, was the first to breach the Helix Unbound tree line, and it was immediately clear that this ring of woods was less developed than the rest. Vincent breached next, about fifteen feet away, where he nearly tripped over a warped sheet of scorched metal. He held the sheet high for Frank to see, then exchanged a thumbs-up to signal this was the place. When General Javez emerged into the overgrown clearing, he paused and assessed his surroundings. This was unknown territory, and as far as he was concerned, that made it hostile territory. He drew his gun and proceeded with caution, Vincent and Frank taking a cue to do the same.

Joseph shifted his walking trajectory upon entering the clearing to join up with Frank, who he stayed near, given he had no weapon of his own. He wanted to shout for Amanda. He wanted to let her know they were there in case she was hiding, or hurt, or preparing to spring a trap under the assumption that the search party was with Project Impulse. But he kept his mouth shut, letting those with more experience in these matters take charge as they stepped slowly toward the clearing's center. Then Vincent stopped, his mouth dropping slightly open as his eyes fixed on something lying on the ground ahead.

"It's a body," he whispered.

That triggered Frank's policeman mode. "Cover me," he told the others.

He shuffled hastily in the direction Vincent was looking as General Javez scanned their perimeter for any signs of movement. Frank reached his destination and prodded the body with his foot. It was surrounded by stains of dried blood on the forest floor, and as expected, it didn't respond. Frank bent down and rolled the body over, getting a good look at Maddox's fatal neck wound. He didn't need to check for a pulse.

"It's a soldier," he announced. Then he examined Maddox's arsenal, paying special attention to the empty counteragent rifle slung around his shoulder. "Definitely with Project Impulse."

"She took one of them out," General Javez said. "Scout around. See what else we can find."

As they did that, Joseph returned to Frank's side. He glanced at Maddox, but only for a moment, the sight of the dead body unnerving. He recalled a vague memory of the soldier, though he couldn't place whether it had been from Helix Unbound, Complex B, or somewhere else altogether. The man had met a gruesome end, and Joseph had to wonder whether it had been Amanda's doing or Project Impulse's. He didn't like to imagine his surrogate daughter as such a ruthless killer, but then again, it wasn't like he'd expected her to come out here and invite Colonel Davis to sing Kumbaya by the campfire, either.

"I've got counteragent darts embedded in the dirt over here," Vincent called from his search zone.

"Me too," General Javez said. "Bullet casings, also."

So the fight had gone down here. But why was there only one body? And where was Amanda? If the battle was over, why hadn't she contacted her family with an update? Or was the battle still underway? Had Project Impulse fled after losing one of its own, and Amanda was still in pursuit? Or had something worse happened, something no one in that clearing wanted to entertain? Frank drifted to a third search zone to look for clues, but Joseph's gears were turning, his scientific brain processing the possibilities and narrowing the evidence required to make a determination. Any counteragent dart stuck in the dirt wasn't a dart that had pierced Amanda's skin. Any bullet casings were simply evidence of Project Impulse's naivety, for such a weapon would have been ineffective against her. Amanda's absence was meaningless. Maybe she'd left the clearing as a prisoner of Project Impulse; maybe she'd left of her own free will. Without more bodies, there was no way to prove the latter. But there was something that could prove the former. An empty injection device, dart or otherwise, would be proof that Amanda had received a dose of counteragent, and that would mean she was in Project Impulse's hands now.

Joseph almost didn't want to look. But he was the only one still standing near Maddox's body. And if this is where the battle had been underway, and subsequently ended, whatever proof remained in this clearing would be there. He shuffled his feet, half-heartedly scouting the patches of dirt between stringy grasses, his mind partially disconnected from his task, telling himself everything would be fine, that there was nothing to see there. But even that wasn't enough to stop him from noticing the glint of sunlight on the glass vial laying only two feet away. Joseph's heart skipped a beat.

Please let it be a dart in the dirt, he told himself. *Please don't let it—*

But reality had a harsh truth to reveal. As Joseph neared, the glass vial took shape, and it wasn't just a dart in the dirt. It was a syringe, and it was empty, save for some deep purple residue and a streak of inky black fluid. The scientist held the syringe up to the sunlight, the weight of his own guilt pushing back against his arm muscles, pressing down on his shoulders and squeezing his tear ducts as his lip trembled with regret. He'd promised Evan he wouldn't let Project Impulse have Amanda back, and now he'd broken that promise. Even worse, the world would soon suffer for it, and it would be his fault. Colonel Davis had predicted as much seven years ago. He'd told Joseph that whatever happened as a result of Amanda's release was on him, and it looked like those consequences would now include worldwide war and devastation.

"What'd you find?" Frank called out.

Joseph couldn't speak, and that was enough to draw the other three over. They saw what was in his hand, and like him, they knew the implications. Out of respect, General Javez kept his comments to himself, though his tactical mind was already charting their next steps. Vincent took the revelation as hard as Joseph, dropping to his knees and examining the syringe himself as if trying to prove it was something different than what it appeared to be. Frank didn't want to be the asshole, but he knew time was ticking now, and no matter what mental struggle Joseph and Vincent were going through, the endgame was approaching.

"We need to find Complex E," he told them. "They've got their weapon back. We need to infiltrate and stop whatever they're planning to do with her."

"Their *weapon* is our *daughter*," Joseph growled. "We were supposed to protect her."

"She chose to protect herself," Frank reminded him. "And she failed. We were always Plan B, and while we hoped we'd never have to execute, it's where we are now."

"How can you be so cold?" Vincent asked despondently, his eyes still fixed on the empty syringe. "You're talking like she's already dead."

Frank took a fortifying breath. "Whether she's alive or dead is irrelevant. She's not on our side anymore. And Project Impulse isn't waiting for the two of you to shed your tears before making its next move."

The detective's words made Joseph's blood boil. He didn't know if it was his own failure to protect Amanda, or that combined with Frank's failure to see through Judas's ruse before it had resulted in Evan's death, but something snapped within him. With a roar, he lunged at Frank, driving him to the ground and hammering him with everything he had left. Vincent and General Javez had to drag him off.

"Let go of me!" Joseph yelled, his arms restrained behind his body.

"Not until you calm down," General Javez said.

"No," Frank said, wiping a smear of blood from his nose. "It's alright. Let him go."

General Javez looked at Vincent, who looked at Frank, who nodded as though he knew what he was asking. They released Joseph. The scientist breathed erratically, his mind in no condition to guide him to rational action. Recognizing that, Frank stepped forward with his hands up to show he meant no harm.

"I'm not trying to be cold. And I know the pain you must be going through."

"You can't know this pain, Detective. This pain... to fail your children... to lose them to the evils of this world... this is a pain only a parent can know."

"You're right," Frank acquiesced. "I can't know your pain, not in the way you do. But I know this: your daughter made it her mission to destroy Project Impulse, and now they're going to use her to get what they want. Unless *we* stop them first."

Joseph shrugged in defeat. "How?"

"We need to find Complex E," Frank reiterated. "Professor, you spent years working for Helix Unbound. Then you got an inside look at Complex B. You were nearly held in containment at Complex C. With all that experience and exposure, there's got to be something, some small detail in that super intelligent head of yours, that could help us find Complex E. Just think. Think about everything you've seen, no matter how insignificant it might have appeared at the time. Find the clue that will get us there."

Joseph's breathing steadied, his emotions giving way to logic. Frank was right. He wasn't focused on what they'd done wrong or what they'd lost, but on salvaging what they still could. And that was going to take finding Complex E. Joseph scoured his mental filing cabinets for anything that stood out from his days at Helix Unbound and its sister facilities, anything that could point them toward a concealed location where Project Impulse could continue its work in secret. But after a few minutes, he came up empty. The others could see it on his face, drawing sighs and diverted eyes.

"I'm sorry," he said.

Frank couldn't be hard on him. "You tried." He then said with encouragement, "You'll keep trying. Maybe something will come back to you."

Joseph shook his head. "They didn't trust me enough to expose that type of knowledge. You need someone closer to the inner circle than me. Someone like Senator Riley's dead husband, or Leonard Guiles, or Colonel Davis, or—" Joseph's words caught as his eyes lit with excitement. "I can't believe I didn't think of it sooner."

"Think of what?" Vincent asked.

"We have an ally in the inner circle. Well, he was in the inner circle. He got out. I don't know where he is but—" Joseph looked at General Javez, his next words fueled by constrained hope. "If I have a person's name, do you and that Drexmore woman have the resources to locate him?"

"Absolutely. Who is it?"

Joseph smiled. "Jackson. His name is Demetrius Jackson."

———

Amanda floated through a sea of endless blackness. There was no ground beneath her, nor sky above her, nor objects near or far on which she could focus. In fact, there was nothing, for she was nothing, a speck of her former consciousness now buried deep inside a mind and body no longer her own. She had no sense of self here, no memory of what she had once been or who she strove to be. And yet, she couldn't let go. She couldn't give herself completely to the darkness. She couldn't let it snuff her from existence in favor of the mindless monster that had taken her place. She held on to life, what little life there was in this world of subconscious existence. Amanda didn't know how she had gotten here, and saw no way to escape, yet her instinct was to fight. She needed to fight for control, fight to return to the mind and body that had been stolen from her. She could feel it, a chaotic ball of rage ready to unleash itself upon the world. She had to stop it.

Amanda willed herself through darkness, toward the mind that no longer wanted her. She reached out, but her mind didn't respond. She tried to force her way into it, but it rejected her, putting up an invisible wall beyond which she couldn't pass. Amanda tried to route around the wall, but it was endless. This wasn't fair. She didn't know much, but she knew that mind was hers. She knew that body was hers. She wanted them back. She needed them back, so she could... so she could... so she could what? Without her memories, she had no idea. But it felt right. So she pushed against the wall with all her might. She felt herself breaking through it, the blackness lifting into the slightest shade of gray as light filtered in from some far off destination...

And then the shockwave hit her. It was a chemical shock, poisoning the path forward and zapping Amanda of what little sense she had. The chemical shock was followed by another of lights and imagery, visions of pain and destruction, of war and death. These must be the images being fed to her brain through whatever contraption now encased her body. Amanda shielded herself from them, and that retreat was enough to fortify the invisible wall that kept her trapped in this subconscious state. When she analyzed her surroundings, she was in a sea of endless blackness once more. There was no ground beneath her, nor sky above her... she had no sense of self here... no memory of what had just transpired, no foresight to see it would transpire again... and again... and again. It was an endless loop of futility, one from which there was no escape, not now, not ever. And yet, Amanda hung on.

———

"What's going on in there?" Albert asked a technician in The Hive's control room. "Her readings are off the chart."

The technician frantically flipped through data streams. Meanwhile, through the viewing window, Amanda could be seen twitching violently in her pod. Her body had partially atomized, bright specks of blue energy swirling around her like she was the eye of a hurricane. No part of her had tried to leave the pod, but Albert worried if something didn't change soon, the pod's integrity would fail, releasing her nonetheless.

"She's overloaded with energy," the technician reported. "Her body is sucking in more Trizorapine than we've programmed the system to deliver. And her pod is drawing double its electricity load."

"Double the electricity?" Albert asked with confusion. "But where is it—" He looked at Amanda, answering his own question. Miniature lightning bolts were firing across the surface of her skin, the sustained charge in her body well beyond anything a normal human being could live through. "We need to reverse the flow before she melts her brain. Is there any way to draw power away from the pod?"

"You'd have to ask Diego."

Unfortunately, Diego was currently missing in action. The Woman in White glanced at the Dark Man. They'd both been watching the exchange, and his silent, responding nod signaled their thoughts were aligned.

"What if we open the drone lines?" she asked Albert.

"We're not scheduled to do that for at least another twelve hours."

"I'm not asking about schedules. She's building up energy because she knows she needs it for what lies ahead. What if we let her start using it now? Is there any risk? Any danger this could blow up in our faces?"

Albert chuckled nervously. "Everything we do here has a risk of blowing up in our faces."

"Let me rephrase the question then," the Woman in White said. "Is it more risky to open the drone lines than not, given what we're currently witnessing?"

Albert considered the inquiry, then replied, "No."

"And is she ready? Forget schedules. Forget programs. If we set her loose, will she do what we need her to do?"

He took a moment to commandeer the technician's screen. After scanning the most recent readings on his genetic lab rat, he answered, "I think so. Yes."

"Then open the lines."

Albert and his technician shared a nervous glance, then he nodded for her to proceed. A few strokes of the keyboard later, and the alarm lights inside The Hive illuminated. A pre-recorded message informed anyone within the main chamber to evacuate it immediately. The handful of scientists and engineers dropped what they were doing and used the cargo exit so they could evacuate in a single wave. Then Albert signaled the rest of the technicians in the control room.

"On my mark." He held up his fingers and counted. "Five."

The technicians watched nervously, their hands at the ready on their keyboards.

"Four."

Electricity hummed throughout the control room.

"Three."

The Woman in White stared at Hurricane Amanda, swirling inside her pod with such ferocity.

"Two."

The Dark Man's black eyes grew wide with anticipation.

"One."

For the briefest moment, Amanda's speck of existence could sense something was about to change, but she didn't know what it was, and she was helpless to stop it.

"Execute."

Each technician sprang into action, their movements precise, every task essential to what was about to unfold. One by one, protective flaps shielding each end of the cables connecting Amanda's pod to the other forty-nine populated pods dilated, opening clear tunnels through which her essence could travel. And travel it did. The whirlwind of energy particles dispersed, several zipping down each cable, where they found identical clones of Evan waiting to grant them life.

"We've got movement in pod seven," one technician announced.

"And pod twelve," another said. "Also seventeen and twenty-three."

The numbers kept coming like a bingo game being called on fast-forward. Then the pod lids started to come off, spilling coolant gases throughout the main chamber. The first drone rose, dematerialized, and darted through the roof. A second and third followed shortly thereafter. With each release, Amanda's storm eased, the energy within her being dispersed among the others. Within two minutes, twenty Impulse drones were already on their ways to their destinations. Within five minutes, the other twenty-nine had followed. Technicians shut off the coolant flows to each drone pod, and the air filtration system cleared the main chamber of opaque gases. The Woman in White checked on Amanda, who, like an obedient soldier, was still at the helm of the ship, leading her forty-nine combatants into a war that had been a long time coming. She breathed a little easier, allowed herself a triumphant smile, then peered at the Dark Man.

"We did it."

CHAPTER 12

THE CHAOS OF CONTROL

The first drone touched down in its target city of Norfolk, Virginia after only two hours. Its slaughter began immediately. Residents of all classes, tourists, vagrants, naval officers... none of them were immune to the attack, not if they'd polluted their systems with DeMarco's narcotics. The drone acted with near-perfect efficiency. It used its own molecules as its default weapons, dematerializing and jetting through target bodies, slicing vital arteries and organs while simultaneously absorbing Trizorapine from their systems to keep itself energized. When targets fought back, the drone would disarm them and use their own weapons for its attack. When an opportunity presented itself to take out multiple targets in one sweep, like it did when they amassed around the explosive artillery on Naval Station Norfolk, the drone didn't hesitate to take advantage. Explosions rang out, buildings collapsed, fires burned, and innocent bystanders who'd never partaken in DeMarco's offerings were lost as collateral damage. But that didn't matter. The drone had a single mission: eliminate all hosts of Trizorapine as efficiently as possible. Collateral damage was an acceptable byproduct.

The second drone landed in Halifax, Nova Scotia shortly after the first. The third and fourth followed, one materializing in Jericho City and the other in Caracas, Venezuela. Like the first, they didn't hesitate in carrying out their orders. Even at an average cadence of one death per second, it would take each of them approximately two days to eradicate a medium-sized city of its target population. Then they would move to the next city, rinse and repeat, and continue on until all cities across the globe had been cleansed. The drones didn't need to sleep or eat or rest between locations. As long as they had Amanda's linked essence to give them life and guidance, and a steady intake of Trizorapine to fuel their Omega Genomes, they could kill in perpetuity. And nothing could stop them.

———

"How far out are we?" Frank asked.

He, Vincent, Joseph, and General Javez were in the back of a military sedan. After leaving Soul Wind Forest, they'd chartered a private plane in Victoria's name and flown to Charleston, South Carolina. According to motor vehicle records, Demetrius Jackson's last known address was in a quaint residential neighborhood on the outskirts of the city.

"It should only be another five minutes at most," their driver replied.

General Javez's phone rang. "Yes, Ms. Drexmore?" He listened intently, then his face turned dour. "Understood." He hung up and shot a nervous look at the others. "It's started."

They each went for their cell phones, opening news sites, social media apps—anything that might give them a sense of what Project Impulse had unleashed. It didn't take long to get their answer. Red headline banners announcing the attack on Naval Station Norfolk were posted at the top of every news webpage. Pictures of black smoke pluming into the sky and dead bodies littering public streets were plastered on every social media feed. Government officials had yet to issue a statement, but rumor was they were treating the attack like an act of war.

"Canada's under attack too," General Javez said as he scrolled through a stream of internal government broadcasts the others didn't have access to. "And there have been sightings in Spain and the U.K."

"Sightings of what, exactly?" Vincent asked.

Frank turned his phone so the others could see its screen. It was frozen on a digital photograph posted only minutes earlier, one in which an Evan clone could be seen disarming a police officer of his pistol. "Impulse children."

Joseph stared at the picture, the image of the boy within it causing his heart to break that much more. "Those sick bastards. They've hijacked everything I created and twisted it for their own deranged purpose."

Vincent looked away, unable to watch Joseph's torment. But as his eyes fell over his own phone screen, he saw something else just as disheartening. "Frank..."

The detective looked, and his gut told him what Vincent was about to show him even before the sheriff turned his phone. It was a video out of Jericho, showing a drone in the distance as it pounced on a street hustler, tore out his throat with its teeth, dematerialized, and then shot its atoms through a fleeing drug gang nearby, each member dropping to the ground as if suddenly pulled from life support. The atoms then pivoted toward whomever was recording the footage, darted toward the screen, and then disappeared as the recording device clattered to the ground and came to a rest, pointing at its owner's lifeless face. Frank dialed Billy.

"I know why you're calling," his partner answered.

"Billy, you've got to get out of Jericho. You, Captain Tipps, Gibbs... you need to grab whatever friends and family you can reach and get out now."

"You know we can't abandon the citizens like that. They'll be defenseless."

"They're already defenseless!" Frank argued. "Don't you understand that? The only thing any of you can do is provide them one extra second of life while you get slaughtered in their places!"

Silence. Then Billy hit him with the one retort he knew Frank couldn't deny. *"Would you run if you were here?"*

Of course he wouldn't. It wasn't in his blood. Frank would fight the good fight, no matter how much the odds were stacked against him. It was the reason he'd chased Ray into City Hall the night of Eden's collapse. It was the reason Vincent and Samuel had to drag him away from the bomb that had initiated that catastrophe. He didn't know how to run away, and Billy didn't either.

"If you stay there," Frank said, "you will die."

Another moment of silence, then: *"I know."* Billy let that linger between them before adding, his voice still harboring a glint of hope, *"But I also know I've got a partner who's already working the case. And if anyone can find a way to stop this, it's him."*

Frank swallowed hard, the weight of Billy's fate falling to his shoulders. "Stay alive until he does. You got that?"

"We'll do our best."

With that, they disconnected, and Frank saw that Vincent was putting down his phone as if he'd just completed his own call. "What's going on?"

"That was Derek. There's no sign of those things in Eden yet. I told him to start preparing anyway, for both a counteroffensive... and an escape plan, should it become necessary."

Frank shifted his gaze to General Javez. "And you?"

"There are twenty-three confirmed hostiles so far. They seem to be spreading in a circular pattern across the globe from some origin point on either the United States's east coast or in the Atlantic Ocean itself. They're targeting cities with critical military forces, critical infrastructure, or both."

"They're crippling defensive responses," Frank followed. He then shook his head in disbelief. "Project Impulse has declared war on the entire planet." Feeling defeated, he turned his eyes to the one person on their team that could offer a glimmer of hope. "Professor, tell me we're not too late. Tell me there's something we can do to stop this."

He frowned, but tried to give Frank what he wanted anyway, even though his logic brain told him defeat was the most likely outcome. "Amanda controls the Impulse army. That would suggest she has the power to shut it down. We've got to find her."

Frank wished he felt relief, but Joseph had unknowingly solidified his feeling of defeat. Because in reality, the professor had been wrong. Amanda didn't control the Impulse army. By her own admission, there was no Amanda anymore. The Alpha child was in control, and the Alpha child was the enemy. It wouldn't shut the army down, and it would kill anyone who tried.

The car slowed, and the driver angled his mouth toward the group. "We're here."

———

Jackson leaned forward in his wheelchair as a breaking news alert showed an Evan clone rampaging through the streets of Berlin. After all these years, he couldn't believe Project Impulse had finally pulled it off. They'd created their army of super-soldiers, though in perhaps the most twisted way possible, and now they'd launched their offensive against the world. That last piece was never part of the original plan. Project Impulse had been under the control of the United States government when Jackson had served it. He'd always suspected his superiors had grander goals than turning over their creations to a political body that would likely underutilize them. But to go rogue against not only the United States, but every government and military body in existence, was sheer madness. If he still had use of his legs, Jackson would consider joining the fight. But perhaps it was best he didn't, for he had a family to protect, and he had no choice but to focus on them.

"I don't know why you're still watching that," his wife, Maya, said as she passed through the living room with a pile of clothes draped over one arm. "You could be helping us pack."

Jackson understood her frustration, but his staring at the television wasn't without purpose. "I'm trying to track the movement of those things. It doesn't do us any good to run if we don't know a safe location to run to."

"I thought there were only two here in the states. Let's just avoid whatever cities those are in."

"There are three now," Jackson informed her. "Another one hit Nevada a little while ago. But it's not about where they are now. It's about where they're going next. They hit Norfolk because of the naval base there. Nevada has Nellis Air Force Base. I have yet to figure out the strategic importance of Jericho. Suffice to say, let's avoid any city that houses a major military complex until we know more."

Maya nodded in agreement and left the room. The breaking news alert shifted to a montage of attack footage from across the globe, but to Jackson, it was all starting to blend together. Dead bodies, smoke, fire, rubble, the occasional clip of one of the drones using its genetic enhancements to murder as few as one or as many as hundreds with a single act of violence. It felt like the end times, even if it was currently limited to a handful of cities. What was going to stop these things from doing the same to the next city, and the one after that? By Jackson's estimate, it was just a matter of time before the world collapsed. Sure, the Impulse army would do the heavy lifting up front, but auxiliary repercussions would also mount. Utilities would collapse. Key supply lines would be broken. The shipping industry would stall. Food and water shortages would follow. Man would turn on fellow man, each in it for the survival of himself rather than the species as a whole. This was how extinctions began.

There was a knock on the front door. Maya had been passing by with another round of laundry for packing, but she froze upon hearing the noise and looked at Jackson for guidance.

"Where are the girls?" he asked.

"In their rooms."

"And the baby?"

"Sleeping."

Jackson rolled his wheelchair to the living room closet and retrieved a pistol from a lockbox. He motioned for Maya to back away, then held the pistol at his side as he used his free hand to unlock, and then slowly open, the front door. Jackson had seen his fair share of crazy things today, but what he saw on his front porch was possibly the craziest of all.

"Hi, Jackson," Joseph said, flashing an uncertain smile.

"You're not here right now, Professor."

He shut the door, but before he could lock it, Frank pushed past Joseph and re-opened it. Jackson rotated his wheelchair to catch the corner of the door with his front wheel, preventing Frank from creating more than a four-inch gap.

"Hey! We're here to get your help!" Frank turned to Joseph. "I thought you said this guy was a friend."

"*Was* is the key word," Jackson said through the gap. "I'm not part of Project Impulse anymore, and I don't want anything to do with it or anyone associated with it."

Vincent tried to reason with him. "Mr. Jackson, you may not remember me—"

"Of course I do, Sheriff. But you're just as much a part of this as the professor. I need all of you off my property now."

Frank sighed. "I'm assuming you've been watching television. If so, then you know there's no avoiding Project Impulse at this point. Its army is coming for all of us. Sure, you can run, but you'll only last so long. Alternatively, you could help us, and maybe then you won't have to run."

Jackson considered his words, knowing there was more truth to them than he cared to admit. He passed his pistol to Maya and motioned for her to hide in a nearby room. Then he shifted his front wheel and opened the door wide once more. "You being here puts my family in danger, Professor."

Joseph nodded in acknowledgement, then countered, "And you not helping us puts them in even more danger. Please, Jackson. We don't need much of your time."

He flipped a mental coin, one side allowing Joseph and his ragtag team inside, the other slamming the door in their faces. But the toss was rigged, for Jackson was still a moral man, and he couldn't turn his back on those he stood to help. "Get in here before someone sees you."

———

Billy leaned across an overhead map of Jericho City and placed a red sticker dot. He, Gibbs, Captain Tipps, and a handful of trusted officers had convened in Frank's Bat Cave to get their heads wrapped around the siege of their city. They'd rolled out the oversized map, then gone through Jericho PD's report logs to trace the drone's progression since touching down. It had started on the southern edge of the city, initially attacking one of Jericho's most economically unstable neighborhoods. Then it had zigzagged between adjacent neighborhoods and commercial districts, slaughtering underprivileged communities in the former and devastating infrastructure in the latter. Next, it had hit the prison. A surviving guard there had estimated a seventy percent casualty rate of convicts and law enforcement officers alike. With no fortified walls or significant police presence left to keep them contained, the convicts who'd survived had fled into the city.

Yousef Kattan and his S.W.A.T. force had tried intercepting the drone shortly after that. They engaged in long-range combat, first firing on it with sniper rifles, then resorting to a shoulder-mounted rocket launcher. The drone took the sniper rounds like they were nothing but a nuisance, the gaping holes they left behind in its flesh instantly healing. Even the round that had landed in the drone's skull was shaken off after only a brief stumble. Whatever was controlling that thing, it wasn't its brain. Use of the rocket launcher, while a good idea in concept, turned out to be the worst decision the S.W.A.T. team could have made. They fired, expecting the projectile to obliterate their target, which hopefully would be too damaged to recover. Instead, the drone captured the rocket in mid-flight with a stream of energy particles, then diverted it into a nearby apartment complex, saving it the trouble of manually hunting down the residents inside.

After that, Captain Tipps issued a *no engagement* order across all units of Jericho PD. They were to observe and help where they could, but it was clear engaging the enemy would at best have no effect, and at worst put cops and innocent bystanders at risk. Yousef and his men continued tracking the drone from afar, providing most of the intel Billy was now using to populate the map. By Billy's estimate, the drone had already covered about a tenth of Jericho's inhabited space. Loss of life for the city alone was already in the five digits. And the physical carnage would take years to fix.

"How long do we have before it takes out the main power station?" Captain Tipps asked.

Billy studied the drone's path. "Maybe another two, three hours. Waste and sanitation won't be far behind that."

"And until it reaches the station?"

"Six hours at best." Billy pointed to Jericho PD on the map, then glided his hand to the residential, commercial, and industrial zones beyond. "And if it gets through us, there's nothing stopping it from taking down the rest of the city."

Captain Tipps chewed nervously on his lower lip. He'd already accepted engagement with the hostile was futile, but it was the only response he knew. "Then we make our stand here, away from the general populace. Send word to any officer still on the streets. They can help evacuate, but in four hours, I want them back in this station, suiting up for battle. Release anyone we have in the holding cells and dismiss all staff. Tell them to get somewhere safe, preferably outside of the city."

"What about Yousef?" Billy asked.

"His team sticks with the hostile. Tell him to provide regular updates and to let us know immediately if it deviates from its current attack pattern. Once the hostile reaches the station, they're free to resume engagement from out there while we hold our ground in here."

A radio voice summoned the attention of an officer in the room. He stepped out to respond.

"I hate to be the bearer of bad news," Gibbs said, "but there's something else we need to consider." He waited for the others to give him their attention. "We've got enough kevlar and munitions to go around, but we're not stocked for the type of prolonged and fully manned engagement this is probably going to take. We'll make our stand, Captain, but it's only going to last until our resources are depleted, which won't take long."

Captain Tipps rubbed his chin in thought. "Clean out the evidence lockers. I don't care if any of it's still under lock and key for an active case. That should give us at least one round of reloading."

"What about the local gun stores?" Billy asked. "Maybe we could use emergency powers to commandeer their inventory."

"And get shot trying," Captain Tipps said. "But it's a good idea. Don't commandeer anything. Tell them we'll buy any munitions they're willing to sell at double the price. Triple if needed. Have them provide itemized invoices the city will pay when this is over."

"They may be hesitant to let us walk off with their arsenal with only a promise to pay later."

"Then tell them they can come back to the station and fight this out alongside us. Pitch it as a way to protect their investment. I don't like the idea of putting citizens in harm's way, but these owners can take care of themselves, and we could use the bodies."

The officer who'd stepped out poked his head back into the room. "Sir?"

"What's going on?"

"We have an urgent situation upstairs."

The group followed him out of the Bat Cave and made their way to Jericho PD's lobby. While en route, the officer informed them that a mob had been spotted marching toward Jericho PD. It was at least thirty people, and some of them were armed. By the time Billy and the others reached the front doors, the mob was in visual range. Its members were sporting tattered prison uniforms, some bloody, and, as reported, there were assault rifles, knives, and blunt instruments such as crowbars and steel pipes disbursed among them. As if Jericho PD needed one more thing to deal with right now...

"Fan out!" Captain Tipps ordered the officers he'd stationed on door patrol. "If they take aggressive action, don't hesitate to wound or kill as needed!"

Despite the line of armed policemen now awaiting it, the mob showed no signs of slowing down. It drew within fifty yards. Then twenty. Billy hadn't drawn his own weapon, but now he felt himself getting itchy for protection. He saw Gibbs resting his hand on his holster, apparently feeling the same way. Ten yards. Now Captain Tipps had joined the itchy trigger finger brigade. He drew his pistol and aimed it at the mob member directly ahead.

"That's far enough!"

"Whoa!" a familiar voice shouted from the back of the crowd. "Stand down, Captain!"

Billy felt the edges of his lips curl upward involuntarily as he exchanged a surprised glance with his boss. Seconds later, Carter pushed through the front line of the mob, his hands up in a traditional *don't shoot me* pose.

"We come in peace," the former officer said.

Billy raced forward and embraced him in a friendly hug. "You don't know how good it is to see you. How have you been?"

Carter shrugged. "I've been surviving." Gibbs was at Billy's side now. He shook his former partner's hand, then embraced with an even tighter hug than Billy had given.

"It hasn't been the same around here without you."

"Yeah?" Carter said with a modest smile. "Well, I'm back, at least for now." He motioned to his mob. "These guys banded with me to escape the prison massacre. They were going to run, but I told them if they accompanied me here, maybe they could earn a little goodwill toward their sentences when this is over." He glanced past Billy and Gibbs. "What do you say, Captain?"

Understanding the gravity of the situation, Captain Tipps didn't hesitate. "Absolutely. Let's get everyone inside."

"And let's get you into a more appropriate outfit," Billy said as he slapped a hand on Carter's shoulder. "I'm sure we can find something that fits. Might even have your name still on it, too."

That turned Carter's modest smile into a full-fledged grin. He joined his former teammates as they all—convict and cop alike—marched into Jericho PD to make preparations for the fight of their lives.

———

Jackson wheeled himself to an open space to the side of his living room coffee table. He used the remote control to turn off the television, which was reporting on a new drone sighting, this one in the Middle East. Tensions in the region had already been high, and it looked as though the drone's arrival had tipped the scales of any existing truces or ceasefires out of alignment. When silence overtook the room, Jackson looked at his visitors, who had dispersed among the room's couch and available chairs.

"I'm not sure what you want from me, Professor. You and I got out of Project Impulse around the same time. There's little I'd know that you don't already know yourself."

Joseph cut to the chase. "We need to find Complex E. That's not information I was privy to."

Jackson scoffed. "You'd better look in imagination land. There is no Complex E. At least, there wasn't during my time with the project."

"Maybe they didn't call it Complex E," Frank suggested. "Was there another location they utilized that wouldn't have been disclosed to Professor Madison?"

Maya entered the room with a tray of ice-filled glasses and pitcher of tea.

Jackson eyed her as if she'd lost her mind. "What are you doing?"

"What's it look like? I'm offering our guests a drink."

"They won't be here long."

"And yet you invited them in," Maya said sharply. "What would your momma say if she knew you planned to let them go thirsty?"

Jackson huffed, but didn't argue. He knew his wife too well to bother with that. "You have until you finish your drinks," he said to his visitors. "Regardless of where this conversation goes, I want you out by then."

"Then let's not waste time," Frank suggested. "Back to my question..."

"Helix Unbound was Complex A," Jackson said before shifting his eyes to General Javez. "From what I saw on the news a year and a half ago, you already found Complex B, which, as far as I knew, wasn't even active during my time at Helix Unbound. To conserve resources, that was the last facility built from the ground up for Project Impulse." He looked at Joseph. "Waxhill was C. They were granted a decommissioned wing inside to manufacture Trizorapine. Complex D —" Jackson sighed. "Well... let's just say that shit show was over before it had even begun. It's under government control now."

"And Complex E?" Frank fished.

"Like I said, there was no Complex E. I'd heard rumors of Project Impulse gaining access to another decommissioned facility, but they were only rumors, and I never learned the location."

Joseph leaned forward. "Please, Jackson, if there's anything at all you can remember... this is our only hope of stopping what's going on out there."

"*Amanda* is your only hope of stopping what's going on out there," Jackson emphasized. No one responded to his claim, but he noticed an uncomfortable energy in the room, and that told him everything. "They've got her, don't they?"

Joseph nodded.

"Then we've already lost," Jackson said, his head dropping in defeat. "Look, I don't disagree with you that Project Impulse has found a new home out there. Call it Complex E or whatever name you want to give it. Colonel Davis called me from there a few days ago." Upon noticing Frank and General Javez reacting, he preempted, "You can't trace the call. Believe me, I've tried. He's made a habit of reaching out every so often, but he covers his tracks every time." They settled down, so Jackson continued. "Anyway, they've clearly got a new base of operations, and they've amassed the resources to launch this attack... your daughter included. But I honestly don't know where that base is. They either kept it extremely well hidden, or they activated it sometime after the destruction of Helix Unbound. Either way, I wasn't in the loop."

A baby's cries carried down from an upstairs room. Jackson asked Maya to attend to the child so he could wrap up with his visitors.

"Jackson," Joseph said, his voice bright with surprise, "you're a father again?"

Jackson smiled. "Guilty as charged."

"But I thought—" He cut his words short, not wanting to be offensive. But his eyes betrayed him as they traveled down to Jackson's paralyzed legs.

"Come on, Professor. You of all people know the miracles science is capable of. Things may not work well down there, but they work enough."

Joseph nodded. "Now I see why you don't want us here. You've always had a protective instinct about you. I'm sorry we put your family at risk."

He stood, indicating it was time to leave.

"Here's my number," Vincent said, passing Jackson a business card. "If you remember anything after we're gone, please call. If you can't reach me directly, call Eden PD. My son will make sure we get the message."

"I will."

They were about to exchange goodbyes, but an unexpected *thump* diverted their attention. Jackson's eyes shot upward, as if concerned the noise had come from the baby's room. But Vincent, Frank, and General Javez looked to the front door, each having triangulated the sound's origin to there. They drew their weapons.

"You don't have anyone else outside?" Jackson asked.

"Just our driver," General Javez replied. "But he wouldn't leave the car." He crept to a window overlooking Jackson's front yard and peered out. "I don't see anyone."

Frank signaled Vincent. "The back door."

Vincent stepped past Jackson's wheelchair and silently crossed the kitchen. He pressed against the wall beside a rear window, then scanned the backyard. "It's clear!"

Frank motioned for everyone else to stay put. Then he crept to the front door, gripped his gun tightly, and yanked it open, raising the weapon so it would be ready for anyone hiding there. But there was no one at the end of his gun barrel. Instead, there was a body at his feet, a body that had been resting against the front door and now tumbled into Jackson's foyer. It was alive, but just barely so. "Colonel Davis?"

The disgraced military leader looked up, and though it took a moment, it was obvious he had processed Frank's identity. "Fuck me..."

Frank grabbed him by the collar and dragged him clear of the front door, slamming it shut so no one could witness what he might do next.

"Take it easy!" General Javez yelled. "He's injured."

"I don't give a shit what he is," Frank said. "I'm going to beat the location of Complex E out of him or watch him die in screaming agony."

Colonel Davis struggled to speak. "I'm not—"

"What's that?" Frank asked.

"I'm not here to fight you, Detective." He rolled to the side, his eyes finding Jackson. "I'm here to see him."

Jackson wheeled forward, his gaze never leaving that of his former commander. He'd never seen Colonel Davis in such rough condition. His face was sporting fresh gashes and bruising. One eye was so puffy it was barely functional. One arm looked mangled beyond repair. An open wound in his torso was bleeding through layers of defensive padding. And his pants were splotched with blood, some dry, some still wet.

"I have nothing to say to you, Colonel."

"I know you don't," Colonel Davis responded. "You owe me nothing. I came... hoping you'd listen." He shifted his body weight as if he wanted to push himself up, but the pain held him back. "I got out, Jackson. I finally got out. I wish I'd done it sooner. I wish I'd left when you left. Maybe then we could have been friends. Maybe then..." He groaned loudly, a mixture of pain and regret that touched even Frank's heart. "I fucked up so badly. I should have never stayed with Project Impulse as long as I did." He looked from Frank to Vincent, and finally, to Joseph. "I'm sorry for my part in this. I never thought—"

"Never thought what?" Frank asked. "Never thought you'd be a victim of your psychotic scheme? You helped unleash an unstoppable army that's out there killing indiscriminately! Did you really think it would spare you?"

Colonel Davis shook his head. "It's not indiscriminate. It's the Trizorapine."

"We already know Thomas DeMarco helped seed the world with Trizorapine," Joseph said. "We know the Impulse army is using it to stay energized."

"Not just energized," Colonel Davis said before breaking into a bloody coughing fit. When it subsided, he explained, "It's their targeting mechanism. The Alpha child is too far away to issue granular commands. We needed something more rudimentary to guide the drones once in action. There might be some collateral damage, but they aren't killing everyone; just those who've been using."

His revelation took a minute to process. Once it did, Frank was the first to respond.

"What kind of bullshit elementary school world domination plan is that? You started a war... against the Earth's degenerates?" He shook his head in disbelief. "That's idiotic!"

Colonel Davis chuckled to the best of his mangled jaw's ability. "No. It's genius." His lungs tried to seize, but he fought off the attack. "What do you think's going to happen when this war ends? The world will be in chaos, and those who survive will be looking for guidance, a leader to see them out of the dark and back into the light. You've seen it yourself with lowlifes like Samuel Collins in Eden. The degenerates, the wicked, the sinners... they're the ones who will step in to seize the power vacuum. They're the competition for global control. By ensuring they don't survive the war, there won't be competition left. And then *he* can take charge. He'll lead the surviving population back to glory, then slowly manipulate it as he sees fit. He'll be a shepherd to the world's only remaining flock, a flock of white-coated sheep that won't even notice they're being tarnished until their wool is so black not even the strongest of moral bleaches can change it back."

General Javez glanced at Jackson for some sign that Colonel Davis might be in the middle of a complete mental breakdown. But Jackson had nothing to offer him, knowing all too well the darkness that empowered Project Impulse.

"I'm glad you got out when you did," Colonel Davis said to his former soldier. "Stay away from the fight, and don't challenge the status quo when it's over. Do that, and you'll be just fine."

"Just fine?" Vincent asked. "You mean we'll be sheep."

Colonel Davis shrugged. "Better to be a sheep than a cow for the slaughter."

Frank kneeled at his side. "Are you sure about that? Because by the looks of it, you chose the latter."

Colonel Davis didn't deny it. "Always the astute observer, aren't you, Detective Holmes?" He squeezed his eyes shut as he fended off a series of stabbing pains. Then he said, "This was my only way out. It's the only way out for anyone he's already gotten his hooks into. Those of us for whom there is no redemption." He shifted his gaze to Joseph. "That's something you're going to have to come to terms with, I'm afraid." He then moved to Vincent. "In more ways than one."

Vincent felt an uncomfortable chill, Colonel Davis's implications not lost on him.

"We're going to stop this," Frank said. "You want redemption? Do the right thing. Tell us where to find Complex E."

Colonel Davis stared at him with weakening eyes. "It's..." His voice trailed. "It's—"

Then a violent seizure gripped his body. Frank and General Javez tried to steady him, but Colonel Davis convulsed, his muscles twisting in unnatural ways and blood spewing from his mouth. As he grew still, he raised a single hand, then pointed a finger at Jackson, and then he was gone. Frank and General Javez let his body sink against the floor. The others remained quiet, disturbed by what they had heard, disturbed by what they had seen, and stewing on the hard truth that they were no closer to discovering Complex E's location than they had been prior to Colonel Davis's arrival.

Eventually, Frank broke the silence. "Why did he point at you?"

The others turned to Jackson.

"Why did he point at you?" Frank repeated. "He was going to tell us where to find Complex E. He couldn't speak, so he pointed at you. What haven't you told us?"

Jackson shook his head innocently. "Nothing. I don't know where Complex E is."

"You said Colonel Davis called you a few days ago," Vincent said. "Are you sure he didn't mention where he was? Or that he didn't say anything that would've given away his location?"

"I'm sure," Jackson said. "It was just his normal rantings about being alone and wanting someone he could trust back at his side. He felt like he was on an—" Jackson froze, realization spreading across his face. He corrected himself. "The colonel *said* he was on an island. I took it figuratively, given his mental state. I've never had reason to suspect..."

"That maybe he meant it literally," Frank said. "What island would he have been talking about?"

Jackson looked at Joseph, who needed no time to figure it out. "Sunrise Isle. But that doesn't make sense. There's an abandoned military compound there, but it's in shambles. It's in no condition to house the complicated machinery required by Complex E."

Jackson shook his head in disagreement. "The surface level compound isn't. But the underground compound could."

Now Jackson had General Javez's attention. "What underground compound?"

"The government built down into the island's core. At one time, the surface buildings and underground structure operated as a single entity. But it was expensive to maintain, and budget cuts eventually shut it down. The surface was lost to the elements, and the underground structure sat unused for years, though, theoretically, there's no reason it couldn't be reactivated. I assumed the government took back control of Sunrise Isle after Helix Unbound's destruction, but if it fell through the cracks…"

"Complex E has excessive energy requirements," General Javez shared. "Would this underground compound have that capability? Being offshore, I'd suspect it would be limited."

"It ran on geothermal power," Jackson said. "It's energy capabilities are essentially endless."

And there it was, all they needed to hear to isolate Sunrise Isle as Project Impulse's newest, most secretive, and ultimately, final home. General Javez pulled out his cell phone and moved toward the front door.

"I'll be in the car. I need to call Ms. Drexmore to make preliminary assault preparations."

Joseph motioned to Colonel Davis's body. "Jackson, what can we do to help—"

"Nothing," Jackson said. "The longer you stay, the longer you endanger the people I care about. I'm friends with the local police department. I'll make arrangements for them to give you space there so you can do whatever you need to do. They'll send someone to take care of the colonel."

"I really am sorry, Jackson. For what it's worth, we'll do our best to end this."

Jackson nodded, but said nothing. The others stepped around Colonel Davis's body and filed out, a solemn air about them despite their minor victory. When they were halfway down the sidewalk, Jackson hollered behind them.

"Hey, Professor?"

The scientist turned.

"Don't come back here until you do." He then clarified, "End it, I mean. Don't come back here until you end it."

Joseph nodded with assurance. "I won't."

CHAPTER 13
FALL OF HUMANITY

Amanda could feel the fear and pain flowing in like an endless stream. All forty-nine drones had reached their target destinations, and many of them had been on the attack for hours. The earliest hit cities now had casualties in excess of twenty-five thousand. The later hit cities were still under five thousand. Nonetheless, the total death toll was well over half a million people, and with all drones deployed, that number would increase at its fastest pace yet. Amanda had to stop it. She pushed through the sea of blackness, toward the mind she could never reach. There had to be a path forward. If the pain of her actions could reach her speck of consciousness, then she had to be able to reach back. She just needed to find the way.

The next wave of chemical shock hit her. It was fresh, and yet it wasn't totally new. With so much Trizorapine flowing through her system, Amanda's fractured psyche had begun anchoring moments into memories. She still wasn't recalling those of the past, but she was remembering the present, and she remembered at least two prior chemical shocks before this one. While that did nothing to dampen the shock's dazing effect on her, it did provide encouragement that she wasn't completely helpless. The shocks were there to feed her aggressive impulses, to suppress and possibly eliminate the portions of her being that didn't align with the monstrosity she had outwardly become. But at least three times now, they had failed. And they had probably failed countless times before that, times Amanda couldn't remember. She was surviving. Now she needed to figure out how to regain control.

Images of death and destruction flooded over her. She saw them, the drones, as they took life after life. Though there was little external bloodshed, Amanda couldn't avoid pictures of sliced arteries, torn open organs, shattered spines... the killing methods were so efficient. Body after body dropped lifelessly, each death piercing her with a guilt that didn't care whether she was being coerced. She needed more strength if she was going to push through the invisible barrier shielding her mind. She needed more of her essence back, more of who she was. She needed her memories. But they were in some other compartment of her subconscious. They weren't here with her, where she could grab them and pull them back inside. She concentrated, temporarily expelling the thoughts of death that plagued her and trying to remember happier times. For a moment, she saw something, a place perhaps, with a tall tower, sprawling neighborhoods, and an expansive young forest. Then, as quickly as it had come, it was gone. Amanda concentrated again, willing the memory forward, calling it toward her, into her, summoning it to merge with her very being. She thought she saw it again, but it was hazy, and before she could grasp it, the next chemical wave electrified her system, plunging her back into darkness. Then, the stream of fear and pain exploded into a raging river.

———

Officers at Eden PD were glued to whatever screens they could find. They were all watching the same breaking news alert, not about the drone attack sieging the planet, but about the nuclear bombs that had just detonated in the Middle East. No one knew who'd struck first, or even who the strikes had been targeted against, but there had been three explosions so far, and world leaders had warned more could follow. Derek had been on the phone with his dad when the alerts started coming in, and after a brief pause to catch the headline, they finished their conversation.

"What's the update?" Stacy asked as soon as he hung up.

"They've found Complex E. General Javez and that Drexmore woman are arranging resources while my dad and Detective Holmes work on assault plans." He looked at Victoria, who was standing nearby. "That Trizorapine you guys have been tracking? Apparently, it's the targeting mechanism for those drones. They'll kill anyone that has it in their system."

"I'll get in touch with my contacts in Washington and spread the word," Victoria said. "If we can disseminate the knowledge quickly enough, maybe we can save lives."

Derek nodded in agreement, then turned back to Stacy as Victoria stepped away with her phone in hand. Stacy looked worried, even more worried than before. In fact, she looked downright scared.

"What's the matter?"

She opened her purse and removed the baggie of Mark's drugs. Derek felt his heart sink.

"Stacy... not you..."

She shook her head. "No, not me. With everything going on, I forgot to show this to you. That day I met a friend for lunch—"

"It didn't go so well," Derek said. "I saw the greasy handprint on your shirt and the blocked number in your phone. I was going to ask you about it, but then all this started happening."

"It was Mark. I met with Mark. He seemed like he needed a friend to talk to, but all he wanted was..." She shivered, not wanting to think about it. "Anyway, he ran off in the middle of our conversation and dropped this on the way out. He's using, Derek, which means he's a target for those things."

Derek scowled as he looked away. Why was it always Mark that caused tension between the two of them? If Derek was a worse person, he'd let the drones have their way with his rival. But he wasn't that person. "I'll send a patrolman to pick him up and bring him back here. That way, if one of those things heads this way, we can protect him."

"You know he won't let a random patrolman bring him in," Stacy said. "I'll go. I'll convince him to come back here."

"I don't want you out of my sight."

"Those things haven't been spotted in Eden. It's still safe out there. It'll take me an hour, tops, and then I'll be back to play Lois Lane to your Superman."

Derek didn't like it, but he knew Stacy was right. "Fine. But if you aren't back in an hour, or one of those things shows in Eden before then, I'm coming after you."

She planted a kiss on him. "Always my knight in shining armor."

Then she took off. Derek watched her leave, then stared at the baggie of drugs now in his hand, contemplating what to do. Rank-wise, he had little authority in Eden PD. But knowledge-wise, he was best equipped to manage the situation.

"Hey!" Diana yelled as he grabbed her desk and pushed it into the middle of Eden PD's lobby, spilling paperwork and office supplies in a trail behind him.

Derek climbed on top of the desk, waved his arms, and shouted, "Listen up!" He waited as conversations slowly died down and all eyes turned toward him. "I know I'm just a rookie, but you know I've been fielding information from my dad since this crisis began. He's on the front line right now, working with Detective Holmes and government representatives to end this war." Derek held up the baggie for all to see. "He just informed me that *this* is what those drones are using as their targeting system. This poison that's infiltrated our streets, our homes, our friends and family... this is what's guiding them. This is what they're after. And that means it's only a matter of time until they come here." He could see nervous shifting in the crowd. "We can't wait until they arrive to get prepared. We need to act proactively, come up with our own defensive plan under the assumption that they *will*, not might, attack Eden. And it starts with isolating the very thing they're after." Derek looked at Diana. "What's the most central point in the building?"

She thought for a moment. "That would be the holding cells."

He turned back to his captive audience. "Scour the building. Find every trace of this stuff that might be around. Evidence room, locker room, private offices, any nook and cranny where it could be hidden. Let's get it in a lockbox and move it to holding." Derek took an unsteady breath. "Now comes the hard part. And it requires complete honesty. Please trust me when I say there won't be any judgment, any consequences, any reason at all not to come forward. We just want to keep people safe." He took another broken breath, then came out with it. "If you've used, even the slightest bit, in the past few months, raise your hand."

Nothing. No one responded with even the smallest movement.

"Come on guys," Derek said. "I know we pride ourselves on our ethics here, but no police station is that clean. This is a matter of life and death. We need to see those hands."

This time, some officers glanced at others, but again, no one confessed. Derek sighed in defeat. He started to climb down from Diana's desk, sensing that he had pushed the limit of authority he didn't have to begin with, when a single hand rose from the crowd. There were a few gasps, and some frowns, but Derek smiled, thankful that someone had come forward. He stood upright and spotted the face that went with the hand. It was a fourth-year patrolman named Eddie. He stepped forward from the crowd, then approached Derek, his hand still held up high.

"I don't want to die," he said.

Derek nodded. "I know. We're going to protect you."

Another hand rose in the crowd. Then another. The confession spout was wide open now, as those too afraid to admit their wrongdoings put life above embarrassment. By the time the hands quit raising, there were fourteen in total.

"These are your fellow officers," Derek said to those who hadn't raised their hands. "They've gone on patrol with you, laughed with you, mourned with you. They're the same people today that they were yesterday, and they need our help." He scanned his eyes over those who'd come forward. "Let's get you to holding also. Work with Diana to reinforce any entryways, erect barriers, whatever it takes to put more obstacles between you and one of those things should it get into this building." Derek shifted his gaze again. "The rest of you, scour the building, then gather whatever firepower we have here in the lobby. If we still have time after that, we can hit the streets and try to bring in others who might need our help. Any questions?"

He half expected someone to question who'd put a rookie like him in charge. But no one challenged him, and a few minutes later, the entire force of Eden PD was executing his commands.

———

"Give it another try!" the convict on his back underneath the generator rack yelled.

Night had settled over Jericho. With the main power station down, there wasn't enough juice to keep the entire city running. Auxiliary stations were pumping what they could, but to prevent overloads, they were cycling rolling blackouts to each region in ninety-minute intervals. Jericho PD had been in a blackout for a little over forty minutes. It had its own backup generator array, but the system was old and rarely used, and this had been the third time it had choked tonight. Billy guided the officer manning the activation panel by flashlight. He reset a couple of switches, dialed down the generator load, and flipped its primary breaker. Nothing.

"Shit," the assisting convict said. "Hang on."

Gibbs was on the floor providing him light as he clanged metal tools against rusted nuts, bolts, and connection wires. Carter, now donning one of his old police uniforms, popped into the room to let Billy and Gibbs know that all deployed units had returned to the station, and that body armor and weapons had been fully distributed. They were still working on assigning strategic placements around the building, but it wouldn't be much longer until that was complete, either. Surprisingly, spirits were high, but that wouldn't last if they couldn't get the lights back on, because every person in that building knew fighting in the dark put them at an overwhelming disadvantage.

"Okay, try again."

The officer at the activation panel repeated his previous routine. This time, the generator array chugged and sputtered like a dying truck engine. The convict whacked something underneath with his wrench, and the system turned over, growling ferociously as it pushed electricity through the walls of Jericho PD and returned light to the building.

"Awesome job!" Gibbs said as he gave their mechanic a hand getting up.

"Yeah, but this thing isn't very stable. We need to go around the building and unplug anything we don't need. Keep the electrical load as light as possible."

"I'll get some men on it," Carter said.

Billy liked seeing him back in *take charge* mode. It reminded him of the good old days when Carter was a core member of his team. He returned upstairs with the others, where they found most of Jericho PD's defensive force assembled in the lobby. Officers who'd already been on duty were still in their uniforms. Those who'd been called in hadn't bothered changing out of street clothes. Convicts whose prison garb had been shredded or heavily stained during their escape had been fished casual wear from storage, the evidence room, and even officers' personal lockers. Those who had made it out of prison in a cleaner state continued wearing their prison outfits proudly. Also exuding pride was the conglomerate of seven gun shop owners who had banded together to supply arms in Jericho PD's time of need. They'd taken the offer to fight side-by-side with their law enforcement officers, some to ensure they got paid at the end of the day, and others because they felt a sense of duty to the cause.

"Billy, come in." It was Yousef's voice on his radio, and it sounded urgent.

Billy whistled for everyone in the lobby to quiet down. "Go ahead, Yousef."

"That thing just deviated from its course. It's headed straight for you."

His words sucked the excitement out of the building.

"Do you have an ETA?" Billy asked.

"It's hard to say. Five, maybe seven minutes at most."

Captain Tipps wasn't going to waste a second of it. Wearing ballistic gear that hadn't touched his body since his sergeant days, and carrying an assault rifle almost as big as him, he stood at the top of the main staircase and addressed all those before him. "Okay, listen up! I'm sure you've all been tracking the news in your downtime. There's a lot of terrible stuff happening in the world, but right now, we need to focus on our own problems here." He glanced at nearby officers. "Some of us in this building have sworn to uphold the law." He shifted his eyes to a group of convicts. "Some of us have chosen to defy it." He then looked to the gun shop conglomerate. "Some are here out of the goodness of their hearts. Others are here for money." Captain Tipps shook his head. "None of that matters now. Because, regardless of our motivations, we are *all* citizens of Jericho. It's our differences that make this city what it is. And I wouldn't have it any other way." He looked at Billy, who nodded in support. "That thing is coming. Those of you who are users—you know who you are—make no mistake, it's coming to kill you. You've all been given assignments. If you aren't already paired with a non-user who can help protect you, find someone to swap with. We won't leave anyone hanging out to dry. As for the rest of you, do what Jericho PD does best: protect and serve." Captain Tipps paused and closed his eyes, as if gathering strength for what he needed to say next. "I wish I could end this speech with some sort of rousing promise that we'll come out of this thing victorious. But that would be a lie. The truth is, I don't know if we'll survive the night. We're up against an enemy with abilities beyond anything we've ever encountered before. But remember this: if that thing walks away from here in one piece, it will take down the rest of Jericho before it's done. Most of us have loved ones out there in the city. All of us have at least a friend or two. No matter what happens, this fight is for them."

Captain Tipps clicked his feet together and raised a hand in salute to those under his command. His officers responded in kind, as did the gun shop owners, and even the convicts. They were a unified force, citizens of Jericho, and they were ready.

———

Death. The visions overwhelmed Amanda's speck of consciousness. She tried to push them away, but they were coming too quickly. Forty-nine separate streams. Forty-nine feeds of innocence being slaughtered. Forty-nine extensions of the mind she couldn't control, the mind doing someone else's bidding despite her desires for it to stop. Another chemical shockwave hit her. They were so frequent that she was almost becoming numb to them. And yet, she could feel they were wearing her down. She had told herself she wouldn't give up. She had kept pushing against the invisible barrier blocking access to her mind and body. She had even tried again and again to recall the memory of that place that had tried to come back to her. But Amanda could sense she was losing the fight. The chemical and visual assault was winning. The darkness was slowly taking her. She didn't have the energy to break the wall to her mind. She would never regain control. But she didn't know how to quit either, even when aware that refusing to quit would ultimately lead to her demise.

A new vision broke through. It was a police station, nestled in the heart of a city, its lights unstable and dim among the night. A drone was advancing on it with unwavering purpose, and though those inside were afraid, they weren't running. They knew what they were up against. They knew the chances of survival were slim. But they were fighting back anyway. Amanda felt her mind order the drone forward. At least a third of those in the building had been targeted for elimination. And given the stand they were making, most of the others would die trying to protect them. Amanda needed to give them a fighting chance. She couldn't let such courage, such nobility, that which represented the good of mankind, be wiped from the planet like a bug from a windshield. Amanda gathered what strength she had left and pushed again. She pushed away from the darkness, into the invisible barrier, reaching out to a mind that didn't even know she still existed...

She pushed for Jericho. She pushed to save humanity.

————

The drone was fifty yards away when the first sniper shot rang out from Jericho PD. It took the bullet in the chest, then let the wound heal as it continued its procession. Yousef's team took the second shot from behind, nailing the drone in the back of a kneecap. Losing support for its body weight, the drone fell to the ground, where third and fourth sniper rounds clipped its shoulder and skull. A wave of assault rifle fire came next. Still healing from its first round of wounds, the drone formed a shield of energy particles to deflect the wave. While distracted, Yousef's team lobbed three grenades at its feet. The drone saw them, but not in time to fully deflect their blasts. Its body was ripped apart, its head, chest, and a single arm staying together and landing with a dull thud over ten feet away. Its other arm flopped in the opposite direction, and everything from the torso down was flung outward as chunks of tattered flesh and bone.

"Advance!" Captain Tipps yelled.

The barrage of assault rifle fire focused on the largest chunk of the drone as a line of Jericho PD's defenses marched forward. Yousef's men targeted their shots on the next largest pieces of flesh scattered about. Yousef himself prepared another grenade, which he tossed next to the loose arm. He assumed the arm was helpless, given it had been separated from the main body, but then he watched with surprise as it dissolved into a cluster of blue energy particles, wrapped around the grenade, and absorbed its concussive blast in a constrained ball of fire. The swarm of energy appeared momentarily stunned, but its physical shock wore off quicker than Yousef's mental shock, and before he could levy another attack, the particles were on the move. They darted toward the line of advancing officers, then through each of their bodies in such speedy succession that the last one already had his vital organs slashed before the first fell to the ground.

No longer defending against an incoming wave of assault rifle fire, the drone's main body dematerialized and joined its arm particles. They went after the S.W.A.T. team next. Yousef ordered his men to run, but it was too late. The particles reached them before they'd taken more than a couple of steps, and one by one, their lifeless bodies collapsed in place. Yousef was the last alive. Determined not to go down without a fight, he unholstered his sidearm and unloaded into the swarm of energy particles. But his bullets did nothing. The next thing he knew, he felt a searing heat as the particles charged into his body. He then felt an impossible entanglement of warmth and cold as half his nerves severed from his spine. Then he felt nothing, and he was gone.

Captain Tipps watched from the doorway of Jericho PD as the swarm of energy particles flew low to the ground, collecting its dispersion of flesh and bone. When it was done, it coalesced in the street, now just thirty feet away, and reformed the naked drone body that had first approached the building. It sported visible wounds upon its initial materialization, but then even those repaired themselves, leaving the drone in pristine condition once more.

"Everyone, fall back inside," Captain Tipps ordered.

Only a handful of Jericho's forces had seen what had occurred outside, yet the somber tone in the lobby revealed those inside weren't oblivious to the loss they'd just taken. Captain Tipps ordered a group of men on standby to barricade the front door. Then he ordered them and everyone else to back away and take up tiered positions across Jericho PD's multiple levels.

"What's the plan, Captain?" Billy asked.

"We can't fight that thing in waves. We need to overwhelm it." He addressed the larger crowd. "When it comes through the door, I want everyone to give it everything they've got! Hold nothing back. If you run out of bullets, grab another magazine. If you run out of spares, grab another weapon altogether. If you have explosives, use them. We're only going to get one shot at this."

As if listening for its cue, the drone's electrical hum rose outside the front door. The lobby was filled with frantic scrambling as those inside readied their weapons and steadied their positions. The front door shimmered with blue energy. Then it blew open, breaking apart the barricade that was no match for the drone's abilities. The creature stood unafraid before its opposing army.

"Fire!" Captain Tipps yelled.

And then Jericho PD lit up like the Fourth of July. Billy saw the drone writhe backwards as the first round of bullets landed. It took no time at all for its entire front side to become a bloody, stringy mess, so many bullets piercing its flesh that there was overlap on every inch of its body. Then an energy shield appeared, and while it blocked most of the incoming fire, some projectiles were getting through, the first sign that the drone was weakening. Muzzle flashes left spots in Billy's vision. Smokey discharge filled the contained space. Some weapons clicked as they hit the end of their clips. Others kept firing. A grenade exploded near the entrance. Then another. Billy heard new clips snap into place and their weapons resume firing as another round ran dry. But the drone hadn't advanced.

Through the smoke and reflective flashes, Billy thought he saw a handful of energy particles break away from their target's mass. The particles dispersed into the lobby walls, and moments later, the overhead lighting grew extra bright, almost as if supercharged. It was then that Billy realized what the drone was doing. An explosion rumbled through the floor beneath his feet as the basement generator overloaded, plunging Jericho PD back into darkness. The sudden cessation of lighting spurred a brief hesitation in those firing upon the drone, and that was the only window it needed to launch its counterattack.

Multiple streams of bright energy particles zipped through the otherwise pitch-black lobby. Gunfire resumed, but it was erratic, and interspersed with screaming and the sound of heavy weapons falling to the floor. Billy ducked as one stream of particles shot over his head. A handful of men behind him fired upon the stream, but it took them out in a single swoop through their bodies. A flashlight beam caught Billy's attention. It was Captain Tipps, who was trying to wrap his head around the chaos so he could issue new commands. Billy crawled toward him, but before he neared, a live grenade rolled to a stop at his captain's foot. It detonated, taking out Captain Tipps and everyone in his immediate vicinity.

More detonations rang out. The gunfire was so erratic that Billy couldn't be certain who was doing more damage to Jericho PD's forces: the drone or themselves. A fire broke out at one end of the lobby. Blue energy particles zipped around like wasps erupting from a fallen nest. And bodies fell. So many bodies, one by one collapsing as Jericho's only resistance faltered.

"Billy!" Gibbs yelled.

Billy spotted him crouched behind a desk. He was still fighting back, taking occasional shots at the energy particles as they whizzed by. Maybe if they could team up, they could find Carter and anyone else still alive and get to safety. Billy took a few shots at an energy stream that had been headed in Gibbs's direction. The stream pivoted away, and Gibbs tossed Billy an appreciative smile. Then that smile jolted as a second stream neither had seen coming pierced his brain, stealing away his life before fleeing out the side of his head.

"No!" Billy yelled.

Gibbs's body joined the others on the floor around it. Billy screamed into the ground, a bleak realization coming over him: no one was going to make it out of Jericho PD alive. The best they could do now was go down fighting. He took several rapid breaths, psyching himself up for what he knew needed to be done. He then slammed a fresh clip into his gun, scanned for the nearest particle swarm, then stood and opened fire. He didn't know if it would do anything. Given how things were playing out, he suspected it most likely wouldn't. But this was the only move he or anyone else in Jericho PD had. Individual swarm particles were knocked out of alignment as his bullets nailed them. The swarm turned toward its attacker in response, then charged just as Billy's clip emptied. He knew he couldn't replace it in time, so he ducked just as the swarm tried to take off his head. Billy then spun to track his enemy. Only instead of the swarm, he saw the face of Officer Steven Keller, a promising young man he'd worked with frequently. The officer now stood lifeless before him, having taken the swarm's impact. He was also holding a live grenade, a grenade that slipped from his now limp grip and bounced off the floor.

Billy tried to run, but he was too close. The grenade detonated, its concussive blast slamming into his backside and throwing him across the room. He landed on his side, the smell of his own burnt flesh filling his nostrils. Through blurry and quickly darkening vision, Billy saw the swarm attack continuing. Jericho PD's forces were down to maybe a quarter of where they had started, and the drone was still going strong, with no signs of stopping. Captain Tipps had warned everyone they might not survive the night. No one had imagined they wouldn't even survive ten minutes. Billy reached for his phone with an unsteady and partially crippled hand. He needed to tell Frank what had happened. He needed to warn his partner what they were up against. But he couldn't read the phone's screen, nor press its buttons. And before he could do anything else, the unescapable hand of unconsciousness took hold of him, and all went dark.

CHAPTER 14
CONVERGENCE

Amanda's last remaining essence sank into the black void. She'd failed to save Jericho. And while she was spending every ounce of energy on that futile endeavor, the defensive forces of at least seven other major cities had also fallen. She didn't understand why someone would desire so much death and destruction. She didn't know why she had been chosen as the vessel of their destruction, either. But Amanda did know she was a prisoner. She was a prisoner of her own mind, a mind manipulated by whoever was behind the worldwide carnage. She'd given everything she had left to take back control of her actions, but she saw now that would never happen. Control was gone. She was nothing more than an observer to the devastating acts carried out by her mind and body. She could do nothing to oppose them.

But what if she could influence them? What if, instead of fighting so hard to stop herself from raining destruction upon the world, she embraced her role? Would her mind accept her back then? Amanda felt a magnetic pull, almost as if it had heard her subconscious thoughts and was opening a channel through which they could connect. It had to be genuine, Amanda knew. Her mind would see if it wasn't and send her back to these depths of nonexistence if not. But how could Amanda genuinely accept a role in the death and destruction she so vehemently opposed? Unless...

She fed off the magnetic energy of her mind and redirected it toward the vault of memories locked deep within her. Her mind pulled back, sensing deception, but Amanda assured it she had a plan, and that plan still involved death, still involved destruction, still served the purpose for which her body and mind had been commandeered. She knew she wouldn't get much leeway, so she latched on to the first memory that emerged, that of the city she didn't know, but which felt so familiar. She drew it into her, and then she felt its name, the name of the place she called home.

Amanda thanked her mind for allowing her to retrieve the memory. Then she gave herself willingly to it, no longer fighting a battle she'd accepted she couldn't win. Her essence was pulled through the invisible barrier, into the storm of chemicals and electricity that fueled her brain. Her senses were consumed by the visual directives being fed into her, and she openly saw the forty-nine extensions of herself spreading chaos across the globe. They were her, and she was them. She had no choice but to continue the attack. The ability to prevent death and destruction was beyond her now. But maybe, just maybe, she could use that death and destruction to humanity's advantage. She felt her connection to the drones strengthen as she accepted the hand fate had dealt her, then concentrated on the one memory she still had of her former self.

Eden...

————

Frank, Vincent, and Joseph were seated in a conference room that had been generously offered by Jackson's friends at the local police station. Joining them via remote video feed was a team of Navy SEALs assembled by Alison Drexmore and currently in transit to Joint Base Charleston, a military outpost shared by the United States Air Force and Navy. General Javez had hooked a government-issued tablet into the room's projector and was displaying a recent satellite image of Sunrise Isle on a pull-down screen. He circled his hand around a section of the island through which square structures appeared to be masked by trees.

"This is the location of the decommissioned surface compound. It's hard to see much detail here, but there's no indication it's been reactivated. It does, however, serve as the entry point to our primary target directly beneath it." General Javez switched the projected view to a cross-section of the facility that had been repurposed as Complex E. "Unfortunately, the only records we have of the underground structure are these diagrams from its initial construction. It may have been modified since then, but we'll have to operate under the assumption that the core layout has remained relatively unchanged." He pointed to an angled line running from ground level to a branching substructure. "This is the entry shaft. As you can see, it's not ideal, leaving no option for coordinated approaches from multiple angles, cover fire, or even a dispersed offensive." He moved his hand to the first level of the substructure. "If we can at least make it here, then our options open up a little more. There are multiple interconnected hallways to use for triangulated approaches and side rooms to use as cover if needed." General Javez slid his hand to an enormous cavity that hung to one side of the underground compound. "This is our destination. Based on all the evidence we've gathered, it's the only room in the compound large enough to host the hub and spoke device we know is central to Project Impulse's plans. Our primary goal is to destroy the device, which will hopefully sever the link to the drones and end the worldwide attack."

"What about that antechamber just before the target room?" SEAL Team Leader Simmons asked from the laptop hosting their video feed. "That design suggests some sort of control room."

"Yes," General Javez agreed. "We came to that same conclusion."

"Could we take it out instead? If the goal is to sever the link to the drones, it would be a hell of a lot easier to blow the computer system running the show instead of the massive hardware it operates."

Joseph looked nervously at General Javez. Clearly, these Navy SEALs hadn't been fully briefed yet.

"We have reason to believe the computer system isn't running the show," General Javez said. "There's a separate... *device* inside the hub and spoke core."

Simmons updated his question. "So we should skip the control room and focus on destroying the hub and spoke core instead? Take it out, the rest of the device fails. Is that the idea?"

General Javez hesitated.

"If I could be blunt, General," Simmons said, "I feel like we're a little in the dark over here. And I don't send my men into hostile territory on partial information. If you want our help, spill it. We need to know everything we might face over there."

Joseph appreciated General Javez's attempt to keep Amanda's role in Project Impulse out of the conversation, but it wasn't going to fly. "There's a genetically enhanced person in the machine's core. She's the one controlling the drones."

Simmons took a moment to process. "And you didn't want to tell us this because—"

"She's my daughter," Joseph said. "Our daughter, really," he corrected, motioning to Vincent. "I created her. He raised her. She's not controlling the drones willingly. She's an innocent, caught in this web like the rest of us."

He was trying to hide his worry, but Simmons was trained to notice non-verbal cues. "I appreciate your candor, Professor. Can I ask you to entertain some of my own?"

Joseph nodded.

There was really no way to sugarcoat the question that followed. "If we kill your daughter, will the attacks stop?"

Joseph couldn't speak, so he nodded again.

"And are you confident that destroying the hub and spoke device will yield the same result, only sparing your daughter's life?"

This time, Joseph's nod was more hopeful.

"Will your daughter let us destroy it, or will she put up a counteroffensive?"

"I honestly don't know," Joseph said.

Simmons grew quiet, his mind churning over the possibilities. Then he said, "I don't normally allow inherent conflicts of interest anywhere near my missions. They aren't predictable. They don't conform to standard probability analysis. But we're a small group, and we need all the manpower and brainpower we can get. So let's table this discussion for the moment. General Javez, tell us about any other resistance we might encounter, besides the professor's daughter."

He switched the projected image to a wider satellite view of Sunrise Isle. A ring of blue dots appeared on the ocean surrounding it. "The primary deterrent is a fully enclosed circle of sonic barriers manufactured by Cannes International. They were prototypes, installed long before the company perfected the technology. They operate at surface level and higher only, leaving the island susceptible to underwater approaches. Their height is also limited, meaning we can fly over them, but doing so will trigger the island's radar system." A two-dimensional icon of a satellite dish appeared over the surface compound. "There used to be gun turret towers along the coast that would respond to any radar incursions." Red dots representing the turret locations appeared. "But reconnaissance imagery shows that all but one have fallen into disarray, and we can easily avoid the one that hasn't." The red dots disappeared. "Other than feet on the ground, that's the only manmade resistance you can expect."

The general's choice of words wasn't lost on Simmons. "Manmade?"

"Yes," General Javez said a with heavy breath. "Professor Madison's genetically enhanced daughter? This island was used as... I guess you could say it was a sort of Petri dish for the prototype chemicals that would one day fuel his work. As a result, nature itself has become a hostile predator willing to defend its territory by any means necessary. We can avoid the sonic barriers, but we'll have little choice but to plow our way through whatever plant and animal life gets in our way."

"What will that entail, exactly?"

General Javez's response was blunt. "Firepower. Lots of firepower."

Simmons muted his audio and conferred with the other Navy SEALs on the call. Everyone in the conference room waited with tense anticipation, Joseph the most tense of them all, well aware that no one here but he and Vincent had Amanda's best interest in mind.

"Okay," Simmons said after unmuting. "Here's our suggestion. We split into two teams: an infiltration team and, for lack of a better word, a decoy team. The infiltration team will approach by helicopter from the southwest, stop outside of radar range, and scuba underneath the sonic barrier. They'll use assistive tech to swim for the nearest beach, then hike to the underground facility, and blast their way in. Their primary mission will be to destroy the hub and spoke device. If that mission fails, or if she forces the team's hand, they'll fall back to eliminating the genetically enhanced girl at its core."

Joseph looked away. He wanted to argue, but he already knew this was the best he could hope for.

"And the decoy team?" General Javez asked.

"They'll approach by helicopter from the northwest and fly over the sonic barrier, intentionally tripping the radar system. They'll land on the coast and proceed toward the underground compound, giving the appearance of an assault mission. With any luck, Complex E will send whatever remaining defensive forces it has to intercept the decoy team, leaving the base vulnerable when the infiltration team arrives. In the unlikely event that Complex E doesn't put up a fight on the island surface, both teams will work together to infiltrate the underground facility."

General Javez nodded in approval. "I guess the only question now is who joins what team."

"Both teams need to present a credible threat," Simmons said. "As far as my men go, we're all equally skilled. As SEAL Team Leader, I'll be on the infiltration team." He pointed to two others in transit with him. "Operator Garrett and Special Warfare Operator Brandt will join me." He then pointed to the remaining two Navy SEALs. "The decoy team will be led by Troop Commander Elliott and Operator Novak. Regarding your side, I'd like Detective Holmes to join the infiltration team."

Frank wouldn't have it any other way, so he nodded.

Simmons was about to continue with his preferences, but Vincent didn't want his position dictated, especially since he could guess which group Joseph would be allocated to, so he spoke up first. "I'd like to go with Frank and the infiltration team. We have experience working together. Where one of us lacks, the other makes up for it." He looked to Frank for support, but all he saw was an apologetic stare. "What?"

"You can't be on the infiltration team," Frank said, figuring the news would come better from him than Simmons. He looked at Joseph. "Neither of you can."

Vincent seethed at the personal betrayal. "You're treating us like we'll compromise the mission because of our attachment to Shortcake. But you know us better than that. Sure, if we see an opportunity to save her, we'll take it. Hell, we're going to be looking for it. But we also know the world comes first. We wouldn't do anything to sabotage that."

Frank frowned. "You're lying to yourself, Sheriff."

"Bullshit."

Frank swallowed hard, not wanting to hurt his friends this way, but knowing full well it was necessary. "Let me ask you something, Professor. If we instructed you to head to the local university or hospital and to cook up a weaponized batch of your counteragent, would you do it?"

Joseph avoided his gaze. "I mean... I don't think it would stop the drones. They're vessels of consumption. They'd drain enough Trizorapine from their victims to negate the counteragent before it could disable their Omega Genomes."

"You know I'm not talking about the drones," Frank said bluntly. "So, would you do it? Would you go right now and make a round of counteragent for us?" Without giving Joseph a chance to answer, he then pivoted. "Better yet: if you were part of the infiltration team, and there was absolutely no way to shut down that hub and spoke device, would you jab a counteragent needle into your daughter's neck to save the world? Knowing it would shut down her abilities? Knowing it would wipe every last memory she had of you from existence? Knowing it would essentially kill her, even if her body remained alive?"

Joseph's lips quivered below watery eyes. "Fuck you."

"And what about you, Sheriff?" Frank said, redirecting his attack. "If we get down in that facility, and I'm forced to put a gun to your daughter's head because it's a matter of her life or the lives of everyone else on the planet, will you stand idly by while I pull the trigger?"

Vincent didn't vocalize his anger, but it was written all over his face.

"Exactly," Frank continued. "The reason you two can't be on the infiltration team is because you still think that's Amanda in Complex E. But she said it herself before she took on Project Impulse. She's dead. That's the Alpha child controlling those drones. That's the enemy. And no one blind to that fact can be trusted to see this mission through."

Simmons waited a moment to let the air settle before speaking again. "Professor Madison and Sheriff Desmond will be on the decoy team. If they see an opportunity to save their daughter, Elliott and Novak will provide support. But *only* if it doesn't interfere with the infiltration team's mission." He paused, ensuring the matter had been put to rest. When no one argued, he continued,

"General Javez, my preference would be to have you on the infiltration team as well, but as I said before, both teams need to present a credible threat. Detective Holmes is a loner-type. His absence from the decoy squad can be overlooked. But no presence from Senator Riley's camp will raise suspicion. Therefore, I need you on the decoy team as well. You can help keep the others safe and hopefully get them back off the island in one piece."

"Speaking of getting off," Frank said, "what's the plan for the infiltration team once the mission is complete? I assume whatever submersible tech we take to the island won't have enough juice to get us back to the mainland when we're done."

"A pilot will hold the helicopter outside of the sonic barriers. When it's time for retrieval, the infiltration team will send up a flare, and the pilot will fly in for pickup. We'll trigger radar, but by then, it should be irrelevant." Simmons's eyes shifted across the video feed, as if he was scanning the faces of those in the conference room. "Are there any other questions?" There were none. "In that case, we'll see you at Joint Base Charleston. We should be ready to leave by dawn."

With that, Simmons disconnected the feed. Joseph immediately stood and stormed for the door.

"Professor—" Frank called after him.

But Joseph ignored him and left, slamming the door behind him. Frank sighed heavily.

"I'll leave you two to talk for a moment," General Javez said.

He followed behind Joseph, closing the door more gently, and leaving Frank and Vincent staring silently at each other, one still hurt, and the other struggling with regret.

"Sheriff—" Frank started.

Vincent held up a halting hand. "You don't need to say anything else. You're not wrong, Frank. I wouldn't let you pull the trigger any more than Professor Madison could push the plunger. We would endanger the infiltration mission. It's just hard... to sit back, knowing that your little girl..." He couldn't finish.

"I'm not going there intending to kill her," Frank assured him. "I'm going to stop Project Impulse, to put an end to this global assault. If I can do that without harming your daughter, please believe I will."

"I know," Vincent said. "And we'll give you the best opportunity we can."

Frank smiled sadly and extended a hand. Vincent stared at it for a moment, then shook it, reinforcing their brotherly bond while they still had this moment to do so. For soon they would head their separate ways, with connected but diverging missions, and whether they would return, or whether their bond would withstand the outcomes of those missions, was anybody's guess.

"This just in," a female reporter's voice announced from multiple televisions tuned to the same station inside Eden PD. *"Reports from multiple cities are claiming the attacking creatures have retreated. We're still awaiting official confirmation, but social media posts from around the globe seem to be corroborating the rumor."* The reporter paused and put a hand to her ear. *"Ladies and gentlemen, I've just been informed that we now have video evidence of the retreat. This comes from Sydney, Australia, which has already seen significant devastation to its HMAS Kuttabul naval base and commercial sectors. Please be advised that some of what you see may be disturbing."*

The broadcast flipped to footage recorded from what appeared to be either a traffic camera or exterior business security camera. It was already the next afternoon in Sydney, but instead of locals and tourists going about their normal Monday routines, panic filled the streets. People were running scared, trampling over each other to escape something unseen. A body flew through the air and landed motionless on the pavement. A drone appeared around a corner, its arm a whip of blue energy that it snapped at the fleeing crowd, picking off those with Trizorapine in their systems as if they were bugs to be swatted. Then, without warning, the drone stopped, and the rest of the people in its vicinity fled without further harm. Its energized whip arm expanded across its chest, down its torso and legs, and up its neck. The drone fully dematerialized, then, after floating in place for a few seconds, shot into the sky and disappeared. The broadcast switched back to the news studio.

"We have no information at this time as to where the creatures are headed. But it seems that, at least for now, all attacks have ceased. We'll bring you additional details as we receive them."

"Whoop-de-doo!" Mark hollered sarcastically. "Does this mean I can go home now?"

He'd been at Eden PD for barely over an hour, and already Derek was sick of him. "You're supposed to be down in holding with the rest of the addicts."

"No," Mark corrected, "I'm supposed to be having sex with your girlfriend." He glared at Stacy, who rolled her eyes nearby. "At least that's the lie she told me."

Derek looked her way with a disapproving frown. "Really?"

"Did you have a better way to entice him over here? I had to promise we'd do it outside your locker just to get him off his parents' couch."

Mark snickered. "I wasn't going to clean up afterwards, either."

Stacy gagged. "When this is over, do you think Professor Madison could cook up something to erase my memories? I don't know what I ever saw in him."

"Hey, Stacy," Mark called.

When she turned, he raised two middle fingers.

"Real mature," she replied. "And a great way to show thanks for saving your life."

"Go back to holding," Derek ordered. "You've caused enough headaches up here."

Mark shared the love of his middle fingers. Then he listened and headed back to holding with the other degenerates, hoping to score a quick fix off of one of them. When he was gone, Derek joined Stacy.

"Sex outside my locker? Of all things?"

She batted her eyes at him. "Maybe if we live through this, I'll extend the offer to you instead."

Derek tried to feign being upset, but his red cheeks gave him away.

"Officer Desmond!" a fellow cop yelled from across the station lobby. "You might want to come look at something!"

Hearing the urgency in his voice, Derek jogged to the window where the officer was standing. Stacy followed, as did Lamar, upon noticing the commotion. They peered out, following the officer's pointing finger to the midnight sky, where against a backdrop of blackness and barely visible stars, a swarm of blue energy particles floated by. Derek knew all too well what the swarm represented, and while he hoped it was just that of his adopted sister, his gut warned him not to be so naïve.

"Is that—" Lamar asked.

"Yes," Derek said.

They watched the swarm sail effortlessly to the north, toward Soul Wind Forest, until it eventually disappeared into the horizon. Derek stepped back from the window and saw that all others had been crowded by bodies from the lobby. They'd seen what he had seen, and now their eyes turned to him for leadership.

"We don't know where it's going," Derek said loudly enough for all to hear. "Let's sit tight until we have more information. It might bypass Eden comple—"

"There's another!" someone called, cutting him off.

Even more bodies than before crammed into the line of windows along that edge of Eden PD. Sure enough, a second swarm of energy particles was floating across the sky, seemingly toward the same destination as the first.

"Hey, look over here!" an officer called from the other side of the building.

Some of the onlookers changed sides. Others continued watching the second swarm as it headed for the horizon. Rebecca and James joined Derek, Stacy, and Lamar as they followed-up on the new call for attention. There was a third swarm, this one originating from the east, but headed toward the same northward destination as the first two.

"What are they doing?" Stacy asked.

Derek had an idea, but he shook his head, not wanting to acknowledge it.

"Are they coming for us?" a citizen who'd been on his way to the holding cells asked aloud.

Derek knew he had to tread lightly. He needed to get everyone prepared, but he didn't want to start a panic, either. "We don't know what they're doing," he said. "But we planned for the possibility that one of those things might come here. Out of precaution, we should execute that plan."

A nervous rumbling broke out among the police officers. Rebecca and James shared a knowing look, then approached Derek as Victoria joined the group.

"We planned for one of those things," Rebecca said, "not three. We should evacuate the city."

That was just the type of overreactive energy Derek didn't want infecting the station. "We don't yet know whether they landed in Eden. Even if they did, we don't know they're coming here. We don't know anything for certain, so we need to stay calm and stick to the plan until we do."

"But we do know," James said. "We know exactly what they're doing." He reached into his pocket and pulled out the drawing he'd taken from Frank earlier that day. Even though they'd all seen it before, he displayed it for the group, its implications far graver now than they ever had been. "We know what they're doing," James repeated. "It's what they were always meant to do. And the only thing we're going to accomplish by staying here is giving them fuel to feed their destructive fire."

Derek took the drawing by one corner and stared at the female-led army marching out of Soul Wind Forest. He mumbled under his breath, "And on that day, few will survive." He didn't want that to happen, not on his watch. So he sought advice from Stacy, who nodded to signal her agreement with the others. Then he yelled into the lobby, "Diana!"

She'd been helping escort newly arrived Trizorapine users to the holding cells. Now she broke away in response to Derek's call. "What do you need?"

He didn't mince words. "The Impulse army is coming. I need you to contact emergency services and have them issue a city-wide evacuation order. Eden's no longer safe for any of us."

Diana wanted to freak out, but she contained herself, nodded, and did as she was told.

"Senator Riley," Derek said, "can you procure government resources to help with the evacuation?"

Victoria nodded. "I'll do what I can. I'm sure resources are thin, but maybe we can pull some in from neighboring cities. I'll let you know."

She grabbed her cell phone and left to find a quiet location.

"The rest of you," Derek then said, "spread the word. Explain what's happening and keep things calm. Those people in holding are still our responsibility. It's up to us to get them out of the city safely."

"Where are we headed?" Stacy asked.

"The closest border is Lakeview Bay." He chuckled nervously. "It'll be like old times."

The others were too on edge to appreciate his humor. Derek instructed them to meet back in the lobby in one hour. At that point, they would begin their evacuation of Eden PD. Rebecca, James, and Lamar agreed, while Stacy gave him a kiss of encouragement, then followed the others to disseminate the news. A flash of light caught Derek's eye. He strolled to the nearest window, where a fourth swarm of energy particles drifted across the midnight sky. Forty-five more would follow throughout the night, and then... then Eden would fall. It was all but inevitable. Derek closed his eyes, concentrated as hard as he could, then threw his thoughts out into the universe, hoping beyond hope they would be received.

Shortcake, if you can hear me, we could really use an assist right about now.

———

Amanda's body convulsed as Trizorapine continued flooding her system. She was awake again, aware of the physical toll the endless flow was taking on her body. It was in a constant state of overdose, forever teetering on the brink of ripping her molecules apart and leaving her body in an irreparable state. Only her link to the drones kept her stable. She exercised her Omega Genome to guide them on their killing spree, each manipulation of their puppet strings burning through the experimental chemical in her system, preventing it from crossing a line from which there was no return. Now that her essence was reunited with her mind and body, she saw a way out. It was a path of self-sacrifice, one in which she let the Trizorapine take her, eliminating the engine that powered this destructive machine. But that path was blocked by neural stimulation being forced upon her by Complex B's Learning Room technology. Amanda couldn't exercise free will inside The Hive. She couldn't self-sacrifice, no matter how much she wanted to. She could only fulfill the homicidal directives of Project Impulse, and in doing so, preserve her own life so that it could endlessly drive the project's army of abominations.

Derek's plea for help was but one of many that crossed Amanda's senses with little attention. Citizens from all parts of Eden had seen the drones arriving. They had seen news reports of the global retreat. And they could do the math as one stream of energy particles after another flew overhead on their way to Soul Wind Forest. They were already fleeing, aware that remaining in the city meant giving in to the death that was lining up on its doorstep. Amanda didn't want to hurt these people. She sensed that many of them had experienced a city-wide tragedy before, and almost all of them had experienced the fear of another potential catastrophe a year and a half earlier. They didn't deserve the burden of yet another looming disaster. But Amanda had to direct the drones somewhere. That, she couldn't disobey. And by congregating them in Eden, perhaps the rest of the world would have time to deploy a counteroffensive. Perhaps they'd stand a chance—

Amanda felt the stimuli in her brain deliver a penalizing shock. Her mission wasn't to give the world a chance. It was to burn it to the ground. Luckily, though her thoughts occasionally betrayed that mission, her actions were in alignment. Eden was on the initial target list. It had only been excluded due to being one drone down. By sending the entire Impulse army there, Amanda would efficiently address the shortfall in the first attack wave. But it was literally killing her keeping the drones that had already arrived at bay. The Trizorapine in her system surged toward lethal levels, forcing Amanda to unleash her Omega Genome in more creative ways.

She broke off additional energy particles from her body, and during a momentary power drain that dimmed The Hive's lighting, she snuck those particles out of the system and through Complex E's walls. She sought anything she could embed them in to help expel the excess energy buildup in her system, and it didn't take long before she found willing recipients in the form of chemically imbalanced plant and animal life. Amanda couldn't pit them against each other—that would go against the programming that prevented her from using the drones to destroy one another. She also couldn't direct them to attack Complex E, yet another brainwashing safeguard to ensure she didn't betray Project Impulse. But she could send the mind-controlled animals after those she hadn't taken hold of, and she could direct the underground and aboveground plant life to lay waste to the island itself, even if it had to maneuver around Complex E in the process.

So Amanda let them serve as the outlet of her chemical-infused fury. She transformed Sunrise Isle into a biological nightmare unlike any other, where nature's delicate balance was thrown so far out of alignment that no animal, no plant, and not even the island's structure was safe from her destruction. Meanwhile, she continued holding the drone army on the edge of Soul Wind Forest. The rest of it would eventually arrive—by early morning based on Amanda's internal projections—and then she'd have no choice but to let it march upon Eden. Until then, however, she had to keep her essence connected to her mind and body. She had to keep that mind and body from tearing itself apart. And she had to secretly hope someone out there was working on a solution to stop her before it was too late.

CHAPTER 15
INFILTRATION

The first rays of dawn were shining through the windows of Joint Base Charleston. General Javez, Frank, and Vincent had already met with the SEAL team, who had put them to work rounding up gear from the facility. Major General Radford of the United States Air Force was the ranking officer in charge that morning, and had received orders to assist in any way he could. Also an old friend of General Javez, he was happy to oblige. They walked down a tarp corridor running the length of the shared airfield between the base and Charleston International Airport. They spoke over the roar of the first civilian planes to take off that morning as they made their way to a remote section hosting their two mission helicopters.

"Are you sure you don't want me to assemble a fleet of bombers?" Radford asked. "You'd be amazed by what the bunker busters we've got on hand can do."

"I'm sure they're more than capable," General Javez responded. "The problem is one of time. The US military designed the Sunrise Isle compound to withstand air attacks. Modern bunker busters would pierce it eventually, but not before the hostiles mount a counteroffensive that would render air attacks useless."

"What'd they do, blanket the island with anti-aircraft cannons or something?"

General Javez scoffed, thinking back to his own experience witnessing reconnaissance choppers being swatted from Eden's airspace by Impulse child-infused magma hands. "I wish it was that simple. You're going to have to trust me on this. Try to bomb that facility, and all you're going to wind up with is a bunch of dead pilots."

"Could we at least clear the path for you?" Radford asked. "We could have fighters perform a single surface sweep to take out any hostiles between you and the underground compound. Your teams could take it from there.”

“While I appreciate the offer, it won’t benefit the mission. We need to draw the compound’s defensive forces out, not give them reason to hunker down.”

Radford sighed. “Is there anything I can do for you, Francisco?”

They stopped by a flap snapping in the wind. Beyond it, Simmons’s team was making final preparations.

“You’ve done plenty just by being generous with your base and supplies. It’s on us from here.”

They exchanged a salute, followed by a friendly handshake. Then General Javez stepped out onto the tarmac. Brisk gusts of morning wind cut through his uniform as he walked across the brightening pavement and joined the others. Both helicopters were ready to go, their pilots just wrapping up safety checks. Simmons, Garrett, and Brandt were already wearing high-tech wetsuits equipped with embedded wrist guidance systems, underwater propulsion devices, safety lighting, compact rebreathing mechanisms, dive knives, and waterproof pockets for their land-based military gear. Frank was still struggling to zip his, clearly a rookie with this sort of thing.

“Here,” Brandt said, lending him a hand.

“You guys do this often?” Frank asked. “It seems like a royal pain in the ass.”

“It is. Unfortunately, so are psychopaths that launch their world domination schemes from remote fortified islands.”

Frank couldn’t argue there. With Brandt’s help, he finished securing his wetsuit. Then Simmons ran him through all the key elements he would need to trigger on his own during deployment, including the propulsion and rebreathing apparatuses. He also stressed the importance of Frank keeping his waterproof pockets properly sealed to not accidentally lose his retrieval flares or surface weapons. Once they were in the field, anything could happen, and each man needed to be prepared to complete the mission on his own should the others fall in combat.

“Detective,” General Javez said once Frank had finished his crash course in underwater incursions. “We need to talk.” He guided Frank over to Vincent, who was waiting by the decoy helicopter. “I didn’t want to bring any of this up, figuring it might distract from the mission. But you’re going to find out eventually, and it’s better I tell you here than you learning about it out there.”

Frank could already sense it was bad news. “What happened?”

“Jericho PD got hit before the drone retreat started. Details are thin. It’s not a total loss, but casualties are significant.”

“My partner, Billy?”

"We don't know. We don't have information about any individuals at this time. All we know is that they were under siege for at least seven minutes. They put up a hell of a fight, but it just wasn't enough."

Vincent placed a hand on his friend's sunken shoulder. "I'm sorry, Frank."

General Javez turned to him. "I'm afraid that's not the only news I have, Sheriff. The drones... they didn't retreat to Sunrise Isle like we thought they might."

Vincent felt his blood run cold. "No—"

General Javez nodded. "They're amassing on the border of Soul Wind Forest. Last count put them at thirty-nine. They haven't attacked the city yet. We suspect they're waiting for the rest of the army to arrive, which, based on sightings around the globe, should be within the next hour or so."

Vincent instinctually reached for his cell phone, but when he clicked Derek's name in his contact list, he was met by a rapid error tone.

"You won't be able to reach him," General Javez said. "Cell lines have been jammed for hours. The only reason I have what little information I do is because the military satellite network is still running."

"What about landlines?" Vincent asked. "I'm sure you have them here. I can call the station—"

General Javez stopped him. "It won't do any good. Eden is under an evacuation order. Satellite images taken a couple of hours ago show a mass exodus from Eden PD. They appeared to be on their way to Lakeview Bay. With any luck, they'll get outside of city borders before the Impulse army reaches them."

The thought did little to comfort Vincent. "What if the Impulse army doesn't stop? What if it pursues them into Lakeview Bay?"

General Javez nodded to the blades spinning up beside them. "That's why we're getting on these helicopters. The best thing you can do to help your son now is to play your part in shutting down the drone device on Sunrise Isle."

Simmons interrupted their conversation. "We need everyone on board. It's time to go."

Vincent looked around for their missing teammate. "What about Professor Madison?"

Joseph hadn't accompanied the group to Joint Base Charleston. In fact, no one had seen him following his angered departure from their mission planning meeting. They'd waited nearly half an hour, assuming he was cooling off with a lengthy walk. But they couldn't wait forever, so they'd left him behind, hopeful that he would come around and join the group before it was time to depart for Sunrise Isle. Now, however, it looked as though that wouldn't be the case.

"He's out," Simmons said with the objectivity of someone with a mission to execute. "He added value to the decoy team, but he wasn't critical to its functionality. Now, unless anyone else is also having a change of heart, it's time to load up."

Maybe it's for the best, Frank thought.

He returned to the infiltration helicopter and climbed aboard. Garrett and Brandt helped him with his restraints and coached him on where to look and how to breathe to best avoid motion sickness. General Javez needed no assistance securing himself in the decoy helicopter, and Simmons confirmed Elliott and Novak had Vincent under control before assuming his own seat. The blades of the infiltration helicopter accelerated, and a few seconds later, it lifted from the tarmac.

"Wait!" Frank shouted.

He'd spotted a uniformed officer emerge from the tarp corridor with waving arms, as if signaling the helicopters to hold their ascent. Simmons ordered his pilot to set back down, and by the time they were stable, a second officer emerged. He was carrying a paper bag in one hand and had his other securely gripped around Joseph's left arm. Simmons told the others to sit tight as he unbuckled his restraints, but Frank didn't listen, and soon he and Vincent were both chasing the team leader across the tarmac.

"This guy tried to force his way through front gate security," the first officer reported. "He said he was with you, that leaving without him would compromise your mission."

Simmons eyed Joseph. He was in the camp that leaving with the professor was more of a compromise than leaving him behind.

"He had this on him," the second officer said, handing over the paper bag.

Simmons peeked at its contents, then looked at Joseph. "What kind of game are you playing?"

"It's not a game," Joseph said. He turned his emotionally conflicted gaze to Frank. "You asked me if I'd be willing to cook up a weapon to stop Amanda. Consider this your answer."

Frank swallowed his pride. "Maybe I underestimated you, Professor."

Simmons instructed the officers to release Joseph, then held the paper bag out for Frank.

"No," Joseph said. "It stays with me. Saving the world might be our priority, but it's not mutually exclusive from saving our daughter." He shot Vincent eyes that pleaded for understanding, given their circumstances. "We're going to bring her home. And if that's what it takes to make it happen—" He motioned toward the bag. "—then I'll be the one to use it."

Simmons looked at Frank for approval. He nodded reluctantly, then watched as the team leader passed the bag back to Joseph, who rolled up its top and held it as though it were precious cargo that needed protecting. Vincent remained silent, the logical side of his brain telling him Joseph had done the right thing, but the emotional side secretly wishing the professor had missed their departure. There was no telling what would happen once they reached Sunrise Isle. There was no way to predict what state they would find Amanda in, what defenses they would have to fight through to reach her, or whether any of them would make it home alive. Maybe Joseph would have to use the counteragent. Maybe he wouldn't. But Vincent had to acknowledge it was probably best to leave the option open. Soon, they were all on board their respective helicopters, Joseph included. Then they lifted into the air and flew toward the rising sun... and whatever physical and emotional horrors awaited them at their destination.

"This way," Derek said to the group of citizens he'd taken under his wing.

The evacuation of Eden PD, and Eden at large for that matter, hadn't been going smoothly. It had taken longer than the hour Derek had established to spread word of the evacuation around Eden PD and to convince everyone inside they would die if they didn't go along with it. Then, once everyone was ready to leave, Derek discovered they'd taken in more citizens than they had vehicles to transport out. A haphazard survey was taken to figure out who inside Eden PD lived closest to the building and had a spare vehicle at home. Then the population was divided. One wave would retrieve the nearby vehicles and evacuate in whatever directions made the most sense from their locations. The other wave would caravan directly to Lakeview Bay in a combination of patrol cars, paddy wagons, and personal vehicles available in Eden PD's parking lot.

Not wanting to separate, Derek, Stacy and her family, Victoria, Diana, Lamar, and Rebecca and James, as well as their parents, had all gone with the caravan. But by the time they'd hit the streets, the rest of Eden had gotten a head start. Roads were jammed at every intersection. Traffic was crawling, rarely exceeding ten miles per hour. And agitation among citizens was leading to unnecessary accidents and hostile confrontations. But it was still faster than walking... at first. Eventually, Derek hit a halt in traffic that had brought him to a standstill for over twenty minutes. Stacy volunteered to scout ahead to see what the problem was, and that's when she'd discovered that, a mile ahead, a handful of residents had gotten too nervous to hold course, and had instead abandoned their vehicles in the middle of the road. Those immediately behind had apparently tried to maneuver around the abandoned vehicles, until they became just as frustrated and abandoned theirs as well. A cascading effect followed from there, leaving the main highway to Lakeview Bay so clogged that no vehicle could get through.

When Stacy reported back on her findings, Derek had contemplated whether to direct the caravan to alternate roads. But he knew those were narrower, and as such would take a far smaller roadblock to shut down. Making the call to proceed on foot was a gamble, but Eden's residents had done it before, so Derek knew they were more than capable. Once word of the decision had been disseminated, Lamar had proposed an ingenious idea: they could use the underground tunnel system. There was an entrance less than half a mile away. The tunnels were well lit, protected from the elements, and would negate having to navigate surface streets where improperly abandoned vehicles, users in need of a fix, and panicked citizens presented unpredictable threats. They would also enable safe passage to within three miles of Lakeview Bay's border. The caravan would have to take its chances with the surface there, but that was better than dealing with it for the entire duration of the trek.

"Watch your step," Derek told those immediately behind him as he passed over a thick electrical cable stretched across the ground.

He and Stacy were guiding the second group of citizens in the caravan. While in vehicles, they had taken the lead. But this was Lamar's territory, so Derek had ceded leadership to him and the group under his watch. They were just ahead, guiding the lengthy caravan through an interconnected network of nondescript pipes that the average person was more likely to get lost in than find their way out of. Along the way, the caravan had picked up some of Lamar's coworkers who'd taken shelter in the tunnels, falsely thinking they'd be safe there from the impending attack. They'd also picked up a random group of residents who'd stumbled into the tunnels on their own here and there, and who were glad to now be under the guidance of someone who actually knew where they were going.

"What do you think's happening up there?" Stacy asked, more to pass the time with small talk than really wanting to know.

"Hopefully nothing," Derek said. "The last report we received before leaving Eden PD was that the drones were still assembling and hadn't yet descended into the city. Maybe everyone will clear out before they do."

"Unlikely," Mark said, butting into the conversation.

Derek rolled his eyes, wondering how exactly his loser of a rival had wound up in his evacuation group. Stacy intercepted before the two of them got into a verbal sparring match.

"Maybe you could try being more positive for a change."

"I am positive," Mark said. "I'm positive those things are going to begin their slaughter well before we're all outside of city limits. It's basic math."

"You still know how to do math?" Derek asked.

Mark glared at him. "You can kiss my ass. I might be down on my luck, but I can still best you in a mental competition any day of the week." He continued laying out his defense. "Those things had to travel here from all around the globe. The first ones arrived quickly because they didn't have far to go. The last ones are taking a while because some are on the other side of the planet. But if you'd watched the swarms go by, you'd have seen they all flew at the same average speed. Regardless of how many drones were already there when we abandoned Eden PD, even the farthest of those remaining should arrive any minute now. We weren't the first to evacuate the city, but we were far from the last, and even we won't come near the border in the next ten minutes." He saw Derek and Stacy exchange a worried glance, then reiterated. "You see? Math."

And this is why Derek and Mark had never gotten along in school, even before their rivalry over Stacy. But just like Mark, Derek had a hell of a brain in his head, even if he was technically a college dropout. And he knew Mark was right. The drones would start their descent well before the masses had escaped Eden's borders.

"You know," Stacy said, "maybe if you applied that intellect of yours instead of laying fire to it with unknown narcotics..."

"Yeah, yeah, yeah," Mark replied, shrugging her off. "Get back to me if we survive this."

"*When* we survive this," Derek emphasized.

"If you say so."

There was no point in arguing further. It would only give Derek a headache. He let Mark's comment slide, and yet, it kept trying to return, nagging at his brain. The fact was, Mark was right again. It was basic math. Survival was a matter of probability, and while probability was on the caravan's side based on currently known information, once that Impulse army started moving again, the odds would shift significantly in its favor. Then survival would be a matter of *if* over *when*. Derek didn't want to consider the possibility, so he pushed the idea out of mind and focused on the trek ahead, telling himself that someone would stop this insanity before then. Someone... anyone... he had to hold on to that hope, however little of it there may be left.

———

Forty-seven. That was the number of drones Amanda struggled to hold at bay as they awaited their final two brothers-in-arms. Her attempts to clandestinely thwart her programming were failing. Eden was small enough that two additional drones made little difference in the efficiency by which it could be eradicated of its Trizorapine infection. Her mind was contesting her decision to wait for them, and with each chemical shock that zapped her system, it came closer to imposing its own will—or rather, the will of Project Impulse—on her. The citizens of Eden had put distance between themselves and the drone army, but it wouldn't be enough. Operating in tandem, Amanda's soldiers would make a clean sweep of the abandoned sections of Eden in a fraction of the time it would have otherwise taken. Then they'd catch up to their fleeing targets and make efficient work of them as well.

Forty-eight. There was only one drone left. A blaze seared across Amanda's mind. Claws tore at her spine. Miniature supernovas consumed her cells, waited for them to regenerate only seconds later, then consumed them again. Amanda recalled something about an endless cycle of death and rebirth. She couldn't remember who had mentioned it to her, or in what context, but she had to imagine that's what she was experiencing now. Would death eventually win, putting an end to the battle she'd so valiantly fought? No. Her programming wouldn't allow it. She had exasperated her energy expenditure on Sunrise Isle's nearby flora and fauna. The island had destabilized as a result, putting Complex E and The Hive at risk, so her programming was now recalling the energy particles she'd snuck into the surrounding environment. Amanda's body couldn't contain its buildup of energy much longer, and there was only one outlet left for her to direct that energy into...

Forty-nine. The final drone had arrived on Eden's doorstep. Amanda wanted to keep fighting the good fight, but she had nothing left. She'd cut a deal with her mind to escape the depths of her subconscious, and now it was time to pay the price. She released her grip, intense relief washing over her as the energy stockpile within dispersed violently to her forty-nine extensions of death. Amanda's exhausted essence became one with destiny, and the Alpha child took charge, claiming a birthright that had loomed over her entire life. She directed the Impulse army forward, into Eden, and into a fate which was now unescapable.

———

Frank watched the building-size pylons grow on the horizon as his helicopter approached Sunrise Isle. They were massive towers of metal and stone that had seen years of elemental wear and tear. Between them stretched a nearly invisible sonic barrier that one wouldn't even know was there if not for its occasional distortion of sunlight as it shined through salty mist to warm the ocean surface. If the helicopter tried to pass through the barrier, it would be vibrated to pieces. Frank could only imagine what that meant for its passengers.

"Roger that!" Simmons said into a radio headset. He looked at the others on his team. "The decoy helicopter is five minutes out from its breach point. We're going to hold just outside the barrier until it arrives."

The infiltration helicopter proceeded forward until Frank could no longer see the pylons from its side door. He was half-tempted to stick his hand out to see if he could feel the sonic barrier that was still mostly invisible, even at this close distance. But he appreciated his appendages too much for that, so he instead joined the others in prepping their water gear.

"When we hit the ocean," Simmons told him, "wait ten seconds for surface disruption and air bubbles to clear. Then check the guidance system on your wrist. You don't need to worry about interpreting the map underwater. A blinking dot in the upper-right corner will steady when you're facing the right way. Once that happens, ignite your propulsion system and hold course until you hit the beach. Garrett will stay close in case you have issues. If for any reason your systems fail, and Garrett loses sight of you, look for our breathing trail and follow. Whatever you do, don't surface until you've reached land. You don't want the current pulling you into that sonic barrier."

Frank nodded. He hid his nervousness well, but inside, his stomach was in knots. If he had wanted underwater action in his life, he wouldn't have joined the police force of a landlocked city. "How do we know their radar won't spot us on the beach?"

"It's designed for vehicle detection. Aircraft and seacraft only. There are predators on that island larger than a man. They'd get too many false alarms at that level of sensitivity."

Frank nodded again, though now his nerves were even more jumbled than before. "Speaking of... I thought we were supposed to bring firepower with us to deal with those predators."

"The decoy team did. As for us, we've each got a gun, some spare clips, a knife, and a pack of explosives." Simmons rattled it off as if itemizing a grocery list. "Unfortunately, we're limited by our underwater approach. Our wits are going to have to be our firepower. Stealth and efficiency are the name of the game."

Frank wanted to barf. "Got it."

Simmons put a hand to his ear, then reported, "The decoy team just crossed over the barrier. They should be lighting up Sunrise Isle's radar as we speak. Let's deploy."

In true team leader fashion, he attached his rebreathing device, leaned out the helicopter's side door, then dropped into the ocean below. Brandt followed, leaving Frank next in line.

"Make sure you don't jump too far out," Garrett told him with a grin. "We wouldn't want you getting mangled by that barrier on the way down."

"Thanks for the advice."

Frank attached his rebreather and looked down at the ocean below. Couldn't their pilot have brought them closer to the surface? Or would the force of the helicopter's blades have risked pushing them into the sonic barrier once in the water?

"Just think of it like jumping from a diving board," Garrett said.

It would have been a helpful suggestion, if not for one tiny detail. Frank spit out his rebreather and replied, "I hate swimming."

Garrett pushed the device back into his mouth. "Then let me help you."

He pried Frank's hands loose from the safety bars adorning the side door and shoved. The next thing Frank knew, he was free falling for what felt like an eternity. Then he crashed through a cold, wet barrier into a world of blue darkness. There was another crash nearby as Garrett followed, and Frank, remembering his instructions, remained still as their air bubbles cleared. Simmons and Brandt were already out of sight, but he could see Garrett checking his guidance system. Frank did the same, spinning in a circle until the flashing dot steadied. Garrett was oriented in the same direction, and tossed him a thumbs-up before activating his own propulsion system.

When in Rome...

Frank activated his system, and soon he was torpedoing through the water like a dolphin on steroids. If swimming had been like this growing up, he might have had an entirely different outlook on it as an adult. Despite charging headfirst into what could turn out to be certain death, Frank found himself having fun. One minute passed, and he felt even more comfortable knowing the sonic barrier was far enough behind him that no simple mistake would end up frying his brain. Simmons must have made the same assessment, for he and Brandt had paused to allow the others to catch up. They floated beneath the waves as Simmons pointed behind them and held up a finger: one. Then he pointed toward their destination and held up multiple fingers: two. Frank got the message. They were a third of the way to their beach landing. Stay the course, and they'd be there in no time.

They reactivated their propulsion systems and continued onward, three professionals and one in-over-his-head detective that had no business being there. Frank couldn't help but wonder what the hell he'd been thinking sticking with the infiltration team after learning of its approach plan. But so far, so good. Who knew, maybe when this was over, he'd pursue a Special Warfare Operator designation himself. After all, he'd been through enou—

A dark figure interrupted Frank's thought as it dashed past his eyes and sunk its oversized jaws into Garrett. Clouds of blood polluted the water as the animal—some kind of shark by the looks of it, though none like Frank had ever seen—shook its prey like a rag doll. Simmons and Brandt responded before he could even fully process what he was seeing. They went for the creature with their knives bared, but before they reached it, a second marine animal grabbed it with tentacles large enough that each could be mistaken for an Amazonian python. It ripped the shark-like animal off of Garrett—or what was left of Garrett—and claimed the remainder for itself.

Frank's limbs locked. His breath hitched. Every part of him screamed to move, but none obeyed. He knew the team had expected to encounter genetically modified predators once on Sunrise Isle. It had never crossed his mind that the chemicals responsible for those predators had likely leaked into the surrounding ocean as well. But as he stared into what he believed were the eyes of a mutant octopus feasting on Garrett, he realized he might not even make it to Sunrise Isle to infiltrate Complex E. Maybe it was for the best that Joseph had hung on to the counteragent, because the decoy team was suddenly looking due for a promotion.

But not if Simmons and Brandt had anything to say about it. They grabbed Frank's shoulders and reactivated his propulsion system, dragging him along as they made a mad dash for the beach. Frank couldn't draw enough oxygen from the rebreather. He was in full panic mode, and his body craved more air than the system could process. He reached up to remove the rebreather, panic overriding logic and telling him if he could just get it off, then he could fill his lungs with the oxygen they desired. Simmons reached back and knocked his hand away before he accidentally drowned himself. Jostled by the push, Frank glanced down, where another shark-like creature was rising from the depths to turn him into its next meal.

He yanked at Simmons's and Brandt's hands, but assuming it was another panicked response, they gripped him tighter. Desperate to get loose, Frank grabbed his knife and jabbed it into Simmons's rebreather tank. The tank exploded outward as compressed gasses fled their prison. The force sent the trio into an uncontrolled spin, but it was enough to dodge the shark-like creature, which zipped past without fulfilling its ravenous desires. Simmons and Brandt must have seen the creature, for they stopped battling Frank and instead braced for an attack. The shark-like creature reappeared and dashed straight toward them. Brandt raised his knife, gauging the closing distance so he could stab at just the right time. But then a second shark-like creature took him from behind, separating his knife arm from his body. Simmons tried to pull him from harm's way, but it was too late. The first shark-like creature had its jaws around Brandt's midsection in seconds, and then Brandt was gone, swept into the ocean's dark depths.

Simmons caught Frank's eye and pointed. There was only one way they were going to survive this. They needed to get to the beach. They launched toward their destination, Frank barely able to catch his breath, and Simmons miraculously holding his. Frank felt a change in the current. He glanced over his shoulder to find one of the mutant octopus creatures closing in fast. Below him, the world was brightening. At first, Frank thought it was an optical illusion. Then he realized it was reflected sunlight off the ocean floor, which was growing shallower by the second. He looked back again. The mutant octopus was only five feet away. It extended a tentacle, which Frank kicked at in hopes of deterring its attack for just a moment more.

The mutant octopus was unfazed. It wrapped the tip of its tentacle around Frank's foot just as the detective felt sand rush up beneath his body. His head broke the ocean's surface, his eyes temporarily blinded by sunlight. Then Frank felt the mutant octopus pulling him backwards. He gulped sea water as his mouth splashed down unexpectedly. Then he grabbed wildly at the sandy ocean floor. But there was nothing solid to grab. His fingers slipped through the wet sand as if it were nothing but water. The mutant octopus got a second tentacle around him, and Frank felt consciousness slipping as oxygen deprivation took hold.

He heard gunshots. They were muffled, but they were distinct to his trained ears. The tightness around his ankles loosened, and then Frank felt something pulling him in the opposite direction. It was Simmons, who'd made it to land before him. He dragged Frank out of the ocean and collapsed just beyond the tide's reach. Frank puked sea water, his body's involuntary attempt at saving his life. Then, just as he finished, the mutant octopus launched itself from the ocean and slapped into the sand less than three feet away. Ever vigilant, Simmons fired upon it, but the creature took the bullets as if just a nuisance and snapped a tentacle around Frank's neck, still determined to have its meal.

The sand beside the creature shifted, and what Frank could only describe as an oversized tree root shot upward like a geyser. It coiled around the mutant octopus, forcing it to release its hold on Frank, then dragged it underground. Simmons and Frank exchanged a disturbed glance, then both men scrambled off the sand and to more solid mud-caked ground beyond the beach's reach.

"What the hell have you gotten me into?" Simmons asked, looking around with his gun ready for the next threat that might come for them. "I mean—what —" His eyes were frantic as he tried to deal with what he'd just seen. "What the fuck, Holmes?!"

Frank fell back against the ground, his body in need of a break. "Welcome to the world of Project Impulse. Glad you signed up for this mission yet?"

Simmons ignored him and reached for his radio so he could warn the decoy team. But his radio was gone, having been lost in the underwater scuffle. He reached for Frank's, but stopped as soon as he saw the bloody white tooth sticking up from its broken casing. He dropped next to his unqualified partner and buried his face in his palms. "We have no way to contact the others. We're on our own from here."

Frank slapped him on the back. "Yeah... that's how these things usually go." He could have lain there for hours. The toll the underwater incursion had taken on his body and lungs wasn't nearly as severe as what his brother had put him through in the heyday of their cat-and-mouse game, but it had drained him nonetheless. He stayed quiet for a few minutes, listening to the distant sounds of animals fighting, plants rustling, insects buzzing... it was like any other of nature's secluded retreats, only with the volume slider turned up to the max. Frank could also feel an odd rumbling, almost like an earthquake deep within the ground, but he chalked that up to his fried nerves. Once he convinced himself that he couldn't lie there forever, and that he'd given Simmons enough time to work through his teammates' unceremonious deaths, he stood and offered his hand. "Come on. We all have plenty to mourn when this is over. Right now, we still have a mission to complete."

CHAPTER 16
ENTER THE ALPHA CHILD

"This is it," Lamar called back from his lead position in the tunnels. "The end of the line."

He pointed toward a hatch overhead that could only be reached by a metal ladder. The hatch was located at a tunnel dead end, the closest the system could bring the evacuees to Lakeview Bay before they had to return above ground. It had been a long trek so far, but there was still a way to go, and Derek knew they had no time to waste. He pardoned his way to the front of the pack.

"I'll take a look."

Derek climbed the metal ladder and released the latching mechanism that secured the hatch in place. He then cracked the hatch open cautiously and peered out, not quite sure what to expect the surface to look like after spending hours underground. To his relief, it didn't look much different than when his caravan had first entered the tunnel system. There weren't many cars here, but there were droves of citizens, all fleeing on foot for the Lakeview Bay border. They looked tired, hungry, scared. There were parents and children, young couples, groups of friends, loners, businessmen, vagrants... their social statuses were irrelevant. All were flowing toward Lakeview Bay with one goal in mind: survival.

Derek pushed the hatch all the way open, drawing a handful of curious stares from those in the nearby vicinity. Then he fully emerged from the tunnels, performed one last assessment of any dangers the surface environment might present, and gave the go ahead to Lamar. "Let's get everyone out."

The tunnels had provided the Eden PD caravan with much appreciated shelter during the night's darkest hours. But now, in the bright glow of the late morning sun, it proved to be a hinderance. Entering the tunnel had slowed Eden

PD's initial evacuation, but not by much. Lamar had identified a ramped construction entrance which evacuees could descend in rows of three. It was a bottleneck for sure, but a wide bottleneck, and one worth the lighting and protection the tunnels had provided since then. This exit, however, was about as narrow of a bottleneck as there could be. Only one person could feasibly climb the metal ladder at a time. Two could fit, but whomever drew hind position risked getting kicked in the face during the ascent and had to pause anyway while waiting for the evacuee in front to climb through the hatch. They were also working against gravity, and though many of the caravan members were in average or better-than-average physical condition, they'd just been through a sleepless night of endless walking, with no food or drink to rejuvenate them along the way.

Derek stayed at street level to assist people as they breached the hatchway. Stacy and her parents joined him to alternate effort. Lamar, James, and, surprisingly, Mark, stayed underground to assist citizens with the initial climb. Victoria, Rebecca, and Diana did the same, stepping in to help females who might not appreciate a male's hands on sensitive parts of their bodies, regardless of the situation. Luckily, there was no drama, there were no major slips, and no one was worse for the wear upon exiting the tunnel. The only drawback was that it had taken so long.

Derek kept waiting for the end of the surface mob to pass them by, but there was no end in sight. The backs of Eden's citizens could be seen as far as his vision allowed when looking toward Lakeview Bay, and the fronts of their faces could be seen all the way to the horizon when looking back at the city. At first, Derek didn't understand how the evacuation could be so much more dense than during The Falling of the Tides, but the answer didn't elude him long. The Falling of the Tides had taken the lives of one-third of Eden's population and injured significantly more than that. That evacuation hadn't been as dense simply because there weren't as many able bodies making the exodus from disaster. Derek supposed he should process that fact through a positive lens, that though the world had been under siege and already lost so much, Eden was, at least so far, surviving.

The last of his caravan made it to the surface, after which those assisting climbed out of the tunnels and got their first look at the fleeing masses. Derek could see they were just as shocked as he'd been, and the sight imparted a sadness upon the group, as they each wondered whether their home would ever be the safe haven they deserved.

"We need to keep moving," Derek reminded them.

He took Stacy's hand and merged into the mob of evacuees. There was no need to maintain a caravan structure at this point. Every citizen on this side of Eden was marching toward the same destination, as part of the same crowd. Up ahead, a fleet of ten military rescue choppers appeared in the distant sky. They grew as they neared, then zipped overhead, their wind shear billowing over the crowd. Derek watched the choppers shrink, then stop about two miles back, where he assumed the exodus mob ended.

"I take it they're with you?" he asked Victoria.

She nodded. "I wasn't sure they'd make it. They're going to start air evacuations from the rear forward to help get people out quicker."

"Sounds good."

Just then, an explosion shattered the solemn peace that had previously hung over the evacuating mob. A fireball turned to a swirl of black smoke where one of the helicopters had been hovering. Derek's section of crowd stopped and looked back, all of them confused at how what appeared to be a rescue operation had suddenly turned violent. But then they saw the first drone. It leaped onto the side of one of the nine remaining rescue choppers, reached in, and sent the chopper into a nosedive into the mass of people below. Screams rang out from the distance. A second explosion kicked off a panicked frenzy in the forward crowd. Multiple streams of blue energy particles shot into the air, picking off rescue chopper pilots, whose unguided aircraft collided in midair, showering the stampeding masses below with deadly shrapnel.

"Run!" Derek yelled.

It didn't need to be said. Lamar, Rebecca, James, and Mark were already on the move, forced into action by the hysterical crowd behind them. Derek, Stacy, Diana, and Victoria followed after almost being trampled. More explosions shook the air behind them. The screams of Eden's citizens grew into a roar. Some were falling victim to the drones, some were collateral damage of the primary attacks, and others were victims of an out-of-control crowd they couldn't keep up with. Blue energy particles darted in and out of the rear mob like snakes making repeated strikes at their prey. Bodies fell. Others flew. Random pockets of gunfire broke out. Light poles were snapped and used as oversized axes to sweep vast numbers off their feet. A gas station exploded, catching a swath of citizens with its flames. Windows blew out, their razor sharp glass slinging through the crowd, slicing necks and wrists deep enough to open major arteries.

Row after row, Eden's citizens fell to the Impulse army. Glancing back, Derek could see the blue energy particles shifting closer. They'd already closed a fifth of the distance between himself and the rear of the crowd. In no time at all, they'd be on him and the others. The gathered exodus was actually making the drones' slaughter more efficient than had they needed to hunt every Trizorapine user down individually. Now, all citizens were in the line of fire, regardless of whether they were targets or not.

That's it! Derek thought.

He was still operating under the mentality that he needed to protect the herd. But he wasn't its protector anymore. He was one of its members, just another cattle running from a looming instrument of death. There was nothing Derek could do for the rest of Eden. But there was something he could do for his own friends and loved ones. Though he might regret it as a selfish act later, his instinct was to make them his priority.

"Veer right!" He yelled to Stacy and Diana. "The woods are close! Angle toward them and stay away from anyone else!" When Stacy looked at him as if she didn't understand, he added, "We're not targets!"

Now she got it. It was self-preservation time. Every citizen for themselves. She grabbed her parents and pivoted on a semi-perpendicular path from the mob. Diana helped Derek spread the word to the rest of their group—all except Mark, who they knew was a liability—and then the group followed suit. The Impulse army was nearly upon them. The screams from behind had nearly faded to silence, mostly because there were few people left alive to vocalize their terror, and those almost within death's reach were too afraid to do anything but stare straight ahead and run.

Lamar took a hard hit to the shoulder, but stayed on his feet. Stacy stumbled, the scrapes from her impact with the ground nothing compared to the kicks and stomps she took from those trampling over her. Her parents and Derek helped her up, and they continued their angled dash for the edge of Soul Wind Forest. Citizens along the edge of the mob had gotten the same idea and were also scattering into the woods. Derek couldn't fault them, but he knew their presence might also endanger his own group. He shouted for everyone to cut left to avoid what appeared to be a growing mass of citizens just beyond the tree line. They broke from the mob just as the Impulse army reached their location, the sounds of gurgled death breaths and lifeless thuds impossible to ignore as they scrambled over dirt and twigs and into the safety of the forest.

Derek paused to allow everyone to catch their breath. He glanced back at the still-fleeing mob, now seeing it from behind as the drones continued their attack in both full-body and dematerialized forms. Dead residents blanketed the street in the Impulse army's wake. Derek couldn't tell where one body began and another ended. It was a river of warm flesh quickly growing cold, a river he and his friends and loved ones were almost a part of. Random citizens were hiking through the woods around them, but so far, none had come close to the group. Meanwhile, the Impulse army seemed focused on the fleeing crowd, rather than the stragglers that had broken off from the masses.

"What do we do now?" Stacy asked.

"We keep on this path," Derek said, unsure if they had any other option. "It'll take longer, but it should still get us to Lakeview Bay."

Lamar stared at the fresh falling bodies in the distance as the Impulse army continued its rampage. "Are you sure that's where we want to go?"

Derek rubbed his head, overwhelmed by all he needed to process. "Maybe not. But for now, let's at least put more distance between us—" He pointed to the Impulse army. "—and them."

Everyone agreed, so they set off deeper into the woods. They tried to stay quiet to not attract attention, and they avoided any other citizens who periodically neared. They thought they were finally safe from harm—at least temporarily. Little did they know, enough Trizorapine-laced residents had sought shelter in the woods that it now warranted a sweep of the Impulse army. Three drones abandoned the larger force, dematerialized, and headed straight for them.

———

The decoy helicopter set down on a flat expanse of beach on Sunrise Isle's northwestern shore. Troop Commander Elliott and Operator Novak were the first to unload, instructing the others to stay put while they secured the area. Unlike the infiltration team, they were armed to the teeth. Each sported an assault rifle and chest strap with multiple spare magazines. They had submachine guns strapped to their belts and two pistols apiece, one on the back and the other in an ankle holster. They also carried Bowie knives, concussive grenades, and trigger explosives. They were prepared for anything, except for what they actually found waiting.

Just beyond the beach, Elliott and Novak spotted an unusual ridge larger than a sedan jutting up from the forest floor. They climbed it, only to discover a fissure on the other side so deep that it exposed years of geological layering. Giant tree roots spanned one side of the fissure to the other, and beneath them, ocean water was pooling from some unseen source. While odd, that alone wouldn't have been enough to make Elliott and Novak think twice about their mission. But the mass extermination of giant animals in the field beyond the fissure was. The dozens of bodies had only just started to stink, their spilled blood still glistening in the late morning sun. There were vicious carnivores, innocent herbivores, species that would never be found living—or dying— together in a natural environment. Something, or someone, had massacred them.

"Professor!" Elliott yelled.

General Javez, Joseph, and Vincent unbuckled themselves and joined the

SEALs on the ridge. They stood in stunned silence, staring at the massacre as if they had just set eyes upon an alien species.

"What the hell is this, Professor?" Elliott asked.

It was only a theory, but Joseph was pretty sure he knew the answer. "It's an outlet. They must be supercharging Amanda with Trizorapine. She needs ways to burn it from her system so it doesn't destabilize her molecules."

"So she killed a bunch of animals?" Novak asked.

Joseph shook his head. "No. She simply controlled them, or some of them, and made them kill each other. It's the same thing she's doing with the drones, only there must be something in her programming preventing her from creating infighting among them."

The ground trembled violently. The group braced as what felt like a miniature earthquake passed beneath their feet. Then they heard scraping, and when they looked into the fissure, they saw the tree roots snaking through packed dirt as though they were giant earthworms.

"Yeah," Elliott said, his nerves rattled, "I think I've seen enough." He turned away from the ravine and confirmed his assault rifle was ready with a live round. "Update our risk profile, Professor. Are we still facing genetically enhanced predators out here, or something else altogether?"

"Oh, there are still plenty of predators out there. The more pertinent question is whether either of you have used illegal drugs recently."

"What kind of question is that?" Novak asked, offended.

"A question of life and death," Joseph said. "You see, the predators on this island will attack anything they view as easy prey, including all of us. But the plant life... it's not after a meaty snack. It will, however, aggressively pursue anything with Trizorapine in its system." He pointed toward the massacre. "Look."

The others followed his gaze to a fallen bear. A thick, thorny vine was wrapped around its torso, slithering and squeezing, digging into its flesh, which oozed with blood.

"My God..." Novak said.

"This is man's work," Joseph corrected. "It's science gone awry. Every living thing on this island has been infected with Trizorapine or some precursor to it. And now it appears they're turning on each other, the way addicts do when their fix is in short supply. So, I'm going to ask again: are you two clean?"

Elliott and Novak both nodded.

"Good," Joseph said. "Then, to answer your question, our risk profile remains the same. The predators will attack us. The rest of the biome will likely leave us alone. And, of course, there are whatever defenses Complex E sends our way."

The ground quaked again. This time, a nearby tree fell.

"And that?" Elliott asked.

Joseph took an uneasy breath. "That... we might just need to deal with. But I'd advise we don't stay on this island one moment longer than we need to."

The others exchanged glances. They were all in agreement on that.

"We've got extra firepower in the helicopter," Elliott said. "I suggest you all load up."

General Javez and Vincent didn't hesitate. Joseph, on the other hand, remained still, observing the war-torn surroundings of Sunrise Isle. He could sense his daughter's pain, the anguish controlling those drones was causing, the turmoil inside of her that had led to such destruction right here outside of Complex E. Was it too much to overcome? Joseph hoped not, but in reality, he had no clue.

"Professor?" Novak asked, grabbing his attention. "Weapons."

Joseph glanced back at the helicopter, where General Javez and Vincent were strapping on a similar arsenal package as the SEALs. Then he scanned the brutal surroundings of Sunrise Isle once more. He'd let those more experienced in combat handle whatever stood between him and Amanda. As for her, Joseph could never turn a lethal weapon on her. He would let her kill him before that. But that's why he'd brought his own weapon to this fight. "I have everything I need right here," he said, patting the brown paper bag that hadn't left his hands since taking flight.

Elliott and Novak didn't care for his response, but this wasn't the time for an argument.

"Let's move out!" Elliott called to the others.

They convened near the unnatural ridge, then hiked alongside it until it narrowed enough to bypass. Elliott kept one eye on a digital guidance system and the other on the woods ahead. Novak, General Javez, and Vincent focused only on the woods, from which they could now hear distant snarls and growls. Joseph kept his eyes on his brown bag. Its contents might be the only thing capable of ending Amanda's reign of terror. He needed to protect them at all costs.

———

"Where is it now?" the Woman in White asked as she stared at an overhead projection of Sunrise Isle.

One used a laser pointer from his seat at the command center conference table to indicate a spot on the coast. "The helicopter landed on the northwestern beach. We don't have the ability to track whomever was inside on foot, but we have to assume they're headed this way."

Three leaned forward. "Is that because you believe a hostile force has infiltrated the island, or because you think Colonel Davis returned and had to make an unexpected landing short of the compound?"

"It would be prudent to treat the intrusion as hostile until we know otherwise."

The Woman in White nodded in agreement. "We have to operate as if Colonel Davis is no longer part of the project. In fact, we may have to treat him as an active threat if he doesn't make contact to explain himself soon." She looked at Four, who was fiddling with a tablet connected to the projector system. "You still don't have the pylon camera footage?"

"It's still transmitting. I've been lobbying for years to have that system upgraded, but we never allocate the resources to make it happen."

The Woman in White wasn't in the mood for his complaints. "We've been a little busy."

She looked at the Dark Man, hoping for advice. But he was standing in the corner of the room, listening to their exchange and waiting patiently for actionable information. He had no advice to share at this time. A shudder tore through the facility, shaking all surfaces and shedding concrete dust from the ceiling. The Sunrise Isle projection flickered.

"Are you sure there's nothing we need to do about that?" the Woman in White asked.

"Structural integrity is still holding," Three responded. "Whatever's going on out there shouldn't be an issue unless it gets significantly worse. Diego's team is monitoring it. He'll let us know if anything changes."

A second shudder, this one less intense than the first, hit them. The Woman in White closed her eyes and clenched her fists, trying not to let the geological activity unnerve her. But it was difficult. When they'd initiated the endgame, she'd thought victory would only be a matter of time. But then she'd learned of Colonel Davis's unscheduled departure from the island. He wasn't forbidden from coming and going as he pleased, but to leave at such a crucial moment, and without telling anyone why, was suspicious, to say the least. That was followed by the Alpha child either fighting her programming or getting its instructions twisted, for she'd redirected the entire drone army to Eden, which the Woman in White had explicitly excluded from the first wave of attacks. Hours of tension had passed where it was unclear whether the Alpha child would actually carry out the assault on Eden, and during that time, Sunrise Isle itself had gone to hell in a handbasket.

The earthquakes had been the first tip that something wasn't right. Diego was concerned the exterior of Complex E had been compromised, and as part of assessing his concerns, he'd sent a team of engineers to the surface. That's when they'd learned about the chaotic battle happening among Mother Nature's creations. They were exhibiting behavior reminiscent of a Trizorapine overdose, actively attacking each other instead of working together to maintain ecological equilibrium. Diego assumed the Trizorapine tanks had been breached. But though they'd taken damage, their leakage was minimal, certainly not enough to explain the sudden shift in ecological dynamics.

It wasn't until the Impulse army had descended upon Eden that the plan seemed to be getting back on track. There had been no news reports covering the invasion, nor social media posts or other amateur information releases to document what was happening there. The Woman in White took that to mean only one thing: the Alpha child was doing what she'd been bred to do. An absence of information suggested no one had the ability to share that information. And with modern technology available to even the most common citizen, the only way that would happen is if they were all dead, or soon to be dead and busy running for their lives.

The Woman in White opened her eyes, the thought stinging her. Derek had been in Eden. She'd warned Vincent to get him out, but the last information she'd seen before Eden went dark was that her son had been rallying a force inside Eden PD. Surely he'd had the sense to flee once he'd learned what he was up against. Surely he could've made it out in time. And if he didn't, then perhaps he at least had the sense to—

The Woman in White cut her thought, feeling the eyes of the Dark Man upon her. She met his gaze. He didn't like that she still harbored this weakness. He'd never approved of the actions she'd taken to protect her son over the years. He'd made it clear, with no words at all, that there would be a time when that weakness would become a liability. Then, the Woman in White would have to make a choice: accept the path she'd taken in life, or join her son on the other side.

"We've got the footage," Four announced.

He replaced the projection of Sunrise Isle with a ten second clip of grainy footage taken from one of the sonic barrier pylons surrounding the island. It began with nothing but sky, then the decoy helicopter zoomed through the center, and then there was empty sky again. At full speed, the footage yielded no information they didn't already know.

"Can you slow it down or something?" One asked.

Four rewound the footage, then played it again, this time at a fraction of its original speed. There was sky, then the decoy chopper, which, as it passed by, revealed the passengers within. Four paused the footage on a frame that perfectly captured those in the helicopter's cabin. Frontmost was General Javez. Behind him were Vincent and Joseph. And they were accompanied by two other military types equipped with an impressive amount of gear.

"The professor's come home," Three said. "And he's brought some friends with him."

"He can't really think a sheriff and squad of soldiers can stop what's happening here, right?" One asked.

The Woman in White shook her head. "He's not coming here to stop us. He's coming to rescue the Alpha child." She pointed suspiciously at the paper bag in his lap. "And he's been spending time in the lab again, by the looks of it."

Four tapped his tablet, splitting the projection between the still image and the overhead view of Sunrise Isle. "Well, he's on the ground already. And now we know for certain he and his band of merry men are coming here."

"We have no defensive force left," One reminded the others. "So, what do we do about this?"

The Woman in White still hadn't taken her eyes off the camera image. Joseph Madison had been a thorn in her side since the early days of Project Impulse, and now he was going to put up one last fight before the project reached its conclusion. But he wasn't the reason the Woman in White was still staring. Vincent was, his posture resolute as he rode beside the professor into battle. He'd honored her request of not letting Derek run headfirst into the firefight, but he'd taken no such precaution for himself. And now here he was, at Complex E's doorstep, a player who'd taken a seat on the opposite side of the game board and openly issued a challenge to compete. The Woman in White felt the pull of the black hole within her. She turned away from the screen, met the Dark Man's gaze once more, and received his message loud and clear. It was time to make her choice.

"Retrieve whatever weapons we have left from the armory," the Woman in White instructed. "Arm the most abled-bodied engineers and technicians we have, anyone not critical to keeping The Hive operational. Turn the surface compound into a kill box. Position everyone in a concealed location, let the five hostiles come, and then open fire once they've got nowhere to run."

"You don't want to take any of them alive?" Three asked. "Not the professor, or..."

"Kill them all," the Woman in White said resolutely. "Nothing stops Project Impulse."

The Plainclothes looked at each other with uncertainty. Then, sensing the Woman in White wasn't going to change her mind, they gathered their gear and left to carry out her orders. The Dark Man watched with pride as another minor earthquake rocked the room. Abigail Desmond was finally gone. All that remained in her place was his progeny, the one that would see his bidding through to the end, and then, when this war was over, stand by his side as he rose to lead his flock. The Woman in White was his now, as was the Alpha child. And they forever would be.

———

Derek pushed twigs and shrubbery aside as he and Stacy led their group through Soul Wind Forest. With the trees still young from Eden's first destruction, they could clearly see other residents hiking alongside them. As much as Derek wanted to avoid anyone they didn't know, it had proven impossible, for too many people had seen the woods as an escape from the slaughter still underway on the streets to Lakeview Bay. The screams were constant, an incessant background noise disturbing to the psyche and unable to ignore. Derek tried, however, as he pulled back a low-hanging branch and guided the others beneath it and then over a shallow hill. He knew they couldn't keep going forever—they were all exhausted, fueled only by adrenaline—but he also had no idea where it would be safe to stop. Once Eden's citizens had been eradicated, there was no guarantee the Impulse army would simply quit and return to Sunrise Isle. More likely, their massacre would cascade to the next city in line, then the one after that, in an endless procession of ruin. It was the way this assault had started, and the way it would continue, only now with the forty-nine drones working as one.

"You've got to stop thinking about it," Stacy said.

"About what?"

"I can see it all over your face. You're worrying about what happens next." She shook her head. "We can't control what happens next. We can only make the best decision for ourselves and hope either your dad succeeds on Sunrise Isle, or the world's militaries figure out a different solution."

The latter didn't seem likely considering how the Impulse army invasion had gone so far. Derek had faith in his father, however. And in Joseph, and Frank, and the qualified team they'd been paired with. He didn't know how they would stop Project Impulse, but he trusted they could. It really came down to how long it would take, and whether he could keep his friends and loved ones alive until then. If not, though, there was something he needed to get off his chest.

"Listen, Stacy, I—" Derek's words were cut off by a swarm of energy particles passing overhead. "Oh, shit."

Everyone froze. They watched the swarm hover over nearby trees, with no clear destination in mind. Then it suddenly swooped down and eliminated one of the other hikers, who'd barely gotten out a yelp before falling lifeless to the ground. A scream, separate from and closer than the exodus mob, filled the air behind the group. They spun in time to see a second dead body fall, and a swarm of energy particles reshape itself into Evan's form nearby. Derek signaled for everyone to get down.

"We aren't targets," he whispered, reiterating the fact more for his own benefit than theirs.

He watched the reformed drone look from side to side as if orienting on its next victim. It seemed confused, almost as if its targeting system had suddenly malfunctioned. A third energy particle swarm passed overhead. Then another scream emitted from the direction of the first, and when Derek looked back, he saw that drone take form as well.

What were they doing?

———

Inside The Hive, Amanda's head twitched as she tried to understand the signals being fed back to her. She was following her programming, forty-six deadly extensions of her mind eradicating Eden's Trizorapine infected population. Thousands of innocents were being slaughtered along with them, but the number was within the acceptable limits of her mission. The problem was coming from the three drones she'd directed away from the main army to hunt down escaped Trizorapine users. They'd already taken out a few, but now Amanda's connection to them was shaky, as if struggling to transmit through some sort of electromagnetic interference. She hadn't lost her grip on the drones, but her commands to them, and their responses back, were garbled. There were more Trizorapine users in the area. But there were also innocents, those not subject to the drones' targeting. And yet, something about those innocents...

Amanda winced as chemicals seared her veins. She tried to focus on her mission. She directed the forest drones to continue seeking their targets, but her mind kept returning to the innocents. Something inside compelled her to pursue them. They had no Trizorapine in them. They were distractions from the overall goal. Yet she couldn't ignore them. She also couldn't force the drones away from them, her directives too unclear through the interference.

———

Five more, Derek counted. There had been five more screams, yelps, or dull thuds as the three drones he'd spotted in the woods continued their attack. But even that raised its own questions. Five more kills in a span of two to three minutes was far below the Impulse army's reported cadence. They were moving slower, less efficiently, as if still uncertain what they should do. They also hadn't gone far. Derek and the rest of the group were plastered against the forest floor, trying their best to conceal themselves, doing nothing that might attract the drones' attention. There was almost no one else around now. And those residents who were must not have been users, for the drones ignored them. Yet they still wouldn't leave.

"I don't understand," Stacy whispered.

Unfortunately, Derek didn't have any answers to give her. All three drones had taken on a physical form now. There was one to the north, another to the east, and the third was to the west. The only direction the group could head to evade them was south, back toward the main road. But even if that was an option, there was no way they could leave their current position without being spotted. Maybe the drones would ignore them, like they were the other passing residents. But Derek suspected they wouldn't, for there was something different about the way these drones were acting. Different meant unpredictability, and unpredictability meant none of them were safe.

"I'll make a run for it," James said. "I've barely touched prescription drugs in my life, much less illegal ones. I'll make a run for it, and that way we can see what they do."

"They might kill you," Rebecca reminded him.

"It's like Derek said, we're not targets. They probably won't do anything."

Derek watched as the closest drone turned toward them, almost as if sensing their whispering. "I'm not so sure about that anymore."

———

Amanda could see them now. She could see through the drone's eyes, see the group of innocents doing their best to hide among the leaves. She didn't know who they were, but she felt like she knew them. They were scared, and though they weren't targets, something told Amanda they had every right to be. She felt a trigger in her mind. It was a subtle piece of programming, implanted by the Learning Room device and left to fester undisturbed unless needed. These people... these otherwise innocent people... had activated that programming. It informed Amanda that they were threats, not because of any chemical in their systems, but because of their opposition to Project Impulse. She was required to eliminate those threats should the opportunity present itself. And though her gut told her she didn't want to, the relentless assault on her mind and body wouldn't let her do otherwise.

———

The drone stepped toward them. Derek felt his heart leap into his throat. If it attacked, they'd be defenseless. The drone took another step. Leaves rustled behind the group. They looked back, only to find that the second drone had also shuffled in their direction. Derek dreaded knowing what the third drone was doing, but he had to find out. He looked toward it, and just like the others, saw it was nearing.

"Get ready to make a run for it," he said.

"We can't outrun those things," Lamar argued.

Derek insisted, "We have to try!" He saw the first drone inch closer. "On my mark."

Lamar glanced nervously at Victoria, who slowly pushed up onto her forearms.

"One," Derek said.

Lamar took her cue and did the same, as did Rebecca, James, and their parents.

"Two."

Stacy squeezed her mother's hand lovingly, then prepped herself for the mad dash to come.

"Three!"

The entire group rose in unison and sprinted southward. The drones hesitated, their garbled messaging making the decision to pursue uninfected innocents unclear. But then Amanda's sleeper programming came through, and they knew they had to eliminate the fleeing group. They dematerialized into energy swarms and darted after their prey. It took less than twenty seconds for them to close in on their new targets. They took aim, one at Derek, another at Stacy, the third at Lamar, each already calculating the most efficient subsequent target in the herd. Five seconds is all it would take to drop them all. The first drone shot forward, its energy particles on a direct path for Derek's heart. He could feel its electricity as it neared. Then he felt the burn of it piercing his skin, merging through his flesh—

"Hey!" a voice screamed in the distance. "Hey, over here!"

Derek stumbled as the energy particles withdrew from him. Stacy caught him, and when he looked back, he saw that all three swarms had frozen in midair. Set back far in the trees, atop a rise in the forest floor, waving his arms as if desperate for attention, was Mark. The drone swarms shifted as if unsure which prey to pursue: the newly targeted innocents, or the dense vessel of Trizorapine that was ripe for the picking. The latter was their ingrained programming. It had to be obeyed, no matter what conflicting orders they might have received.

"Mark!" Derek yelled. "Get the hell out of here!"

He smiled, but didn't move. "I figure I owe you for all the times you've tried to help me this past year." His watery gaze shifted to Stacy. "I'm sorry I was such an ass. You deserved better."

The drone swarms bolted toward him.

"Keep her alive!" Mark shouted to Derek as he turned and ran in the opposite direction.

There was no way he would outrun the drones, and if Derek, Stacy, and the others stayed put, there was no chance they'd outrun them either. They resumed their sprint south, back toward the forest edge and river of death that awaited there. Along the way, though it might have been his imagination, Derek thought he heard an echoing whimper from behind, as the drones caught Mark and stole whatever promising life still existed within him. If it was real, then the clock was ticking before the drones caught them again as well.

———

Amanda was watching through the lead drone's eyes. They'd been momentarily distracted by their primary mission, but were now back on the prowl. The rear-most innocent was only thirty yards ahead. The drones would break formation in a matter of seconds, coordinate which would take out each target, then proceed with their attack, finishing the job they'd started minutes earlier. Amanda sensed her superiors observing her. They were in The Hive's control room, still pleased with her progress, and yet... worried about something. Amanda opened herself to their thoughts. Intruders were coming. They were coming for her. A small army was being assembled to combat them, but the army was inexperienced, hardly an effective defense against the heavily armed group headed their way.

Ten yards. The forest drones had split apart for a triangulated attack. They'd picked their first of the opposition targets and were calculating who to take out second and third. Amanda felt her mind trigger again. The intruders were opposition targets as well. She could sense that from her superiors' thoughts. Only unlike those in Eden, these targets were here, on this island, ready to strike. The makeshift army wouldn't stop them. They'd break through, infiltrate The Hive, destroy that which Amanda was bound to protect.

Five yards. Amanda couldn't leave her defense to an inept group trained in science and engineering rather than warfare. There was only one qualified person on this island who could defend it against the intruders. There was only one person she could trust to get the job done. One yard...

———

The Hive's fluorescent lighting pulsed erratically. An electrical cable split, showering the main chamber floor with sparks. Coolant lines re-opened, their gasses spilling from the drone pod array. Computers inside the control room glitched, gibberish from their fried CPUs running the length of their screens. An energized charge filled the air, and through the observation window, all those present could see Amanda's body burning brightly as the storm of energy particles enveloping her swelled.

"What's she doing?" the Woman in White asked frantically.

A technician tried to get her computer to respond, but to no avail. "We don't know."

The glass cover to Amanda's pod exploded outward. The energy storm consumed her, dematerializing every remaining molecule in her body.

"We need to contain her!" the Woman in White yelled.

This time, Albert responded. "We can't!"

Amanda's swarm pulsed in place, sucking in enough electricity and Trizorapine to fuel its coming fight. Then it oriented on the approaching threat and shot through the wall of The Hive, merging and unmerging until it reached the surface, where it would achieve the mission it had been given. A stunned silence hung over the control room. No one knew how or why the Alpha child had escaped its pod, and it was obvious now that it—not them—was in control. The Woman in White spun to face the Dark Man, who'd been watching from behind her. But all she caught was the closing control room door, and emptiness where he'd so often stood.

———

Lamar squeezed his eyes shut. Out of shape relative to the others, he'd fallen to the back of the group as they'd fled the approaching drones. He heard them coming, felt the electricity of their swarms as they neared his skin, and knew he was as good as dead. But then—nothing. Lamar felt no piercing of his body, nor a blunt impact that would send him tumbling. He was also still breathing, his heart still pumping, and as far as he could tell, fully intact. When that fact finally dawned on him, he risked slowing. When harm still didn't befall him, he stopped altogether. Then Lamar looked back—and there they were. All three drones had returned to bodily form. But instead of pursuing, they were standing motionless in the woods, as if in a catatonic state.

"What the hell are you doing?" Derek hollered over his shoulder.

"They've stopped!"

Derek thought he was hearing things, but then he glanced past Lamar and saw what the geologist had seen. He slowed down, nearly tripping Stacy and Rebecca, who'd been hot on his heels.

"We have to keep going!" Stacy said, tugging at him.

Derek pointed. "Look."

She and the others paused and followed his finger's trajectory. The drones were still frozen in place. They'd reverted to dormant organic lifeforms, the same as they'd been before Amanda had been stolen away to give them life.

"Listen," Rebecca said.

Something had changed in the air. The exodus mob was no longer screaming. There were cries, there were whimpers, there were expressions of anger and sadness, but there wasn't any fear. The slaughter had stopped.

"What's happening?" Stacy asked.

Against his better judgment, and her discouragement, Derek stepped cautiously toward the lead drone. He waved a hand in front of its face, but it didn't even blink in response. Derek then stared into its eyes, where he saw microscopic specks of energy floating in stasis.

"Are they dead?" James asked.

"No," Derek said. "It's like they've exhausted their instructions or something." He pondered over his own statement, then clarified, a smile slipping across his lips, "It's Shortcake. She's stopped guiding them."

The others took the news with relief, some dropping to the forest floor to catch their breath. But Stacy wasn't so quick to read into the revelation. She joined Derek near the drone, examined it, and noticed the same glowing energy deep within its pupils. If it wasn't dead, then it could resume its attack as soon as it received a new set of orders. But those orders needed to come from Amanda, and for whatever reason, its connection to her had been severed for the time being.

"What do you think this means?" Stacy asked.

Derek hadn't the foggiest idea. "That's the million dollar question, isn't it? But if these things are still alive, then Shortcake's still alive. So there's hope."

"Or death," James said, souring the mood. His spiritual channeling of Frank Holmes grabbed everyone's attention. "The question isn't what the stoppage means. The question is who's behind it. If it's your sister, Amanda, then I agree, there's hope for us all. But if it's the Alpha child, then what we've witnessed so far is just a taste of things to come." He swallowed hard, disturbed by the thought he vocalized next. "The fate of humanity is in one of their hands." He motioned toward the frozen drones and their glowing eyes. "I imagine we'll find out shortly whose that is."

CHAPTER 17
CHOICE

Frank and Simmons stepped lightly. Through the trees, barely twenty yards away, a panther with oil slick fur was chomping on a mound of bloody remains on the ground. This was the third lethal predator they'd come across during their hike across Sunrise Isle. So far, they'd managed to skirt each without detection, and were hoping to do the same with this one. Frank and Simmons hadn't encountered a mass extermination like the one found on the northern end of the island. But they'd seen numerous signs of violent confrontations, from disturbed foliage, to ripped fur and lost teeth, to trails of blood that were still fresh, but which they avoided so they wouldn't find out what was at the end of those trails. They'd also felt and seen evidence of ongoing geological disturbances. There was no way the disturbances were natural, for they were tearing the island apart, and Frank wondered just how much more the land mass could take before chunks of it started breaking off into the ocean.

Simmons stepped on a twig hidden beneath damp leaves. The panther's head jolted upright, strings of flesh and fur dangling from its jaws. It glanced around, and Frank and Simmons held still except for tightening their grips on their pistols. The panther's eyes locked in their direction. They could see it, which meant it could see them, no matter how still they remained. The predator growled, a warning not to come anywhere near its food. Simmons motioned for Frank to keep walking—away from the panther—and Frank obliged, sidestepping to avoid taking his eyes off the threat. The panther watched for several more seconds. Then, apparently comfortable Frank and Simmons were only passing by, it returned to its meal.

The ground shook. Frank braced against a tree while Simmons kneeled to lower his center of gravity. The panther's head snapped up again. It looked around with fright, then yelped as the ground beneath it split open and a battalion of thin, hairy roots reached out of the depths to ensnare its legs. The panther snapped ferociously at its attackers, but the roots slithered around its neck and squeezed, cutting off its oxygen supply. The panther contorted and pulled, but it was no use. The roots had a stranglehold on it, and a few seconds later, they retracted like a cable being wound by a winch, breaking the panther's bones and compressing its limbs in unnatural positions so they could squeeze it through the crack from which they'd come. Then the predator was gone, and Frank and Simmons were left rattled by something they'd likely never get used to, no matter how many times they saw it.

Ever since the beach incident, they'd been expecting a genetically modified root network to come after them. But neither the roots nor the plants to which they belonged seemed interested. It was as if Frank and Simmons either weren't threatening enough or appetizing enough to be hunted... at least for now. They didn't complain, however, for while they felt confident in their ability to avoid, and if necessary, fight, surface predators, there was absolutely no way to evade or overcome the island's vegetation should it set its sights on them. The earthquake passed, so they continued their trek.

"It should be just beyond that ridge," Simmons said, checking his guidance system.

They marched up the indicated incline, reached the top, then looked ahead through the trees. They saw a barbed-wire fence surrounding a military compound that had seen better days. The central building was in disarray, plant life slowly reclaiming territory that had been commandeered by man. The camouflaged bunkers that surrounded it were exposed in several places, animals, plants, and likely the weather having shredded large swaths of tarp over the years. There were vehicles lined along one edge of the compound, but they looked in even worse shape than the buildings, with layers of grime and rust peeking out from the shrubbery that had consumed them. As for the barbed-wire fence, it was overgrown as well, and a section of it had been flattened by a fallen tree, negating the need for wire cutters or concentrated acids, which Frank assumed Simmons was carrying in one of his gear pockets. He started for the open path, but Simmons held him back.

"Wait. Something's happening in there."

Sure enough, Frank heard a commotion from somewhere deep within the compound. It sounded like people arguing, though they were too far away and too muffled to confirm that was the case. Then, as if sightings on this island couldn't get any weirder, a swarm of bright blue energy particles shot upward from the roof of the central building. Frank knew instantly the swarm could only be one person: Amanda, who was heading north on an intercept course to the decoy team. Simmons wasn't as informed, but he'd seen enough footage of the drone attacks to know the energy swarm represented a threat, and for his part, he was glad it was headed away from them.

The commotion suddenly grew louder. Then someone exited the central building. The individual was wearing clothing akin to a mechanic's uniform. He shouted something about *not signing up for this*, then threw a pistol to the ground and stormed away from the building. Two more individuals followed, one in a similar uniform, the other in a lab coat. They had weapons as well—which they kept—though it appeared they had no intent of using them to defend Complex E. A man Frank recognized as the Plainclothes he'd interrogated on the way to Complex B marched after them, barking orders for them to return to their posts. But they ignored him. Then, a small mob of their coworkers emerged from the central building. Two more Plainclothes flanked them, each begging them to return inside. A leader broke from the mob.

"Come on, everyone," Diego shouted loudly enough for Frank and Simmons to hear clearly. "The emergency boats are this way. I've got a manual override code for the island barrier."

The Plainclothes continued their protest, but they could do nothing to stop the worker exodus. Armed with most of what remained of Complex E's arsenal, they set off through the compound's front gate and marched into the jungle. The Plainclothes shouted obscenities of frustration, then collected the few weapons the workers had left behind.

"Are you ready for this, Holmes?" Simmons asked as he checked his pistol.

Frank nodded. Then Simmons took off for the fallen section of fencing. Frank stayed hot on his heels as they crossed over the smashed foliage and metal, their stomping drawing the Plainclothes' attention. Three was the first to assess the incoming threat. He raised one of the guns he'd picked up, but Simmons planted a bullet in his head before he could pull the trigger. Four had no interest in risking his life, so he bolted for the entrance to the central building. But Simmons didn't let him get there, nailing him in the back with two bullets, the first of which incapacitated him, and the second of which ended his life. One wasn't focused on Simmons. He had his eyes set on Frank. Unfortunately for him, he had no weapon. And by the time he'd lunged for one on the ground, Frank had already taken aim and fired, landing a bullet in his side. One screamed in agony as he skidded into the grass. Frank stood over him and took aim again.

"Wait, wait wait," One pleaded through the pain. "I can help you, Detective."

Experienced in his ability to weasel, Frank wasn't buying it. "You've done enough, already." He centered his sight on One's forehead. "This is for my brother."

And then he pulled the trigger. One's body collapsed against the jungle floor. The adrenaline-fueled moment over, Frank felt a jolt as the realization of what he'd done hit him. He'd taken the life of a person who'd already been incapacitated—an adversary, but a person nonetheless. Even with his track record of questionable law enforcement tactics, this was a line he'd never crossed before, and it left his mind clouded.

"Holmes..."

It was Simmons's firm voice, and it was followed by an approving nod. The SEAL member was silently reminding him that they were engaged in a war, and that One wasn't a person, but an enemy combatant. There was too much on the line to leave loose ends, including him. Accepting the hard truth, Frank helped Simmons check pulses to confirm the three Plainclothes were dead before proceeding into the central building. There was no resistance, Project Impulse's entire makeshift army having walked off the job. And as icing on the cake, the Plainclothes had left the hidden floor entrance to Complex E wide open when scrambling to stop them. So Frank and Simmons descended into the facility unimpeded, ready to face whatever defensive force remained there. One thing Frank knew for sure was that they wouldn't need to worry about Amanda putting up a fight, though the same couldn't be said for their friends to the north. He thought about Vincent and Joseph, about their determination to save their daughter, a daughter that was undoubtedly on her way to kill them. He said a silent prayer, wishing them luck on their mission, and resolute on completing his in case they failed.

The energy swarm touched down on a bed of damp grass and leaves to the north of Complex E. Amanda reformed her unstable body, which was still crackling with electricity despite being disconnected from The Hive. She'd supercharged her physically exhausted cells before departing, supplementing their lack of caloric fuel and adrenaline with controlled pulses of electrical energy. It was the only way to ensure she'd have enough stamina to both defend Complex E and return safely. Amanda had essentially turned herself into an organic battery, but like all batteries, she had her limits. She was still inhabiting the drone army, but she couldn't actively direct it without the continuous feeds of Trizorapine and power The Hive provided her. She also had full use of her own genetic enhancements, but they would deplete her stored charge quickly. She needed to subdue the approaching threat before that happened.

Amanda stared straight ahead, honing in on her targets. There were five of them. They were armed, but their ammunition had been significantly depleted from encounters with aggressive predators. Their mental states were... difficult to comprehend. All five were scared, but not for the same reasons. Two had been shaken by something devastating they'd seen upon arrival, a feeling that was subsequently compounded by their encounters with the island's native inhabitants. One was afraid solely of failure, his mind repeatedly reminding him of the larger consequences of that failure, consequences for which Amanda herself would be responsible. The last two... they were the most difficult to understand. They weren't afraid for themselves. They'd come to this island already accepting they might die here. No, they were afraid for Amanda. They were afraid she would never again be the person she once was. She didn't quite know what to make of that. She recognized there was more to her than that of which she was consciously aware. But it was buried inside of her, suppressed by chemical barriers, and tucked away into a dark recess she couldn't access.

She had accessed it, though. It's where she had gotten the idea to focus the drone attacks on Eden. Whether that particular decision had been a misstep for Project Impulse remained to be seen. But the efficiency with which the drones had been eliminating Eden's infected prior to Amanda cutting their feed had been impressive, suggesting it had been the right call. Either way, whatever was buried behind the chemical barriers wasn't something Amanda could readily access of her own accord, even if a piece of it had slipped through before. And if these two hostiles were hoping to release more, then their mission had failed before it had even begun.

Amanda started toward the targets. But after only a few steps, she sensed more threats closing in on her. These were animal, not man. The first, a grizzly bear, pushed through foliage ahead and to the left. It was joined by two others of its kind, one by its side and the other to the right. A panther appeared, its fangs bared and hungering for the chemicals within Amanda's body. Then came the killer bees, a swarm large enough to take down most mammals. They were followed by a tiger and pair of hyenas, none typical of those found in other parts of nature. These animals had either been directly exposed to Project Impulse's experimental chemicals or were the spawn of those that had. In both cases, their minds and bodies had been genetically altered in ways that made them mentally unstable, but also even more bloodthirsty than they otherwise would be.

Amanda considered how best to handle the blockade of flesh that had erected itself before her. In her heightened state, these creatures didn't stand a chance against her, even working in unison. But they weren't alone. Amanda sensed something else on the prowl for the Trizorapine she harbored. Whatever it was, it was all around her: in the ground, standing high overhead, all across the surface from one end of the island to the other. The plant life wanted her as much as the animals did. And it was closing in on her, roots shifting, vines slithering, even tree trunks and blades of grass bending in for their share of the prize. Amanda felt a vibration beneath her feet. These creatures needed to be taught their place. They needed to know what fate awaited them if they proceeded with their attack. So she shot a dematerialized arm into the earth, snagged the thick root that had been preparing to seize her legs, and ripped it out of the ground. She reformed her arm and held the struggling root high for all creatures to see, then snapped it in half and tossed its bleeding pieces onto the forest floor ahead of her.

Amanda let her eyes burn bright with energy as she dematerialized both hands, her arms stretched outward as if inviting the next challenger. The island's native inhabitants saw her for what she was: an alpha predator, the ruler of this genetically altered kingdom, and one which they must respect. The prowling vegetation pulled away, and the assortment of mutated surface predators retreated from sight. They wouldn't bother Amanda again.

"How far are we?" Vincent asked as the decoy team entered a small clearing.

Novak checked his guidance system. "We should be there in a few minutes. If this Complex E of yours is going to send human resistance after us, this is its last chance."

"I'm starting to think they don't have any human resistance left," General Javez commented. "Between the losses of two other facilities and Colonel Davis's defection, their military resources may be strapped."

"Let's hope so," Elliott said. "Because we don't have enough ammunition to—"

Before he could finish his sentence, a spear of energy particles thrusted into his chest, through his heart, and out his backside. Elliot's body seized, his mouth hanging open from speaking, his eyes blank as death ripped his soul from its fresh corpse. The energy particles pulled back, Elliot's body dropping with a thud to the damp ground, and rematerialized as Amanda's arm. The chaotic child of science stepped out of a dense wall of foliage and into the clearing, her predatory eyes set upon her targets, her mental faculties in a heated contest over what to do about them.

Novak made the decision for her. He shook the shock of Elliot's death in a matter of seconds and responded as his training dictated he should. He fired upon Amanda with his assault rifle, but she absorbed every round into an energy shield, expending energy to tune out the pain of impact, yet simultaneously recovering it by feeding off each projectile's kinetic charge. She swung a whip of energy particles to disarm Novak, then snapped that same whip around to knock him off his feet. General Javez had taken aim before Novak hit the ground, but Amanda had turned her free arm into another spear of energy particles that she launched at his chest. He shifted his assault rifle to take the brunt of the attack, and though the energy particles dispersed through it instead of his body, their impact was powerful enough to knock him ten feet backwards, where the back of his head slammed into a tree trunk and left him unconscious on the ground. Amanda brought the spear around and pointed it at Novak's head.

"Shortcake, no!" Vincent said.

Her head snapped in his direction. This was one of the two hostiles with such confusing intentions. Amanda's programming told her he was a threat to Complex E, yet some gut instinct and her own assessment of their current encounter told her he wouldn't attack her. As if reading her thoughts, Vincent held up his hands in a gesture of peace. Then he slowly disarmed himself, dropping all weapons to the ground and stepping away to communicate he had no intent of using them against Amanda. Her mind told her the gesture was meaningless. Her battery was discharging with every second that passed away from The Hive. She should finish what she'd started and get back to resume the attack on Eden. But the conflict within her was too real to ignore. Where was it coming from? Had she been infected by something previously imprisoned behind the chemical barrier of her subconscious? Regardless of what she did about this hostile, or the other that confused her so, she knew she should still eliminate the active threat in her grasp. She focused on her energy spear.

"No!" Vincent repeated, this time more sternly than before.

Was he really telling her what to do? Did this mere man, who bore no special talent, no genetic enhancements, no ties to Amanda's superiors, really think he had authority over her? What gave him that right?

"Please, Shortcake. You don't have to do this. This isn't you."

She stared at him, uncertain what he meant by those words. If this wasn't who Amanda was, then who was she? She was the Alpha child; that's what her programming told her. She was the one who would ensure Project Impulse's success, and then... and then what? Amanda's programming hadn't implanted a projection of the future in her mind, and with no memories on which to base such a future, any vision of it was simply blank. She glanced at Elliott's body on the ground, then at the unconscious lump nestled in the trees just outside the

clearing. Then she looked at Novak, helplessly pinned down by her energy particles, shivering with fear as the instrument of his death loomed inches from his
head. This was who Amanda was. She'd assumed the mantle of death incarnate.
She'd brought it to the world, brought it to Eden, brought it to this island, and
she would continue bringing it, wherever her superiors directed her, until there
was no more death to deliver.

"Shortcake," Vincent said, his voice pleading, "come back to us."

Something inside of her wanted to listen. But her programming told her it
was nothing but weakness. She needed to shut it out. She needed to finish this
mission. She needed to eliminate the sources of conflict within her. Vincent could
see that Amanda was struggling. He took a chance, knowing it could mean his life,
and stepped toward her with an outstretched hand of love. Amanda saw it
coming. She recognized the gesture, and though she didn't understand why this
stranger would make it, she knew accepting it would be the end of her. She
screamed with internal strife as she consolidated her spear of energy into a
bowling ball she lobbed at Vincent. It struck his torso, and like General Javez,
blasted him across the clearing, leaving him incapacitated. He wasn't dead, though
he should have been. But something inside Amanda wouldn't let her kill him, at
least not with that first strike.

She heaved a series of deep, unsteady breaths, refocusing her mind to ignore
the conflicted force within her. Then she heard something odd: the rustling of a
paper bag. It was Joseph, though Amanda only knew him as the second member
of the hostiles who'd come for her. He'd seen his partner go down, and was now
scrambling to retrieve something from an innocent looking brown bag he'd been
carrying. Amanda couldn't see nor sense the nature of the weapon inside. That
made it even more dangerous than any gun, knife, or explosive ordinance the man
could have been carrying instead. She couldn't take any chances that he'd brought
with him a way to subdue her.

Amanda redirected the energy particles that had immobilized Vincent. She
snared them around Joseph's neck, then lifted him high into the air. He had the
paper bag open, and had even managed to slip a hand inside. Amanda shook him
from side to side, her programming ordering her to end his life now, before he
deployed his weapon against her. But some speck of recognition inside of her
refused to let her carry out that command. Joseph clung to the bag with every
ounce of strength he had. Amanda tightened the grip around his neck, depriving
him of oxygen. Joseph struggled, one hand on the lip of the bag, the other still
inside of it, trying to reach just a little farther...

It was no use. Amanda was a trained soldier. Even when using non-lethal
force, she knew how to incapacitate an enemy combatant. She applied more pres-

sure to Joseph's neck, cutting off the blood flow to his brain. The speck of recognition inside of her faded into the darkness, no longer able to fight, leaving the Alpha child to do what she had been born to do. The paper bag fell from Joseph's empty hands. It crashed hard against the ground, the bag ripping open, and its contents spilling into the dirt and leaves. Amanda had wasted enough time humoring these hostiles. They were an impediment to the war she was still waging, and it was time to eliminate them. She would start with the most dangerous one of them all, the one she had suspended in midair, turning blue, nearly unconscious as he used every last morsel of strength, hope, and love to point a single finger toward the ground near Amanda's feet. She knew she should ignore him, but that was where his weapon had fallen, and if it presented some unforeseen threat...

Amanda glanced down, expecting to see a gun or bomb of some sort, perhaps something more reliant on chemistry and genetics rather than explosive or concussive force. She could have never foreseen the flimsy plastic container that had broken open upon impact, nor the dessert that had once been inside, but now lay sprawled across the jungle floor. That bright white cream speckled with dirt. Those lush strawberries that looked right at home among the island's greenery. That pale, moist cake that had served as their bedrock...

The speck of recognition in Amanda's mind suddenly burst with life. It reached into the darkness, latching on to the earliest and most precious of her memories, then pulled them forward with a might unlike any Amanda had ever felt before. Her memories shed themselves of their black cloak, crashed through the chemical barriers that had imprisoned them, and stormed her mind with a fury no mental reprogramming could withstand. Her body loosened as her essence took charge once more, ousting the Alpha child from her throne, and resuming reign over her actions and thoughts.

Amanda immediately withdrew the energy particles threatening Novak and Joseph, gently lowering the latter to the ground. She was woozy, her memories of new and old colliding with the violence of asteroids in deep space, merging into a unified history of experiences and emotions. Her true self had just woken from a long and dark dream, and though the terror was behind her now, awareness of the atrocities she had committed while under the spell of Project Impulse were at the forefront of her mind. She shook feverishly, overcome with self-loathing and detestation. How could she have let herself slaughter those innocent people like that? Why hadn't she been stronger, fought harder, forced herself into a state of self-destruction for the sake of humanity?

The answer was clear. It was for the same reason Evan had done all those awful things in Eden so many years ago. It was because *he* wanted it that way. He had implanted himself inside Evan, and it wasn't until Amanda had graced her counterpart with unconditional love that his true self was able to regain control. Now he'd done the same to Amanda. She'd let him in when taking revenge on Judas, and he'd festered inside of her until she could no longer withstand his call. She was awake now, however, the way Evan had awoken in his deranged tower of flesh and bone, and she could see the world the way he had seen it: a vulnerable collection of people seeking their place, their happiness, who never asked to have their lives disrupted by monstrous abominations of science. Evan had begged Amanda to kill him so he couldn't hurt anyone else. But she'd foreseen more good in his survival and had spared his life. She dropped to her knees, sobbing quietly, realizing that she couldn't foresee the same for herself.

Novak scrambled to his feet and aimed his assault rifle.

"Wait!" Joseph choked through a strained voice. "She's not the enemy."

"Like hell she isn't!" Novak retorted.

Joseph motioned to Amanda, curled into herself like a child with no one to turn to. "Look at her. That's not the same person who attacked us."

Novak had trouble understanding. She sure looked like the person who had killed his teammate, knocked out the sheriff and general, and was about to kill him and the professor had she not... stopped. That part didn't compute. She'd stopped of her own accord, and she was making no sign of attacking now. Novak stared at the crumpled girl, no longer popping with electricity, no longer bearing a predator's eyes, and he realized Joseph was right. She was different somehow. She wasn't the genetically enhanced soldier that had come to kill them. She was his daughter, and he was pleading for her life. Though he might live to regret it, Novak lowered his rifle.

"Thank you," Joseph said. "Can you help the others?"

Novak nodded and made his way to Vincent, checking the sheriff's pulse before rousing him. Joseph approached Amanda slowly, unable to imagine what conflicting thoughts must be going through her head, or what internal punishment she was exerting on herself. He kneeled by her side, then placed a fatherly hand on her shoulder.

"It's okay," he said. "You're back now."

Amanda turned her head, her eyes wide with heartbreaking turmoil. "But I—those people—all those people!"

"That wasn't you," Joseph assured her. "That was the Alpha child, and you defeated her."

"Not soon enough," Amanda gasped through hyperventilating breath.

Joseph embraced her, holding her tightly as her tears flowed freely. Moments later, another set of arms joined his as Vincent shared his adopted daughter's burden. They each closed their eyes and leaned their heads in, providing what little comfort they could as Amanda sobbed into her palms. She didn't know how she could live with herself after everything she'd done. She didn't know if she deserved to live. But despite the terror she'd caused, she felt loved. And whether she lived or died, she could ask for nothing more.

By the time she and her fathers broke their embrace, General Javez was back on his feet. He and Novak swapped fresh clips into their guns, preparing for the next leg of their journey. "We need to get back to the helicopter."

Joseph and Vincent helped Amanda up.

"I need to return to Complex E," she said. "There's a machine there they used to control me. They call it The Hive. I need to destroy it."

"We've got another team on the ground taking care of that," General Javez informed her. "Besides, I don't want you anywhere near that machine right now. The best thing we can do is put as much distance between you and it as possible."

Uncertain, Amanda looked at Joseph and Vincent for advice. They nodded in agreement. With everyone now on the same page, Novak checked their bearings, then joined General Javez in lead positions, their weapons at the ready. Amanda stepped ahead of them, however. She knew she couldn't ever fully repent for the tragedy she'd caused, but from now until her dying breath, she was going to make sure she used her abilities for good.

"Stay behind me," she told her military companions. "I'll clear the way."

———

Simmons and Frank rounded a corner deep inside Complex E. So far, there had been absolutely zero resistance to their intrusion. Frank was starting to suspect there wouldn't be, for it seemed Complex E was having its own share of troubles right now. Mild earthquakes kept rocking the facility. Hairline cracks had opened in several walls. Concrete dust mixed with particles of dirt littered the hallway floors. Lighting was erratic, as if the facility's power had been compromised. And the only people Simmons and Frank had seen were civilians who'd cowered at their weapons and begged to get by, swearing they were just trying to get out with their lives intact. After patting each of them down to protect against unexpected bullets in the back, Frank and Simmons had let them go.

They cleared side rooms as they followed Simmons's guidance system to The Hive. Most contained supplies, a few were sleeping quarters, and some were empty closets. Most importantly, none harbored threats to their mission, except for one sleeping quarter from which Frank had heard an ominous scratching against the door. He stood ready with his pistol as he opened it, and a pack of mutant underground beetles, each the size of his fist, scared him shitless as they skittered out. Luckily, they ignored Frank and Simmons and instead followed the hallway leading to The Hive, until they turned a corner and disappeared. The room they'd come from was a wreck, bloody sheets atop the bed, a pair of bloody pants in the middle of the floor, supplies scattered about, and a trail of mud leading from the door to a hole busted in the side wall. Frank didn't want to know what had happened here.

He and Simmons continued down Complex E's main corridor. They eventually reached The Hive's control room, which they expected they would have to break into, but were pleasantly surprised to find wide open, as if whatever civilian worker had been inside last hadn't bothered securing it behind them. Frank and Simmons passed the arrays of abandoned computer terminals and stared through the viewing window that overlooked The Hive's main chamber. They'd obviously known about the hub and spoke device's scale and had brought the ordinance necessary to destroy it, yet it still struck them with awe when they came upon it in person. This thing was a marvel of technology. Albeit, it was some seriously twisted technology; but it was impressive nonetheless.

Frank tried the airlock door that led to the main chamber, but it wouldn't budge. He scanned for an access panel, finding none. Simmons checked the computer terminals, which were either fried or resting on lock screens he didn't have the password for. They shared a *guess we'll have to do this the hard way* shrug, then opened fire on the viewing window. Their bullets marred and cracked the glass, but didn't break it. Simmons removed a small explosive from his vest pocket. He peeled a film backing, exposing a layer of adhesive, and stuck the explosive in the middle of a web of cracks. He then adjusted a dial on the face of the explosive and motioned for Frank to join him in the hallway. Thirty seconds later, the explosive detonated, shattering the viewing window and taking out the front row of computer terminals.

Simmons and Frank climbed over jagged glass and located handholds and footholds they could use to scale the main chamber wall. They reached the floor, then looked at the massive device looming before them. Despite the damage to Complex E and the device itself, it appeared as though it were still functional. Sparks occasionally shot from a split electrical cable, and some sort of images flickered rapidly from a pair of high-tech goggles in the central pod, whose glass was also in pieces. But the lights were on, electricity was humming, and coolant gases were still flowing, creating a dense layer of fog over the ground below. If Amanda returned, the machine would be here waiting to embrace her, so she could continue her war against the rest of the planet.

"Check your top right pouch," Simmons told Frank. "You should have three explosives. The dial on the top tells you the countdown. You have one rigged for seven minutes, another for six, and the last for five. We need to start with the longest and work our way to the shortest, synchronizing as we go." He held out his wrist guidance system, which now displayed a wireframe overlay of The Hive. There were four blinking dots on the overlay. "If we hit these four points in unison, it should collapse the chamber, rendering the device useless. I used my extra to get us in here. I suggest you use yours on the central pod for good measure."

Frank nodded. "I'll take the right half; you take the left?"

"Let's do it."

They went their separate ways. Simmons made it to his first demolition target a few seconds ahead of Frank. He attached his seven minute explosive, waited for Frank to catch up, then counted aloud so they could initiate at the same time. They repeated with their second demolition targets, Simmons again counting aloud not just so they could initiate their six minute timers in unison, but so they could also do so right when the first pair of explosives reached the six minute mark. That was it. The four critical points had been rigged to blow. Simmons met Frank near the central pod and counted down to the five minute mark. Frank initiated his final explosive at the indicated time, then threw it into the open pod, waiting a moment to confirm it didn't bounce back out. Then the shotgun blast came.

Simmons's body jolted forward. He slammed face first into the floor ahead, temporarily displacing its fog, which revealed his back had been torn to shreds by the close range pummeling of pellets. Frank spun to find the Woman in White standing behind him. He caught her mid-pump and leaped out of the way just as she fired at him. He felt the blast of pellets skirt by before tumbling through the fog and hitting the cold surface beneath it. Frank had to assume the Woman in White had seen where he'd landed, so he rolled toward the nearest pod, knowing the fog would continue to billow above him, but hoping the pod's spillage would camouflage his movement.

The Woman in White fired into the floorspace he had just left behind. Then she fired again, this time landing the blast close enough that Frank felt a pellet ricochet into his thigh. He pivoted his roll to the side, where he felt fresh coolant gas falling on him. The Woman in White fired again, this time farther away from him. She'd lost his trajectory.

"How long did you rig those explosives for, Detective? Ten minutes? Five? Less? However long it is, I'll make sure it isn't long enough for you to make it out of here alive."

Frank held still. As long as he didn't move, the coolant gasses wouldn't give him away. He tried to spot the Woman in White's feet, bracing to tackle her as soon as she got close enough, but all he could see was dense mist.

"Let's make a deal, shall we?" she called out. "You shut down the explosives, and I let you walk. We both live to see another day."

She obviously didn't know him very well. Frank would rather die knowing he'd put an end to Project Impulse than provide it an opportunity to continue its sadistic endgame. But if he could make it out alive, that was certainly preferential. The only problem was that he was blind. He thought if he could keep the Woman in White talking, he could triangulate her position. But this chamber was so massive, every word echoed from multiple directions. He could try standing with his pistol ready, and hope he had it pointed close enough to her to get a shot off before she shot him. But his single projectile required much more accuracy than her spread, and she already had a superior position, leaving him with less than desirable odds.

"Come on, Detective," the Woman in White said. "Time's ticking."

She was right about that. Frank didn't know exactly how long he had left to evacuate The Hive, but he guessed it was probably less than three minutes. He gripped his pistol, debating whether to fire a few blind shots to at least get his target's feet moving enough to disrupt the wall of fog between them. Then he wondered why she wasn't doing the same. One possibility was that she was waiting for an opportunity to present itself. Another was that she was low on ammo and knew reloading would leave her vulnerable. Maybe Frank could capitalize on the latter...

He pointed his pistol perpendicular to him, stretched his arm as far as it would go, and fired as close to the floor as possible as not to leave a revealing streak on the fog's surface. The initial discharge echoed throughout the chamber, masking its origin, but the bullet's impact into a far wall startled the Woman in White, who fired another round in its direction. Frank switched his pistol to his other hand, stretched toward the opposite wall, and fired again. As before, the Woman in White spent a shell chasing his ghost.

"I don't know what you think you're accomplishing, Detective. Pretty soon, we'll both die down here."

Frank had slowly swung the pistol ahead of him. He took a nervous breath, then pulled the trigger. This time, the Woman in White actually jumped, her feet briefly disturbing the fog ahead as she discharged her shotgun once more. Its pellets landed close, one nicking Frank's hand and another ricocheting into the side of his scalp. It didn't hit with enough force to cause a major injury, but it burned, and that burn was soon smothered by the warmth of blood.

"Shit," the Woman in White said.

There was a loud clack, then seven spent shells clattered to the hard floor, barely ten feet from Frank. He launched himself forward as the Woman in White got her first fresh round loaded. She abandoned the reload procedure, locked the shotgun, pumped it, and took aim. But Frank was already on top of her. He ripped the weapon from her grasp and rammed her backwards until she slammed into the chamber's front wall. Then he stood back and centered the shotgun's barrel on her chest. The Woman in White released a defeated scoff.

"I always wondered which of you would finally pull the trigger... you or my husband." She slid down into a seated position, knowing it was pointless to fight. "Once my identity was out of the bag, the others thought it would be him. But I knew better. Vincent could never kill me, no matter how much he might want to. But you, Detective... you have the darkness in you, just like your brother. You try to be an honest cop. You try to respect the law. But when push comes to shove, you'll do whatever it takes to shape outcomes as you see fit. You'll lie, you'll oppose the system, you'll cheat, and you'll kill. Because make no mistake about it: you are a killer, Detective. You and your brother are the same."

If she wanted Frank's mercy, she had a hell of a way of showing it. "It's fitting that you bring up my brother. I spent so many years of my life chasing him, running from him, trying to capture him, not wanting to become him... but family is complicated. He got away with torturing me because he knew he could push that line between hatred and love. If he had been any other criminal, I would've had him in jail or in the ground years before he had the opportunity to destroy Eden. But he was family, and, well..." Frank fought back a wave of emotion as he steeled himself for what needed to be done. "I won't let you do that to the Desmonds any longer. They're good people, and they deserve better than I had."

The Woman in White stared hard at him, not an ounce of remorse left on her face. "Then let's not keep wasting each other's time."

Frank tightened his grip on the shotgun and fired, keeping his eyes fixed just long enough to witness its pellets tearing open her chest before turning away. A tremor rippled through him—guilt, chastising his homicidal action. But Frank pushed it away. He couldn't have risked leaving the Woman in White alive, not at this critical juncture, and not with the Desmonds', or the world's, future well-being at stake. She'd proven her resilience too many times already. The chaos needed to end here and now.

Cognizant of the time, Frank threw his weapon aside and ran to the central pod, where he scoured the floor for Simmons. He found the SEAL buried in the coolant fog, but he was already dead, likely killed upon impact. Frank raced back to the viewing window and climbed. He pulled himself haphazardly over shards of glass, slicing his hands and torso before tumbling back into The Hive's control room. Then he pushed himself up and sprinted for the main corridor. He didn't look back as the explosive timers hit zero, their subsequent detonations crippling key support beams before the main chamber imploded under the strain of earth overhead.

———

Amanda and the decoy team reached the beach just as the rumbles of The Hive's cave-in shook the ground beneath their feet. The helicopter's pilot was hanging out its side, a sniper rifle in his hands, having spent the previous ten minutes fending off random predators that had gotten too curious for their own good. As for the team itself, a number of those same predators had lined their path back to the beach. They hadn't attacked, for they saw Amanda had taken the team under her wing. But she sensed that might change if they didn't leave soon. She was no longer brimming with the same power she had been when trekking out of Complex E. She was still the island's dominant predator, but not so dominant that the next in line couldn't challenge her claim to the throne. Its natural inhabitants could see that, and it would only be a matter of time before one of them acted upon it.

"Get those blades spinning!" Novak yelled from across the sand.

The pilot scrambled into his seat and began the helicopter's startup routine. An earthquake struck, this one more violent than any that had preceded it. It knocked everyone except Amanda off their feet. She looked behind her and saw trees rustling violently. Then she saw the predators scatter, each of them running in Complex E's direction. A screech louder than anything Mother Nature could produce emanated from the distance. It was followed by snarls and growls, then the sounds of animalistic combat, which only multiplied in the minute that followed. The peak of the earthquake passed, but the ground was far from still.

"What is that?" Vincent asked, referring to the ongoing growls, snarls, and whimpers.

Amanda placed a palm against the sand and opened her senses. There was a war raging outside of Complex E. Something had happened. Something was drawing the island's flora and fauna into a makeshift arena of jungle and barbed wire. It was intoxicating, something they felt they needed, something they were willing to kill each other to obtain. But the plants had the advantage. They were the ones with direct access. Aside from a handful of earth-dwelling creatures, they were the ones absorbing the prize that had been released into their underground ecosystem during The Hive's collapse. They were spreading it, overdosing on it. *And they wanted more.*

Amanda knew the feeling all too well. "Trizorapine. The island's root network was just flooded with Trizorapine." She saw Joseph's worried look, his first thought that of the Trizorapine flowing through her system. "It's okay. It hasn't reached the beach yet. We just need to leave before it does."

The earth quaked violently again. This time, everyone could hear the pain of it cracking open, not just in one location, but several across the island. Distant trees fell. The animal arena slaughter continued.

"Come on!" General Javez yelled.

He crawled on all fours across the beach, unwilling to let these quakes prevent their escape. The others followed suit, Amanda falling behind them even though she was the only one who could maintain her balance as the ground trembled. There was something else happening on the island. It was something unrelated to the Trizorapine release or predator battle. It was darkness, whisking its way across the surface, fleeing its own destruction, so that it might return another day. Amanda let her mind follow the darkness. She saw the jungle crumbling as even the plants turned on one another, each in service of its own chemical needs and willing to kill the rest to fulfill them. She saw the eastern shore and a flat stretch of land hanging over the ocean. Amanda saw a helipad at the end of that stretch, and a host vehicle waiting upon it for a passenger it couldn't refuse. He was going to get away. He was going to escape Project Impulse's destruction. He was going to move on to infect others, the way he had her, Evan, Judas, Abigail Desmond, Raymond Holmes, and countless more. And then, when he'd rebuilt his forces and was ready to see humanity's fall through to the end, he would come for her again. And there was no guarantee she'd be able to resist him then.

"We need to go now!" Vincent yelled.

He and the rest of the decoy team had made it to the helicopter. They were on board, most strapping in, and the pilot preparing for takeoff. Amanda walked calmly up to the helicopter's side hatch, but didn't board.

"What are you waiting for?" Joseph asked.

She looked at him with solemn, loving eyes, then said what she already knew would be the second most painful words to ever leave her mouth. "I have to stay."

Everyone aboard the helicopter froze, uncertain they'd heard her correctly.

"What?" Vincent asked. "No—"

Amanda took his hand and gave it a heartfelt squeeze. Then she repeated, "I have to stay." She recalled the night she had first escaped from Helix Unbound. She remembered Joseph's pleading tone, his battle to fight the sadness within him as he set his little girl free into the world, not knowing at the time whether he would ever see her again. A serene, but sad, smile formed on Amanda's lips as she quoted his own words from so many years ago back to him. "I have to stay... so that you can live." She motioned over her shoulder. "*He's* still out there. I can feel him. And if he gets away now, this circle of violence will never end. I have to stop it, right here, right now, while there's a still a chance."

Joseph protested. "But... the island."

"I can handle the island," Amanda said confidently. "You raised me to be a survivor." She looked at Vincent. "And you raised me to be courageous." She stepped back and addressed them both. "Now I need you to trust me to finish what I started."

Joseph started unbuckling his restraints. "We're coming with you."

"No, you aren't."

Vincent followed suit. "We're not giving you a choice."

Amanda frowned, fresh tears in her eyes. "I'm not giving you one, either."

She released two streams of energy particles from her fingertips. The first pushed Vincent back into his seat and refastened his restraints. The second did the same to Joseph. They fought back, each one pulling at their buckles with futility while begging for Amanda not to do this. She fused their restraints shut before retracting the particles into her hand. Then she caught the pilot's eye.

"Get them out of here."

He glanced at Novak and General Javez for confirmation.

The latter stared hard at Amanda, then spoke to her, one soldier to another. "Are you sure you can do this?"

Amanda nodded resolutely. General Javez relayed the nod to Novak, who then relayed it to the pilot. Joseph and Vincent continued their protests as Novak shut the side hatch. Then the helicopter lifted and hovered out over the ocean. Amanda watched it shrink as it moved farther and farther away. She could still hear her fathers' voices in her mind. They pleaded for General Javez and Novak to cut them free. They begged the pilot to turn around. But the others were obeying Amanda's request, and they would do so until Joseph and Vincent were clear of harm's way. She closed her hearing off to their pleas, then stared as the helicopter grew ever smaller, and finally said what she'd already known would be the most painful thing she would ever have to say. It was the one word she couldn't bring herself to vocalize to her fathers' faces, but which she had to speak aloud now, given the one-way trip she knew lay ahead.

"Goodbye."

CHAPTER 18

THE LIVING DARKNESS

rank exited Complex E to the sounds of a raging war zone. He'd barely made it out, first getting clipped by The Hive's implosion, then bobbing and weaving his way around mutant plant roots as they broke through every room and corridor of the facility in search of a narcotics fix, and then almost being swallowed whole by a fissure that had split open in the exit tunnel. Despite the deck being stacked against him, he'd made it to the surface in relatively good condition, though he promised himself a vacation when this was over... assuming it would truly be over.

Frank's initial plan was to launch rescue flares from the surface compound. He would find a way to climb onto the roof of the central building and wait for retrieval. But now he saw that was no longer an option. The surface compound was a bloodbath. The bodies of dozens of large predators were sprawled across the ground, and dozens more were in active combat, biting and clawing at both each other and the aggressive plant life that had overrun the facility. With no desire to become collateral damage after everything he'd already survived, Frank hightailed it for the fallen barbed-wire fence. He thought he was in the clear, but then a massive grizzly bear came charging over the fence, on course directly for him. Frank readied his pistol and prepared to dodge the grizzly, in hopes of then either outrunning it or wounding it enough to scare it off. But the grizzly didn't engage him.

It veered at the last second, avoiding Frank altogether, more interested in joining the drug-induced battle for predatory dominance. He felt its rough fur as it grazed past him, then heard its jaws snap with primal rage as a pair of vines intercepted it mid-charge. Fascinated, Frank watched those vines lift the grizzly into the air, then tear it in half, spilling its guts on the compound floor. Smaller animals and plants raced in to claim their share of its chemical-infused innards.

Okay, Frank thought to himself, *fascination over. Time to get the hell out of here.*

He continued into the jungle, where he dodged falling trees, leaped over expanding cracks in the ground, and steered clear of any other creatures heading into battle. Frank reached a clearing just large enough to accommodate the infil-tration helicopter, then fired a red flare into the sky. He waited two minutes for the pilot to start on an initial bearing, then fired another flare to help him hone in on the exact retrieval location. Frank heard spinning blades approaching, then jumped and waved as the helicopter passed overhead. It looped around, then lowered just enough for him to climb aboard without touching down on the jungle floor.

"Where are the others?" the pilot asked.

"They didn't make it. Let's go."

The pilot didn't need to be told twice. He pulled the helicopter high over Sunrise Isle, outside the reach of its dangerous inhabitants, then started back toward the ocean. Frank stared out of a side window, finally getting a grasp on the insanity unfolding below. Predators were still charging in from all directions, converging on Complex E, where they were being slaughtered by each other and the even deadlier foliage in the area. Catastrophic fissures covered the island surface, displacing trees and earth, erecting impassible barriers, and plummeting trapped animals into rocky depths. Rivers of saltwater had breached what had previously been solid ground, and Frank watched as a southern chunk of Sunrise Isle broke off from the larger mass, then bobbed precariously on the ocean surface before sinking into a watery grave. A second chunk, this one along the western shore, followed shortly thereafter.

"Holy shit," the pilot said.

Yeah, Frank thought. *Holy shit was right.*

Sunrise Isle's out-of-control plant life had destabilized its entire system, both ecologically and geologically. Its vegetation seemed oblivious to its own self-destructive behavior, drilling countless holes through the earth that harbored it, breaching the surface to attack land animals, and even fighting amongst itself, killing the very fabric that held the island's foundation together. A third chunk broke off and floated away before sinking into the ocean's depths. Saltwater rivers were growing, fissures were widening, and soon, Sunrise Isle itself would be nothing more than a memory.

———

Amanda stood on the boundary between beach and jungle. The path ahead was one of chaos, a violently changing landscape surrounded by deadly plant life that could smell the Trizorapine in her blood and was poised to strike the moment it sensed vulnerability. It was a path no sane person would dare traverse, yet it was one Amanda had no choice but to face if she wanted to reach the Dark Man before he escaped. She reached into her shirt and exposed Evan's fang necklace. Then she wrapped a palm around it and closed her eyes, her mind reaching out beyond the boundaries of mortality, calling to her fallen lover, willing him to her side.

"I don't know if you're out there," she whispered, "but if you are, I'm ready. This task is our burden to bear, our last chance to make things right. Let's do it together, and when it's over, we'll be together once more."

She stood in silence, tuning out the noises of destruction around her, until she felt a mental warmth touch her skin. It spread over her hand, embracing her the way she was embracing Evan's fang. It caressed her head, her lover's phantom presence holding her as he once had, sharing his undying love for her, a love that knew no bounds, not even death itself. Amanda felt his embrace transfer through her skin, carrying its warmth to her heart, providing her with one last remembrance of the bond they'd shared. She experienced a flutter, then a surge of exhilaration that accelerated her breath, and opened her eyes.

Amanda was once again by herself in this collapsing hellscape, but she was no longer alone. She stared at the jungle path ahead, along which surface predators were now gathering. They were the same ones that had tracked her to the beach, the ones that knew she wasn't the Alpha child any longer. And they were waiting for her. Amanda yanked on Evan's necklace, snapping its woven thread. She then adjusted her grip on the fang, holding it like a knife, her mind refocused on the end goal, and her body and soul determined not to let anything stand in her way. She took a deep breath, released it, and spoke her final words:

"I will fear no evil."

Then she charged into the fray. A panther attacked first, but Amanda ducked beneath its leap and used Evan's fang to slice open its gut. A pack of hyenas thought they could surprise her while her attention was diverted, but Amanda swung around a whip of energy particles that penetrated their flesh and sliced open their hearts. The trees must have sensed the land predators couldn't take her alone, for they formed a temporary alliance and joined the action. A heavy branch swung toward the back of Amanda's head. She felt the distortion in wind and turned in time to catch the branch with an energy shield. She then wrapped the shield around it like a vise and snapped it clean from its trunk. A grizzly bear and wolf charged from her left, and Amanda used the snapped branch to impale them both.

Vines along the ground snaked up her feet. Amanda felt their mutant teeth sink into her ankles. She briefly dematerialized the atoms in her legs, sending the vines flailing. Then she whipped a stream of energy particles downward, slicing their heads from their bodies. Four paws slammed against her back. The next thing Amanda knew, she was on the ground, some sort of jungle feline on top of her. The animal sunk its teeth into her shoulder, and through the pain, Amanda could feel those teeth sucking the blood out of her like vampiric fangs. She stabbed a hand behind her, Evan's fang finding the feline's neck and tearing it open. The feline yelped and pulled back, giving her time to stand. But the next set of vines was already on her. They restrained her ankles and wrists, their own teeth chewing into her flesh. Amanda dematerialized her appendages to loosen herself, but as soon as she reformed them, a new quartet of predatory foliage bound her. Its prey helpless, the feline came back for a second attack, this time burying its fangs into Amanda's thigh.

The child of science considered dematerializing her entire body and making a flying dash for the far edge of the island. But she didn't know if she had enough strength to make it, her Omega Genome far past exhaustion, and her Trizorapine levels being drained even quicker than planned by the vampiric nature of her enemies. She couldn't risk landing short of her goal, surrounded by predators, and with no defenses left. She dematerialized one arm, shaping it into a lance she used to pierce the feline's skull. Then she snapped the lance into a snaking whip and sliced through her restraining vines. She progressed farther down her path, slicing with Evan's fang on one side and her energy whip on the other, stealing back what Trizorapine she could with each lash. The land predators were thinning, but increased plant life was taking their place. The island was also in a constant state of intense quaking, and Amanda could hear layers of ancient rock splitting open all around her.

The vines slipped past her defenses and grabbed her again. An Anaconda dropped from a high tree perch and sank its teeth into her side. Another grizzly bear emerged from the jungle ahead. The vines pulled Amanda to her knees. She could feel herself weakening. She needed to do something to exert her dominance, to show these creatures she was still their Alpha. It was the only way they'd let her pass. But to do so... Amanda couldn't guarantee she'd have much energy left when it was done. She realized it was a moot point, however, for if she didn't do something drastic now, Sunrise Isle's chemical atrocities would drain her not only of her Trizorapine, but of her life. And she couldn't let that happen. Not yet.

Amanda concentrated the molecules within her. She ignored the sharp grip of the vines, the stabbing pain of the Anaconda as it pressed its fangs deeper into her, and the hungry eyes of the grizzly that was now running straight for her. She dematerialized her body, drawing every pulsing particle inward, creating an unstable core of raw energy. Then she allowed her molecules to collide, and her collective mass exploded outward, energy particles shooting in all directions like shrapnel from a grenade. They sliced through every organic lifeform within a quarter-mile radius, killing most and incapacitating all others. Then they slowly collected where Amanda had stood and reformed her body, which fell to one knee in the center of a wide, circular burn on the jungle floor.

Amanda had never done something like that before, and she wasn't sure she could ever do it again, at least not without the type of supercharging The Hive's machine had provided her. Her vision tried to fail her. She lacked balance and felt nauseous. But she couldn't show weakness now, not after such a drastic measure to display her strength. She pushed through her body's resistance and stood, faking stability as she took in oxygen as rapidly as she could. The plant life surrounding her was still. The land animals were on the ground, dead or dying. And a quarter mile ahead, those that waited cowered from Amanda's path, no longer interested in challenging her reign over a collapsing kingdom.

Amanda limped forward, her body having failed to come perfectly back together following her outburst. She tasted blood on her lip. It was running down from her nose, evidence of the trauma her brain had endured. The glare of sunlight filtering through tree canopies brightened until it was almost blinding. Then it dimmed, leaving Amanda's vision obstructed by black spots. A deafening roar rose to her left. The ground cracked and lifted, and another section of Sunrise Isle released into the ocean. Amanda stumbled, hardly able to see where she was going. She could feel the land predators returning, their chemically enhanced senses piercing her facade.

Just a little farther, she told herself.

Her mental encouragement then assumed Evan's voice. *You can make it.*

Something dripped to Amanda's right. It was more blood, this time seeping from the vine wounds that had reopened around her wrist as her healing abilities faltered. The blood was running over her palm and across Evan's fang, which was still tight in her grasp, then dripping off its point in repeated pitter patters against the damp dirt and leaves below. The blood attracted the ants. They emerged from their nests, wave upon wave on the prowl for the source of their stimulant. Amanda could hear them scurrying behind her. More roaring, and another chunk of the island sank away, taking out a sixth of the remaining jungle.

The ants were closer now. Their mandibles clicked with ravenous hunger. Nearby, a pack of the remaining land predators neared, fanning out to box in their wounded prey. Amanda coughed, her lungs under too much strain. Evan's voice told her to keep going. It reminded her that she wasn't a quitter, that no matter how far she fell, she would always have the strength to rise back up. Amanda felt a throbbing in her temple. The deterioration inside reminded her of her Trizorapine overdose when battling Judas. But this wasn't an overdose. This was quite the opposite. She'd pushed her Omega Genome too far. The last time she and Evan had done that, their abilities had gone dormant for years, shutting down as a protective measure to save their lives. But Amanda wouldn't let them shut down this time. She needed them, whatever little was left of them, for her confrontation with the Dark Man. And her body was paying the price.

Something growled to the right, preparing to strike. Something else growled to the left. The ants were on her heels, scurrying over one another in a race for the first bite. Then came the tree line, and Amanda broke through to blinding light, beyond which were the remains of the island's eastern shore. The ants and land predators didn't pursue her farther, almost as if they were afraid to leave the confines of the jungle. That, or they were afraid of what waited in the clearing beyond. Amanda's eyes adjusted, and then she saw the stretch of flat land with the blurry helicopter parked at its far end. Its blades were spinning, and the Dark Man was climbing aboard with what appeared to be a temperature-controlled steel briefcase in his hand.

Amanda flailed her arms as much as her broken body would allow. The helicopter pilot spotted her and signaled the Dark Man, who glanced back with indifference. Amanda hobbled across the clearing, too weak to show aggression, too far gone to present a threat. The Dark Man watched her come, his indifference yielding to curiosity. He stepped down from the helicopter and observed Amanda's struggle. She knew what she must look like: a battle-worn soldier far past her prime, ready to be put down to make way for fresh blood. But she also knew the Dark Man believed in her. He believed in her strength, her ability, her determination to survive at all costs. He wouldn't judge her by her ragged appearance. He would see the fight within her, and if there was any way to fix her, he wouldn't let the opportunity pass him by. He started down the stretch.

This was it. Amanda had him now. All she had to do was reel him in, capture him with her lure, and then let nature take its course. She dragged one foot behind the other, every motion an excruciating toll on her crumbling skeleton. She ignored the increasing blood loss, the multiplying head throbs, her now nearly nonexistent vision. It was all irrelevant, for her goal was right in front of her. He closed the gap. Fifteen feet. Then ten. Amanda paused and held out her empty hand, a plea for his help, an acknowledgement that she was his, if only he would save her. Five feet. Then one. The Dark Man examined Amanda. She feigned inner strength despite having none left, then looked from his black eyes to her open hand, unable to beg with her voice, but trusting he would get the message anyway.

The Dark Man extended a hand of his own. It was radiating with power, a force of evil that had mastered pulling the proverbial strings of death. Amanda braced herself for contact, telling herself she only had to resist him for a few seconds at best. Then they touched, and she felt the darkness taking her, enveloping her broken soul and claiming it for its own. Time was running out. She had to make her final stand against the dark. And she had one last move at her disposal...

Channeling the combined strength of her inner essence and Evan's love, she swung his fang overhead, jamming it through the back of her hand, driving so hard that it broke through her palm and pierced the Dark Man's flesh. He tried to pull away, but Amanda held tight and pushed the fang deeper, until it broke through the other side, binding them together. Then she let her defenses fall. She stopped trying to hold her molecules together. She stopped fighting the rapid deterioration of her physical being. And she let her blood flow, from her wrists, from her hemorrhaging brain, from the Anaconda bite that had reopened in her side, and from the puncture wound in her hand. It mixed with the Dark Man's blood. Her chemical imbalance spread to his open wound, infecting him, tainting him with the same Trizorapine he'd subjected her to since the day she was born. And then the predators came...

The swarm of ants was first. Whatever fear had been holding it back from this clearing dissipated the moment Amanda had struck the Dark Man. He kicked and squirmed as the ants climbed up his legs and pelvic region, nibbling with their mandibles, but saving plenty for the land predators and plants that soon followed. Amanda couldn't feel the pain of their bites or any others from the larger creatures that pounced upon them both. Her spine and nerve network had already deteriorated beyond that point. But she did manage a relieved smile as thick vines and roots encircled her and the Dark Man. He panicked as they squeezed, trapped in a machination of his own making, for the first time ever facing the same death he had cast upon so many others. And Amanda... Amanda had won. She accepted the tight embrace that would soon end her life, as one last peaceful thought floated through her mind:

Evan... I'll see you soon.

On the edge of Soul Wind Forest, Derek and the others sat waiting. They could have continued running while the drones were disabled, but they knew it would only delay the inevitable. If the Alpha child resumed control, there would be nowhere left on Earth to hide. The drones would finish their mission, eradicating all those infected with Trizorapine, as well as those they had targeted for other reasons. No one spoke while awaiting their fate. Victoria occasionally tried her phone, but between clogged networks and the electrical anomaly in Soul Wind Forest, it was a lost cause. Stacy sat quietly with her parents, primarily to comfort her mother, who was having a difficult time accepting this might be the end. Lamar stared at the trees in quiet contemplation. Rebecca and James were near their collective parents, holding hands, while Diana watched them, having trouble figuring out whether they were simply good friends or something more. And Derek sat with his head hung between his knees, his mind swirling with the possibilities of what might be happening right now on Sunrise Isle, his heart still hoping his dad and adopted sister would be okay.

"Look," Rebecca said, drawing the group's attention to the drones.

There was movement, not in their muscles, but on the surface of their skin. It was flaking in places, almost as if it was disintegrating. Derek stood and approached the trio.

"Be careful," Stacy told him.

He motioned for the others to stay back, then leaned in for a closer examination. Behind the disintegrating skin was blood seepage. Then wounds began to open. They were different for each of the drones, and Derek realized these must have been the wounds they'd sustained during their global assault, but which their genetic enhancements had healed. Did their reopening mean—

The others could tell whatever was happening didn't present a threat. They gathered around Derek and watched as the drones continued deteriorating. Then Lamar pointed to their eyes, where the bright blue glow of energy particles was dimming. It transitioned to a darker shade of blue, then a barely blue shade of gray, and then it was gone. The drones collapsed, their bodies breaking into dust particles upon impact with the ground.

"Listen!" Diana said.

Something was happening back on the road to Lakeview Bay. It was cheering, cheering that soon grew into an impromptu celebration. The other forty-six drones were also dying. The threat to Eden, and the world, was over. James and Rebecca embraced gleefully. The parents of the group exchanged grateful hugs with them and each other. Diana sported a grin that might split her face if she didn't rein it in. And Lamar stood with a quiet smile, simply relieved to have survived. Derek didn't participate in the others' joy, however.

He stood over the piles of dust, watching their top layers skimming into the breeze. He wanted to rejoice. He wanted to celebrate having been granted another day of life. But he had seen the energy particles in those drones' eyes fade. Fade—not withdraw to their owner... and he knew exactly what that meant. Stacy didn't understand why Derek wasn't jumping for joy with the rest of them, but then she saw the sorrow on his face, and followed his gaze to the drone dust, and in that moment, she knew what it meant, too.

"Oh, God, Derek... I'm so sorry."

She slid her arms around him, and as he struggled to hold back his tears, he gripped her as if he would never let her go.

———

The decoy helicopter hovered just beyond the sonic barrier, its passengers watching the last chunks of Sunrise Isle split apart and slowly sink into the ocean. Joseph and Vincent had convinced the others it would be safe to wait there. They wanted to give Amanda a chance to evacuate with them, should she complete her mission and not have the ability to evacuate herself. But where she was among the free floating chunks of dirt, foliage, and stone was anyone's guess. A helicopter had taken off from Sunrise Isle's eastern shore just before the final collapse. Novak was able to get a clear view through his binoculars and confirmed that there was only a pilot on board. There were also boats circling around the south of the broken island, but they appeared to be carrying civilians, and had been on the move before Amanda had set off into the jungle. Finally, there was the infiltration helicopter, which the decoy team pilot had been in communication with, and which had already relayed the status of its mission and members. Amanda wasn't with any of them. She was simply... gone.

"We should return to the mainland," General Javez said. "We don't want to risk running out of fuel over the open ocean."

Vincent shook his head. "We can't leave yet. Shortcake could still need us."

General Javez looked to Joseph for a voice of reason, but it was clear he was on the sheriff's side.

"We can wait three more minutes," Novak told him. "Then we won't have a choice."

General Javez sighed and leaned back in his seat. Joseph and Vincent scanned the sinking landmasses littering the ocean. They knew the chances of Amanda still being alive were slim, but naturally, they were in denial. They were her fathers, and they wouldn't give up on their daughter without some sort of confirmation

—positive or negative—regarding her fate. If only they'd known that confirmation was about to come, they might have braced their emotions more.

"There's new information coming across emergency satellite channels," their pilot called back. "I'll feed it to the cabin speakers."

A few seconds later, a low-quality broadcast played for everyone to hear. "*—threat seems to have subsided at this time. The U.S. military is in communication with its partners around the world and will release new information as it becomes available. For those of you just joining in, we have confirmed reports that the hostile army that had congregated in Eden after launching a global assault has been defeated. Every one of its soldiers is dead. It's still unclear how the army was defeated, or who was behind the initial attack, but we can say for certain that the threat seems to have subsided at this time. The U.S. military—*"

The pilot cut the feed as it started its loop, leaving the helicopter's passengers in tense silence. Vincent had already started making excuses in his mind: Maybe Amanda had killed the drones remotely. Maybe she'd been hurt and channeled her damage into them in order to save herself. Maybe she'd reversed the flow of energy, and consumed the drones to fuel her ongoing battle. He looked at Joseph, assuming the scientist would be going through the same mental exercises as him. But aside from a single tear that ran from one of his eyes, Joseph was a blank slate. Vincent silently pleaded with him to help reason through what they'd heard, to explain how the drone army death and Amanda's survival couldn't be mutually exclusive events. But Joseph's intellectual mind knew better, and as such, he had nothing to offer the struggling sheriff. He was empty on the inside, a childless father who'd lost everyone he'd ever loved to a project he himself had once championed. It was the purest form of destruction, not physical in nature, and yet so overwhelmingly devastating that there was no coming back from it.

Joseph's head slumped against his headrest, his eyes processing nothing, and his heart aching beyond what he'd ever thought was fathomable. Upon seeing the professor's reaction, Vincent dropped his own denial, releasing the floodgates that had been holding back an unrelenting wave of anguish and despair. He shook his head as the tears flowed, pounded his seat in hopes it would ease his pain, then curled forward in an uncontrollable weep. General Javez signaled Novak, who instructed their pilot to take them home.

CHAPTER 19
LEGACY OF DESTRUCTION, LEGACY OF LOVE

Weeks passed before the world returned to some semblance of normalcy. Eden and the other forty-nine cities that had come under attack cleared their dead, arranged burials, and began repair efforts. Leaders across the world called for government inquiries into the global attacks and their cascading effects, especially those in the Middle East, which had permanently displaced large swaths of the population, and where tensions would remain high for years to come. Fingers were eventually pointed at the United States, which admitted to being the source of the hostile force, though it denied any involvement in creating and unleashing that force.

Victoria, General Javez, Joseph, Vincent, and Frank were ushered from one interrogation to the next. They testified before a House of Representatives panel, the Senate Black Book Review Committee—which was largely for show—the National Security Agency, the Central Intelligence Agency, and the Federal Bureau of Investigation. They were farmed out to United States ally countries, whose equivalent government bodies and agencies grilled them even more harshly than their own. Jackson was also questioned, though given his personal situation, he was allowed to field that questioning remotely. And those with less direct involvement were summoned for one or two rounds of their own interrogation. That included Novak, Derek and Stacy, Lamar, James and Rebecca, and the surviving technicians and engineers from Complex E, who'd been rounded up by the United States Coast Guard upon reaching shore.

Most questioning was made public, an attempt to appease unrest among the global populace. But more sensitive matters, such as the origination of Project Impulse as a government-backed super-soldier effort, were kept behind closed doors, and those with knowledge of such sensitive matters were *strongly encouraged* to leave them there. Joseph was the most knowledgeable about the entire series of events that had transpired over the course of seven years. But he was also the least cooperative, more inclined to stare into space, wallowing in a misery that knew no end. Victoria and General Javez offered what overlapping information they could, leaving Joseph to simply state whether their version of events was accurate before returning to his emotional void. The others rounded out the bigger picture, providing personal details from each of their unique points of view, until each inquiring body was satisfied it understood enough not to press further.

The final stop on the interrogation tour was the United Nations headquarters in New York City. By then, every participating government had already documented its own version of the Impulse war, as it was now being called for ease of reference. They'd drafted an accord voluntarily banning any and all research into genetics-based super-soldier technology. No participating country had been left untouched, directly or indirectly, by the Impulse army, and the overarching perception was that such technology couldn't be controlled, and presented too great a risk to humanity to be perpetuated. Every nation had already informally agreed to sign the accord, but some were uneasy with one key detail: that a single man had the power to defy their agreement and resurrect Project Impulse, should he so desire...

"Professor Madison," the delegate from France addressed, "thank you for joining us today."

Joseph said nothing. He was flanked by Vincent and Frank on one side, and Victoria and General Javez on the other. They weren't expected to be asked questions directly during this meeting; they'd been summoned to help clear the air if Joseph refused to play along.

The France delegate continued. "In a few hours, we will sign one of the most unifying world agreements ever to be forged. All in this room have acknowledged the dangers inherent to combining genetic manipulation with militaristic goals. Fifty cities from across the globe were nearly wiped out by such dangers, and the rest of the world would have followed if not for the lead Impulse soldier turning on her army. We were helpless to stop them." The representative lowered her gaze to her clasped hands. "All evidence suggests Project Impulse is over. And yet, the man without who it could have never reached the heights it did is sitting in this room, having faced no punishment for his actions, and capable of repeating them should the opportunity present itself." She returned her gaze to Joseph, steeled for her next statement. "Many in this room would feel much more comfortable with you in confinement. Some have even suggested you deserve worse. Your actions led to the death of millions. Some would like to see atonement for those actions."

Joseph stirred, quietly suppressing an anger he knew would only hurt his case.

"Well?" the France delegate asked.

"I didn't hear a question," Joseph told her.

The delegate from Russia spoke up. "Should you atone for your actions? Should you give up your life to bring comfort to those who now live in fear of having their lives taken from them?"

Several other delegates in the hearing chamber shifted nervously, apparently not entirely on board with the implied capital punishment. But others sat stoically, awaiting his answer and ready to pass judgment. Joseph glared at his inquisitors, their lack of empathy astounding.

"You say I've faced no punishment," he said after a few moments. "How many of you have lost a child? How many of you have lost two of them, the only two you had, and ever will have?"

No one responded, but some adjusted their postures, and others cleared their throats, tells that they hadn't, and that they were uncomfortable with the prospect.

"No punishment?" Joseph repeated. "My children are dead. They're dead by the same hand that brought them life. My hand. A dead man's hand." His lip quivered involuntarily as he eyed the France delegate. "If you want to lock me up, fine." His eyes watered as he shifted to the Russia delegate. "If you'd prefer to take my life, fine. In fact, it would be a relief. Because while you sit there thinking I've faced no punishment, I can assure you I feel punishment every second of every minute of every day. I feel punishment with every breath I take, every thought I think, every movement of my limbs, and every pulse of blood through my body. I exist in a living Hell. And the only thing that could make it worse... would be to repeat the mistakes of the past all over again." He let that thought sit with his inquisitors for a moment, then concluded, "Do with me what you will. Frankly, I just don't care anymore."

The France delegate exchanged silent communication with her nearby colleagues, then leaned into her microphone. "Thank you for your candidness, Professor."

Few questions followed after that. The inquisition was adjourned, and Joseph and the others were permitted to return home.

———

The United Nations accord was signed as planned. Vincent and Frank watched the televised event together from their hotel restaurant later that day. They'd invited Joseph to join them, but he'd declined, citing his desire to pack and return to Eden as soon as possible. Vincent bounced an idea off of Frank to help the scientist. The detective admitted it would be a gamble, but worth it to potentially claw their friend back from the depths of sorrow in which he was drowning. Vincent finished his meal, and when the signing was complete, he excused himself to intercept Joseph before he left. The scientist's suitcase was standing ready at his door when Vincent arrived outside his room. He was doing a final check for personal belongings when he heard the knock, and reluctantly let Vincent in, suspecting this wasn't a casual visit.

"How can I help you, Sheriff?" Joseph quickly held up a correcting hand, then said, "Sorry, I'm so used to saying it the old way. How can I help you, Mr. Mayor?"

"*Acting* Mayor," Vincent emphasized. "And you know you don't need to use formal titles with me."

Samuel Collins had already punched his one-way ticket out of office when Amanda had confronted him during the Rose Parade. But he didn't change his ways. And when the Impulse army descended upon Eden, he'd ignored the evacuation order, deciding instead to ride out the attack in his office, high as a kite on Trizorapine-laced drugs. He was dead before he even knew his life was in danger. Authority for choosing a successor fell to Eden's city council, whose remaining members unanimously agreed to offer the job to Vincent. He'd debated declining, but then realized he could do more good for the city in the near term through political directives than through law enforcement. So he accepted the temporary position, leaving open the prospect of running for official reelection once he saw how his first term went.

Joseph stepped aside and motioned to a rolling chair. "Would you care for a seat?"

Vincent chuckled. "We both know you're not going to give me that long. How about I just cut to the chase?"

Joseph gave him a nod.

"I've been having discussions with Senator Riley outside of this grand tour of ours. Assuming we all come out clean on the other side, which it looks like we will, I wanted to see if she could fast-track a deal between Eden and the federal government."

Joseph's curiosity piqued. "For?"

"For the land that hosted Helix Unbound." Vincent shrugged. "It's part of

Eden, after all. And the government hasn't used it in years. With all the disaster spending it's doing, I figured it could use a decent influx of cash for a property it has no interest in anyway."

"Humph," Joseph replied. "You plan on building a campsite or something? City park, perhaps?"

Vincent shook his head, his teeth pressing nervously into his lower lip. There was no sense beating around the bush. Joseph was going to find out one way or another. "I'm commissioning to have Helix Unbound rebuilt."

The professor turned white. "Excuse me?"

"Let me explain," Vincent said, trying to head off the heated response he knew was coming. "Helix Unbound was never meant to be a breeding ground for war. Its intent was scientific advancement. Sure, that advancement was concentrated around military applications, but it didn't have to be. Project Impulse and the people who ran it... they corrupted the facility, commandeered it for their own purposes. They weaponized it, but just think what it could have been had that never happened. Think of the cutting-edge genetic research that could have been done for the betterment of humanity."

Joseph's knees buckled. He fell against his bed, Vincent's words knocking the air from his lungs.

"This is a chance for Eden to give back to the world," Vincent continued. "We unleashed so much terror over these past five years. What if we could repent, shower the world with cures for previously incurable diseases, new agricultural techniques, genetic solutions to physical impairments—the list goes on and on." He smiled warmly, hoping the gesture would open Joseph's mind to the idea. "This is our chance to give back, to right the sins of the past."

Joseph, who'd been despondent to all he'd heard, slowly lifted his eyes. "You'd be better off turning that land into a parking lot."

Vincent sighed. "I was hoping to get you on board with this."

"Don't you understand? It's too risky. What's to stop what happened with the original Helix Unbound from happening again? You put the wrong person in charge and it's going to be Project Impulse all over again."

"That's why I need someone ethical in charge, someone who knows the risks and will put the appropriate mitigations in place to address them."

Joseph scoffed. "You'll never find someone you can trust that much."

Vincent met Joseph's eyes, steady and unblinking. "I already have."

It suddenly registered what he was asking. "Me?" Joseph questioned. "You want me to run a resurrected Helix Unbound? You've lost your mind."

"Can you name one person more qualified for the job?"

"Yeah," Joseph said. "A groundskeeper, for when you turn that plot of land into the outdoor activity space it should be."

Vincent took a heavy, frustrated breath. "I know you're in a dark place right now. I get it. You know I do. But Shortcake gave her life to protect ours. Are you really going to spend yours wasting all that talent you have?"

Joseph avoided his gaze. "I'm done with this conversation."

Seeing he wouldn't get anywhere by pushing, Vincent returned to the door. "You've got time to think about it. We still haven't finalized the deal for the land. Once we do, there'll be at least a few months of construction. Then there's stocking the facility, finding the right talent... I can put together an advisory team to help with the latter, but at some point, Helix Unbound is going to need a director. I'm hoping you come around by then."

Joseph stared into space. "Don't count on it."

At least Vincent had tried. He told Joseph he'd see him back in Eden, then left quietly. The professor didn't move for several minutes. Logic told him that rebuilding Helix Unbound made perfect sense. The land was a great location for activity that needed an isolated environment. The scientific breakthroughs that could be made had the chance to change lives for the better. Sure, the initial cost would be a hit to Eden's fiscal budget, but the subsequent profits would provide an ongoing revenue stream for a city that once again had a long road to recovery ahead of it. Under the right leadership... Joseph shook his head. He couldn't do it. Even though it wouldn't be the same building, nor the same work, he just couldn't step foot in that place. There were too many heartbreaking memories to bear.

He put the conversation out of mind and stood. Then he finished checking his room for personal belongings, grabbed his suitcase, and started into the hallway. The phone beside his bed rang unexpectedly. Joseph considered ignoring it, figuring it must be a wrong number or a courtesy call of some sort from the front desk. Then again, given the nature of his visit to New York, it could also be important. He returned to his bed and lifted the receiver.

"Mr. Madison?" the front desk clerk said. *"I have a Demetrius Jackson on the line for you. He said he didn't know what room you were staying in, but that you would want to take his call. Should I put him through?"*

Jackson? Joseph thought. *Why would Jackson have tracked him down here?*

"Yes," he told the clerk. "Please put him through."

There was a click as the clerk patched in the line. *"Mr. Jackson, you're on with Mr. Madison."*

Jackson waited until he heard the clerk disconnect before speaking. *"Hello, Professor."*

"Jackson... why are you calling me? The last time we spoke, you told me to stay away."

"I told you to stay away until you ended it. I've been watching this coverage of the U.N. accord. They're claiming it's over. Tell me, Professor, is it really over?"

Joseph swallowed hard, because to admit it was over was to admit Amanda was gone forever. "Yes. It's over."

There was an extended pause, as if Jackson was contemplating his response. Then: *"When are you flying back to Eden?"*

"Today. I'm actually about to head to the airport."

"Change your ticket," Jackson said. *"Come here instead."*

Joseph didn't understand. "What? To Charleston?"

"That's right. We need to talk."

Joseph considered the idea, but he wasn't sure he could face anyone else associated with Project Impulse right now. "Jackson, I'm not in the best mental state."

"I know. I could see it in the public hearings. Regardless, you need to come see me. It's important."

There was a strange tone to Jackson's voice. It wasn't urgency or fear or anything else Joseph should worry about. But there was an anxiety there. Whatever this *important* matter was, it was weighing on his former colleague, and he clearly didn't want to discuss it over the phone. Given Jackson's help in finally stopping Project Impulse, agreeing to his request was the least Joseph could do.

"I'll be on the next available flight."

———

It was late evening by the time Joseph stepped up to Jackson's front door. He questioned what he was doing there, having spent his flight trying to come up with plausible reasons his former colleague would need to see him in person, but finding none. He told himself he would be in and out. He'd listen thoughtfully to whatever Jackson had to say, then he'd leave on the next flight to Eden. What Joseph would do from there... well, even he didn't know that. He'd planned on returning to Pine Ridge, but he was fairly certain they wouldn't take him back until he could at least fake a better attitude in front of students. He had Vincent's offer to run the new incarnation of Helix Unbound, but in the time since receiving that offer, his warmth for the idea had gone from cold to subzero. Joseph couldn't rejoin that world, or any variant of it, and that left him aimless. He knocked, ready to get this over with.

"Good evening, Professor," Maya greeted him with a friendly smile. "Come in."

She stepped aside, revealing a spotless floor where Colonel Davis had died mere weeks earlier. Maya was either an extremely skilled cleaner, or she and Jackson had hired a service suited for mopping up after hitmen. She showed Joseph to the living room, which looked as he remembered, save for a closed laptop sitting atop its coffee table.

"Have a seat. Demetrius will be in soon."

Joseph sat in a chair next to the couch as Maya disappeared into the kitchen, he suspected to grab an offering of iced tea. He could hear Jackson's daughters chatting and giggling over the clangs of silverware on ceramic, and realized he'd shown up right at dinnertime. Feeling even more like he shouldn't be there, Joseph looked around nervously. The living room walls were adorned with family photos. One was a professional shot of Jackson in his military uniform that must have been at least twenty years old. Several were selfies of Maya and the girls from various vacation spots, trips they'd taken by themselves while he was in the relentless service of Helix Unbound. And the more recent ones showed a family reunited in the wake of Eden's destruction. Joseph reminded himself that even the worst of disasters could have a positive impact if you looked in the right places.

"Thanks for coming," Jackson said, wheeling himself in from the kitchen. "It's spaghetti night. Maya and I need to trade out supervision duties to make sure sauce doesn't go flying unexpectedly. Sisters at this age... one minute they're laughing, the next they're bickering and pulling each other's hair." He smiled and shrugged. "I suppose I wouldn't have it any other way." Jackson wheeled himself over to Joseph. "Did you have time to eat at the airport? Maya can bring you a plate if you're hungry."

Joseph hadn't had time to eat, and he was hungry. But he didn't want to stay here any longer than necessary. "I'm okay. Besides, you didn't have me fly down here for a plate of pasta. What's going on, Jackson?"

He swallowed nervously. "It's uh... it's probably best if I let Amanda explain it to you herself."

What? Joseph must not have heard correctly. But then he saw Jackson open the nearby laptop, and when it woke from sleep, Amanda's face was on the screen, staring at him from a still of an unplayed video. She looked as though she was wearing pajamas, and the lighting was concentrated on her, as if provided by an artificial source in a dark room. Then Joseph realized it wasn't just any room. It was *this room*, the room he was seated in at this very moment. She'd recorded the video from Jackson's couch, and the timestamp in the lower left corner indicated she'd done it barely a month ago.

"What the hell is this?" Joseph asked, his skin going prickly.

"You'll see."

Jackson used the laptop trackpad to click the play button, bringing Amanda back to life. Joseph covered his gaping jaw, the sight of his little girl breathing, moving, and staring at him almost too much to take. Then she spoke, and her voice was both heartwarming and earth shattering at the same time, a simultaneous reminder of the daughter that had graced his life, only to be stolen from it.

"*Hello, Father,*" Amanda said through a worried frown. "*If you're watching this, there's something you need to know.*" She took a stuttered breath. "*There are so many places I could start, but I think it makes the most sense to pick up where we last saw each other.*"

Joseph braced himself, the memory of Amanda's departure from Eden one he didn't cherish like others.

"*I was devastated by Evan's death. As you probably know, our connection went far beyond one of physical or emotional love. We'd bonded on a level unique to our Omega Genomes. I was him, and he was me. And when Judas killed him…*" Amanda's voice cracked. "*He killed a part of me, too. He unbalanced me, sent me spiraling down a path I would have never traveled otherwise. I thought opening myself to the darkness would be a onetime event, a way to avenge Evan and nothing more. But even after my bloodlust had been fulfilled, the darkness never left. It haunted me, reminding me of the killer I'd let myself become. I'd taken lives before, but—*" She shook her head. "*Something was different this time. This time, I wanted to kill. I used the darkness to kill. I'd become what Project Impulse had always wanted, and I detested myself for it. I left Eden to protect the rest of you, but I also left in hopes of escaping my destiny.*" Amanda frowned again. "*But that's the funny thing about destiny. There is no escaping it. It always finds you.*"

Joseph snuck a glance at Jackson to get a read on him. If he'd watched this video before, he had a hell of a poker face hiding that fact.

Amanda continued. "*I didn't know where to go. No matter how many cities I visited, how many remote places I stopped in, I could feel the darkness chasing me. It wasn't until I stumbled into this quirky little hotel a month or so after leaving Eden that I finally found direction. It just came to me, something I'd known all along, but which my mind had hidden from consciousness, so the darkness wouldn't find it.*" Amanda held up a newspaper. Printed among a handful of other police photographs taken that fateful night at Renewed Hope was a phrase written in blood, Evan's final message before dying. "*I finally understood the meaning of Evan's last words. Contrary to their appearance, they weren't for you, Father. They were for me. And once I knew that, I had purpose again.*" She put the newspaper down. "*Please don't be upset with Jackson. I swore him to secrecy the night I showed up on his porch. He's a good man. He protected me when I was at my most vulnerable all those years ago. And I needed him to protect me again.*"

Joseph stole another glance at Jackson. "What's she talking about?"

Jackson bit his lip and stared at the carpet, not ready to answer.

"I can't tell you how hard it was to go through this transition alone, to not have you or the Desmonds by my side. But just like I needed Jackson to protect me, I needed to protect you. You had to remain oblivious for your own safety." Amanda's eyes were welling with tears. *"I thought I could start a new life. I did start a new life. But the darkness just kept coming. And I knew the only way to protect her was to finally face it head on, even at the cost of my own life."* Now the tears were streaming. *"I promise it wasn't a suicide mission. If there had been any way to win this battle and return, I would have done it. I didn't want to leave any of you. But I had to protect you... and if you're watching this, then I succeeded. Jackson promised he wouldn't show it to you otherwise."*

Joseph looked again at Jackson, who'd clearly known more than he'd been letting on or that he'd divulged during his interrogations. Despite knowing he should be thanking his former colleague for sheltering Amanda, he couldn't help feeling his veins fill with rage. How could Jackson have deceived him like this? Why hadn't he said something when Joseph had turned up at his house weeks ago? If he was so loyal to Amanda, why not come clean when she was in the clutches of Project Impulse? Of course, Amanda had already given Joseph the answer. She'd sworn Jackson to secrecy, and he'd maintained it, even when the opportunity to spill had presented itself.

Joseph heard the cries of Jackson's baby filtering down from an upstairs bedroom. The cries calmed him, holding him back from speaking his mind, as Jackson wheeled back to the kitchen. Maya ran through the living room, apologizing for the interruption, and hurried upstairs. Joseph was alone now, Jackson back on dinner duty, as Amanda wrapped up her tearful recording.

"I don't know when we'll see each other again," she said. *"Evan shared that you aren't exactly a religious man. But I think it's safe to say we've both seen and experienced things that leave the door open for belief. I want you to know that I'm choosing to believe. I believe that we'll be reunited one day. And until then, I want you to know just how much I loved you, how much you made me feel love in return, and how I trust that you'll show her the same love you showed me."* Amanda nodded with encouragement. *"Be the father you were meant to be, and just maybe, she'll bring you the peace you deserve."*

Joseph blinked with confusion. *What was she talking about?* This was the second time Amanda had referenced some other person, some girl or woman... what did she know that Joseph didn't? He waited for her to explain, but no explanation came. Amanda leaned in toward the camera and cut the recording. A black screen took over as the slider on the digital video file reached its end. Joseph fiddled with the keyboard and trackpad, searching the open file folders for some other video, a continuation, or maybe additional information, but he saw only the one video file.

Maya came downstairs carrying her baby, who was cooing peacefully now. Joseph barely paid attention to her as he continued searching the laptop's file system. Maya crossed through the living room, but she didn't exit into the kitchen. She stopped next to Joseph, who, upon glancing up, saw her watching him with empathetic eyes. Something triggered in Joseph's mind. He looked back at the family photos adorning the living room walls. Despite some of them being quite recent, none featured Jackson and Maya's baby. Joseph looked at Jackson as he came wheeling back in from the kitchen, nothing from the waist down exhibiting any sign of life.

"No..." Joseph whispered, his instinct denial.

Jackson smiled with understanding.

"But you—" The scientist shook his head vehemently. "You said yourself things worked well enough down there. You said it was a miracle of science."

Jackson shrugged. "It was a miracle... just not mine."

Maya sat on the couch, lowering the baby enough for Joseph to see. Its skin was fair, a far cry from Jackson and Maya's shade.

Joseph's throat tightened. "But she—I—This can't—" He had difficulty forming even the most basic thoughts, much less the sentences to express them. When he finally could string together a set of words, it was to plea for Jackson to stop the pain, the pain that what he now saw to be true might not be something he could handle. "Please don't do this to me. I'm not ready."

Maya smiled and gently pushed the baby into his arms. "We never are."

Jackson wheeled up beside him as he cradled the child. "I'd like to introduce you to your granddaughter, Professor. Her name is Josephine."

Joseph's trembling lips cracked upward at the revelation. "Josephine..."

"Amanda said Evan named her."

Joseph's heart skipped a beat. He pictured Amanda holding up the newspaper with a copy of the same photograph he'd seen the night of Evan's death, those cryptic letters scribbled in his surrogate son's blood. "He knew..." Joseph struggled to swallow the thick saliva collecting in the back of his mouth. "Before he died... he knew."

But of course he had known. Amanda would have already been pregnant, and Evan had taken Trizorapine at The Red Room, opening his senses to even the most invisible sources of life. Amanda would have known too had her senses not been distracted by loss, then vengeance, then darkness. Her body had hidden her pregnancy from her and had even protected that pregnancy during her violent battle with Judas. But Amanda had eventually figured it out, and then she'd turned to the one person she knew would not only see her through her pregnancy, but who would also protect her and Evan's baby when she left to finish the war that would eventually claim them all if she didn't.

Joseph gently stroked the cooing baby's head. "Hello, Josephine."

Jackson squeezed his shoulder. "We'll help you get the logistics sorted out. We've already got most of the basics: diapers, formula, pacifiers, a car seat. I'll carpool with you back to Eden if you don't want to make the drive alone." He looked at his legs. "Well, you'll be doing all the driving. But at least you'll have some company."

Maya cleared her throat, as though he was forgetting something.

"Right," Jackson said. "You may want to invest in some additional homeowner's insurance. Josephine has inherited—how do I say this—some of her parents' more unusual traits. She can be a handful at times."

Joseph stared at his granddaughter's smooth face. She opened her eyes wide, as if taking him in for the first time. That's when he saw them: those giant emerald orbs, just like her mother, surrounded by a ring of black, just like her father. When Josephine blinked, there was a brief twinkle in her eye. It was the same twinkle he'd seen in his own reflection all his life, the same twinkle he'd seen in Amanda, and which had made him fall in love with her. This was Joseph's granddaughter, and just as Amanda had asked, he would love her unconditionally.

He took the most relaxed breath he had taken in weeks. "I can handle that."

———

Joseph spent that night and several more with Jackson and his family. They ran him through Josephine's routine, prepped him for the most fatherly duties he had ever had to perform, and shared stories from their year and a half with Amanda under their roof. When the day came for Joseph to begin his journey back to Eden, he declined Jackson's offer to carpool, insisting Project Impulse had stolen enough of his own family time, and encouraging him to make the most of it now that its looming dangers had passed. Maya and the girls helped Joseph pack a rental car with baby gear. Joseph thanked them for everything, and expressed his inability to find words strong enough to articulate his gratitude to Jackson for everything he'd done to protect Amanda over the years. They shared a firm handshake of respect. Then Joseph was on his way, Josephine in her carseat in the back, staring at the passing world with those emerald green eyes of hers.

Joseph's mindset had undergone a transformation during his stay with Jackson. He would always miss his children, but they'd left him with a miracle of life that, though not replacing his loss, would bring him endless joy to mask the pain it caused. The only problem now was that babies were expensive. And by the sounds of it, Josephine might be more expensive than average. Joseph would need a stable source of income to properly care for her. Luckily, he'd come to peace with that too.

"Hello?" Vincent answered when Joseph called his cell phone during the drive.

"How's your mayorship treating you?" Joseph asked, his tone noticeably different from the last time they'd spoken.

"I can't complain yet, but I'm sure that's coming. What can I do for you, Professor?"

"Is the Helix Unbound directorship offer still open?"

"Of course. Are you reconsidering?"

"Under two conditions," Joseph stipulated. "Have the blueprints for the new building been drawn up yet?"

"They're in progress, but it's still early enough to make changes. What do you need?"

"My first condition is that there has to be an onsite cafeteria."

"It's already in the plan," Vincent told him.

"That wasn't the entire condition. There has to be an onsite cafeteria, and it has to serve strawberry shortcake. Not that premade store-bought crap, either. It has to be prepared fresh, on premises, every day. It doesn't matter whether it sells, whether it's profitable... hell, give it away for free as an employment perk if you want. But it needs to be in writing. Strawberry shortcake, starting on opening day and in perpetuity until the facility shuts down some far off time in the future."

Vincent gave no pushback. *"Okay. Condition two?"*

"There needs to be an onsite daycare for working parents. Again, make it an employment perk. It'll help us attract bright minds torn between their love of research and familial responsibility."

Vincent paused before giving his response this time. *"Um... I don't think that'll be a problem. If you don't mind me asking, what gave you the idea?"*

"I'll explain when I see you," Joseph said. "I'm out of town, but I'll be back in Eden in a few days. We should do lunch and hammer out the details. Just understand that these are dealbreakers. If you want me, make them happen."

"Yeah, sure. Consider them done." Vincent paused again, his policeman instincts on the prowl. *"Are you sure there's nothing else you need to tell me?"*

Joseph looked in his rearview mirror at the reflection of Josephine, who'd fallen fast asleep, her tiny chin dipping to meet her tiny chest. "Nothing that can't wait. I'll call you to set up that lunch meeting."

He disconnected, then focused on the stretch of road ahead. It was long, certainly marred by bumps and potholes, but it was also bright, bathing in the sun of a new day. It led to a future of hope, a future of happiness, a future of love, and a future of peace. And Joseph would have Josephine by his side every step of the way.

CHAPTER 20

THE FINAL TIDE

Six months later...

S tacy moaned in sleepy protest as she rolled over in bed. Luckily, it was still pitch black outside, which meant she had time for additional shut-eye before rousing Derek for work.

Or did she?

Stacy glanced at the dim alarm clock Derek had installed on her side of the bed to prevent him from oversleeping. His logic had been questionable, but then again, Stacy knew if the alarm blared on Derek's side, he would just shut it off and pretend as though he'd never heard it. With it being on her side, he was guaranteed enough prodding and scolding to get him moving... at the cost of her beauty rest, of course. The clock's digits were blurry to Stacy's tired eyes. She almost gave up, not wanting to wake her body prematurely, but then the first digit—a seven—sharpened. That was later than Stacy had anticipated based on the lack of dawn's glow outside. When the second set of digits sharpened—a five and a three—her brain kicked into high gear.

"Derek!" she said with a shove to his back. "We overslept!"

He turned groggily. "But it's still dark outside."

"It must be stormy weather or something."

Stacy leaped out of bed and searched for her phone, but couldn't find it. That was odd, considering Derek had been making an effort to keep his room tidy in recent months. She pulled back bedsheets, checked under her pillow, under the bed itself—

"What are you doing?" Derek asked, his voice less groggy than before.

"My phone. I thought I put it on the nightstand last night."

He sat up and pointed to his closet. "I don't remember you taking it out of your jacket pocket when we got home."

Stacy was pretty sure she had, but she would check anyway.

"Can you grab my uniform while you're in there?" Derek asked.

"Sure."

Stacy opened the closet door and turned on the light. Her jacket was hanging right where she'd left it the night before, and there was a bulge in its right pocket. Relieved, she stuck her hand in to get it, only to feel something unfamiliar and not at all phone shaped. It was a box made of padded leather. When Stacy pulled it out, she saw it was a jewelry box. She opened it, and found it was empty. "Derek, what is—"

Her words caught in her throat as she turned to find Derek on one knee, a diamond ring that refracted the closet light outstretched toward her. His lip was quivering with nervousness, though Stacy knew he had nothing to be nervous about.

"Stacy Fitzgerald," Derek said, his voice cracking, "will you marry me?"

Her first instinct was to mess with him. After all, she'd never have an opportunity like this again, and she had so many options at her disposal. She could tease Derek about how ridiculous he looked proposing in his pajamas, and how such ridiculousness was unworthy of her. She could point out that he was hazardous to her health, having almost gotten killed three times now since hooking up with him. She could tell him she was just using him for the shelter and some really great sex, but wasn't actually interested in anything serious. Or she could take a much more mature, and more appropriate route...

"What took you so long?" she asked with a teary grin.

"Is that a yes?" Derek asked, his common sense clouded by his nerves.

"Of course it's a yes!"

Stacy held out her hand so he could place the ring on her finger. He'd gotten her size just right. Then she wrapped her arms around Derek's neck and planted a long, passionate kiss on his lips. There was a double-tap on his bedroom door, which cracked open. Vincent poked his head in, his hand shielding his eyes.

"Is everyone dressed?"

It sounded like there were other people with him. Stacy shot Derek a curious glance.

"I set the clock ahead two hours," he admitted. "You almost ruined my plan. I elbowed you for a good five minutes before you finally woke up."

"Well?" Vincent asked with pent-up excitement.

Derek chuckled. "Yeah, Dad, come on in."

Vincent threw the bedroom door wide open, revealing Diana and Stacy's parents. Their eyes darted to the young woman's hand, which she held up proudly, showing off the ring now sparkling on her finger. Elation filled the air as hugs, kisses, and congratulatory handshakes were exchanged. Psychologically and emotionally, it had been a difficult six months in Eden, which was still recovering from the mass loss of life the Impulse army had taken. But its citizens had found small nuggets of joy and hope along the way, nuggets that would serve as the foundation for the city's future. It had been a difficult six months in the Desmond household as well, for they'd lost one of their own family members and were now proceeding through life a little emptier than before. Derek and Stacy's engagement was the first of their nuggets. Thankfully, it was a strong nugget, setting a high bar for the foundation of their future. And with the support of their families, and the tiniest bit of luck, there'd be many more nuggets to come.

———

Jericho PD was still sporting the sharp tang of fresh paint and sawdust. Carter breathed it in as he stepped through the front door, the thought of complaining never entering his mind. He could have been back in prison, where he was certain the odor would be far less pleasant despite it also receiving a recent remodeling. But he didn't have to worry about that anymore. His heroic actions during the Impulse army attack had earned him and a few other surviving prisoners full pardons. As an extra bonus, Carter's criminal record had been sealed, enabling him to rejoin Jericho PD. It wasn't the same. He'd lost his partner, his captain, and countless others he'd previously worked alongside. But someone had to keep Jericho safe, especially during the years it would take to get back on its feet. Carter was more than happy to serve, especially if it meant contributing to his family's finances again. After all, those off-broadway shows they enjoyed weren't cheap.

"Carter, is that you?" Billy hollered over construction noise from an office across the lobby. "Get in here. We need to discuss a case."

Well, it was nice to see some things never changed. There had rarely been a dull moment at Jericho PD before its destruction, and it didn't appear there would be many now. Carter handed his duffel bag of personal belongings to a rookie cop, who agreed to drop them off in the locker room. Then he trekked up to the half-built office.

"What's up, Billy?"

Billy seemed taken aback by the greeting. He cleared his throat and motioned to the nameplate on his desk with a hand that still bore burn scars on its backside.

Carter rolled his eyes. "Really?" When Billy didn't back down, he adjusted his greeting, which he accompanied with a sarcastic smile. "How can I help you, *Captain Meadows*?"

Billy sighed with ecstasy. "I just love the sound of that."

Carter wasn't amused. "This has got to stop."

"Just give me a few more weeks of it," Billy pleaded. "I promise, you can go back to calling me Billy after that."

"That's what you said a few weeks ago."

Billy shrugged. "Eh, who's counting?" He shuffled through a stack of paperwork on his desk and passed a report to Carter. "The real reason I needed you in here was this. It's the latest intel on Thomas DeMarco. It appears both he and Dietrich Wessler survived Project Impulse's global coup. With Jericho in tatters, he's likely to resume operations here. Rumor has it he may even try to set the city up as his new home base. I need my best man on it, and that's you."

Carter skimmed the report, eager for a shot at redemption, and yet hesitant, knowing how this had played out in the past. "I know it's below your pay grade now, but don't you want to reach out to Frank about this? Maybe form an interagency task force or something?"

Billy smiled, but behind it, Carter saw sadness. Frank had been overjoyed to learn that, despite one half of his body being covered in more scars than a plastic surgery addict, Billy had survived the assault on Jericho PD. But even that hadn't been enough to get the band back together. Whatever Frank had been through on Sunrise Isle, it had brought him a fresh sense of closure, and he was ready for a new chapter in his life, a chapter that took him away from Jericho PD. In hindsight—or maybe in Frank's foresight—it had worked out well for Billy, for Frank would have likely gotten the captain promotion over him, and he dreaded having to address his former partner as an uptight administrator. Come to think of it, maybe it was time he let Carter off the hook in that regard...

"Frank's got a new life. Let's let him enjoy it." Billy motioned toward the report. "The DeMarco case is yours now. Don't screw it up."

Carter nodded, then looked at Billy with sincerity. "Aye, aye, Captain."

———

Lamar, seated before a central computer terminal in Eden's underground tunnel system, looked over the paper resume in his hands. "It says here you've won several science awards over the past few years. Care to tell me about those?"

The nervous interviewee standing next to him explained. "The first award is nationally recognized. My teammate and I created a more efficient method for separating solids from liquids in hospital environments. It hasn't been widely adopted yet, but we're hoping for the best." He tried to get a read on Lamar, but couldn't. "The second award isn't really much to speak of. The third one, though, that's a global award. My teammate and I were up against some of the brightest minds from around the world." He was getting excited speaking of it. "We'd proposed a theoretical method for reversing arctic ice melt and counteracting humanity's carbon footprint on the world."

Lamar raised his brow with interest. "And when it was tested?"

The interviewee slumped. "It didn't work." He recovered energetically. "But the theory was sound. With some tweaking, we can probably get to a working implementation eventually."

Lamar nodded. "You keep speaking of a teammate. Has any of your work been your own?"

The interviewee swallowed hard. "No, but I promise we're equal contributors. I'm not riding on someone else's coattails."

"Hmm..." Lamar's eyes scanned toward the top of the page. "Normally, I expect the people I hire to have some sort of college degree."

James laughed nervously. "Well, I am working on it. These things take time."

Lamar smiled, done putting him through the wringer. "How many hours per week can you give me? And don't say forty. Finishing your education is important. The moment this job interferes with your grades, I'll fire you."

"Maybe fifteen, then?"

"Fifteen sounds like a good number."

Lamar held out his hand, which James shook gratefully.

"You won't regret this, Doctor Reed. I'll be the hardest part-time research assistant you've ever had."

"I'm counting on it," Lamar said, setting the resume aside. He then passed James a lab coat. "So, ready to get started?"

———

Above their heads, and much farther north, Rebecca parked her car on a freshly paved lot set deep within Soul Wind Forest. The car had been a present from her parents following the defeat of the Impulse army. With a new outlook on life, they wanted nothing holding their daughter back from the world of opportunities before her. She checked how she looked in the rearview mirror, stepped out and adjusted her suit, then grabbed a professional briefcase her parents had bought her along with the car.

The building looming before Rebecca barely resembled its predecessor. It was still boxy, but a little shorter and painted tastefully with vibrant accents. It had a ground floor surrounded by glass, windows on every level, and an inviting entrance with a large sign that read:

HELIX UNBOUND
TOMORROW'S TECHNOLOGY FOR THE GOOD OF TODAY

Rebecca took a calming breath and proceeded inside. She gave her name to the admin at the front desk, who provided her with a temporary security badge. Then she was escorted to a second-floor conference room that overlooked the woods, and offered a beverage and snack while she waited. Rebecca declined, too nervous to eat or drink. She had been in this room before, about a month earlier, when the finishing touches were still being put on the building. She had met with a panel of two science personnel and a human resources representative, each of whom participated in what felt like a grueling hour-long interview.

Helix Unbound would host its first intern this coming winter, and if all went well, they would institute a permanent internship program going forward. Rebecca had applied, but she knew the competition was fierce. It wasn't just her peers at Pine Ridge, either. When word had gotten out that Eden was investing in a new cutting-edge research facility, students from all around the country had applied. The candidate field had been narrowed to fifty, then twenty. As bright as she was, Rebecca couldn't imagine making it through the cut of ten, then five. Now Helix Unbound was down to its final three candidates, and they were bringing them back in to have a second round of face-to-face interviews.

"It's nice to see you again, Rebecca," Doctor Fischer greeted upon entering the conference room.

He was an older gentleman, someone who'd retired from academia but still wanted to make a difference in the world. He was followed by Doctor Martinez, a younger woman who'd already made a name for herself in the scientific community, and Mrs. Hall, Helix Unbound's head of human resources. The others exchanged greetings as well, then took their seats in traditional interview style, a three versus one quiz show competition where the dominant side got to ask a lopsided number of questions.

"Has anything changed that we should be aware of since you first applied?" Mrs. Hall opened as she passed out copies of Rebecca's application materials.

Rebecca skimmed her materials, then shook her head. "No, ma'am."

"As you know," Doctor Martinez began, "we invited you back here today because you are one of three finalists for our upcoming intern position. One reason we wanted to meet again in person was to check if we needed to incorporate any new information into our decision. Another was to get a better sense of each candidate's character. Helix Unbound's mission is to push the boundaries of scientific possibility. That carries the potential for great good... as well as great harm." Given the recency of the Impulse army's global attack, she didn't need to elaborate. "So, is there anything you want to share about your character? Anything we haven't seen in your application materials or that you didn't divulge during our previous interview?"

Rebecca got the sense that she was fishing, but not blindly. "No. Not that I can think of."

Doctor Martinez seemed displeased with her answer.

Mrs. Hall extended an olive branch. "You know, in my line of work, I see all kinds of situations where people don't necessarily realize they've done something wrong. Sometimes it's not even intentional. They don't see the significance of an action or a relationship. They don't perceive conflicts of interest or similar threats where they might exist, and as such, they fail to disclose pertinent information."

Rebecca waited for more, but after a few moments of silence, it became obvious Mrs. Hall was done. "I'm sorry," she said timidly. "I'm not sure what you're talking about."

Doctor Fischer cut to the chase. "Why didn't you tell us about your relationship with Director Madison?"

His revelation caught Rebecca by surprise. "How did you—" She caught herself. "I mean, Professor Madison was one of my teachers. I didn't disclose any of my other teachers in my application."

"None of your other teachers run this facility," Doctor Fischer said. "It's a little odd that someone as smart as you didn't think it was worth mentioning."

Rebecca felt her cheeks growing warm. She had intentionally withheld her association with Joseph from this group, but not for nefarious reasons. Now she looked guilty of what was essentially fraud by omission. If they wanted someone with good moral character for their internship, she had just excluded herself from the list. "I, uh... I think maybe I should withdraw from the candidate process."

Doctor Martinez cocked her head with curiosity. "Is that because you have something to hide or because you're afraid we might not like your answer to our question?"

Rebecca felt herself clamming up. "I just don't want to waste your time. I'm not a bad person; I promise. But I know how this must look."

"So correct our view," Doctor Fischer said. "Tell us why you withheld your relationship with Director Madison from the application."

Rebecca glanced nervously at her feet, feeling both silly and ashamed for letting something so meaningless spiral into such a point of contention. "I didn't want you giving me the internship for the wrong reason. Professor—" She stopped and corrected herself. "*Director* Madison is your boss. I figured if you knew I was his student, or if I asked him for a letter of recommendation, you would feel obligated to award me the internship, even if I wasn't qualified." She returned her gaze to her inquisitors. "I wanted to win the internship on my own merit, not based on my network."

Doctor Martinez smiled with a hint of smugness as she looked at Doctor Fischer. "I told you."

Doctor Fischer nodded, then fixed his eyes on their candidate. "Well, Rebecca, you just did."

She wasn't sure she'd heard him correctly. "What?"

"You are officially Helix Unbound's first intern... assuming you accept the position, that is."

"You're not just saying that because I was Director Madison's student?"

"Of course not," Doctor Martinez assured her. "We gave him the applications of each finalist. That's when we learned he knew you. But when we asked him for an assessment of you, he refused. He told us if you didn't volunteer the information, there must be a good reason for it, and that we should assess you based on our own observations." She paused, then added, "Though he did mention something about ignoring the B on your most recent transcript..."

Rebecca sighed with relief, the tension flooding out of her body.

"You have plenty of merit for this position," Doctor Fischer said. "And that you didn't take advantage of your network to get it tells us all we need to know about your character."

"Thank you," Rebecca said, barely able to speak the words.

The three interviewers stood and offered congratulatory handshakes.

"Mrs. Hall here has some paperwork for you to fill out," Doctor Martinez then said. "That way, we can have all our ducks in a row when you come back this winter." She checked her watch. "But we did finish a little early. So... would you like to take a tour of the facility first?"

Rebecca nodded with wide-eyed elation.

"Follow us," Doctor Fischer said.

Rebecca did, and as she stepped through the sterile, high-tech hallways of a refreshed Helix Unbound, only one thought persisted in her brain.

This is so cool!

———

Later that day, Diana sat with her head down on her desk at Eden PD, her landline phone propped in the crook of her elbow as Vincent droned on and on about the red tape he was having to cut through to have the city scrubbed of Samuel's name and likeness. He had made it one of his many missions as mayor, resolute that for Eden to fully move on from its past, it couldn't have that asshole's memory tarnishing nearly everything that made the city great. Normally, Diana would have been happy to engage in the conversation, but Vincent had caught her with only ten pages left in her latest mystery novel, and she really wanted to know who'd shaved the Persian cat the night of the diamond heist.

"He's got layers of business contracts with fine print requiring his name to be displayed in prominent places. It's going to take a team of lawyers to find holes in these things before I can remove a single letter!"

Diana eyed her book, calling to her from only a few inches away. She wondered whether she would need a team of lawyers to draw up an agreement that Vincent wasn't allowed to interrupt her during intense moments of suspense.

"Oh, and get this. An architect showed up today with designs for a statue that was supposed to be built on the ground floor of City Hall. The thing was over nine feet tall. I don't remember him being that tall!"

Diana beat her head against the desk, hoping if she knocked herself unconscious, she might sleep through the rest of Vincent's rant and then wake to return to her book. When that didn't work, she tried a more direct approach. "Honey? Honey, you've got to stop."

"What's wrong?"

"It's going to take you years to wipe the city clean of that man's filth. And I'll be glad to listen to your stories as you do it. But right now, I need about ten minutes of me time."

"You're about to find out who shaved the cat, aren't you?"

Diana giggled guiltily. "We're still taking the kids out for a celebratory dinner tonight?"

"Absolutely. I'll call you when I leave City Hall." Vincent would have hung up, but then he heard something crash down what sounded like the stairs leading to his former office. *"What was that?"*

There was another crash, and Diana watched as paperwork fluttered out of broken filing cabinets piled at the bottom of those stairs. "Your replacement. He's decided to do a little cleaning of his own around here, since there's nothing better to do. I think it's his way of releasing aggression. He ran into some snags when rebuilding his family home."

"How would you know that?"

"I like to eavesdrop on his phone calls. I did it when you were sheriff, too."

"Maybe I shouldn't have asked. Anyway, tell him my desk is off limits. I had to pay out of my own pocket for that thing. I might bring it home one day."

Diana watched as the desk in question took a fatal tumble down the same stairs as the filing cabinets. "I'll be sure to do that."

She hung up, then grabbed her book and opened it to where she'd left off. Not five words in, however, someone stopped at her desk. It was a citizen, youthful, dark-skinned, looking somewhat uncomfortable, as if he wasn't sure he was in the right place. "Can I help you?"

"I'm looking for Sheriff Holmes," the citizen said. "I was told I could find him here."

Diana pointed toward Vincent's old office, which Frank had just cleared of its last piece of furniture. "Be careful; he might be in a mood."

She'd been joking, but she wasn't sure the citizen had caught on. He walked toward the office with trepidation, eyeing the pile of discarded furniture as he climbed the stairs. Then he knocked on the frame of Frank's open door.

"Yes?"

"Are you Sheriff Holmes?"

Frank shrugged. "That depends. Are you here to kill or otherwise hurt me?"

The citizen shook his head.

"In that case," Frank said as he extended a hand, "Sheriff Holmes. And you are?"

"My name is Darnell. Darnell Tipps."

Frank froze, the last name drawing immediate recognition. "You're Captain Tipps's kid?"

Darnell nodded.

"I'm sorry about your dad. I looked for you at the funeral—"

"I didn't go," Darnell admitted. "Me and my pops... we didn't exactly get along."

"Yeah, he kind of mentioned that."

Darnell paced uneasily. "Look, I won't take up much of your time. I felt bad about missing my pops's funeral, so I went back to Jericho and visited the police station there. Some of the guys who survived that night... they told me my pops sent you to stop what was happening. They told me he did it because y'all knew those things would come to Eden, and that he was trying to protect me. Is that true?"

Frank nodded solemnly. "Yeah, it's true. I just wish I had stopped them sooner. I'm glad to see you're all right, though. It's what he wanted."

Darnell fidgeted with his fingers, avoiding eye contact. "This is going to sound crazy. And feel free to tell me no. But... would you mind meeting with me every now and again? I was hoping you could tell me more about my pops. After I left

Jericho, I cut off communication with him. Now what I wouldn't give for just five more minutes of his voice..."

Frank placed a consoling hand on his shoulder. "How about we start now?"

Darnell's eyes lifted. A minute later, Frank informed Diana he was headed out to lunch and asked her to find someone to clean up *that crap at the bottom of the stairs*. She heard, but ignored him, as her novel revealed the cat victimizer as none other than its owner, which made about as much sense as teaching a mosquito to talk. She tossed the book aside in frustration, then watched Frank leave with his guest in tow, wondering what the heck that had been about.

———

Alison took a deep breath as she silently read the final line of the report in her hands. She was on a video call with Victoria and General Javez, who had their own copies of the report, but who had read them in advance. They remained quiet, allowing time for Alison to absorb and awaiting her response, which they hoped would be favorable.

"Well," she said as she flipped the report back to its front page and set it on the desk before her, "what can I say other than job well done? I think this should sufficiently close the record on Project Impulse. Barring any new developments, which I presume there won't be, we can all sleep easy tonight. It's been a long road getting here, but I can't say I'm sorry we've reached the end. Though—" She bobbled her head as if rocked by brief emotion. "I might actually miss these little virtual get-togethers of ours. They've been such a staple of my routine these past two years."

General Javez replied, "Forgive me for saying, Ms. Drexmore, but I don't think we share that sentiment."

Alison chuckled quietly. "I can't blame you. So what's next for you two? Planning to stay in politics, Senator?"

"Not when my term expires," Victoria said. "I've achieved what I'd set out to accomplish. It's time to let someone else deal with the daily tedium of political issues."

"And you, General?"

General Javez shrugged. "I finally got my win. I'd say that's earned me some much needed vacation time. Where things go from there..."

He let the thought hang, unsure himself how that sentence would conclude. But Alison thought she caught an unusual nonverbal response from Victoria, a bodily shift perhaps, maybe nothing at all, but then again, maybe—

"If you don't mind me asking, Ms. Drexmore," the senator said, "while I still have the authority to do so: what happened to the civilian workers from Complex E? Our sources tell us they were detained by an unknown agency following their formal testimonies. Where are they now?"

Alison had wondered when this question would arise. "I had them questioned further about their roles in Project Impulse. Most were released after signing confidentiality agreements. Some that had more active roles are under house arrest to ensure they don't present an ongoing threat to the country."

"And the others?" Victoria pressed.

"Who says there are others?"

Victoria wasn't letting her off so easily. "The others, Ms. Drexmore?"

Alison sighed. She could have kept dodging, but she'd been to war with these two, and they had earned enough goodwill for an honest answer. "Let's face it, there was too much talent there to let go to waste. We've redeployed them within our own military research divisions. But rest assured, they're under constant supervision."

"And the United States's recent agreement with the U.N.?" General Javez asked.

"Our country plans to uphold its end of the accord." Alison's lip curled at the edge, not quite a smile, but not without pleasure. "But there's quite a spectrum between creating a genetically enhanced super-soldier and doing no genetic experimentation at all." Having given them all she was willing to give, she then changed subjects. "I can't help but notice some similarity in the backgrounds of each of your video feeds. If I didn't know better, I'd say you were taking the call from the same house."

Victoria and General Javez, despite being in separate boxes on her screen, glanced at each other, as if looking straight through the divide separating their feeds. There was something to their gaze, their body language, the hidden smiles betraying their otherwise stoic faces... Victoria turned her eyes back to her camera to give the appearance of looking at Alison.

"I'm sure we'll speak again one day, Ms. Drexmore."

Alison actually wouldn't mind that. "I'm sure we will."

And the feeds went dark.

———

That evening, Joseph finished reading a proposal for a new research project Doctor Martinez wanted to trial at Helix Unbound. It was a sound experiment, though he'd left her some questions and comments to address before he'd approve it. He gathered his personal belongings and turned off his office light, then locked the door behind him and proceeded to Doctor Martinez's lab. She'd already left for the day, so he deposited the marked-up proposal on her desk. Then he made his way down to the first floor daycare center, where he could watch Josephine playing through an observation window. She was rocking on her back on a plush mat on the daycare floor. Her caretaker was dangling a toy with plastic rings and metal bells just out of reach, and Josephine giggled each time she reached for it and the caretaker pulled it back. Joseph smiled, the sight of her playing filling him with warmth. He opened the daycare door.

"Oh, Director Madison," the caretaker said, standing to greet him, "Josephine has had a great day today. We read books, watched a nature video, played with toys..."

Joseph bent down and lifted his granddaughter, who cooed happily and snuggled against his neck. "When did she eat last?"

"Let me check." The caretaker turned toward a nearby podium, then paused in confusion. "I thought I left the log right here."

He checked the floor around the podium, then passed through a baby gate to the daycare's kitchen area. Joseph felt a gentle tap on his arm. Josephine, eyes sparkling, was holding the clipboard like a prize. She cooed again as microscopic energy particles retreated into her fingertips. Joseph stifled laughter as he waggled a half-hearted *no no* finger at her. He then took the clipboard and tossed it onto the padded mat.

"Is that what you're looking for?" he asked, pointing at the clipboard.

"Now how did it get over there?" The caretaker retrieved the clipboard and read through Josephine's log. "She'll be due in about an hour. Maybe sooner. She's had quite an appetite today."

Joseph smiled at his granddaughter. "I know what we can do about that."

He thanked the caretaker and left, Josephine and his belongings in tow. They proceeded down the main first floor hallway until they reached the onsite cafeteria. Joseph didn't need to order. The staff on duty greeted him and Josephine by name, then delivered a fresh slice of strawberry shortcake to their table. Joseph performed what he referred to as *the fork test*, slicing through the shortcake with its blunt edge and watching for the appropriate springiness in response. The dessert passed. Joseph ate the test bite, which was too large for Josephine, then cut a more appropriately sized sliver and held it near her mouth. If she had been any other baby, he would have never risked feeding her a dessert with so many components. But Josephine took the sliver and gummed it until broken down enough to swallow. Joseph took his second bite, then gave her another, and the process repeated, as it always did, until they were full or the shortcake was gone, the latter usually coming first.

Joseph couldn't help remembering Amanda at times like these. They'd made so many memories in the kitchen of the first Helix Unbound, and now here he was, making new memories in this new Helix Unbound with Josephine. The only thing that could make it better was if Amanda and Evan were there to share those memories with him. He often thought about their sacrifices, Evan to protect Amanda, and Amanda to protect everyone else, including a secret daughter Joseph hadn't known existed at the time. He understood now why she'd been so resolute to face the Dark Man. She needed the cycle of death to end for Josephine's sake. She wanted her daughter to grow up in a world without that darkness, without that constant threat hanging over her life.

No one, not even Joseph, had seen what had transpired between Amanda and the Dark Man. But he knew in his heart she hadn't died in vain. She'd stopped him. She'd ended the cycle. Sometimes, as Joseph sat in Helix Unbound's cafeteria, eating his strawberry shortcake, he thought back to that day on Sunrise Isle. He recalled Amanda's repetition of his own words, the mature young woman she'd become, a child of so much ability, yet who'd experienced so much hardship in life. She had looked weary. And she had known the trek across Sunrise Isle was one from which she wouldn't return. Yet she went anyway. She went because she loved him, because she loved the Desmonds, because she loved Josephine, because she had come to terms with what needed to be done, and because she was the only one with the strength to do it.

Joseph could only imagine the toll her battle through that hellscape had taken. She'd likely reached the Dark Man with nothing but sheer will fueling her. She wouldn't have had the ability to stop him on her own. But she had a secret weapon at her disposal: the island. Iteration after iteration of playing this scenario out in his mind, it was the only logical conclusion Joseph had come to. Amanda had turned the island against the Dark Man. He didn't know how she had done it, but it had involved giving herself to the island as well.

She would have been battered. She would have been bruised. She would have been bleeding. But she would have been at peace. Joseph recalled the way chunks of broken island had floated apart, ocean waves lapping at their surfaces until waterlogged enough to sink into the murky depths below. He pictured Amanda on one of those chunks. He pictured her broken body among the foliage, abused in ways only she could endure. He pictured the restful smile on her face, a smile she would take with her into the afterlife, whatever that happened to be. She would greet Evan with that smile, and he would know that, in death, she had won.

Joseph pictured Amanda transitioning from this world to the world beyond as the waves came to claim her. Her body remained on Earth, but her soul, a soul that, against all scientific evidence to the contrary, Joseph was confident existed separately from the body that had hosted it, was gone. Amanda's was a soul of tranquility, a soul free from pain and fear, a soul of endless love and care, a soul that had moved on to a better place. And as that soul reunited with the part of her she'd previously lost, waves lapped at the ankles of the body she'd left behind. They climbed her legs, then her torso and chest. They eventually covered her body like a watery shroud. Then, as the tides fell, they carried that body out to sea, gently lowering it into the depths of an embracing tomb, from which it would never be seen again.

AUTHOR'S NOTE

Thank you for reading *Shortcake: Prophecy Fulfilled*!

This trilogy began with a young girl on the run, unsure of who she was or her place in life. During her journey, she learned to love, to stand up for herself, and to fight back against the evils of the world. Though the ending was bittersweet, this is what the tale has been building towards since page one, and I couldn't imagine it concluding in a more fitting way. Amanda's story is over, but the world she lived in and the characters that shaped her life will return in a future incarnation. I hope you've enjoyed *The Shortcake Trilogy* and that you'll join me again when that time comes.

———

Reviews are the lifeblood of independent authors. If you have a moment, a star rating and review would mean the world to me.

Leave a review:

———

Ready for a new type of thrill?

I invite you to explore my other series, including the adventure thriller *Artifact Manor* series and supernatural suspense *Chance Hotel* series, by visiting my author website at the link below.

Thank you for supporting my creative endeavors,

Christopher Gorham Calvin
www.christophergcalvin.com